I0588641

# PENTARK

## THERE IS STRENGTH IN US ALL

## T.L. BRECHIN

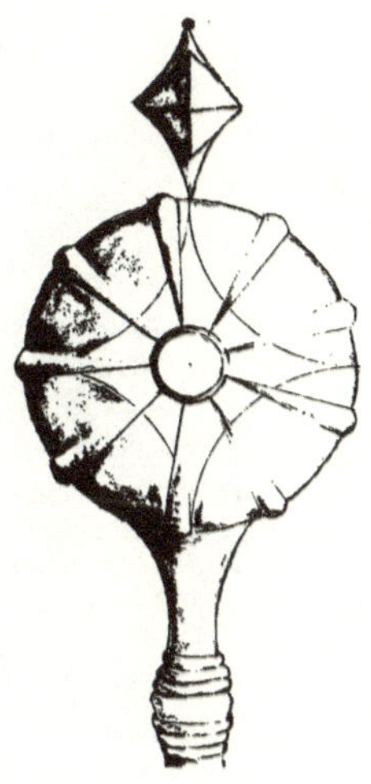

T.L. Brechin grew up on a farm near the sea, with a free and adventurous childhood. From an early age she would lose herself in magic and mystery. A ride to the forest would have her dreaming of mythical creatures in the trees. The author was creative and curious, and as a child would read until her eyes hurt. After raising children and having life's standard adventures, a story was bubbling inside and she thought "wouldn't it be wonderful to share this with the world".

All rights reserved: no part of this publication may be reproduced or transmitted by any means, electronic, mechanical, photocopying, recording or any information storage and retrieval systems or otherwise, without the prior permission in writing from the author.

For avoidance of doubt, Author reserves the rights, and [Platform/Publisher] has no rights to, reproduce and/or otherwise use the Work in any manner for purposes of training artificial intelligence technologies to generate text or illustrations, including without limitation, technologies that are capable of generating works in the same style or genre as the Work, unless [Platform/Publisher] obtains Author's permission to do so. Nor does [Platform/Publisher] have the right to sub licence others to reproduce and/or otherwise use the Work in any manner from purposes of training artificial intelligence technologies to generate text or illustrations without Author's specific and express permission.

With respect to any audiobook created or distributed, Author shall not permit or cause the Work to be narrated by artificial intelligence technologies or other non-human narrators, without Author's prior and express written consent.

With respect to any translations created or distributed, Author shall not permit or cause the Work to be translated into another language with artificial intelligence technologies or other non-human translators, without Author's prior and express written consent. For purposes of clarification, a human translator may use artificial intelligence technologies as a tool to assist in the translation, provided that the translation substantially comprises human creation and the human translator has control over, and reviews and approves, each word in the translation.

The Authors Guild*

This novel is entirely a work of fiction. The names, characters, places and incidents portrayed in it are the work of the author's imagination. Any resemblance to actual persons, living or dead, events or localities is entirely coincidental.

Pentark and image are registered trademarks*

ISBN: 978-0-6459042-0-8 (book)

ISBN: 978-0-6459042-1-5 (e-book)

Text copyright © 2024 T.L. Brechin.

Map art and interior illustrations copyright © T.L. Brechin

USA copyright © 2024

The author asserts their moral rights in this work throughout the world without waiver

Book cover and design by Julia Dineen

Edited by Sheelagh Wegman BA, AE  IPEd

First published by T.L. Brechin 2025

Website: tlbrechin.com

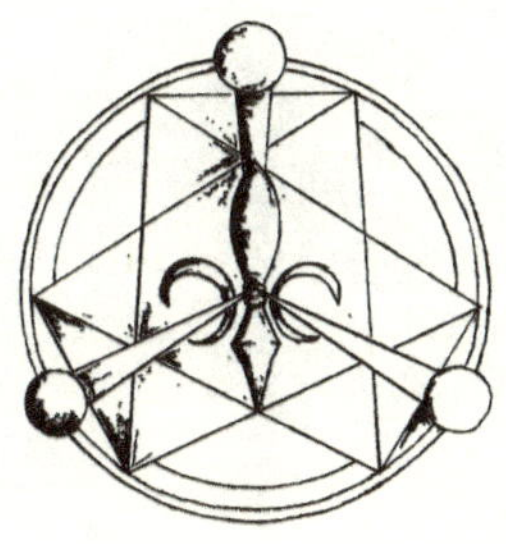

for the seekers of light...

# Acknowledgements

To Liz: my teacher, critic and writing guide.
I could not have done it without you.

Special thanks go to my editor Sheelagh Wegman who
happily decorated my initial draft in red and polished the
manuscript until it shone.

To Julia Dineen: the reaction of readers seeing the
cover for the first time says it all.

To my wonderful parents, children, grandchildren and partners. You
fostered my dream until it became a reality.  You have taught me much
and have a special place in my heart.

Heartfelt gratitude must go to the generous families and individuals who
gave me shelter when I sorely needed it and helped guide my ship to
calmer waters.  They know who they are.

## Animals

To the animals in my life. I loved them all. Those with outstanding
personalities made it into the book.

Apache, Cinnamon, Whisky, Poppins, Snowball, Sooty, Snip, Tibbs,
Rufus, Cadbury, Stitch, Ruby, Kip, Sam, Spot, Bobby, Wallace,
Jasper, Caesar, Joe, Boston, Scruffy, Jess, Ruby, Meeko, Tilly, Lilo …
and numerous bovines.

Lastly, to my readers.  Thank you for your support.
I hope my story takes you to faraway lands and expands your mind.
You are the reason I put pen to paper and the reason
I could finally write, The End.

# GLOSSARY

## PENTARK

Structure built on the top of Way Fell near Mirraway Castle.

## CHARACTERS

**Artorus:** Master of the Knights of Power.

**Attricus:** A soothsayer. He grew up and was educated in Elodom Monastery.

**Boris:** A 70 year old teenage dwarf, fraternal twin brother of Ferdy. Lives in Banters Den in the Land of Magirus with his parents Ester and Leopold.

**Elvendor:** King of the elves. Lives in Alfura, the elven enclave in the Norfolk Woods in the Land of Magirus.

**Ester:** A dwarf, Boris and Ferdy's mother. Lives in Banters Den with her husband, Leopold.

**Ferdy:** A 70 year old teenage dwarf, fraternal twin brother of Boris. Lives in Banters Den in the Land of Magirus with his parents Ester and Leopold.

**Ferryman/fisherman:** Owns the ponies that take Attricus and Volgor across the Abyss River.

**Frovin:** A European badger. His family live in Greenwood Forest.

**Hermit of the Living Waters:** The hermit grants permission to cross the Intrepid River using his barge.

**Henry:** Resistance fighter.

**Ikoseer (Eye–ko–sear):** Female sage. She lives in White Timber Mountain in the Land of Arctus and rides Helios, the golden stallion.

**Jester:** Lives in the Tangled Woods.

**Knights of Power:** Protectors of the Pentark. There are twelve Knights of Power, based in the Ascension Mountains.

**Leopold:** A dwarf, Boris and Ferdy's father. Lives in Banters Den with his wife Ester.

**Mafasat:** A lion. Connected to the Sarsen Stones.

**Maria:** Marta's deceased grandmother.

**Marta:** Daughter of Roselin, granddaughter of Maria. Lives near Brechin Village in the World of Man.

**Mortimer (Lord):** From Mawdark Castle in the World of the Dark Night. He invades the World of the Soul for the Prince of Darkness. During the invasion he murders King Gordir and Queen Eleanor.

**Nipper:** A young sailor on the tall ship, *Sirius*, in charge of tying and untying the anchor ropes.

**Norfolk Elf:** The guardian elf of Norfolk Woods and the spiritual elf of the elves of Magirus and of the Isle of Spheres.

**Onysius (Earl):** Duke Tardor's son. Ally of Lord Mortimer.

**Patrayus:** The youngest member of the Knights of Power.

**Potsy:** A very old and wise dwarf. Lives in the Lux Mountains.

**Ranger:** A bullock owned by the elves of Alfura.

**Rannoch:** A Knight of Power. Horse marshal to the King of Gorthonomir.

**Raven:** Ikoseer's animal helper.

**Rhyll (Rill):** A goblin from the goblin enclave, Hammerlock in the World of the Dark Night. He rides anomirs for the enemy.

**Roselin:** Marta's deceased mother, daughter of Maria.

**Scithios:** Commander of the Knights of Power. Second in command to Artorus.

**Sheen:** Ikoseer's owl helper.

**Thrim:** Ghost dwarf ancestor to Boris and Ferdy.  Master forger to the Isle of Spheres.

**Tibbs:** A ginger tomcat.  Captain of the tall ships.

**Tom:** This elf drives Ranger the bullock.

**Toros:** The black bull of the Abyss River.

**Volgor:** A kurr.  His family live and fish on the Bleak River near the Raven Mountains.

**Wallace:** A wolfhound belonging to Marta's family.

**Yoska:** The nomadic name given to Prince Mir.

**Yellow Man:** This character rides a horse of air.  He dresses in varying shades of yellow and has purple hair.

**Zagar (Zaygar):** A Knight of Power.

# ROYALTY

**King Farmir:** Ancestral king of the Kingdom of Gorthonomir.  Fought in the Battle of the Stones.

**Prince Galway (King in waiting):** Son of King Gordir and Queen Eleanor. He and his family went into exile when Lord Mortimer invaded the World of the Soul.

**King Gordir:** King of Gorthonomir, father of Prince Galway and husband of Queen Eleanor.  He and Queen Eleanor were murdered by Lord Mortimer when Mortimer invaded the World of the Soul.  He is first cousin to Duke Tardor (father of Onysius).

**King Hord:** The goblin king.  Lives in Hammerlock, the goblin enclave which is part of the World of the Dark Night.

**King Jigs:** King of the gnomes.

**Prince Mir:** Son of Prince Galway and Princess Helena.  Grandson of King Gordir and Queen Eleanor.  Older brother to Princess Moira.

**Princess Moira:** Daughter of Prince Galway and Princess Helena. Granddaughter of King Gordir and Queen Eleanor. Younger sister to Prince Mir.

**Duke Tardor:** Father of Onysius and first cousin to King Gordir. As a coronation gift, King Gordir annexed off an area of land from Illingaith and entitled him Duke. Tardor named the land Asilodor and built Jimpiragh Castle. He was a respected member of the royal family. Deceased.

**Earl Onysius:** Son of Duke Tardor. Lives in Jimpiragh Castle.

## SPIRIT BEINGS

**Queen of the Sun – Solara:** A sun being. Her spiritual home is in the Ascension Mountains in the World of the Soul.

**Prince of Darkness:** Nemesis of Solara, the Queen of the Sun. He is a dark being from the World of the Dark Night.

## CREATURES

**Anomirs:** Anomirs are raptors with razor sharp claws and are large enough to carry goblins into battle. They have scaly head and legs, and a feathered body. They are able to fly either in daylight or at night, although their night vision isn't good. They can fly much faster than a snow eagle. Their natural enemies are the sword Honorex and the Firebird. They can't fly through the Arkfeld, the force field between the three 'Worlds'.

**Boorlings:** Wrake horses. They were created by the Prince of Darkness but their ongoing breeding is overseen by Lord Mortimer from the World of the Dark Night. They are usually only ridden by master wrakes. Onysius rides boorlings occasionally. They have a pacing gait and can travel 100 miles per day with a wrake or human on their back.

**Kurrs:** Short creatures (about dwarf height), but thin and wiry. Families of kurrs live and fish along the Bleak River between the Dukedom of Asilodor and the Raven Mountains, close to the World of the Dark Night. Salmon is their favourite fish.

**Rock Giants:** They created the Isle of the Spheres and the archipelago in the Mother Sea.

**Wrakes:** Humanoid creatures created by the Prince of Darkness and bred by the Lord Mortimer in the World of the Dark Night. Used by Lord Mortimer when he invaded Illingaith in the World of the Soul. Master wrakes ride boorlings. Wrakes are carnivorous and especially like to eat young dwarves, badgers and ponies.

## Mythical Creatures

**Firebird:** Connected to the Pentark.

## Stones

The central stone of the Pentark is called the Lightenstone and there are 12 smaller outer stones.

## Place Names

**Ageless Forest:** In the Land of Illingaith between the Intrepid and Abyss Rivers.

**Alfura:** The elven enclave in the Norfolk Woods in the Land of Magirus. Home to King Elvendor, Yahdra and Tom.

**Aramark:** An ancient temple in the Dukedom of Asilodor. The Well of Forgetfulness is in this temple.

**Banters Den:** A dwarf mining village. This is where Leopold, Ester, Boris and Ferdy live.

**Brechin (Bree–kn – Scottish pronunciation):** A village in the World of Man near Greenwood Forest.

**Calligan's Plain:** A lush plain between the Norfolk Woods and the Intrepid River.

**Elodom Monastery:** A monastery in Wetwood Forest in the Land of Magirus. Attricus was raised and educated here.

**Greenwood Forest:** In the Land of Magirus. It borders the World of Man.

**Glen Bain:** A narrow valley in the mountain range called The Veils.

**Hammerlock:** The goblin enclave in the World of the Dark Night.  Rhyll comes from here.

**Norfolk Woods:** The elven woods.  The trees in these woods are Norfolk pines (Araucaria heterophylla).

**Riverbend:** A small fishing village on the Abyss River (Land of Illingaith side).

**Rolling Hills:** North of Banters Den in Greenwood Forest.  The cousins of Boris and Ferdy live here.

**Sarsen Plains:** In the Land of Illingaith, between the Ageless Forest and the Abyss River.

**Sarsen Stones:** Standing stones on the Sarsen Plain.  Mafasat the lion lives here.

**Tangled Woods:** In the Dukedom of Asilodor.

**Way Fell:** A hill close to Mirraway Castle.  The Pentark is on the apex of this hill.

**Well of Forgetfulness:**  In Aramark Temple in the Dukedom of Asilodor.

## HORSES

**Aster:** A scruffy moor pony. Galloway type bay mare with a small white star on her forehead.  Ridden by Boris the dwarf.

**Bloss:** A draught Shire mare. Owned by Marta's family.

**Famrod:** A black Friesian stallion.  Ridden by Artorus, a Knight of Power.

**Helios:** A gold coloured stallion. Ridden and owned by Ikoseer, the Sage.

**Poppins:** A scruffy moor pony.  Galloway type bay mare with black markings.  Ridden by Ferdy, the dwarf.

**Snowball:** A white pony.  A Welsh Mountain type mare. Ridden by Marta.

**Farasi:** Onysius' warhorse.  A dapple grey Percheron.  This horse isn't named in the story.

**Acer:** Patrayus' Shire warhorse.  Chestnut with a white blaze.  This horse isn't named in the story.

**Annunse:** The yellow man's horse of air.  This horse isn't named in the story.

**Skarn and Flint:** The ferryman's ponies.  Not named in the story.

## WATERWAYS

**Abyss River:** This river is fed by a massif of the Arifer Mountains and flows into Werthyn Harbour.  It is the natural border between Illingaith and Asilodor.

**Bleak River:** A river between Asilodor and the World of the Dark Night.  Bleak, catfish and salmon can be found in this river.

**Berthing Gates:** Security gates at the narrow entry to Werthyn Harbour.

**Glacial Lake (Blue Lake):** A bifurcation lake meaning that it flows in two directions: east into the Intrepid River and west to the Mother Sea.  Turquoise in colour.

**Intrepid River:** This massive river is fed by the glacial lake, Blue Lake and the Gorthwain Mountains.  It separates the Lands of Arctus and Magirus from the Land of Illingaith.  It eventually flows into Werthyn Harbour.

**Iscador River:** This river is fed by the Lux Mountains.  It flows into the Intrepid River.

**Lake Mirraway:** A lake on the plateau below Mirraway Castle.

**Mother Sea:** This sea surrounds the Isle of Spheres and all islands in the archipelago.

**Rubicon River:** This is a spiritual river and a 'real' river.  Crossing the Rubicon means 'no going back'.  To cross the Rubicon is to go into a new realm.

**Werthyn Harbour/Port:** A saltwater trading port fed by the fresh waters of the Abyss and Intrepid Rivers. The narrow entry to this harbour is via the Mother Sea. The entry is secured by the Berthing Gates.

## CASTLES

**Jimpiragh:** This castle was built by Duke Tardor in Asilodor after the annexure of this land from Illingaith.

**Mawdark:** In the World of the Dark Night. Lord Mortimer lives here.

**Mirraway:** The royal castle of the King and Queen of Gorthonomir and their family. Built in the Land of Illingaith.

## MOUNTAINS

**Arifer:** Part of the natural border between the Dukedom of Asilodor and the Land of Illingaith.

**Ascension:** A group of three mountains in the Land of Arctus. The home of the Knights of Power and the Queen of the Sun.

**Gorthwain:** The natural border between the Lands of Arctus and Illingaith.

**Lux:** The natural border between the Lands of Arctus and Magirus. The home of Potsy, the dwarf.

**Raven:** The natural border between the World of the Dark Night and the World of the Soul.

**The Veils:** A massif of mountains around Mirraway Castle.

**White Timber Mountain:** In the Land of Arctus. The home of Ikoseer, the Sage.

## LANDS AND KINGDOMS

**Arctus:** A land in the Kingdom of Gorthonomir in the World of the Soul.

**Asilodor (Ass–eye–lo–door):** The Dukedom of Asilodor was originally part of the Land of Illingaith. This land was annexed off as a coronation gift to Tardor after his cousin Prince Gordir was crowned King of

Gorthonomir. Tardor built Jimpiragh Castle here. After Onysius aligned with Lord Mortimer, Solara referred to Asilodor as the 'Land of the Half Light.'

**Kingdom of Gorthonomir:** Consists of the three lands, Arctus, Magirus and Illingaith in the World of the Soul.

**Illingaith:** A land in the Kingdom of Gorthonomir in the World of the Soul.

**Isle of Spheres:** An island in the Mother Sea. Part of an archipelago.

**Magirus:** A land in the Kingdom of Gorthonomir in the World of the Soul.

## WORLDS

**World of the Soul:** Created after the Treaty of Spheres was signed.

**World of Man:** Created after the Treaty of Spheres was signed.

**World of the Dark Night:** Created after the Treaty of Spheres was signed.

## WEAPONS

**Adamas:** Created by the Prince of Darkness to breach the Arkfeld.

**Arkfeld:** A force field. There are two Arkfelds in the Isle of Spheres separating the World of the Dark Night and the World of Man, from the World of the Soul.

**Honorex:** An ancient sword used in the Battle of the Stones. This sword can repel anomirs.

**Thrust:** A magic dwarf sword forged in the Lux Mountains.

**Toil:** A talisman created by the Prince of Darkness.

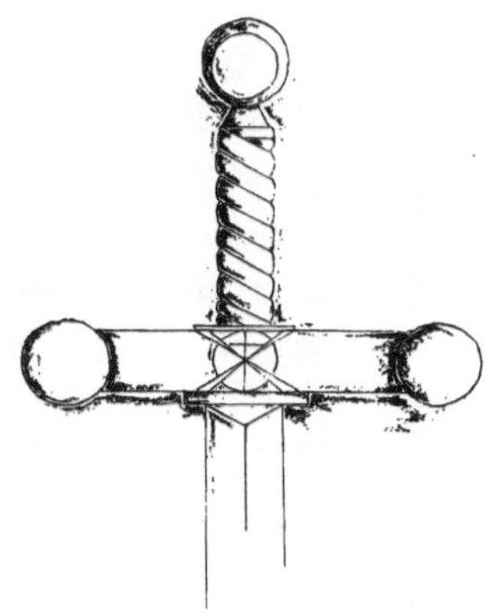

# Knights of Power

There are twelve Knights of Power but only a few are named in the story.
The following list is complete.

Arius

Arnos

Artorus – Knight master.

Carthos

Gresten – Knight champion.

Nebarus

Orta – Knight champion.

Patrayus

Quanos

Rannoch – Horse marshal to the King of Gorthonomir.

Scithios – Knight commander.

Zagar

## BATTLE AND TREATY

**Battle of the Stones** On the Isle of Spheres 200 years prior to the beginning of this story, the Queen of the Sun, Solara, strengthened the light impulse on the Isle. This created conflict in the hearts and minds of many inhabitants which led to a civil war called the Battle of the Stones, initiated by Solara's nemesis, the Prince of Darkness.

During this civil war three basic factions emerged:

1. Those who were ready to live in a higher world of light;

2. Those who were good of heart but unaware of a higher light;

3. Those who rejected a higher world of light.

To make peace the Queen of the Sun instigated the Treaty of Spheres. She decreed that the Isle of Spheres be split into three separate worlds:

1. The World of the Soul – comprising the lands of Arctus, Illingaith and Magirus (Asilodor was annexed later);

2. The World of Man – formerly part of the Land of Magirus;

3. The World of the Dark Night – originally part of the Land of Illingaith.

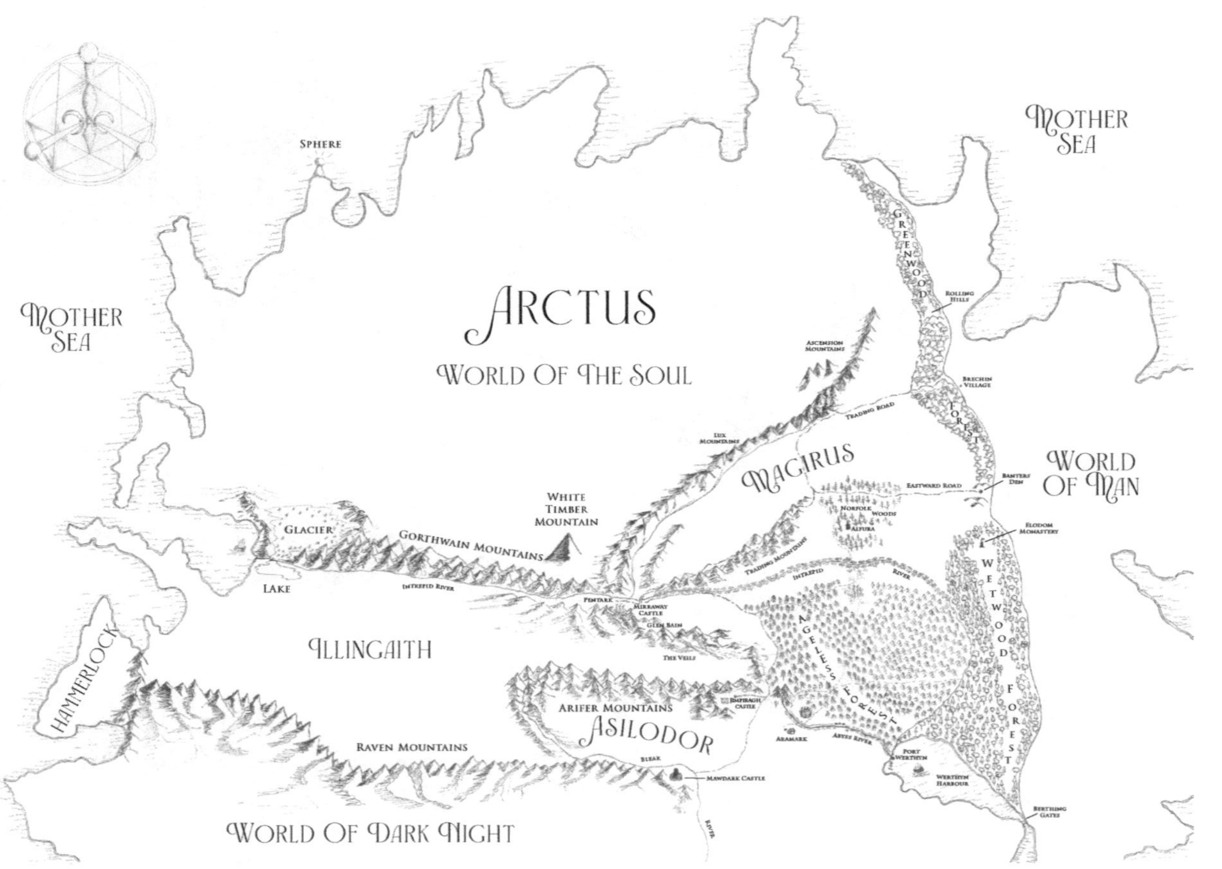
ARCTUS
WORLD OF THE SOUL
MOTHER SEA
MOTHER SEA
SPHERE
GREENWOOD
ROLLING HILLS
ASCENSION MOUNTAINS
BRECHIN VILLAGE
FOREST
TRADING ROAD
LUX MOUNTAINS
MAGIRUS
EASTWARD ROAD
BANTERU DAM
WORLD OF MAN
NORFOLK WOODS
ALFURA
ELDOOM MONASTERY
WHITE TIMBER MOUNTAIN
GLACIER
GORTHWAIN MOUNTAINS
TRADING MOUNTAINS
INTREPID
RIVER
WETWOOD FOREST
LAKE
INTREPID RIVER
PENTARK
MERRAWAY CASTLE
GLEN BASIN
AGELESS FOREST
ILLINGAITH
THE VEILS
HAMMERLOCK
ARIFER MOUNTAINS
EMPRAGH CASTLE
ASILODOR
ARAMARK
ABYSS RIVER
PORT SWIFTRIVER
RAVEN MOUNTAINS
BLEAR
WERTHYN HARBOUR
MAWDARK CASTLE
BERTHING GATES
WORLD OF DARK NIGHT
RIVER

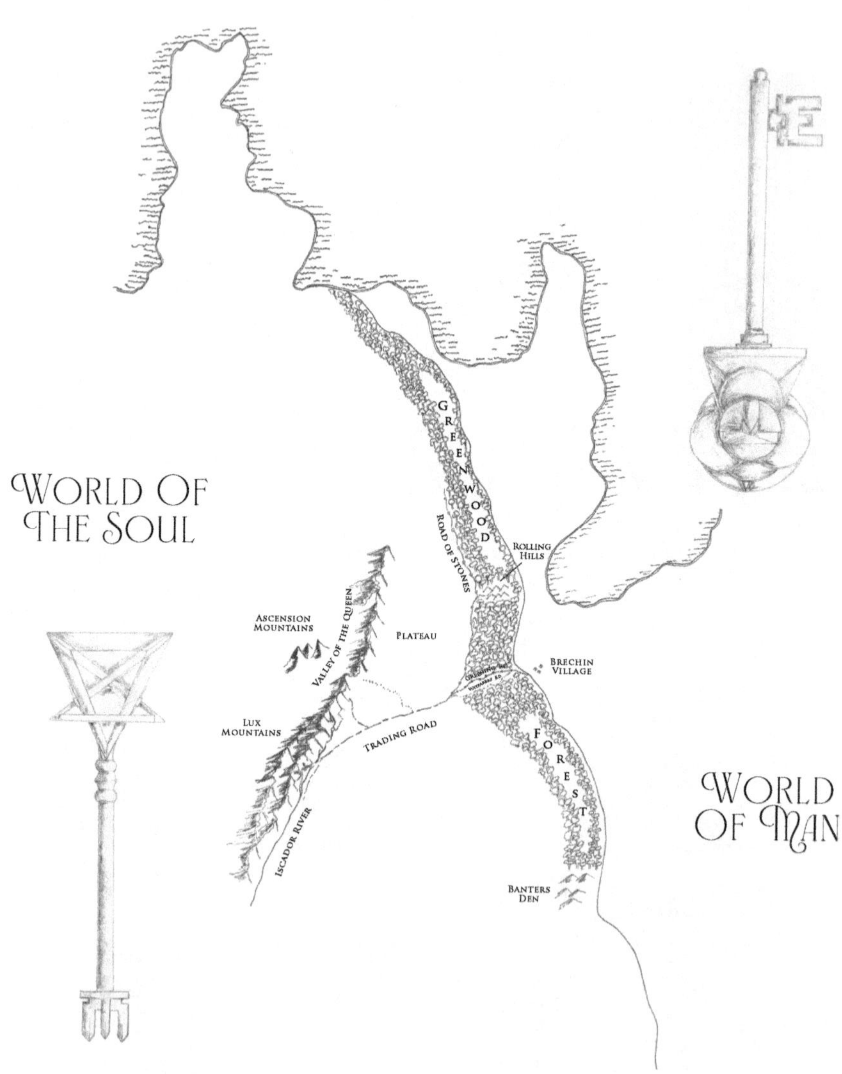
WORLD OF THE SOUL
WORLD OF MAN
GREENWOOD
ROAD OF STONES
ROLLING HILLS
ASCENSION MOUNTAINS
VALLEY OF THE QUEEN
PLATEAU
BRECHIN VILLAGE
LUX MOUNTAINS
TRADING ROAD
FOREST
ISCADOR RIVER
BANTERS DEN

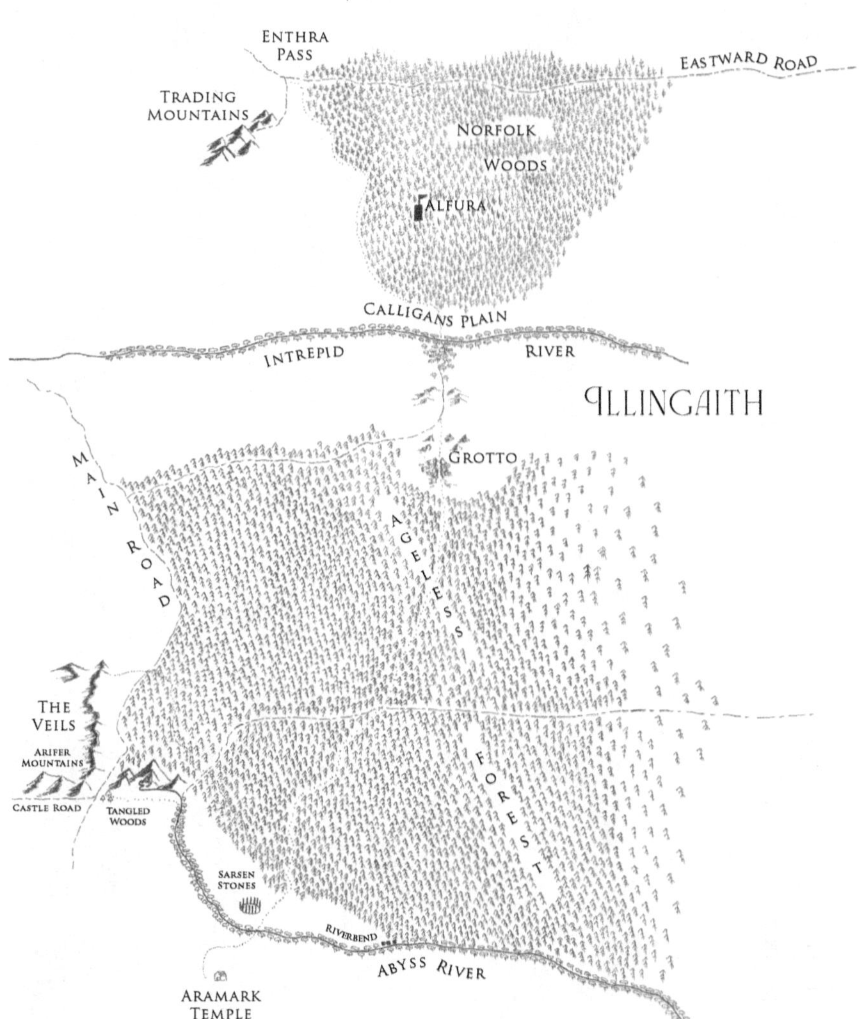
ENTHRA PASS
EASTWARD ROAD
TRADING MOUNTAINS
NORFOLK WOODS
ALFURA
CALLIGANS PLAIN
INTREPID RIVER
ILLINGAITH
GROTTO
MAIN ROAD
AGELESS
THE VEILS
ARIFER MOUNTAINS
FOREST
CASTLE ROAD
TANGLED WOODS
SARSEN STONES
RIVERBEND
ABYSS RIVER
ARAMARK TEMPLE

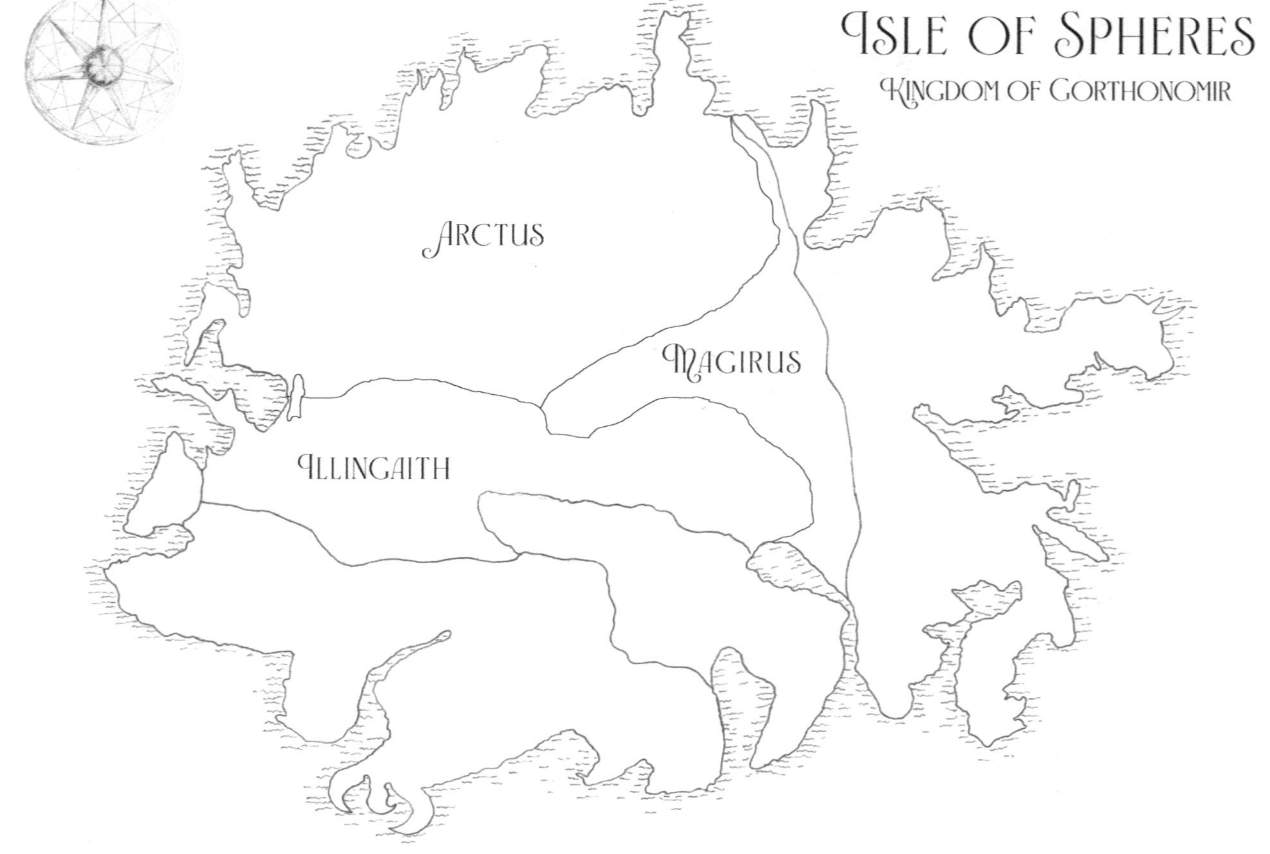

ISLE OF SPHERES
KINGDOM OF GORTHONOMIR
ARCTUS
MAGIRUS
ILLINGAITH

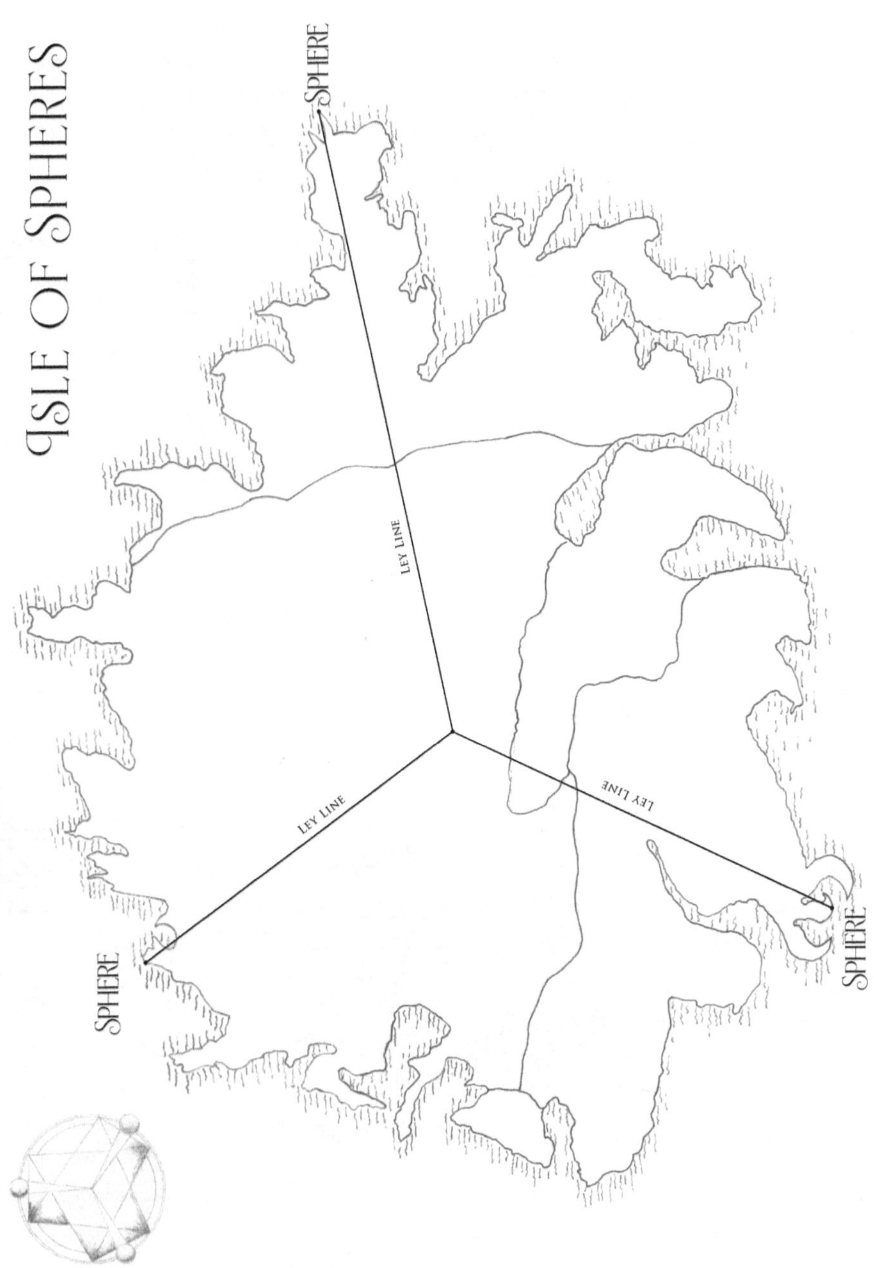
ISLE OF SPHERES
SPHERE
SPHERE
SPHERE
LEY LINE
LEY LINE
LEY LINE

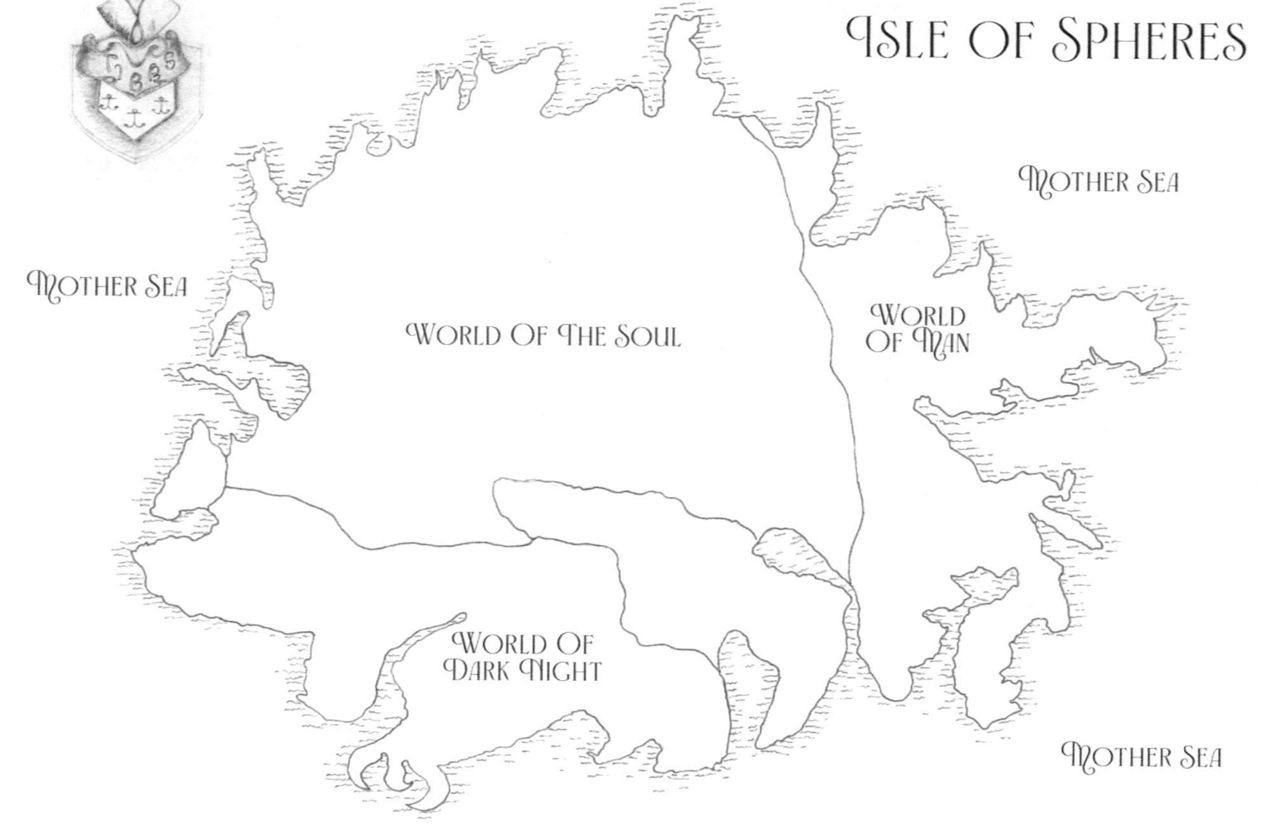

ISLE OF SPHERES
MOTHER SEA
MOTHER SEA
WORLD OF THE SOUL
WORLD OF MAN
WORLD OF DARK NIGHT
MOTHER SEA

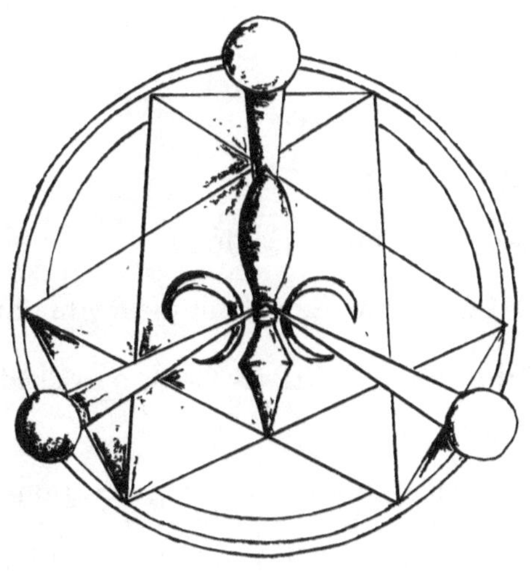

# PROLOGUE

It took some effort to push through the worn oak door—I flinched at the creaking hinges, my boots echoing on the old wooden floor.

Confronted by walls of books, stacked column high, it was impossible to move any further into the room. It seemed other-worldly and I wrinkled my nose at the aging tomes.

'Hello ..?'

'Can I help you?'

I jumped. The voice was strong and clear.

I craned my neck. 'I wanted to learn about the myths of this island.'

'Have you visited the ruins of Mirraway Castle or walked up the fell to the site of the Pentark?'

'Yes. I went there yesterday. It was a stunning view from the fell.'

'Locals believe this area was once the scene of two battles. The Battle of the Stones and then two centuries later, another—the Battle of the Pentark. There are artifacts among the ruins—mostly strange arrowheads. Some say they belonged to a race of elves.'

'Oh?

'And what were the battles about?'

'The same as always. Greed and power. There was a queen who lived among the mountains. Solara, the Queen of the Sun. She had a vision, instructing her to increase the spirit light on this island.

'She used magic to boost the power of the Pentark. But not everyone on the island embraced the change. The Queen had a spirit nemesis called the Prince of Darkness and he brought revolt in the form of battles.

I heard a rustling sound and a column of books swayed as if pushed from behind. I started as a seemingly ethereal statuesque woman suddenly stepped in front of me, holding a tattered book. With a knowing smile she searched my face.

'Many believe that the Pentark had mysterious stones in it. One of them, the central stone, was the most potent. After the first battle, the Queen oversaw a treaty—the Treaty of Spheres—so named after the three light spheres on the headlands of this island. They were like lighthouses that guided ships. They too are in ruins.'

'Yes … I saw them too. Didn't the Treaty bring peace?'

'That was the Queen's hope. The Treaty separated the island into three worlds—the World of the Soul, the World of Man and the World of the Dark Night. Peace reigned for two hundred years.'

She sighed.

'But of course darkness never rests and history repeats itself…'

'And then there was the second battle? The Battle of the Pentark?'

She nodded and held the book out. I opened it to the first page.

*Pentark.*

'Oh. Thank you.'

'Return the book when you've finished reading it.'

With that, she turned, revealing a single band of strange symbols embroidered down the front of her robe.

But I never saw her again.

# PART 1

# MIST

# CHAPTER 1

The crowing of a rooster outside her window woke Marta with a start. Remembering what day it was, she scrambled out of bed, pulled on her best breeches and wrapping up against the cool morning air, grabbed two woven baskets by the back door. With arms full, she pushed open the wooden gate at the end of the garden path and headed down to the orchard. As she passed the barn, Wallace the wolfhound whined and tugged against his chain. Feeling sorry for him, Marta released him and he ran ahead, scattering rabbits as he went.

It was late summer and the apples were still plentiful. She picked the best ones, polished them until they shone and carefully placed them in the baskets. She lugged the baskets back up the laneway to the barn where her father was buckling the last straps on the draught mare's harness.

Soon he was hoisting large sacks of potatoes across his shoulders, grunting, and rolling them onto the dray. He stacked them into neat rows, while Marta put five new twisted ropes and a small wooden crate of mature cheeses along the other side. Then she filled a nosebag of oaten hay for Bloss to eat later and laid it on top of the cheeses. She climbed onto the seat next to her father and gave Bloss a light slap of the reins. Bloss responded, and straining against the load, headed down to the orchard gate. Wallace bounded alongside the dray to the farm gate, and then lay down and sulked when Marta told him he must stay.

It was a slow journey from Broadmeadow Farm down to the village of Brechin, but Marta loved the crunch and rumble of the wheels, and the rhythmic sway and jolting of the dray. The ruts in the road were well worn and the cobblestones and rough granite made the track arduous for Bloss. Her load was heavy but she had made the trip down the valley many times before and she knew how to pick her way along the crown of the roadway.

Within the hour they reached the arched village gates. The clouds that earlier threatened rain had cleared and sun shone down on

the valley's patchwork quilt of green vegetables, wheat sheaves, oats
and fallow ground.

Just as it always was on the village's monthly market day, there was a lot of
*to-ing and fro-ing* and a *Much-to-do* and *Can't-be-wasting-any-time* attitude
among the busy folk arriving in an orderly manner to set up their stalls.
Peaches, plums, apricots, and greengages sat full and ripe in willow baskets
and the delicious aroma of freshly baked bread wafted through the air.

Bolts of fine cloth: yellow, green, red and blue were on display in the
tailor's window. Sacks of beetroot and carrots stood in neat rows in front
of the farmers' stalls and further along were piles of roughly stacked gourds
and casks of mulled wine. Horses that required shoeing were tethered in
a row outside the local blacksmith's. A young apprentice in leather apron
and with sweat beading on his brow, pumped the bellows until the coals
glowed orange and red in the gloom of the shop. Soon the ringing of
hammer on anvil was added to the hustle and bustle.

Bloss patiently made her way through the throngs of farmwives, villagers
and roustabouts streaming through the gates. Some were there just for
the outing but most wanted to trade or barter their goods. They found an
empty spot and Marta's father unhitched Bloss from the dray. As Marta
handed her father the nosebag the mare tried to snatch a mouthful of the
oats before being led to the nearby stables. Marta stayed behind with their
display. As soon as he returned, Marta hoisted the first basket of apples
onto her hip, and headed towards the bakery.

'Bread for lunch and some milled flour,' he reminded her as he watched
her go, 'and a small bag of onions wouldn't go astray …'

'Yes Father,' Marta called over her shoulder.

When apples were in season, the local bakers made delicious pies
throughout market day, preferring to use Marta's tart apples and always
most grateful to exchange them for some of their finest ground flour. By
lunchtime she was pleased to see that all the apples in the basket had been
replaced by the ordered goods, together with some plums and peaches as
a special treat.

As Marta came near her father's stall she saw a few other vendors gathered nearby, all drinking warm spicy mead from tankards brought by the publican of The Cock 'n' Bull as a token of thanks for the trade they brought his way. She sat by her father on the back of the dray, swinging her legs as they shared their simple lunch. There was a bit of idle chatter among the men at first. But then there was a lull in the conversation.

One man leant forward and said in a low voice, 'Shouldn't we be talking about what's been happening in Greenwood Forest?'

He looked around the gathered group. 'And a few even stranger things have been seen around here of late. You know, it's a curse Brechin's so close to it.' He pointed with his tankard in the general direction of the forest, and a shiver spread through the group.

'You may be right,' said the publican, looking down and shuffling his feet. 'But I've seen nothing myself—and I live right here. Anyway there's naught we can do about it. If you ask me, we'd best keep ourselves to ourselves.'

'Can't just ignore it,' said the wheelwright. 'I think we should be arming ourselves. I've been told that there's even elves and dwarves appearing out of the forest. What could they possibly want from *us? They're* the ones who have magic.'

'But we have *food*,' the farmer reminded them. 'Rumour has it, ever since the World of the Soul was invaded by the World of the Dark Night, more and more crops have been failing each year. Perhaps the inhabitants are slowly starving.'

'I think it's more than that,' said the wheelwright. 'The breach in the Treaty of Spheres was twenty years ago now.'

The publican shrugged. 'People see things in the dark all the time. Their imagination runs wild. Where's the evidence?'

'As if those vile and nasty creatures from the World of the Dark Night would be leaving any evidence,' retorted the wheelwright.

'And don't forget, the border into the World of Man is still protected by the Arkfeld,' said the farmer.

'And I'd take a bet any day that the force field's too weak by now to stop them from coming here through the forest,' insisted the wheelwright.

Marta listened with great interest. Rumours of the ongoing conflict within the World of the Soul were often shared on Brechin's market day, but she had not noticed people being so worried before. The villagers generally seemed satisfied that the Arkfeld's protection was holding, and that any attacks from the World of the Dark were a problem only for the World of the Soul. She watched the men now as they whispered to each other, and then looked across at her father. He had told her about this rumour of strange creatures being seen in the village, but he had assured her not to be concerned about it. She turned back to the wheelwright.

He nodded at the village elder who had been listening silently all the while. 'Tell us again about the mysterious woman you saw on a golden stallion that had obviously come through the Arkfeld.'

He raised his hand. Everyone was quiet, waiting for the elder to speak.

'It was the most beautiful horse I've ever seen. A kind of glowing golden colour. I was a boy. Over sixty years ago. It was night time, but there was a full moon so that I could see quite well. I was walking along the track to my grandparents' farm when I heard horse's hooves and looked up to see a woman riding bareback, cross the track and disappear into the forest. But I swear that she turned her head and gave a kind of nod, looking straight at me. Aye, for just a moment, I admit. But there was something in that look. What she were doing there I don't know, but I still think somehow she were on our side.'

The elder took a deep breath and then shocked them all by adding, 'And I saw her again, just yesterday. And she gave me that same look, as if she was telling me not to be afraid.'

Marta's father jumped from the dray. 'Come Marta, try and sell the rest of those apples, eh? And then we can go home.'

Marta noticed the change in his mood. Ever since the Treaty of Spheres had been breached, every new child in the valley had been warned by their parents that they must never go near Greenwood Forest, the boundary between their World and the World of the Soul. But Marta and her father had a special reason to be concerned about the danger. For long ago, when her mother had given that warning to Marta, she had added that she herself had grown up in the World of the Soul.

They packed their leftovers into a sack and put them in the front of the dray. Marta hitched the last basket of apples onto her hip and headed to the only place she hadn't been to today: Jester Alley.

The alley was mostly a ragtag lot of buffoons, beggars and vagabonds trying to eke out a living by playing games and tricks on their audience. There were tumblers and jesters; a fiddler and a minstrel who acted out ballads from a temporary stage; and in a small dim tent a card reader sat at a round table with a crystal ball. In the crowd were also villagers and peasants playing various games: noughts and crosses, draughts, chess, Fox and Geese, and others trying their luck at archery.

Marta made her way through the scattered groups trying to barter her apples, but there were no takers save a young pickpocket who helped himself to an apple and ran off laughing. Annoyed, she pulled the basket closer to her body. A gust of cold wind rustled the nearby treetops drawing her gaze to the forest, but there was nothing to see. With a shiver, she turned to go back to her father.

But as she weaved her way back through the alley, she noticed a hooded stranger sitting at a wooden crate turned upside down to form a table. As she passed he looked from under his hood and caught her eye. With a sweep of his arm, he invited her to sit opposite him. Marta stopped in her tracks.

'Would you like to try your hand against me?'

Marta noticed a roll of leather, some game pieces and two bone dice placed on one side of the crate. So he was a gambler.

'I have no money and I don't know how to play,' she replied. 'Besides, I came here to barter my apples. All I've got so far was a thief who helped himself. So I'm leaving.'

'Ah … and who could blame you?' the stranger replied with a sudden smile, rattling a leather pouch full of coins. 'But I've fleeced enough people for today. Let me strike a bargain with you: play for free against me and if you win, I'll pay you for all your remaining apples.' He placed two coins on the crate, indicating that to be a fair price for her goods.

'I don't know,' murmured Marta, still ill at ease.

His hand hovered over the coins. 'Isn't my offer fair?'

Marta wavered. 'Umm … Yes … but what if I lose?'

The stranger gave a light shrug. 'Then I keep my money and you keep your apples.'

She looked up and saw her father passing the alley on his way towards the stables to fetch Bloss. That meant she had some time to spare. He would groom and water Bloss before he brought her back to the dray.

'One game?'

Marta made up her mind. She swung her basket of remaining apples to the ground and sat down on an upturned wooden barrel opposite the stranger. She had a quick glimpse of sunken cheeks and a pinched mouth. Then he unfurled the leather roll before him. It looked like a map with roads, lakes, rivers and mountains, and other strange symbols or numbers either carved or inked onto the leather.

He picked up two small silver game pieces. Keeping a skull for himself he handed Marta a small silver apple. He placed two dice in the middle of the map.

'We start here,' he pointed to one corner of the map. 'We take turns to throw the dice. Before you throw them you must call out a number. If the two dice make up your number, then you can move that number of spaces. There are two paths to choose from. Both paths will take you to the mountain in the middle. Here.' He tapped the spot with a long fingernail. 'The right hand path is longer but if you take it and land on this circle, you have a free turn. The first one to the top of the mountain wins.'

'Five!' The stranger grabbed the dice. 'Ah,' he said. Taking the left path he moved his small silver skull five places to a space with the symbol of an hourglass.

'Eight,' guessed Marta.

She threw the dice, watching as they rolled to a stop showing eight. Relieved, she decided to take the other path and moved her tiny silver apple eight spaces, and onto the number thirteen. She looked up at the shadowed face.

He picked up the dice and as he rolled them in his hands he said nonchalantly, 'I promised to meet an old and dear friend of mine here in the village. She rides bareback on a fine golden stallion, a palfrey. Perhaps you have seen her?'

Marta started and then shook her head. She felt for the amulet that hung from her neck.

'There are no gold coloured horses around here.'

'You couldn't mistake this one. It's a magnificent beast.' The man's tone hardened.

'I haven't seen her or her horse,' she said.

Marta stared at the map, clasping her amulet closer. Her heart pounded in her chest. She was aware that the stranger was now watching her expectantly. She glanced at him and caught his thin, insincere smile before he looked down. Her mouth felt dry. She wanted to run but sat frozen on the barrel, wishing that her father would appear with Bloss.

'I don't believe you.'

Marta's eyes flickered. 'But I'm telling you the truth.'

'Villagers do gossip …'

'I've heard nothing.' She shook her head nervously.

Just then she felt something brush across her back. A fierce voice above her right ear whispered 'Go! Now!'

The hooded stranger snatched his coins, shoving them back into his pouch. He yanked on the string to secure it.

All Marta could think of was getting back to her father. She stood up and grabbed her basket, knocking over the barrel in her haste. The stranger lunged at her, bumping her arm and spilling apples everywhere. Marta scrambled for the basket again but the furious figure snatched it from her grip, the menace in his laugh assaulting her ears. Then, as she bent to pick up a fallen apple and hurl it at him, someone stepped in front of her, and thrust a sword into the stranger's breast. As Marta stared horrified at the slumped body on the ground, the owner of the bloodied sword retrieved it and turned towards her.

Only now did she become aware of a commotion coming from the entrance to the village. Shoving the apple in her pocket, she ran down the alley towards the screaming voices where mothers were running to their children, gathering them up and making for the nearest buildings, while their husbands were grabbing whatever they could find to use as a weapon.

Marta stood watching in a daze. Then she saw, beyond the mayhem, a troop of strange men on horses, pushing and trampling, slashing and destroying as they went. The village was under attack! She had to get to her father.

She started running towards the stables, but her legs felt heavy. Behind her she heard the sound of horses and fleeing people, getting louder and louder. With a frantic burst of speed she reached the front of the stables, but before she could open the door, she heard the swordsman's fierce voice again: 'No! This way!'

She barely had time to draw a quick breath before he grabbed her hand. 'Come! The back doors will be safer.'

Marta stumbled and almost fell as he dragged her along the outer wall of the stables to the back doors. And as he lifted the crossbeam and the doors swung open, she stood, holding her sides, trying to catch her breath. Then she was pulled through the doorway. The nearest horses were already fidgeting in their stalls.

'Open as many stall doors as you can!' the swordsman yelled, running down one row of stalls. 'We must free the horses. Now!'

In a daze Marta ran along the line of stalls closest to her, sliding back the latches and flinging open one door after another. As each horse was freed, snorting and stomping, they rushed towards the back doors, and out into the sunshine in all directions. There was the sound of splintering wood and squealing as the remaining animals tried kicking their way to freedom.

Marta caught sight of her father, trying to control Bloss in her stall. She yelled at him through the wall of horses.

'Father … Father! The village is being attacked! Get out!'

Just then Bloss broke from his grip to join the throng of escaping animals.

'Marta! Marta!' Her father bellowed, her name almost lost in the screaming of the horses.

But as Marta began to run to him, the swordsman, now on a huge black horse, swept her up onto his horse and placed her in the saddle in front of him. The stallion spun on his powerful haunches, creating a cloud of dust, just as the rider commanded, 'Go, Famrod!'

And the great horse responded at once, surging forward towards the wide open back doors, away from the advancing danger. With both hands gripping the pommel, Marta clung on. She strained to look back towards her father. As the stallion propelled himself out towards the dark forbidden forest she let out one last yell: 'F-A-T-H-E-R'.

As the horse and its two riders moved deeper and deeper among towering oak trees, they soon left the village far behind. The further they travelled, the closer the trees crowded in around them. But the stallion maintained his firm footing and sped onwards, mile after mile, with a strength and purpose guided by the swordsman.

At last Marta felt a sudden shortening of the stallion's stride and his body tensed. The swordsman spoke urgently, 'Get ready Famrod … NOW!'

The stallion lurched forward and Marta knew they had crossed through the Arkfeld into some kind of alien realm. Even though they were still in Greenwood Forest the surrounding trees looked and felt menacing. Just then a tree branch reached out, as if to snatch her from the saddle. She shrank back in fear as the grasping branch ripped her pocket, dislodging the forgotten apple. It dropped from the flying steed and rolled into the leaf litter on the forest floor.

A thickness, a quick overwhelming tiredness swept through her body and her head began to droop. She fought against it, but her eyelids felt heavy and began to close. Meanwhile, Famrod didn't miss a beat; his hooves thudded and struck the overgrown track, pushing further into no-man's land.

In the empty stable, her father stood shocked and afraid, wondering whether he would ever see his daughter again. Into his mind came the image of the black stallion that had swept past him in a dream just two nights ago, with its rider bearing a glowing crest at his shoulder.

# CHAPTER 2

It was almost dark before Marta and the knight could halt their frantic escape, and she found herself being taken through a screen of tangled briar and hawthorn onto a worn flagstone path, leading to a doorway concealed in the surrounding rock face.

With Artorus leading Famrod, they entered a huge cavern, its only light a flickering candle on a rough wooden table pushed up against one wall. At the table was an old woman seated in a wicker chair. She was wearing a vibrant blue hooded robe and scribbling notes in the margin of one of the papers scattered across the table top. The old woman immediately rose to greet them, revealing a single band of mirror-imaged symbols embroidered down the front of her robe.

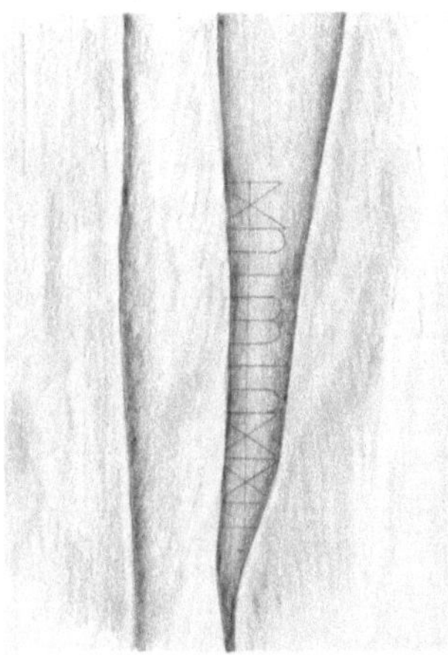

'I've been expecting you, Artorus, but not quite so soon. You've come from the World of Man?'

'Yes. Onysius' scouts and wrakes attacked the village of Brechin, just beyond the forest. One of his spies was in the market. He was a gambler and was about to capture Marta when I intervened ... But he'll have nothing to tell the Earl with my sword to his heart.'

Marta flinched at the news. The old woman looked down at her with a comforting smile. Now that she was closer, Marta could see her strong features and a high forehead, and although the Sage's face was lined, the rest of her appearance belied her age. As the woman pulled back her hood, Marta saw that her long hair was almost the same colour as hers, red, but lighter, a pale orange tinged with grey. And hugging her skull was an intricate aqua blue metal headpiece held in place with woven hair. Marta had never seen this kind of metal and wondered if it was a type of crown.

'Welcome to our humble cave Marta.' She paused. 'I'm Ikoseer the Sage, of White Timber Mountain.'

Marta looked at her wide eyed.

'There's no need to be afraid …'

'I'm not.' Marta stepped back a little. She felt the intensity of the woman's gaze and wondered if she was any safer here than in Brechin.

'You had a terrible experience today, and I have no doubt you've had to leave family behind. But I sense that your father survived the attack.'

Marta's tears welled. How could this woman know about her father? They had only just arrived.

The hot breath and soft lips of the warhorse tickled the woman's palm as she offered it a piece of apple before taking the reins from Artorus. 'Were you followed?' she asked.

'No. Onysius' scouts and wrakes were behind us but we evaded them.'

'Can't be too sure. I'll take a look after dark. Let me attend to Famrod while you make a meal for the two of you.'

While they spoke of things she did not understand, Marta had been looking around and now she noticed several horse stalls lining a far wall. Standing in one and tearing at oaten hay was a handsome stallion. In the adjacent stalls were two sturdy bay ponies with wide, deep chests, and a taller, finer, white mountain pony.

Marta studied the stallion. As he shook his mane the candle flame picked up a hint of gold shimmer. She stared, remembering the gambler asking her if she had seen an old woman and a golden horse. Folding her arms across her chest, she kept the woman within her peripheral vision.

After a simple meal of bread and cheese Marta bedded down in a small alcove off the main room while Artorus joined Ikoseer, relaying the details of what had happened in the World of Man. There was much to discuss and plans to make. With dusk now upon them, the knight made a bed near Famrod, and Ikoseer left the cave to make sure that Artorus had not been followed.

Ikoseer headed out into the cool night air. The tops of the trees swayed against a canvas of brilliant stars as she walked along the old travelling route. When she was satisfied they were not in immediate danger, she turned back. But nearing the cave she heard laboured breathing and the low thud of running feet. She was scanning the steep bank above her when a blurred tangle of bodies dropped in full flight over the bank, rolled and landed at her feet. It was two young dwarves that she knew to be from Banters Den, with one of her own faithful animal servants, Frovin the badger.

'Aha!' She peered down at them with interest. 'What do we have here?'

Amid much cursing, the trio caught their breath and untangled themselves. The light from the old woman's staff threw a soft glow over their shocked faces. Ikoseer thought they looked rather comical. One dwarf had bits of dried fern and thicket twigs poking out of his beard, and the other's clothes were covered in sticky clivers and stringy moss. Even Frovin looked unkempt. Ikoseer leant down and affectionately scratched the top of his head.

Badgers never run from a fight, so she knew Frovin had deliberately led his companions towards the safety of the cave. And although for now the dwarves were a mystery to her, she did not dismiss their arrival as accidental.

A distant howling broke through the forest and as if in response, the wind dropped and the treetops stilled.

'What was that?' asked one of the dwarves, startled.

'Wolves.' Uneasiness stirred in Ikoseer's heart. 'Come, we mustn't tarry!'

Without waiting, she strode ahead of them, the glow from her staff brightening as she led the way through the tangled plants that hid the rock face of the cave. But just outside the door that Marta and Artorus had entered she turned right onto a narrow path that followed the natural curve of the outer rock. Frovin kept close on the woman's heels with the two exhausted dwarves dragging along behind as best they could.

They entered a hidden opening at the back of the cave, and were led through a short passageway past two small rooms, and finally emerged into a large room strewn with straw. The two dwarves threw off their rucksacks and slumped onto the straw, overwhelmed by the strangeness of it all, until the old woman lit a candle and they were comforted by the eerie dance of the warm flame against the cavern walls—it reminded them of the mining tunnels of home.

Slowly they began to pick themselves clean and took in their new surroundings. They eyed off the stranger who had brought them here, and was now building a fire and making a pot of nettle tea.

She poured out two cups and handed them to the dwarves. 'You're a long way from Banters Den.'

As they looked up in surprise, Frovin added hastily, 'Ikoseer, may I present Boris and Ferdy.'

Now the dwarves were amazed.

'Ikoseer? The Sage of White Timber Mountain?' Boris asked.

'We've never met a sage before. But we've heard stories about you from home,' Ferdy added.

'One should never take too much notice of stories my young travellers. There are many things left out of stories that should be in and many things put in that should be left out. But you are too tired—and no doubt too hungry—for us to share any stories now. Let us prepare some food, and then you can all go to sleep, safe and warm on the straw in the corner here.'

Boris remembered he had a few remaining biscuits his mother had lovingly cooked and a sticky mess of broken nuts, seeds and elderberries with bits of dried apple and prunes squashed together. He took it from his pack and put it out to share. The Sage poured her own tea and laid out some figs, mushrooms and cheese, along with broken crusty bread. They tucked into it with a will, and afterwards, bone weary and glad of a dry bed, they fell into a deep slumber, quite unaware of the two other guests in another room.

Now, having checked that all these guests were asleep, Ikoseer moved into one of the small rooms near the back entrance to the cave. But she could not settle. She could still hear the wolves of Skag howling in the distance. It did not bode well; the wolves were a long way north of their home in the World of the Dark Night. In the early morning mist she left the cave again and searched the surrounding trees. There was no sign of Onysius' scouts or the wolves. They were safe for now.

Marta woke early. Her back ached and the air was cool. She pulled the warm blankets about her. The night gone, she watched a moth settle into a crack in the ceiling. From her bed she could see the horses in their stalls. Famrod was standing in the closest one, with head bowed and back foot resting, his tack straddled over a low wooden door.

The scene took her back to the chaos in the stables at Brechin. She remembered the thick, musty smell of straw bedding, ground oats and millet filling her nostrils when Artorus pulled her through the back door. And then the panic of the surging horses as she released them from their stalls. But the hardest memory to bear was the rush to get to her father before Artorus tore her away. She couldn't help but think of him now and wonder if he really was as safe as Ikoseer had assured her.

She clutched at her mother's amulet, the most precious thing she owned. Since her mother died nine years ago, the amulet had hung around Marta's neck. She still felt her loss deeply. And now she may have also lost her father. As she stared again at the rock ceiling, tears welled and ran in tiny rivulets onto her pillow and into her ears. She blinked the tears away and lay quietly for a few more minutes, to gather some inner strength. When she heard Artorus start to make breakfast, she got up to help.

At the back of the cave Ikoseer was peering in on the other three travellers, all snoring, with a cacophony like musicians tuning their instruments before a performance. She left them to it and joined Artorus and Marta in the main room. Marta was by now wanting to set the table, and so Ikoseer picked up a map she had left there the night before and began examining it.

'When can I go back to the World of Man?' Marta asked, three plates in her hands.

Ikoseer met her gaze. 'It may be some time before you can go back. It will not be safe there for a while. Artorus and I will be travelling on further into the World of the Soul, and you will need to come with us … for now. I have a task to complete here. Artorus is helping me and now, it appears you have joined us.'

Marta's eyes widened and she felt her pulse quicken. But now Frovin, Boris and Ferdy were rousing themselves and, following the sound of voices, were wandering dishevelled and half asleep into the main cave, where one end of the table had been set with plates and cups and the delicious smell of frying onions and mushrooms with lots of butter filled the air.

Marta was sitting at the table with her back against the cavern wall, and started at the sight of them coming in. First came a badger, a familiar animal in the World of Man, but behind him were what looked like dwarves, like the ones that her mother had drawn for her as a child, both with long bushy beards and pointy green hats. She wondered how they came to be here with a badger.

'Ah,' said Ikoseer, turning to the trio and beckoning to them. 'Do come in my dear friends and meet your new companions.'

But they were just as bewildered as Marta, and crowded together with their backs pressed hard against her robe. Ikoseer introduced them all by name, and guided them to the table where they all sat down to breakfast. Artorus hastened to get more plates and served the food he had bought in the market. Bread and cheese were now added to the fried mushrooms and onion, prompting Ferdy to remember the apple still in his pocket. When he pulled it out, battered and bruised, and plonked it down on the table, Marta was startled.

'How did you come by one of my apples?' she asked.

'How could it be yours?' bristled Ferdy. 'I found it in the forest.'

'It's why we're here,' Boris added. 'And what a pickle we got ourselves into because of it.'

Marta reached over the table to examine it, but Ferdy kept a firm grip on the fruit.

'It's from Father's orchard. In the World of Man. I must have dropped it in the forest. I remember it fell as we were leaving the oak trees.'

Ferdy and Boris shifted their gaze to Artorus and back again.

'It was you we saw charging past us on the horse!'

'I was threatened by a gambler while I was selling our apples at the Brechin market. Artorus … killed him, and then he helped me escape from foreign soldiers invading our village.'

There was a long pause as they took in this news.

Marta looked at the dwarves, puzzled. 'Is it safe for dwarves to travel through Greenwood Forest?'

'Good heavens. No!' said Ferdy. 'It's not a nice forest anymore.'

Ikoseer leant towards them. 'Perhaps you could enlighten us about how you have arrived at just the right time.'

All eyes were on Boris. He squirmed on his chair.

'Arrived at the right time? I'm not sure I understand what you mean,' he said.

'I can tell you how we got here.' Ferdy stabbed another buttered mushroom and popped it in his mouth. But when he saw the look Boris gave him he changed his mind.

'Those foreign soldiers that invaded your village must have come straight from Banters Den, where we used to live. Our parents panicked when they arrived because they had wrakes with them, so they sent us off on a trek north through the forest to our cousins in the Rolling Hills …'

'Even though that was over two hundred miles away and would take us more than a month to get there,' Ferdy cut in. 'And even though we'd never left Banters Den before.'

Seeing Marta's bewildered look, Boris added, 'Wrakes are humanoid beasts that like to eat young dwarves when they're hungry enough.' Boris cleared his throat. 'Father told us to stay within the corridor of oak trees that runs the full length of the forest bordering the World of Man. He said that since they removed the stones from the Pentark, it was the only part of the forest that was safe. And then we were tired after walking all that way and had just got off to sleep when the thudding of a horse's hooves woke us up and you charged past us.'

Ferdy leant forward. 'When I saw this apple on the ground outside the oak trees I ran to grab it. But I was caught up by a birch branch and then captured by Onysius' soldiers …'

'They were following not far behind you,' Boris added, 'but I kept out of sight and they didn't see me,' Boris added. 'I had to watch them put Ferdy up in front of one of the wrakes and then ride off. I didn't know what to do.'

'I didn't mean to get caught.' Ferdy gave Boris a furtive glance. 'But you know that I love apples. I love the way when you cut one in halves how Mother does, you get the beautiful star pattern in the middle.'

'And then you met Frovin in the forest?' prodded Ikoseer.

Boris nodded. 'I was just standing there, when I heard someone or some thing making a snoring noise nearby.'

'And so Frovin, you helped Boris find Ferdy?'

'Yes, once he explained what had happened, I followed the scent of the soldiers and wrakes to their camp, and while they were building a huge fire we looked around, and found Ferdy up a nearby tree, bound and gagged.'

'So before the wrakes could roast me and eat me, Boris and Frovin cut me down and we all ran for our lives.'

'I was leading the way when we fell down the bank …'

'And landed at my feet at just the right time. And all because of an apple,' said Ikoseer with some satisfaction.

'I'm sure it has nothing to do with apples,' cut in Boris. 'Father says all the trouble is because they took the stones out of the Pentark. They should have just left them there. Onysius would've left Banters Den alone and … and we wouldn't have had to leave home and …'

Ikoseer raised her eyebrows. 'The royal family had no choice. Do you think they should have left the stones for the enemy to use?'

'No, but Father says that at least we'd still have good harvests and the forests would be safe.'

'Perhaps. But all is not lost. There is still a little magic left. Eight of the twelve outer gems remain in the Pentark. The power is weak in the World of the Soul, but nevertheless everyone will just have to manage.'

'It's all because Earl Onysius broke the Treaty that we're in this terrible mess,' said Ferdy, quoting his father verbatim.

Lord Mortimer was behind the civil war,' corrected Artorus. 'And Onysius is his accomplice.'

Ikoseer locked eyes with Ferdy, making him shrink back in his seat. 'It is dangerous to leave powerful stones in the hands of your enemy. One never knows what they might do with them. But now, my dear friends, fate has brought us all together … has it not?'

Ikoseer cut a slice of cheese and looked meaningfully at each of her guests, except Artorus.

'Fate?' squeaked Boris. 'Disaster more like. We are most grateful for your help but Ferdy and I must be on our way. We have to continue on to the Rolling Hills and we intend to get there.'

With Boris' sharp jab to his ribs, Ferdy nodded in agreement.

'I suppose we must go,' he added, shoving a thick slice of bread loaded with fried onion and mushrooms into his mouth.

Ikoseer continued without pausing. 'And I must remind you that we are all now in the World of the Soul. That means that none of us is safe outside this cave.'

She leant down and focused on the dwarves. 'I was hoping that perhaps one act of kindness might deserve another. Just a few days travel is all I ask of you … unless that is asking too much?'

Boris squirmed, and Ferdy almost choked on his mouthful. At this point Artorus leant forward, took up one of Ikoseer's maps and, making room on the table, spread it out and began pointing as he spoke.

'Here's the cave where we are now, and here's the Wayfarers' Road that we're going to follow through the forest. We'll emerge here, at the junction of the Greening Road, the Trading Road and the Road of Stones. Ikoseer, Marta and I will be taking the Trading Road, which leads up to and follows the length of the Lux Mountain range.

'But Boris, you and Ferdy will take the Road of Stones,' said Artorus, returning his finger to the junction. 'You can see that it runs in the opposite direction, following the western edge of the forest.

'Now the pack ponies need to remain with us, so you'll have to continue on foot. It's seventy-five miles. Should take you about ten days, until a track turns off the road and back through Greenwood Forest and on to the Rolling Hills. That will be another two days' journey. But it will be much safer than going along the Road of Stones.'

He turned to Frovin. 'I would appreciate your help getting through the forest—you know it so well. But once we reach the junction you will be free to return to your sett or continue with Boris and Ferdy to the Rolling Hills.'

'I will definitely come with you to the junction. I'm sure they will too.' Frovin turned to Boris and Ferdy. 'Won't you? We haven't come this far without trial, but there are more of us now—and we'll have Ikoseer with us!'

'And you also have Thrust, do you not?' asked the Sage suddenly, raising an eyebrow at Boris. 'It is always handy to have such a weapon on our side.'

Alarmed, Boris felt for the short dwarf sword his father had given them to take on their escape.

'We'll come with you as far as the junction,' he said, already vouching for Ferdy. 'But don't expect us to continue on with you along the Trading Road. Our debt to you will be paid once we reach the end of the Wayfarers' Road. Then we'll travel along the Road of Stones towards the Rolling Hills where our cousins live.'

'Very well.' Ikoseer gave a faint smile. She turned her attention to Marta, aware that she was unsettled by all the talk.

'This is very new to you Marta. Is there anything you would like to know?'

Marta felt overwhelmed. Her bottom lip quivered.

'Our worlds are so different from each other. Everything is more ...' She struggled for the word ... 'unpredictable. Until yesterday, I'd never left the World of Man. Or seen knights or sages. Or dwarves. And I had no idea that badgers could talk. It's normal for all of you, but not for people in my world.'

Marta took a deep breath. 'My mother was a refugee from this World of the Soul. Somehow she escaped into our world at the start of the civil war.'

Her voice softened, and her eyes misted over. 'She died when I was nine. Shortly before her death she showed me a strange but beautiful pattern in a book. She called it a Pentark. All I can remember is that it had a central stone with other stones around it. She said that it powered the light sphere on our headland to keep our country fertile and our coastline safe for passing ships.

'But I know that our sphere is not the only one. She told me that there are three spheres in total around the Isle, each looking after one of the three worlds.'

She gave Ikoseer a questioning look. 'But what I don't understand is that if some of the stones have been taken from the Pentark, then why has it affected your world and not mine?'

Ikoseer hesitated. 'That very same question has drawn the attention of Lord Mortimer.'

'I know why!' Boris butted in and dropped his knife on the metal plate, making Marta jump. 'I overheard Father say that the only reason the World of Man is still so fertile must be because the Pentark stones are hidden there. And that's why our home was attacked and we had to leave ...'

Marta was startled by Boris' outburst. She could see tears brimming along his eyelids.

Boris lowered his voice. 'And that's because we're miners and live close by. The enemy thinks we had something to do with helping to hide them.'

Ferdy sat to attention. 'Maybe the stones are hidden in
our mining tunnels.'

'Don't be ridiculous,' said Boris sniffing.

Artorus gave Ikoseer a sharp look. 'Boris is right. The enemy seeks, in
particular, the Lightenstone, the central Stone of the Pentark. But your
father is mistaken. It is not in the World of Man.'

'Where is it then?' asked Ferdy scratching his head.

'Why is it that some dwarves ask far too many questions?' Ikoseer raised
her voice, peering down at Ferdy. 'First they want nothing to do with
things and then they want to know everything there is to know! There is
little I can tell you except that we are on our way to the Lux Mountains.
And, as we shall be parting company with you at the junction, it is really
of no consequence to you what we are doing and why we are going …'

She paused, and then continued in a gentler tone, 'But three more pairs
of eyes keeping a lookout for trouble in the forest will be most helpful. It
seems all three of you have already come through one clash with Onysius'
scouts, which shows your fighting spirit.'

'Scouts and wrakes,' corrected Ferdy running his stubby fingers around his
plate and sucking off the remnants of buttery juice.

'And wrakes,' confirmed Ikoseer, amused. 'These things must not be
dismissed lightly and I am most grateful for your company. But now there
are ponies to be packed and saddled and much more to do before we go. If
we can rouse ourselves after such a splendid breakfast and be on our way,
the forest mist will be our friend. The Wayfarers' Road is old, slow and
overgrown, but I know the way.'

∽

Without waiting for more discussion Ikoseer stood up and headed to
the back of the cave to pack up. Within the hour breakfast was cleared
and Famrod and the ponies were attended to. They were all ready to go.

Artorus swung open the old cavern door and they passed through, with Ikoseer leading out her stallion followed by the three ponies and Famrod.

Artorus pointed to the ponies. 'Boris and Ferdy, you can ride Aster and Poppins. Marta and Frovin can ride Snowball.'

Famrod stamped and jingled his bit while Artorus helped Boris and Ferdy onto the two bay ponies. Marta mounted the white mountain pony and Frovin was lifted up to cling atop a pack behind her saddle. Ikoseer swung onto the bare back of the golden stallion, then intoned an incantation to seal the door.

At her words, 'On, Helios,' the shimmering horse stepped out onto the Wayfarers' Road, leading the motley caravan into the morning mist.

# CHAPTER 3

Standing at an arched window in the North Tower of Jimpiragh Castle in the Dukedom of Asilodor, Earl Onysius was tapping his fingers on the cracked stone ledge. In the fading afternoon light he scanned the desolate plains, cursing the hot dry winds that swept across the baked earth. He fixed his gaze on the horizon along the castle road, looking for any signs of movement. But there was none. His jaw tightened.

It had been weeks since he had sent his scouts and wrakes from Mirraway to invade the World of Man, and there was still no news from them. And what about his spies? Why hadn't they reported back? He turned away from the window and sat down at the great stone table that filled the room. He picked at a plate of food and then rattled his empty tankard. A kurr, a stunted goblin-like creature, crept forward to refill it with spiced mead before slinking back into the shadows … waiting.

A small group of kurrs had been found wandering on the border fringes between Asilodor and further south in the World of the Dark Night, looking for bleak, catfish and salmon in the cold waters of the Bleak River. This one, Volgor, had been captured and brought to Onysius as a sort of amusement, a gift, caught only because he was young, small and weak. Kurrs were considered to be unpredictable—and therefore untrustworthy.

Onysius mulled and fidgeted. War and battle had taken their toll, and his ageing bones complained as he rose from the table and returned to the arched window. He stared out onto the barren landscape, but saw nothing, his mind elsewhere. His dark eyes were sore and red from the persistent winds and all-pervading dust around him.

'Bring me the soothsayers!' he barked.

'Soothsayers, my Lord?' squeaked the kurr from the corner of the room. He ventured out a few tiny steps so that he was now just visible in the fading afternoon light. 'We only have one left my Lord … the other two … well they …'

Onysius felt his anger rising as he turned and clapped his watery eyes on Volgor. 'Well they what?' he demanded.

'The trolls are very hungry and they thought the soothsayers looked positively delicious and ready for a proper roasting down there in the kitchen … only one escaped my Lord.' Volgor took a step back to safety and spread his hands in resignation.

'WHAT!! The trolls ate my soothsayers?' Onysius sent dagger stares to the terrified creature as if it was his fault.

'S-s-still one left my Lord … 'came the apologetic reply.

'Well don't just stand there cowering. Bring him to me NOW!' By this stage Onysius was boiling with rage.

'Y-y-y-es! My Lord … ' Volgor made a race for the door, pulling it back just as Onysius' flying tankard clipped his ear, smashed against the wall, spraying an arc of mead before crashing to the floor.

Volgor scurried down the cold stone steps. It had become unbearable to be near his master. But he was not free of him yet.

The news about the eaten soothsayers had, understandably, not been well received. However trolls have to eat just like every other creature and food was scarce. Save Onysius, everyone in Jimpiragh Castle was hungry.

The civil war that Lord Mortimer had engineered years ago against King Gordir, in order to gain his Kingdom of Gorthonomir, had resulted in death and starvation and had spread throughout Illingaith and the adjoining Lands of Magirus and Arctus.

Volgor had been serving Onysius faithfully ever since, but this only delayed the inevitability that before too long he too would be roasting on a spit in the main kitchen, surrounded by salivating trolls. He shivered just thinking about it. Looking for a single soothsayer in a huge castle was a dangerous game. He would have to be careful.

He came to the bottom of the stairs, waiting and listening. There was much activity in the scullery; the banging of pots and pans and a foul stench of cooking permeated the air.

He began to feel queasy as he sped deeper into the castle. He hugged the walls, his feet quiet on the stone floor, slipping into quarried alcoves to avoid detection. Of course, Volgor did not expect the soothsayer to be anywhere near the kitchen so he crept away from the North Tower then turned left towards the library.

At his crowning, the new King Gordir had annexed a mountainous area of land in the south of Illingaith, and presented it as a coronation gift to Duke Tardor, his cousin and Onysius' father. And his consort had given valuable books for a library.

There, upon a mountain, Duke Tardor built Jimpiragh Castle and named the annexed land Asilodor. As a man of war he had no time for books and libraries, and the tomes had been left to gather dust in the undercroft. But now Duke Tardor was gone, a skeleton in a crypt deep under the castle floor.

And Earl Onysius had need of soothsayers. Books, he had discovered, were used by soothsayers. So he cleared out a small armoury and made it into a library.

Volgor knocked on the library door, not expecting a reply. He was right. He knocked again, this time a bit harder and whispered loudly, 'It's Volgor. Onysius wants you … NOW! Gather your things and open the door. Hurry up!'

Volgor put his ear to the door and heard faint rustling, but the door stayed locked. He could not blame the soothsayer. If he left the relative safety of his library his life was at risk. If he did not leave, then Onysius would send Volgor with some loyal thugs to drag him up to the North Tower and demand an explanation.

On the other hand Volgor did not want to consider what his own punishment might be if he came back without the soothsayer. He kept listening, tapping now and then until he heard heavy breathing. The inner bolt slid back, releasing the door from the stone arch and opening it just enough for Volgor to slip in.

He had been in the library only once before and nothing had changed. Far too many books and not nearly enough room. A small, rough wooden desk was jammed into one corner with a narrow path winding to it through a forest of stacked books. He noticed a cascade of melted wax hanging from a spent candle; a cowl hung from a crude hook hammered into the stone mortar, teetering on collapse. An inkhorn and quills cluttered the desk amid rolls of paper.

Attricus, the soothsayer, was podgy with grey unkempt hair, and was dressed in a plain brown habit that hung to the floor. He wore simple strapped sandals and a frayed twilled rope around his stomach, the rope seeming to droop without any real purpose. He looked rumpled and worn as he shuffled past Volgor to the desk and slumped into his chair. They looked at each other: the scrawny kurr and the podgy soothsayer.

Finally Attricus spoke. 'I know what Onysius wants … But my crystal ball is silent. There is nothing I can tell him.'

Volgor didn't know what to say. Soothsayers did not confide in kurrs and he had visions of Onysius pacing furiously back and forth in the North Tower. Concerned about his own skin, he just wanted Attricus to hurry up.

His eyes darted back to the door. 'I have to take you to him.'

There was nothing more he could say and the soothsayer would just have to make something up … wouldn't he?

With resignation Attricus sighed, wrapped his crystal ball in a cloth, and hugged it to his protruding belly. He appeared to give one last loving glance around at the mountain of books as if it might be the last time he saw them. Then he closed the door behind him, and trundled after Volgor.

The trek back to the North Tower was uneventful. As Volgor and Attricus slipped past the scullery door at the bottom of the stairs and began climbing, they could hear the trolls noisily tucking into their roasted meal, licking their lips and sucking fat off their fingers. The stench followed them up, making them both retch.

The spiral stairs to Onysius' room were very steep and Volgor wondered if the soothsayer would make it. He was breathing hard and so they rested at the first landing, but Volgor wasted no time moving again.

The door to the upper room was partly open and Volgor paused. He took a deep breath and slipped through the gap into Onysius' presence. Without a word he hurried to the shadowed corner as the soothsayer nervously entered behind him, placing his scrying ball onto the huge stone table.

Onysius was still standing by the window, staring, fists clenched. He remained silent.

Attricus wavered, then with trembling hands, unwrapped the crystal ball, working the cloth around the base, protecting it from the harshness of the cold stone and taking up as much time as he could. Then he stared into the ball, willing it to bring him something. But the crystal, empty and silent, stared back.

Nothing.

Beads of sweat gathered along the deep furrows of the soothsayer's forehead; his palms became hot and wet. A whole minute went by.

Still nothing.

Volgor peered out from his hiding place. Onysius' fingers were drumming on the window ledge once more. But suddenly the soothsayer caught his breath and his mouth opened a little, just enough for Volgor to realise that he had seen something. Attricus' eyes widened and he began blabbering. The words were gibberish, tumbling over each other like polished stones in a raging river, making no sense whatsoever.

Onysius turned from the window and within two strides was bearing down on him, his watery, bloodshot eyes glaring with contempt.

'Stop speaking nonsense! What is it you see?' he demanded.

Attricus felt the cold rise of fear. 'I see the deathly shape of a gambler, with a sword to his heart. From the grave he points to a cloaked knight with the Crest of Power upon his shoulder. There is also another … an apple seller.'

'So did my spy find what we seek before he died? Speak up … What more do you see?'

Attricus answered in halting speech, his head down, keeping his gaze on the crystal ball.

'I cannot … tell more than that … my Lord … Perhaps by tomorrow noon … more will come.'

His voice faded away. He was hoping against hope that this would be enough to satisfy Onysius' thirst for news.

'BAH! … you can tell me nothing! So, one of my spies is dead. There are plenty more. Perhaps it is you the trolls should have roasted. Take your useless ball and get out of my sight. I will see you back here tomorrow. You will hope it is more forthcoming then. LEAVE me!'

Onysius turned his gaze to the darkest corner of the room.

'Volgor, see to it he makes it back alive. Bring him to me again in the morning.'

'Yes, my Lord.' Volgor crept out of the shadows and shuffled towards the door, following Attricus out onto the landing and trotting down the stairs behind him.

Each of them was thinking that his life was on a knife edge and if he wanted to be alive to see the sun rise in two days' time, then it would be best to try to escape tonight. And yet each one kept the thought to himself lest the other should betray him.

Attricus saw himself being trussed by a pack of trolls as they prepared a roasting dish in the scullery of the North Tower and he was not waiting around to see if the vision came true. It was a warning. His life was in danger—he knew he must disappear.

As they reached the bottom of the stairs all they could hear was loud snoring, farting and the occasional stomach scratching from contented full-bellied trolls. And the stench of cooking still hung in the air as they hurriedly turned down towards the library where Attricus' comforting books awaited him, piled high behind the thick oak door.

# CHAPTER 4

Volgor was outside the library in Jimpiragh Castle, twisting a loose tassel on his threadbare shirt. He had just escorted Attricus back after his meeting with Onysius. But, as soon as the soothsayer closed the door, a scraping and clattering had begun.

Volgor stopped to listen, wanting to return to his own room but curious about what was going on inside this one. He had an escape plan to make and time was running out. Darkness would be his only friend.

He felt homesick, wondering if his family still fished in the Bleak River and if they had survived the attacks of trolls and wrakes. He closed his eyes, remembering the joys of grabbing the slimy catfish splashing in the shallows. And the wonderful smell of them cooking on the campfire.

He was startled by the groaning creak of rusty hinges. He pushed his ear hard against the wood. Another creak, then complete silence. He strained to hear the slightest sound.

Nothing.

His curiosity was piqued. He thought of knocking but reached for the ringed handle instead. He gave a light push, surprised when the heavy door gave way slightly. He pushed again, harder this time and the door opened a bit further. Yes, the soothsayer had forgotten to bolt it.

He stopped and listened again. All was quiet but he could smell a strange musty odour. A slight draught of cool air blew through the open door. He had no idea why, but he whispered, 'Hello?'

No one answered.

He pushed again hard, and the door opened far enough for him to poke his head around and look in. The towers of books remained, but there was no rustling of papers, no faint glow of candle flame and he assumed, no Attricus.

Volgor squeezed his scraggy body through the gap, slammed himself hard against the door to close it and slid the bolt across.

Where was Attricus? Volgor crept forward. His nostrils flared at a strange smell in the room and he followed it, his calloused feet silent on the cobblestones. When he rounded the last tower of books he was expecting to see piles of rolled papers on a desk, but was astonished to find the desk moved and the papers gone. He swung around and fixed his bulging grey eyes on the opposite wall. A column of books had been shifted and it took him a moment to make sense of what he was looking at.

There was another door, but it was not fully shut and a cool breeze from an underground tunnel was bringing the musty odour with it. He felt a blend of excitement and relief welling in him.

Volgor wondered what to do. He knew if he was going to follow Attricus he had to do it now. There was no time to go back and get his things. He looked around. Looked for something useful to take. A rope—anything. But all he could see were umpteen columns of books and the soothsayer's inkhorn and goose quills for writing. The candlestick was gone, and so was the cowl that had hung from the hook in the wall.

He made for the tunnel doorway and poked his head in the gap. As he peered into the gloom through his thin fringe, his hooked nose wrinkled in disgust. Damp clung to the stones like beads of sweat and the tunnel was cold and uninviting. He gave a small shiver and without looking back, slipped through into the darkness, leaving the door ajar.

Ahead of him was the soothsayer, shuffling along the cold tunnel that led from the library. A hessian sack hung from his right shoulder and he held an unlit candle.

Attricus pulled his cowl closer around him and wished his sandals wouldn't slap against the stone floor. He knew the way as far as the underground room, but from there he would be travelling blind. He patted his pocket, reassuring himself that his flints were still there.

∽

35

The soothsayer's thoughts turned to how he had found this way out of the library a few months ago. While searching in a book of spells, he had stepped onto his hem, lost his balance and collided with a large jumble of books stacked against the wall behind him.

The books collapsed around him and as he was restacking them he felt a slight breath of cool air that seemed to be coming from a tiny crack in the wall. He turned his cheek to the crack and felt it again, checking to see if there was a loose stone. Then he stepped back, staring at the wall.

Running his hands over the stones, he reached behind the lowest books, feeling, prodding, until his fingers touched on a small metal lug near the floor. He dragged the books away and attempted to move the lever, but it was jammed. He tried again and again. Nothing.

Looking around for something heavy to help move the lever, he realised that this room had been a small armoury. He remembered seeing a rusty battleaxe in a corner. Finding it, he slammed the handle down hard onto the metal lever, and kept striking it. But it would not budge. Hoping to lubricate the lug, he dripped precious candle wax onto the lever and kept on striking.

Finally, with sweat dripping from his brow, he heard it release, revealing the outline of a secret door. The hinges were old and layers of iron scale jammed the mechanism. But a short while later, and after more effort, he could swing the door almost fully open, revealing a tunnel.

Cautiously, he followed the tunnel to the undercroft, a room that housed the many goods that Onysius kept for himself including grain, cheese, olives, honey and dried fruits. The discovery of these stores had led over the intervening months to the podginess that Volgor had noticed.

∽

Now that he was using the tunnel to escape from the castle, Attricus wished he had also searched beyond the storeroom. Behind him Volgor's eyes soon adjusted to the darkness and being small, he was nimble and quick. He also noticed that the passage narrowed as he went.

Before long he saw Attricus' hunched body trundling along up ahead, his head bent as he kept close to the walls. Sometimes he would slow down and stop, cocking his head to one side, listening for any noise behind him. But all he heard was the dripping of water and the scurrying of rats.

Once, the soothsayer turned right around and peered through his glasses into the darkness, but Volgor kept hidden.

Eventually the tunnel joined the undercroft, but the entrance was blocked off. On one side, barrels of wine were stacked up to the ceiling. Sacks of potatoes were heaped together on the other side and Attricus began to clamber up them, reaching for the gap at the top. He lay flat against the sacks, peering over them, surveying the room below. Several of Onysius' soldiers and wrakes were working. The soldiers held flaming torches and barked orders and the wrakes lifted and carried.

As he watched, a wrake slung two large sacks of potatoes onto his broad shoulders. He was about to walk up the stone steps to the kitchen but something made him stop. He sniffed the air and looked towards the tunnel. He moved closer, staring at the gap above for several minutes. The wrake's nostrils flared and a long low growl gurgled from his throat, deep and menacing.

Attricus froze. His heart pounded in his chest and fear spread through his body. But then a soldier struck the wrake's legs with a whip, biting hard into the flesh. He spun to face the soldier and with a warning snarl moved off, lumbering towards the stairs. The soldier glanced up, swept his torch several times across the face of the mound, and turned away quite satisfied, before following the wrake and the rest of the party and plunging the undercroft into darkness.

Attricus breathed a sigh of relief. Without waiting, he slung his hessian bag over and down the stack, wriggled his body through the gap and slid carefully down the other side into the storeroom. Crouching on the floor, he groped for his bag and pulled out the candle, pushing it down into the holder.

Volgor was by now watching from above as Attricus searched in his pocket
for his flints to light the candle. He frantically struck the stones. He
fumbled, unable to get a spark, and Volgor decided that it was time he
revealed his presence.

He slipped down the sacks and standing behind the soothsayer said,
'Can I help?'

Attricus opened his mouth to scream but Volgor stifled it with his hand
and hissed in his ear. 'It's Volgor. I've come to join you.'

It took some moments for the soothsayer's breathing to slow and he tried
to look at the kurr. Volgor gently released his grip, struck the flints, and
lit the candle. He held it to Attricus' face and they stared at each other in
the eerie light.

Volgor held a long withered finger to his lips and the soothsayer nodded,
mouthing the word 'food'. Volgor understood, handed the candle back to
him, and crammed a small leather sack with nuts, dried fruits, potatoes
and a round of wax-coated cheese.

A short coil of rope was hanging on a hook nearby, so he slipped it
over his neck and grabbed a sharp knife from a nearby table, securing it
under his belt.

Attricus was shoving dried meat and hardtack biscuits into his larger sack.
When he discovered a box of candles he took what he could, while Volgor
stood ready and expectant in the middle of the room. Apart from the stairs
leading up into the kitchen and the tunnel to the library, there were two
tunnels ahead, one apparently running south, one east.

When Attricus was ready he joined Volgor, peered down at him and spread
out an upturned hand in a questioning gesture. Volgor looked up at the
raised eyebrows and furrowed forehead. A cold realisation hit him. He had
assumed Attricus knew where to go.

The kurr swallowed hard. Here they were, daring to escape from the clutches of Onysius, master of Jimpiragh, and stealing from his storehouse as well. But they had no idea which way to go from here.

He returned the questioning gesture with one of his own and pointed to the tunnel to his right hoping it would take him south towards Bleak River and the Raven Mountains to his family. Attricus pursed his lips and pointed to the other tunnel hoping it would take him east to the Jimpiragh Hills, and then to the Tangled Woods. He intended to head as far away from Onysius as possible.

Volgor yearned for his family. He missed them and he looked up at Attricus with pain in his eyes. He was torn between the two. The soothsayer understood. In the flickering candlelight Volgor bowed his head, whispering 'Sorry.'

He picked up his sack and not wanting to look back, headed towards the tunnel on his right. Attricus watched as the kurr melted into the blackness. Then he sighed, hitched his bag onto his shoulder and walked towards the other tunnel. Burdened with night blindness and a heavy load he looked ahead to get his bearings, blew out the candle and stepped into the dark.

The tunnel seemed to go on forever. On occasion, he put his hand to the wall, feeling his way forward. His fingers slid over the cold wet stone. Numbness spread up his arms and into his core. But eventually stone gave way to earth. Cobwebs hung in strings from the ceiling and festooned the walls. They stuck to his fingers when he reached out for support and he shivered, recoiling when he touched soft, squishy bodies and they scurried away. Spiders!

He felt a change in the air … as if there was a greater space before him. He waited for a moment, thinking he heard a sound far behind him, a soft scurrying … then it seemed to stop.

He had no time to think and nowhere to go. Hoping he was right about the space, he spread his arms out in front. Swinging them from side to side and feeling that the wall came to an end, he moved left into another opening and out of sight. He stood still, listening. The pattering sound continued. He was puzzled. He heard it come closer and closer until he was sure it was almost beside him in the tunnel. He tensed and held his breath.

'Attricus?'

'Volgor … is that you?'

'Yes,' he hissed.

'What are you doing here?'

By now Volgor was beside him. 'I … I changed my mind. Nasty things in these tunnels … very nasty things.'

'But what about your family?'

Volgor swallowed hard. 'Perhaps they're not there anymore.'

'Don't worry. You'll meet them again. Besides, it's much safer if we travel together. You can be my eyes in the dark.'

Attricus paused. 'It feels like we're in another cave. Can you see anything?'

'Yes. The tunnel's opened out into another cavern. Then it branches off again. I don't know, but I think we're standing in a crypt.'

'Duke Tardor's crypt?'

'Is Onysius' father buried down here?'

'Yes … he's here somewhere … or what's left of him after twenty-five years. Come on. We've got to get out of Jimpiragh. The sun will be gone soon. We can travel by moonlight.'

'Why don't we just go and have a look?' stalled Volgor. 'Seeing as we're here.'

'No! We should not disturb the dead. And we haven't the time.'

But Volgor had already sneaked past Attricus, leaving him standing in the dark.

'Volgor …?'

All was quiet. The soothsayer waited for several minutes until he heard the soft pattering of the kurr's returning feet.

'We have to go now. It will soon be nightfall,' he insisted.

Volgor tugged at the soothsayer's sleeve, excited. 'But it's the Duke's crypt. Don't you want to come and have a look?'

'No I don't. It'll just be a pile of old bones.'

'Ah yes … but these bones are well dressed. The pile of old bones has royal garments … Come!'

With that, Volgor grabbed Attricus by the hand and pulled him further into the crypt.

The soothsayer stumbled along behind until the kurr stopped and then, without waiting, grabbed the candle and struck the flints. As its warm glow lit up the darkness, he handed the candle to Attricus. With some trepidation, he swept it over the skeleton.

The haunting eye sockets of the dead Duke stared into nothingness. There was no crown upon his head but his royal red robe, dull, fragile and coated in dust, showed who he was. A small inscription was carved into the stone slab he lay on. Volgor pulled himself up for a closer look.

'See. Just a pile of old bones.' Attricus shivered and turned to go.

'Wait!' said the kurr looking down. 'Bring the candle closer. Here.'

Attricus moved the light, holding the tip of the candle down, so that it dripped wax into the thick layer of dust along the edge of the stone. At first they saw nothing, but then a tiny glimpse of colour became visible from underneath a fold in Tardor's robe.

'What is it?'

Without answering, Attricus moved the light closer and reached for the object. Cloth, soil and dust fell away to reveal a short sword. A cut jewel was set in the centre of the elaborate gilt handle and the Royal Crest of the Isle of Spheres adorned the top. They both stared. Such a beautiful object in such a terrible place!

With his thumb Attricus gently rubbed the dust off the jewel, revealing its true beauty. His hands began to tremble. He locked eyes with Volgor and without a word and before he could change his mind, slipped the sword into a secret pocket inside his tunic.

'Now, we must go!'

Without delay, Attricus took the lead, holding the light as far in front of him as he could. The candle flickered across the earthen walls where the black gaping mouths of two more tunnels bore into the earth. One appeared as if it would take them back towards the main castle; the other headed off at right angles.

'This one,' said Attricus. 'I can feel the cool evening breeze coming from the Jimpiragh Hills.'

For a moment he held the candle high at the entrance before extinguishing it and then Volgor led them into the gloom.

It did not take long to reach the tunnel's end. Cold, hungry and weary, they ate a small meal from the supplies in their sacks and slept, huddled together for warmth among the rocks as they waited for the sun to set and the full moon to rise.

$\infty$

Standing atop the tower of the outer north wall, Onysius was looking along the castle road leading to the Tangled Woods. The last rays of sunshine bathed the baked earth. On a huge perch beside him was an anomir.

He was stroking the creature when it jerked its scaly head towards the east. Vulture-like eyes fixed a stare towards the Jimpiragh Hills, and then throwing its head back and with curved beak to the sky, it let out a piercing scream.

Onysius followed its gaze. He saw nothing but turned to the creature: 'What is it my beauty? What is it you see?'

# PART 2

# GLIMMER

# CHAPTER 5

Onysius stood staring into the flames of a campfire near the massive Lux Mountains, contemplating his next step. The fire crackled and the stars twinkled in the clear night sky. Snow covered the mountain caps that rose like rock giants behind him.

Dressed in light armour, Onysius was an imposing figure despite his advancing years. He stood tall and strong. His once black hair, now heavily peppered with grey, fell to his collarbone and the dark bloodshot eyes that focused on the fire were set beneath a jutting brow. A light breeze ruffled the red cloak that fell in soft folds from a clasp at his broad shoulders. A sheathed dagger hung from a wide brown belt and his hand grasped the decorated pommel of his sword, out of its scabbard and with the tip resting on the ground.

As soon as he had discovered that Attricus and Volgor had escaped Jimpiragh, he sent an armed band of soldiers, wrakes and mounted anomirs after them. Then, on an impulse and impatient for news from his scouts in the World of Man, he saddled a boorling—a steed normally only ridden by wrakes—and sped towards Mirraway Castle.

He disliked boorlings. They were obstinate, especially when in pursuit of prey and uncomfortable to ride due to their pacing gait, but he had almost two hundred miles to travel and over open ground they were much faster than horses. He arrived at Mirraway by noon on the third day. Once there, he immediately made the necessary preparations to leave for Magirus with his most trusted men. Still smarting at the escape of Attricus and Volgor, he sent for the old crone who lived in a hovel outside the castle's walls.

Now his mind wandered back to that day.

∽

Dressed in filthy garb, the crone sat cross-legged on the cold stone floor in front of him, her grey hair hanging in strings.

'Bring me a bowl of water,' she snapped to the frightened scullery boy. 'Make it quick!'

Black nails tipped the gnarled fingers that reached out to snatch the bowl when the boy returned. As he scurried away she held the bowl in front of her and sniffing, stared into the tiny pool in the bowl.

'I suppose you want to know about the Lightenstone?' she rasped. 'Is that it?'

She raised her eyes to meet his. 'In revenge—or spite—for being overlooked as leader of the Knights of Power, you leave your Order and then grovel in front of that mongrel Mortimer as he gloated on the murdered King's throne.'

Onysius lifted his chin in defiance. 'You have no right to judge me!'

'You were an ambitious fool,' she hissed.

'So what have you done since you were expelled by the knights? You teamed up with Mortimer, raiding and pillaging the land for him while it dies. Look at it … everywhere things are barely growing.'

The old crone waggled an accusing finger at him. 'And why ever did you promise him that you'd help him find the Lightenstone, eh?'

Onysius rose from the throne and circled the old woman so closely he could smell her. If she felt his intense gaze she didn't show it. As her breathing deepened, her body began to rock. Onysius returned to his seat and with a sweep of his arm dismissed the two guards who stood waiting nearby, leaving him alone with the old woman.

'What can you tell me about the scouts and spies I sent into the World of Man?' he demanded.

She began to speak in a deep slow voice. 'How long have they been gone now?'

'Too long.'

'Hmmm … you should follow 'em.'

'I leave tomorrow.'

The old crone stopped rocking. She lifted her eyes and studied him.

'Wise. Wise,' she crooned.

Onysius' voice quickened. 'So. The Lightenstone's hidden there then?'

She pursed her lips, thinking. 'Don't know what the connection to the Stone is. But somehow, it seems right.'

She looked back down into the water. Her eyes narrowed. She sucked her tongue and drawing up the spittle smacked her lips together.

'Ah … the Sage's close by. Now ain't that interestin'? But I must warn you—she's not to be messed with. Got the power of light about 'er.'

Onysius bristled. 'I'm not afraid of her.'

'Course not, my Earl, course not.' She crooned again, looking up and gestured with her hand in agreement.

'Do you see a cloaked knight with the Crest of Power on his shoulder … or a dead spy?'

Placing a hand on each knee, she leant forward over the bowl. 'Yes … perhaps he's a former comrade of yours.'

Onysius turned away.

'There's nothing more I can tell you other than something has happened in the World of Man. It's to do with the Stone,' she reiterated. 'And I see that the forces of light are gathering strength.'

He glared down at her, thinking about what she had said and then dismissed her with a wave of his hand. The crone struggled to her feet. Then she grabbed the bowl, cupping it in her trembling hands and lifted it to her thin lips. She gulped down the water as if to swallow what she had seen.

Without more ado she turned her back on Onysius. Tucking the bowl under her right arm she shuffled to the door and shouted to the guards, 'Let me out!'

∽

The next day, once a warhorse was freshly shod, Onysius left the blacksmith's shop with his men.

'Open the gates! Open the gates!' yelled the watchman from the keep.

A porter standing atop the flanking towers ordered the portcullis to be opened. The wrakes put their full weight to the winch. The groaning wheels began to turn and the chains bit into the wooden drum.

Onysius and his small entourage of men passed through the barbican of Mirraway Castle and onto the Lake Road. They had a long journey ahead.

∽

A sudden commotion in the camp snapped Onysius out of his daydream. A loud shout came from the watchman and he instinctively grasped his sword, unsheathed his dagger and moved towards the noise. Soon he heard the low growl of a wrake and noticed that the horses were unsettled by the visitor. Then he saw the dismounted wrake standing by his boorling.

The watchman, hearing Onysius' footsteps, turned to face him. 'There is news, my Lord. Our scouts crossed into the World of Man. One of the spies that you sent with them has been slain … by a knight …'

Onysius held up a hand to halt the watchman and turned his attention to the wrake. 'Speak!'

By the time the wrake finished his report, Onysius was furious.

The wrake stepped forward. 'But we think they had help,' he sneered, curling his top lip and releasing a foetid stench from his mouth.

He glared at the beast. 'Help?'

The wrake spat on the ground. 'We heard rumblings of a sage …'

Onysius tightened the grip on his sword. *Ikoseer!* The wrake turned to go.

'Return to Greenwood Forest. Continue your search,' he commanded.

The wrake returned a hateful look and snarled, intending to disobey.

Before striding back to the warmth of the fire, Onysius turned to the watchman. 'We leave in the morning. Have the men ready at daybreak.'

The watchman bowed. 'Yes, my Lord.'

Meanwhile, the wrake was caressing his boorling's leathery neck with long slow strokes as he watched Onysius disappear. The boorling was drooling with pleasure and emitted a high-pitched groaning sound.

'Not today my pet. We'll find you something else to eat.'

# CHAPTER 6

Ikoseer sat on a fallen log looking in awe at the majestic Lux Mountains before her. The shadow of a snow eagle glided across the white-blanketed slopes before soaring up towards the peaks. She breathed in the cool mountain air, pleased to be leaving the confines of Greenwood Forest.

She knew she would soon be faced with a new challenge, that of travelling through open country until they reached their destination. But she hoped that Onysius' scouts had grown weary of looking for them.

They had been following the Wayfarers' Road for a week. The old track was overgrown and dangerous in places, but a slow and steady pace brought them to the junction of the Greening Road, the Trading Road and the Road of Stones.

It had been a sad time for Marta. She missed her father and was worried that he would not know she was safe. And somehow she did feel safe. Even though everything in this land was strange and mysterious, she felt an increasing inner sense of belonging and familiarity that she could not explain.

Boris, on the other hand, had been pensive the last few days, knowing that he and Ferdy would soon be leaving the group. Their plan was to head north-east towards the safety of the Rolling Hills.

Ikoseer looked fondly at the activity before her. At sunrise, Boris and Ferdy wandered off to find wild mushrooms. Folding up the bottom of their vests into makeshift baskets they returned laden, tipping their find into a hot buttery pan. Marta made flatbread, adding some herbs that Frovin found nearby. Artorus was saddling the horses and checking their feet for stones. Despite the serenity of the scene before her, Ikoseer was unable to shake off an increasing sense of unease.

Breakfast was soon ready and they sat around the fire eating in silence.

Ikoseer looked over at Boris. 'We'll be parting soon my dear friends. I wanted to thank you and I offer my gratitude for your companionship on our journey through the forest. I hope your travel on the Road of Stones will be a safe one and that you reach your relatives in good health and good cheer.'

With a wavering heart Boris looked down at the dying flames of the fire.

Sensing his conflict, Ikoseer continued. 'Should you choose, you are of course, most welcome to come with us …'

'We can?' piped Ferdy, sitting bolt upright, a hopeful expression on his face.

Boris frowned at his brother. Ikoseer smiled gently at the excitement bubbling up in Ferdy. Boris squirmed, remembering his blunt refusal to go any further than the end of Wayfarers' Road.

What was it he had said? 'But don't expect us to continue on with you along the Trading Road to the mountains. Our debt to you will be paid once we reach the end of the Wayfarers' Road, and then we'll travel along the Road of Stones towards the Rolling Hills where our cousins live.'

Boris had made a promise to his mother that they would go straight to the Rolling Hills, but so far all these adventures had left his promise in tatters. He knew that if Ferdy had not been captured, they would already be in the relative safety of the Rolling Hills. And yet deep within him he had a strange yearning for something more.

'And what of you, Frovin?' enquired Ikoseer.

Frovin looked at the dwarves. 'I'm sorry. I'll miss both of you, but I've decided to go with Ikoseer.'

Marta saw Ferdy's excitement fade, and her heart went out to him.

'Boris, why don't you and Ferdy come too?' she said. 'You're very good at finding mushrooms. Besides, it's a long walk from here to the Rolling Hills and how will you protect yourselves if you're attacked by a wrake?'

Boris shot back. 'I'm sure there'll be just as many wrakes where you're going.'

The walking would not have bothered Boris. Riding horses was not natural for dwarves and Boris now had a sore backside and legs that he was sure would never straighten properly again. But they were by nature mountain dwellers and perhaps it was the sight of the Lux Mountains that tugged at his heart.

'Come on Boris,' pleaded Ferdy.

Boris looked up from the fire and turned his gaze towards the mountain range. High up, the wind blew drifts of snow from the peaks and the early morning sunshine bathed the massive slopes in a rich golden hue. The moment they emerged from the gloom of the forest and saw the mountains for the first time, Boris was overcome by their majesty. He also had the oddest feeling that the mountains were calling to him.

'Oh … alright then,' he sighed, defeated. 'I'll come.'

The Sage and Artorus exchanged looks.

'Wonderful. It's settled then. You will all be most valuable to us on this journey,' said Ikoseer. 'But I sense that Onysius' scouts aren't too far away. If we depart straight away we can stay perhaps one … maybe two … days ahead of them.'

'But I still don't know where we're going.' Ferdy was frustrated.

Ikoseer nodded. 'Our journey will take us through the Lux Mountains to where Thrim, your ancestor, forged Thrust, and then to the foot of the Ascension Mountains where his headstone still stands.'

Ferdy scratched his head, wondering. *We're going to a cemetery?*

'To reach the mountains we'll first travel by the Trading Road as planned. But we'll leave that before we get to the road through the pass. I have a feeling that road won't be safe. So we'll be crossing the mountains by another route.'

By now everyone was paying attention.

'We'll camp on the plain tonight,' Ikoseer continued, 'but we must leave there before daylight tomorrow. Who knows where the wrakes and wolves will be? With an open plain before us we'll be vulnerable. At least for a time.

'As we cross the plateau rocky outcrops will give us some cover, but between them the ground is flat and exposed. If we're to make it to the foot of the mountains, we must keep our eyes and ears open. The enemy could appear from anywhere. So now let's pack up and make haste.'

The unease in Ikoseer's heart hadn't abated and she was anxious to get going as soon as possible.

Full of excitement, Ferdy pulled Boris to his feet. 'Come on Boris, we've got mountains to explore.'

Ferdy wasted no time gathering the breakfast pans before shoving them into a thick hessian sack. Boris kicked dirt over the fire, mulling over his decision. Had it been wise? he wondered.

They were soon ready.

Boris was still deep in thought when Artorus picked him up and dumped him into a saddle. With a quick tug on the bridle and a slap to Aster's rump he was jerked forward and on his way.

A feeling of panic arose in him, as he found himself staring at the golden rump of Helios and the flowing robe of the Sage. Frantic, he turned around looking for Ferdy. But all he saw was the black nose of Famrod and above it, the face of Artorus looking down on him, amused.

He was sandwiched between them, and Ferdy was somewhere behind.

They covered over ten miles along the Trading Road that morning. The road was wide and level, with grassy plains stretching for twenty miles on either side, and an occasional stand of windswept trees dotting the verge. At midday, Ikoseer led them down into a grove of bent and twisted trunks for a short rest and a bite to eat. The horses drank from a small spring near the edge of the trees and Marta re-filled their skins with the cool clear water. As they sat together eating leftover bread and drinking water a forest raven flew over them, and landed on a branch.

'Kraa! Kraa!' Ikoseer held up a hand to greet the bird.

Accustomed to forest creatures and knowing that the raven had come as a messenger, Frovin leant towards Ikoseer, while Artorus tensed, hoping for good news. Boris and Ferdy fell quiet.

Marta wondered what the Sage was doing. She sat still and stared at the bird as if connecting her mind with the bird's mind and after a short while said, 'Thank you my friend.' With that the raven departed as abruptly as it had come.

'My worst fears have been realised,' she said. 'It appears that Onysius is travelling along the Trading Road from Illingaith, with a troop of about twenty soldiers.

'Last night, he received a visit from a master wrake on his boorling …'

Ferdy froze. 'I've never seen a boorling, but I've heard of them. I don't want to get carried away on one of those …'

The Sage looked directly at Ferdy. 'And neither should you, so try not to get tangled up with one if you can help it. They are a vile savage creature that I hope none of you will ever meet. Nothing bred by Lord Mortimer is to be trusted.'

She paused and then began again. 'Last night a master wrake visited Onysius. It seems he now knows that his spy was killed in a raid in the World of Man. He has heard a rumour of a sage in these parts and that a knight is involved, but I doubt he knows more than that. For the moment the rest of you are unknown to him … and I'd like to keep it that way.'

'What will we do?' asked Ferdy, full of concern. 'Will we make it to the mountains before they see us?'

'Yes, I think we will … if we go now. We have a head start. We'll be turning off the road in a few hours. Then we'll make camp and rest until midnight, leave in the early hours tomorrow and cross the plains of the plateau under cover of darkness. We'll need to put as much distance between us and Onysius as possible.'

'But what happens if they see us before we turn off?' Ferdy's mind conjured up all manner of nasty things that might happen should they be set upon.

Artorus stood up. 'We can only hope that they're more than a day's ride away so they won't see us.'

'Now look what we've got ourselves into,' Boris whispered fiercely to Ferdy, annoyed with himself for agreeing to come. 'We should've just gone on the Road of Stones. Much safer.'

Ferdy could not look at him. Perhaps Boris was right.

They travelled another ten miles without incident before turning off the road and down a steep embankment onto the open plain.

There was no road or path to be seen, but patches of small white pebbles were showing through the moss on the ground and Marta wondered if it had once been an old trade route. Despite their tiredness, Ikoseer kept them moving towards the mountains for another hour before stopping at a large outcrop of jagged white rocks. The rocks looked odd sticking straight up out of the flat ground, but behind them was a natural semicircle with room for all the horses and an area to camp. It sheltered them from the wind and they were out of sight of the road.

Boris, Ferdy and Frovin scampered over the rocks gathering enough kindling for a fire, while Artorus helped Marta make fresh bread. It was safe to light a fire. Onysius could not have seen the smoke. He was too far away.

As they all sat down to eat, Boris could contain himself no longer. 'So are we going to the mountains, just to visit a gravestone?'

Ikoseer handed him a piece of steaming bread.

'I want to know too.' Ferdy shoved a piece of hot bread into his mouth.

'I'm sure you do and now that you two have joined us on our way to the mountains, perhaps it's time I told you a little more.'

The Sage paused. 'Do you remember we talked before about Onysius' scouts searching through our two worlds for the Lightenstone because it will give them great power?'

'Yes,' said Boris. 'They're the ones who invaded Banters Den and separated us from our family.'

'But I thought that the gambler in Brechin was searching for you and Helios,' interrupted Marta.

She tried to read the Ikoseer's face, convinced that their lives were in danger because the Sage was with them.

Marta watched Ikoseer put aside her bread and with a tiny twig, smooth a patch of sand in front of them. The firelight was like magic playing upon Ikoseer's intricate headpiece as she drew a semicircle and marked one end with an X. Then she drew a steep ragged line up and away from it, scribing a circle at the apex. 'This is a Way Fell, a hill, and the circle here … is the Pentark.'

'The semicircle represents a range of mountains called The Veils and the X … here … marks Mirraway Castle.'

Around all of this she drew another oddly shaped outline. 'And this is the Land of Illingaith. By road, the border is around four hundred miles south-west of here.'

Further west and adjoining Illingaith, she drew another outline and another X saying, 'This is the Dukedom of Asilodor. And this is Jimpiragh Castle.'

'Where Onysius has come from.' Frovin reminded them. Marta felt his reassuring paw touch her back.

Ikoseer nodded.

'So does Onysius still live in Jimpiragh?' asked Ferdy frowning.

'He uses both castles now, but Mirraway belongs to the royal family. When the civil war started they fled from there into exile.'

Ferdy leant forward. 'Where did they go?'

'To the Lux Mountain and then later to the Ascension Mountains.'

'Are they still in the Ascension Mountains? Is that why we're going there? To visit the royal family?' Ferdy's curiosity was now piqued.

Ikoseer gave the dwarf a steady glare. Ferdy reddened and gave her an apologetic look.

'The dark forces have increased their efforts to locate the Stone,' she continued. 'So, in order to save the Isle of Spheres, the Lightenstone must be found and returned to its rightful place in the Pentark. And I was hoping … that you might help me.'

No one spoke. They scarcely breathed. Boris was the first to break the stunned silence.

'Is that why we're here? You want us to help you take the Lightenstone back to the Pentark? But we're just dwarves. H-h-how is it p-p-possible for us to be of any help to you,' he stammered. 'I don't even know what to look for.' He was feeling a little angry.

'Me neither.' Ferdy looked puzzled. 'But what I don't understand is why you need us at all. You said it wasn't in the World of Man, so you must know where it is.'

'Must I?'

Ferdy looked down at his boots.

'Ah. So that is our true task.' Frovin took on a steely determination.

Ikoseer nodded at the badger. 'But it will not be easy to find the Lightenstone. It has remained hidden since it was removed twenty years ago …'

Ikoseer paused. 'And … it's not the only Pentark Stone that needs to be found.'

The dwarves looked at each other in dismay.

'The four outer gems that were removed,' Frovin reminded them.

'Yes.'

Boris was dumbfounded. 'What! Are we expected to find them as well?'

Marta was taking in the gravity of their undertaking.

Hesitant, Ferdy dared to ask. 'Do you know where the gems are?'

Artorus stood up and began to explain. 'The outer gemstones represent the twelve signs in the zodiac belt across the night sky.' Four were removed, one from each of the four elements—Earth, Water, Air and Fire and are being held in trust. I can reveal to you now that two of them were each cast into a river.'

'You want us to help you find five stones that were all hidden in different places twenty years ago?' asked Boris in exasperation. 'And the enemy has been searching for them ever since and never found any of them?'

'Yes. That is what I'm asking of you.'

In a huff, Boris folded his arms and glared.

'But how can I help?' Marta was bewildered. 'I'm only a young woman from the World of Man. This isn't my world.'

'Perhaps it is because you are from another world that you can help,' replied Ikoseer gently. 'All four of you have something to give. I see courage, strength and light in each of you. Even if you can't see it yourself.'

A strange silence fell over them again as they struggled with their own doubts and thoughts, knowing that what they were being asked to do was fraught with great danger.

'But, you're the Sage of White Timber Mountain,' spluttered Ferdy, trying to make sense of it all.

'Sometimes, even sages need help,' said Ikoseer looking at him. 'Why do you think Artorus was in the World of Man? I can't be in all places and see all things, despite what you might think. We all need help at some point.'

The Sage continued. 'But we're never alone. There is someone of great power who can help us find all five stones. That's why we're going to the Lux Mountains and then onto the Ascension Mountains—to visit her.'

'So now you can see the massive task before me … before us … should you choose to go on this journey with me. And remember, no task is ever given to someone that isn't capable of handling it.'

Ikoseer was by now overwhelmed with tiredness. She sighed and then rose, leaving them with their thoughts. Boris and Ferdy finished their meal in silence while Frovin busied himself by digging a hollow to sleep in. Marta, deep in thought, drew patterns in the sand with her finger.

It was a clear night and Marta felt prompted to stop what she was doing and look up, searching for the huge Great Bear constellation, the Seven Sisters, and of course the star Sirius. Like all farmers in the World of Man, her parents planted their crops by the moon and stars, and these three were their favourite signs to look for. Now, as she thought of her parents, she saw a falling star and made a wish for a safe journey. So much was uncertain.

She looked back at Artorus, sharpening his weapons on a leather strop and thought of the evil men following them. She watched as he stopped and held up each blade, flicking his thumb across it, testing the sharpness before returning it to its sheath. He had saved her from the gambling spy, and helped her escape from Onysius' scouts. She had no choice but to trust him now—and Ikoseer.

She turned to see Ikoseer adjust her hood and lie down. With her back against a rock and facing the fire, she nestled her staff against her chest, with the point just under her chin. Marta hoped that if the Sage was drawing the enemy to them, she was also powerful enough to protect them.

By the time the sun sank over the horizon, everyone was bedded down, ready to rise again just after midnight and head towards the mountains, hoping to put distance between themselves and the enemy. Boris and Ferdy were unable to sleep and stared into the dying fire thinking of many things.

'What's a zodiac belt?' murmured Ferdy.

'I don't know. We're miners, not magicians.'

'Why does Ikoseer want you and me to go to the mountains with her? I don't know how we can be of any help … '

'I don't know that either,' Boris replied.

Somehow he and Ferdy had joined in a perilous quest. But determined to go to sleep, he closed his eyes and rested his hand on Thrust. His hand felt the sword begin to pulse and a tingling sensation spread up his arm. Startled, he looked down. The handle was vibrating. Alarmed, he pulled back his hand and the vibrating stopped.

'Boris?' whispered Ferdy rolling over and putting his back to the fire.

'What!'

'We're miners. We should at least be able to find the Earth gem.'

# CHAPTER 7

The sun was beginning to set behind the Lux Mountains, when Onysius and his troop passed the same place on the Trading Road where Ikoseer had turned off the previous day. One of the wrakes halted and sniffed the air. They were travelling towards the Greening Road junction, hoping to meet up with the scouts sent earlier into the World of Man.

'What is it?' asked Onysius.

'Dwarves … and horses,' he replied dismounting. He looked down the embankment at the hoof prints, both large and small. 'And ponies.' He squinted, looking across the flat plains of the plateau into the distance.

'And humans … ' he added, screwing up his nose.

'When?' Onysius followed the wrake's gaze.

'One … maybe two days.'

A marshal came forward. 'Why didn't they take the proper road to the mountain pass?'

'Because they wanted to avoid something,' replied Onysius as he swung out of his saddle. He made his way to the verge, joining the wrake.

'How many horses and ponies?'

'Two of each,' grunted the wrake.

Something caught his eye. He jumped down the embankment and grabbed it before putting it up to his nose. He drew in a deep breath, saliva running from the corners of his mouth. With glistening eyes, he placed the object into Onysius' outstretched hand.

'Young dwarf …'

It was a small handkerchief. Onysius unfolded it, noting that one corner was embroidered, in bright red, with a Dwarfish word that none of them could read. Curious, he rubbed his thumb over the raised stitching as he walked back to his horse. He shoved the handkerchief into a small leather pouch attached to his saddle, and remounted while he evaluated his options. He looked again towards the Lux Mountains. A feeling of unease came over him but he dismissed it from his mind. He needed to find the Lightenstone.

He turned to his sergeant. 'Is there a route through the mountains other than using the main pass?'

'It's not on the map, but dwarves are mountain dwellers so perhaps they know another way.'

They were still a half day's ride from the Greening Road junction and the sun had already sunk further behind the mountains. It would soon be twilight. The air grew cooler and the horses were tired.

'We'll camp here tonight.' Onysius pointed to the track down the embankment.

As he lay by the crackling fire, he considered whether he should follow the dwarves.

They all rose the following morning as the first rays of the sun bathed the plateau with long pale streams of light. By then, Onysius had dismissed the idea that the travellers might be of any real importance to him. He thought they were all fleeing from the scouts, and heading towards the mountains for safety. It explained why they had avoided the main pass. Nevertheless, Onysius looked towards the mountains and cursed them.

Alone by the fire, he dipped a small piece of hard unleavened bread into a bowl of hot broth. He was tired and somewhat discontented. As he ate and brooded, he watched his soldiers tend to the horses and break camp. His sergeant approached and waited for him to speak.

'We continue onto the Greening Road and from there into the World of Man. I need to find the scouts I sent there earlier. They should have more news. Inform the men we're leaving as soon as possible. Have them prepare.'

'Yes, my Lord.' The sergeant bowed.

'Wait! Instruct the wrake to follow the dwarf trail, but the horse stays with us. And if he finds the travellers, he's to capture … not kill. Then he's to return to me with any prisoners. He knows the consequences if he disobeys.'

Within half an hour the horses were packed and ready to go. The soldiers mounted and moved up the steep embankment onto the Trading Road. But Onysius sat on his dappled warhorse, watching the lone wrake jogging across the open plains towards the mountains. He knew that even on foot, it would make good ground in a day.

The group journeyed uninterrupted on the Trading Road. They met no one and by noon they reached the junction with the Greening Road and the Road of Stones. Sitting around a fire cooking their lunch was the small group of scouts and wrakes that Onysius had sent before him into the World of Man.

The men rose the moment they realised who it was. The Commander stepped forward and greeted Onysius as he dismounted and directed a scout to take his warhorse. The two groups, Onysius said, would stay the night. As his eyes swept the campsite, he noted there were no prisoners.

Wanting privacy, he moved away from the camp, directing his Commander to walk with him.

'What news do you have?'

The Commander looked surprised. 'I sent the master wrake to Jimpiragh … and to give you news. Of course, I had no idea you'd left the castle. Haven't you seen him?'

'Yes, I have … but some days ago. He tells me one of my spies was killed in a village in the World of Man.'

The Commander nodded and repeated the details.

Onysius mulled over the Commander's words. 'Perhaps I know this knight you speak of. He served in King Gordir's court. And the knight took someone with him?'

The Commander wavered. 'Yes … a young … woman …'

'A woman?' scoffed Onysius, cocking his head. 'But you lost them.'

'Yes. The warhorse was very fast and the rider knew where he was going.'

'I don't want excuses! But the dwarf in the tree interests me. I sent one of my wrakes across the plateau to follow a dwarf trail. And the master wrake also mentioned a sage.'

'Because the trail went cold, I suspect the rider had help. We've searched the forest for more than a week but there's been nothing. Even the wolves of Skag went hungry and have moved on. It's obvious that the spy was compromised. Somehow, there's a connection between the knight and the one he took back into Greenwood Forest.'

'And the Stone …' finished Onysius.

'I agree. If they've left the forest, I think they'd make for the mountains.'

Onysius looked towards the snowy peaks. They seemed to look back at him, cold and uninviting. Intense frustration rose in him. He got the feeling that the forces of light were gathering strength, as if to taunt him.

He clenched his fists as rage surged within him. As he roared his displeasure to the mountains, a forest raven took flight.

# CHAPTER 8

Attricus pushed his glasses further up his nose as he squinted into the morning sky.

'Anomir!' he yelled to Volgor, sending both of them scrambling into a hollow of prickly briar that grew along the border of the Tangled Woods.

Despite their exhaustion, they pulled their legs close to their bodies and tucked their heads down to their knees. They tightened into a ball and kept perfectly still. High above, they could hear the piercing scream of several anomirs wheeling overhead.

It had taken them eight arduous days to travel from Jimpiragh Castle to the Tangled Woods. Onysius must have flown into a terrible rage when he found that they had escaped. They had seen wrakes brandishing battleaxes in the distance, but it was the anomirs, the fiercest creatures of all, that Attricus and Volgor feared the most. The massive birds flew hard and fast over Asilodor, able to detect ground movement from several miles away, and their treacherous talons could crush the bones of their living victims on impact.

For safety, the pair journeyed by night and rested during the day. From the castle they trekked through Jimpiragh Hills and then continued on to the Tangled Woods. The Hills provided them with caves and depressions for protection and sleep. Although Attricus often cursed the route they had taken, it was the only way they could have gone. Had they escaped into the mountains behind Jimpiragh, it would have led them deeper into danger. And the plains in the other direction were flat for twenty miles, giving them no cover at all.

They stayed huddled in the briar and as the screaming of the anomirs faded, Volgor heard a scuffle coming from behind him. Eyes darting, he stood up and turned around to see what had happened. He was dumbfounded. Attricus was gone!

'Attricus?' Volgor hissed, staring at the empty space.

Frantic, he searched the spot where Attricus had been hiding. There were no broken branches and the ground was undisturbed. He didn't know what to do. A dreadful chill seeped into his bones.

He hissed louder, 'Attricus?'

'Looking for someone?' asked a quiet voice behind him.

Startled, Volgor spun round and looked up. Standing before him was a tall thin man dressed entirely in various shades of yellow. He had a kind face, a pointy nose and a wild shock of purple hair that defied his quirky hat.

Volgor's mouth hung open.

'Have you lost someone? I may be able to help,' offered the man.

Volgor swallowed hard and backed into the briar.

'Has someone by any chance … disappeared?' The yellow man had a quizzical expression on his face. Volgor's reaction gave him the answer. 'Aaah. I am a boundary rider of the Tangled Woods. It is my business to know … if someone has been swallowed.'

'What do you mean … swallowed?' Volgor stole a quick glance around, wondering whether more yellow men were lurking about.

'They only swallow some, you know. Does he meddle with magic by any chance?'

Volgor remained tightlipped.

Reading Volgor's face he clapped his hands in glee. 'Yes he does!'

His quirky hat wobbled as he bent from the waist and lightly touched Volgor's nose with a finger, making it tingle. 'But it's not his fault for being caught. Magic is an inexact art and a matter of interpretation. Even good magicians can be fooled by what they see … or perhaps he had no warning.'

He stretched and stood up. 'So, where are you going?'

'Nowhere,' blurted Volgor. 'We're just travellers.'

The man smiled. 'So, do you want to find your travelling companion …
the … errr … swallowed one?'

Volgor looked down at his scruffy feet.

'Yes … of course you do. Come!'

The yellow man turned and began walking along the edge of the woods,
beckoning Volgor to follow him. Volgor hesitated for a few moments but
then adjusted his rope, slung his sack over his shoulder and trotted to
catch up, warily stepping in beside him.

'It's so sad, the story of the Tangled Woods,' began the man. 'It was once
a magical place of earth spirits. Fairies and sprites were common and the
animals could talk. The trees were alive and vibrant. But now the light
magic has almost gone …'

The man slowed his pace, glancing at Volgor. 'I saw the anomirs … and
many wrakes. I knew they must be searching for something. Or someone.'

Defeated, Volgor gave a slight nod.

'Terrible creatures. But there's naught can be done about them. And
we're almost at the entrance to the woods, so I'm afraid it's where we
must part company.'

Volgor frowned. 'But you said you'd help me.'

The man patted him on the head. 'Oh, but I am helping. To find the
swallowed one, you have to go into the woods alone.'

Volgor was mortified.

'But I warn you. You mustn't venture off the road. The one you seek
must come to you. He must come onto the road and join you, and then
the passage out of the woods will be safe. The way is narrow and the
illusions are great.'

'Illusions?'

'Nothing will be as it seems. If you stay on the road then you have no need for concern. But you must remain vigilant!'

They stopped as the road leading into the Tangled Woods came into view, and hid behind some briar, making sure they were alone. Volgor stared through a gap in the thicket at the road junction ahead. He could see the castle road leading west, back towards Jimpiragh and the road that branched north.

That was the main road to Illingaith but was too dangerous, snaking its way through the Arifer Mountains. And the road into the Tangled Woods continued on, eventually reaching the Abyss River, the natural eastern border between Asilodor and the Land of Illingaith.

Still crouching, Volgor tried to muster up courage to leave the briar and make for the road. In resignation, he steeled himself, muttered a small prayer to his mother, and turned to thank the man. Blood drained from Volgor's face. He was gone.

Then he heard the yellow man's voice in his right ear saying, 'Good luck Volgor.'

Volgor started.

'Yes,' he whispered. 'I even know your name.'

But Volgor had no time to react. He was pulled from the briar by unseen hands, and pushed down a small embankment, tripping and rolling until he came to rest on the road. Dizzy, he staggered to his feet and with skinned knuckles and grazed forehead, he stood swaying before the entrance to the Tangled Woods. Then he heard something in the distance: the thud of approaching boorlings and the battle cry of wrakes. Gripped with fear, he stared into the woods.

The yellow man's words repeated in his head: 'Stick to the road! Stick to the road! Stick to the road!' He willed his legs into action and ran as far and as fast as he could. Suddenly a tree branch reached out, knocked him off his feet, and slammed him face down on the gravel.

Coming to, he groaned and opened one eye into a tiny slit, but all he could see at first was a thick blanket of large tangled tree trunks. When he turned to the other side, he thought he saw movement.

But it was the eerie silence that bothered him. Even his breath seemed to resound and echo through the trees. Rubbing his battered head and sitting up, he realised he had fallen close to the edge of the road, so he shuffled on his backside until he sat squarely on the crown.

Shivers ran up his spine and remembering his knife, he yanked it from under his belt. Holding it out in front of him, he stood up and inched forward, hearing the crunching of his feet on the gravel. He felt as if a thousand eyes were watching him. Sometimes he caught a glimpse of movement, first on one side and then on the other, but whenever he turned to look there was nothing.

Suddenly, further ahead and to his left, he saw a court jester sitting on a stump beside the edge of the road. He was clothed in a jacket of red and yellow checks and underneath were tight breeches with one leg yellow and the other one red. On his head was a fool's hat, and the three red and yellow arcs that sprang from the centre each had a gold bell attached to the tip. Two of the bells almost touched the top of the jester's shoulders. His hair was yellow, his skin white and his full lips were bright red.

Volgor stared, wondering if the jester had been following him all this time. Keeping to the middle of the road, and still firmly holding his knife, he hesitated before walking towards him, and stopped before getting too close.

'Can I help you?' The jester spread his luscious red lips into a thin broad smile. 'Are you looking for someone?'

Remembering the yellow man's warning, Volgor remained silent.

'People only come here because they're looking for someone. And I have seen someone wandering through the trees. Just now. He looked like a magician. Are you looking for a magician?'

'Didn't say I was looking for anyone,' retorted Volgor.

'No … so you didn't. But if you were, it would be a magician you'd be looking for. I must say the poor fellow looked terribly distressed. Wondering where he was. How he was going to get out … ' The jester cocked his head to one side, making his bells jingle.

'I … I wouldn't know …' Volgor stammered, avoiding his gaze.

'Mmmm … What a strange little creature you are. Wandering through here all alone with your rope and your sack. So where did you say you were going?'

'I didn't.' Volgor decided to ignore him and move on.

But as he was walking past and watching the jester from the corner of his eye, he was caught off guard when the jester asked, 'Did you speak to the yellow man?'

Noticing the falter in Volgor's step, he leapt off the stump and cartwheeled along the roadside, shouting with laughter: 'Terribly distressed, terribly distressed, terribly distressed.' Then he disappeared into the trees.

By now, Volgor's nerves were on edge, but there was no one to help him. He had never felt so alone. A part of him wanted to give up and run back as fast as he could to the entrance, but he could not leave Attricus wandering about, lost in the Tangled Woods forever.

Summoning up as much courage as he could, he tightened his bag and started to run, yelling, 'Attricus, Attricus!'

The stillness broke. Whipping into a frenzy, the trunks swished and swayed, slapping their branches hard against the ground. A whirlwind appeared, spewing leaves through the air, stripping bark. The trees moaned and wailed in pain. The dreadful sound gathered into a screaming crescendo that swept along the road ahead of Volgor.

Shoving his knife back under his belt, he clamped his hands hard over his ears as he ran, squinting to keep the debris out of his eyes. On and on he went and the wild wind followed. Cracks began appearing along the roadside, opening and closing at will like gaping hungry mouths. Willowy branches lurched and snatched at Volgor, trying to drag him into the tangled mire.

As he jumped a crack, further up ahead and to his left, he spotted Attricus standing among the swirling trees. His heart skipped a beat and he yelled as hard as he could against the wind, 'Onto the road, Attricus! Onto the road!' But the wind swallowed his words.

As Volgor kept running towards Attricus, he moved deeper into the trees, beckoning Volgor to follow him.

'No. I can't!' yelled Volgor. But Attricus paid no attention. Volgor realised it was an illusion and forced himself to look away as he passed by.

In an instant the figure reappeared, this time on the right, then on the left and on the right again. He was everywhere; holding onto the swinging branches, waiting by the side of the road, sitting on a tree stump, walking along the road verge hunched over and dragging his heavy sack behind him.

Volgor kept his focus on the road ahead. *How terrible it would be to pass him by and not know him! What if I can't find him?*

When he heard malicious laughter coming from behind him he turned and caught sight of the jester dancing and jeering at him before disappearing again. Anger rose in Volgor and tears began to sting his eyes, and blur his vision. But still he ran on and on. Then without notice he heard Attricus calling to him, but the sound came from within his head. Slowing down, he looked around but saw nothing.

'Attricus?'

'I'm here, Volgor!'

Volgor halted and trying to catch his breath, scanned the tree line to his right. Further ahead he could see a single hand emerging.

'Attricus, is that you?'

'Yes! Grab my hand and pull me onto the road!'

Volgor hesitated. The voice sounded warped.

'Now, Volgor!'

He shook his head. 'No! You're just another illusion …'

'Take the Duke's sword! Hold it up so the jewel shines into the trees and you will see me. That's how I found my way to the road. Hurry!'

Volgor crept along the crown of the road and towards the outstretched hand. He saw the short sword, and the jewel, shining iridescent green and with a halo of shimmering light. As he stared at it he felt a warm calming glow come over him.

All around him the maelstrom whipped his face and branches clawed at his body, but he stood firm and strong. Fascinated, he reached out his long bony fingers, grasping the hilt of the Duke's sword and taking it from the outstretched hand. When he turned it into the trees, he saw Attricus standing before him.

With that, Volgor grasped the soothsayer's hand and pulled with all his remaining strength. For a moment they lay on the road together. Then, willing himself to stand, Attricus pulled Volgor up too. 'We have to get out of here!'

'I can't,' Volgor replied over the din and the chaos. 'I'm so tired.'

'You have to. We can't stay here. Hold the sword in front of us and shine the light onto the road. Come on … we've got to go!'

They went on for miles, pushing against the unrelenting wind with Volgor in front and Attricus guiding and holding him steady as they went. Then as they turned a corner, Volgor saw an opening ahead. But as he peered through slitted eyes, he noticed a wall of grey mist begin to form across the road, and he baulked. Attricus looked up. He saw it too and realising they had come to the end of the woods, he pushed harder against Volgor.

'Run!'

Holding the short sword steady, Volgor took the lead. His sluggish legs burdened him the closer they got to the opening. His sack dug deep into his shoulder. His rope chafed his neck. His strength was being sapped.

With rays of sunlight streaming through the thickening mist, they made a final push and passed though the opening and out into daylight. In utter relief and exhaustion, they sank into a heap on the road. They were free. They lay on the road heaving until their breathing slowed enough so that Volgor could hear the slight sound beside him, and looked up alarmed. Returning his stare and mounted on a strange horse made of air and light sat the yellow man. With a knowing smile he tipped his quirky hat, spun and disappeared.

Volgor tugged the soothsayer's sleeve. 'Did you see that?'

Attricus lifted his weary head. 'See what?'

'A yellow man.'

Attricus chuckled. 'What are you talking about? There are no yellow men, it's just another illusion.'

But resting on the ground the kurr saw a mustard yellow coin carved with a strange symbol. Hesitant at first, he wrapped his fingers around it and slipped it into his pocket.

# CHAPTER 9

Ikoseer stood at the foot of the Lux Mountains and looked up at the cliff face as the sun rose over the horizon, gilding the upper snowline with rays of light. She dismounted, muttering as she scoured the scattered boulders that looked like marbles thrown by a giant hand.

'It's been a long time since I was here, a mighty long time.' She moved further and scrambled onto a large rock. To get her bearings, she pointed her staff towards the summit, swept her eyes along the cliff and then looked down.

She smiled and turned to the others. 'Come! I think I've found it.'

And with that, she slid off the rock and strode over loose scree, until she stood in front of a section of cliff covered by briar. Artorus guided Famrod through the boulders and rubble to join her, and the others followed.

Boris and Ferdy scanned the mountains until they disappeared from view, while Frovin peered over Marta's shoulders, expecting to see a pathway. But there was none.

Artorus dismounted and stood beside Ikoseer, discussing what to do before they started pulling and slashing at the thicket, prompting the others to join in.

Boris found pickaxes in one of the packs and he and Ferdy got to work immediately, driving the spikes hard into the base of the briar, and scooping away the loosened rubble with their hands. Frovin used his long claws to help them dig and Marta grabbed the broken brush and dragged it out of the way. They quickly worked up a sweat, and it was not long before the briar was removed.

Everyone but Artorus and Ikoseer was astonished to see solid rock. But the Sage started muttering again, put her ear to the wall and with a circular motion ran her right palm over the surface. She stepped back and scribed an arc on the rock with the point of her staff.

'Hmmm … it's here somewhere.'

Ferdy whispered to Boris. 'What's she looking for?'

Then out of nowhere, they heard the whoosh of wings. A forest raven swept past them, and flying a little too fast, hit the wall and fell to the ground.

With great care the Sage picked up the dazed bird in her hands, cradling it and stroking the glossy black feathers until it recovered enough to perch on her arm. The raven shook and ruffled its feathers, cocked its head to one side and began to 'kraa' softly.

Tuning in, Ikoseer nodded in acknowledgment of a message, before relaying it to the others.

'Onysius has continued on the Trading Road and met with some of his scouts at the entrance to Greenwood Forest, but he found our tracks leading off the main road, and he's suspicious. He's sent a wrake after us.'

Ferdy shuddered. Horrified he said, 'On a boorling?'

'No. This one's on foot but we still have to move on as soon as possible.'

The raven began to flap and clutching Ikoseer's hand, tugged urgently at her sleeve with his beak, pulling her towards the rock wall.

'Yes, and you should be more careful where you land, my young messenger,' she chuckled.

Marta noticed a sudden change come over the Sage's face.

'Ah … she said, 'There it is!'

With that, the raven took flight, swept between Marta and Frovin, glided underneath Snowball making her squeal, and then was gone.

Uttering incantations, Ikoseer touched her staff on the wall revealing an amber hole encircling a black vertical slit. It looked like a cat's eye. 'Boris, come!'

Boris looked confused but Marta sensed the urgency in the Sage's voice and gave Boris a push forward, making him stumble. Before he had time to protest, the Sage grasped him by the shoulders and turned him to face the cliff.

'Quick! Slide Thrust into the keyhole.'

Boris felt tingling spread down his arms, and he trembled as he grasped Thrust by the hilt and drew it out of the sheath. His hand shook as he pointed it towards the hole, before plunging it hard into the rock. It clicked into place.

'Now turn it!'

With all his strength and with both hands on the hilt, Boris twisted the blade to the right, until the slit was horizontal. At first nothing happened, but then he heard the slow grating of rock on rock as a door rolled away revealing a wide passageway leading into the mountain.

Ikoseer faced the cleft in the rock. 'Hurry! Take the horses! It's a time lock. Everybody in before the door closes again!'

Artorus and Famrod went first. Marta grabbed Snowball and Aster, followed by Ferdy, Frovin and Poppins, and then Ikoseer and Helios. Boris was about to step into the mountain when panic gripped him. He had left Thrust in the keyhole and the moving blade had almost returned to the top!

Planting both feet firmly on the wall and grasping the hilt, he pulled with all his strength. It seemed to be stuck fast in the rock, but then it suddenly came free. Boris fell backwards, landing with a thump on the ground, just as the keyhole disappeared and the door began to close. He was scrambling to get up, when he was seized by the scruff of his neck, pulled through the door and dumped on the rocky floor inside.

'Keep your wits about you. This is no time for dwarfish foolery,' scolded Ikoseer, as she hauled Boris to his feet. Then the soft light of her staff began to glow, and Artorus started to lead them all along the passageway.

The only sounds were the occasional dripping of water and the ringing of horseshoes as they walked on in silence for many hours. Then they turned a corner and ahead saw a dim glow as the tunnel opened out into a spacious cavern.

As they approached, Marta was amazed to see, a podgy old dwarf sitting at a roaring fire toasting his toes and reading a large book. His high-backed gilt-framed chair was covered with well worn brocade. When he made no attempt to acknowledge them, she wondered if he was blind or deaf. But it appeared that he was neither, because all of a sudden he jumped up and greeted Ikoseer with great excitement.

He clasped the Sage's hands and shook them vigorously. 'Welcome, Ikoseer, my dear, welcome. I have almost been expecting you. The sight of a sage and a small travelling party crossing the plateau was brought to my attention just yesterday.'

He gave the Sage a mischievous grin. 'And it was my dearest wish that you should call ... and here you are!'

'Are you still spying on the enemy?'

'I am indeed. Mountain cats and mice—stealthy, quick and quiet.'

'Then perhaps we have information to share.'

'Marvellous!' he chortled. He turned to the knight and shook his hand. 'It's Artorus ... if I'm not mistaken?'

Without waiting for confirmation, he moved along, 'Now let me see ... who else is travelling through my mountain?'

Ikoseer introduced the others.

'This is Frovin of Greenwood Forest.'

'Most pleased to meet you Mr Frovin, I'm Potsy.'

'And this is Marta.'

'And where are you from young lady?'

'I'm … from Brechin.'

'In the World of Man? Bless me. You are a long way from home!'

'And lastly, Boris and Ferdy.'

Potsy's eyes glistened as he looked between the two.

'Did someone else turn the key today?' he asked raising his eyebrows, but directing the question to Ikoseer. The Sage smiled her confirmation.

'I knew it! I cannot believe it. One of you must have Thrust,' Potsy said excitedly.

Boris and Ferdy blinked in astonishment.

'So, the blade of Thrim survives! And who is your father?'

Ferdy blushed. 'Our father is Leopold … of Banters Den.'

'Ah. And your mother?'

'Ester … of Banters Den too,' said Boris.

'Yes indeed. I do believe it's true. Such fine young dwarves, and who better to carry the blade of Thrim than ones such as yourselves. Let us all be glad it is in good hands. Perhaps you could visit Thrim's gravestone …'

He spun to Ikoseer. 'You are going that way? Aren't you?'

'Yes, we're on our way to the Ascension Mountains on urgent business.'

'Indeed, I believe you are. How long has it been, five years?'

'I was last here on my way to a meeting of the Council of the Silence.'

'Ah, I remember it well … but it's been far too long between visits. Now that you're here, you will stay won't you … at least one night?'

'It's a generous offer,' said Artorus stepping forward. 'But there are many of us and food is short.'

Potsy gave a dismissive wave. 'The Maslin bread has already risen …'

Ferdy's stomach stood to attention. 'You have grain for bread?'

Potsy clapped his hands in glee. 'Aha! A dwarf with an appetite! But don't concern yourselves, my dear friends. My stores are adequate; brought here by resistance fighters. In exchange I offer them respite and tend to the sick and wounded. The monks of Elodom Monastery in Magirus have a way with plants, so I have grain and vegetables to share. Even Banters Den is a source of hops for my yeast …'

The twins' eyes widened as he winked at them.

'I've a huge pot of soup on the stove and we can't let that go to waste. Besides, much has happened since we last met and a cup of tea with honey oat biscuits simply won't suffice … if you understand.'

Ikoseer nodded as Potsy continued. 'There are some terrible goings-on and much to be done, but as you can see, I'm too old to fight with club and shield anymore … so much the pity …'

The Sage would have preferred to get further ahead of the wrake, but she could see the benefit of a well-earned rest, not just for the riders but for the animals as well. She noticed Potsy had also sourced fresh hay and water for the horses and had prepared beds for the others. And the enormous table that sat in the middle of the cavern had been set with cutlery fit for a king.

'Your hospitality is gratefully accepted Potsy, but we must continue on tomorrow.'

'Wonderful! Unburden your horses at the stalls over there and make yourselves at home. I have bread to bake and soup to stir.'

Potsy busied himself in the kitchen. He loaded the oven with more wood, slid in the risen loaves, then stood on the thick wooden bench, and bringing the soup to a simmer, stirred it with a large ladle.

Once the loaves were done, Marta watched Potsy slide them out of the oven and rap his knuckles sharply on the top as she had seen her mother do. Satisfied they were baked, he tipped them onto the bench. She helped him slice the hot crusty bread. He spread it with so much butter, that it melted and pooled on their plates. As they took their places at the table, he put down bowls of steaming vegetable soup, followed by apple tart, wafers and vintage cheese. Mead was in plentiful supply and they all had a wonderful dinner. Then, when the horses were fed and groomed, they sat around the fire as the old dwarf mesmerised them with tales about the slaying of dragons and crowning of kings from faraway lands.

Then, with full bellies and weary from travelling and sleeping under the stars, Boris, Ferdy, and Marta snuggled into warm downy beds with fluffy pillows, while Frovin curled up at Marta's feet. Artorus, Ikoseer and Potsy stayed by the fire, where they spread out maps and talked long into the night. Boris listened to their hushed tones, but was unable to keep his eyes open. Within minutes he was fast asleep and dreaming of home.

They woke early the next morning to buttered toast and honey, dried cranberry muffins and strong hot tea. Extra muffins and toast were placed into their packs, along with a small ceramic pot of honeycomb. A small block of cheese wrapped in cloth was handed to Ferdy, slices of dried apple to Marta and much to Ferdy's disappointment, three small bags of honey oat biscuits to Boris.

As they replenished their water supply, Potsy and Artorus checked Potsy's map of the tunnels, deciding which one they would follow.

'I'll go with you to the first junction and if you keep following the map you'll come out of the mountain onto the old pathway you were initially going to take. From there you will still have perhaps an hour of travel before you reach the ridge above the valley,' said Potsy.

He lit two torches, handed one to Artorus, and strode ahead. Within the hour they reached the turnoff. Potsy hugged them all, wished them good luck, told them to be careful, and bade them a tearful goodbye.

'I do hope that it's less than five years before I see you again.'

Ikoseer rested her hands on Potsy's shoulders. 'Much is uncertain my dear friend, but we know there is safe passage through these mountains should we need it and we may yet call on you again. Farewell for now.'

It took them the rest of the day to wend their way through more tunnels, but by nightfall they had made it to the last cave. Boris had been expecting another wall of rock with another keyhole, but the cave was open and there in front of them was the ancient pathway.

'Is that the hidden path through the mountains?' asked Boris. 'The one we could've taken?'

'Yes,' said Ikoseer leaning against the wall.

'Except we found the mountain door. Just as well we had Thrust to open it,' added Boris.

Ferdy was rubbing his tummy. 'It was a most pleasant night.'

'I wasn't suggesting it wasn't … I'm just curious. That's all,' said Boris.

'Do all the mountains in the World of the Soul have hidden doors?' asked Marta.

Ferdy butted in. 'Never heard of such a thing 'til yesterday.'

Ikoseer chuckled as Boris elbowed Ferdy in the ribs. Then her face became solemn. 'All mountains are a door but not all mountains have a door. The bearer must earn the key to open the door. Until then, the door remains a mystery.'

Ferdy was befuddled. 'How can Thrust be a key? It's a sword …'

Marta frowned. 'Could you have opened the mountain door yesterday without Thrust?'

The dwarves sat up straight.

Ikoseer paused. 'Yes. I could.'

Ferdy's jaw dropped.

'How is that possible?' Boris spluttered. 'You needed my help to open it.'

'My staff, would have sufficed. As it did five years ago.'

'I was tricked!'

'It was no trick,' replied Ikoseer sternly. 'Didn't your father tell you Thrust was forged in this very mountain and hammered …?

'Of course he did,' shot back Boris.

'So now the connection has been restored. The guardians of this mountain, the rock giants, from whom the precious ore was sourced for the blade, recognise both you and Ferdy as the current bearers. If we hadn't used Thrust to open the door, the giants would be none the wiser … although I expect they would have felt the presence of the blade somehow. I was simply alerting them to the current state of affairs.'

Ikoseer gazed at the glowering dwarf.

'It was a test Boris. I was encouraged, however. Your instinct is strong as is your inner fire, although sometimes a little too much so …'

Marta stifled a giggle at Boris' scowl, breaking the tension.
They all laughed.

'The World of the Soul is a strange place,' said Marta. 'I've never heard of rock giants. Did they create the mountains here?'

'They created all the mountains on the Isle of the Spheres,' said Ikoseer sweeping her arm across an invisible landscape. 'They were here from the beginning of time. They are the oldest of creatures. They created the archipelago in the Mother Sea, of which this island is just one of many.'

Marta wondered if the rock giants could somehow help them find the stones.

'Are the rock giants awake?' Ferdy wondered if that was why his mother insisted on blessing the mining tunnels at their yearly festival.

'They are aware, rather than awake. They slumber most of the time.'

Artorus decided it was safe to light a fire and left the cave to gather wood. After supper he laid out the map, showed them where they were, and where they were heading—across the Valley of the Queen and on to the Ascension Mountains.

'Will we be safe crossing the valley?' asked Ferdy.

'Not as safe as I would like. The claws of the enemy have reached far and wide so we must remain alert. Potsy said soldiers, wrakes and wolves have been seen in the Lux Mountains and let's not forget about the wrake following us across the plateau. Our trail stops where we entered the mountain door, but that's not to say it won't find the ancient path and still be in pursuit.'

'I don't understand,' said Ferdy. 'Can't you just use your staff … er … to kill the wrake if it finds us?'

'I have no intention of killing anything, unless I am forced to,' replied Ikoseer in a grave tone. 'Wrakes have no choice but to be what they have been bred to be. If I can avoid confrontation with them I will.'

'But you will protect us … won't you?'

'Unless I am forced to,' repeated the Sage. Ferdy reddened and stared at his boots. Marta broke the silence. 'Will it take us long to get across the valley?'

'A full day's ride,' said Artorus. 'If we leave early in the morning and have safe passage, then by nightfall we'll reach the gateway …'

'There's a gateway into the Ascension Mountains?' asked Boris.

'Yes, it marks the entrance,' replied Artorus.

'Can the wrakes and wolves go through the entrance too?' asked Ferdy.

'No, once we're inside the gates, we'll have full protection.'

Although scolded by Ikoseer, Boris was excited by the idea of passing through mountain gates and things he had never seen before. Days earlier, he had berated Ferdy for wanting to come on such an adventure, and now he was in the thick of it.

He looked back at the map. 'Where's Thrim's gravestone?'

'Here,' pointed Ikoseer. 'It's not marked, but it's in a cemetery just inside the gates.'

'Why is he buried across the valley? Shouldn't he be buried here in the Lux Mountains where Thrust was forged?

'He's buried amongst kings and queens of old, knights and elven lords. He kept fine company indeed.' Ikoseer paused. 'Thrust isn't the only blade he forged and tempered. He was the master craftsman to many a king in the Isle of Spheres. He clothed King Farmir in chain mail for the Battle of the Stones. He hammered his sword Honorex, as well as twelve swords, one for each of the Knights of Power.'

Boris went quiet. 'Father didn't tell us that.'

'Who are the Knights of Power?' asked Ferdy.

Frovin looked at Artorus and their eyes met.

'They are the protectors of kings and queens … among other duties,' said Ikoseer. 'But it's not important for dwarves to worry about such things. All will be revealed in good time. Now we need to sleep. We have a long day ahead of us.'

'If it's not safe to travel across the valley, why are we going in daylight?' piped Ferdy.

'The wolves of Skag hunt at night and if they've left Greenwood Forest and are roaming these mountains, we'll be easy prey. It's far better that we travel by daylight, giving us a better chance to protect ourselves. One wolf is bad enough to deal with, let alone a pack. And we won't be stopping to eat … so prepare what you'll need before we go.'

Marta shivered. Her sheltered life in Brechin had not prepared her for this kind of adventure and she pined for home.

They bedded down for the night on the cavern floor and set out at daylight into heavy mist. Ikoseer led the small company of riders along the old path, but it took longer to reach the edge of the valley than she would have liked, as the stones and shale made it slippery for the horses.

By late morning they reached the bottom of the valley. The mist remained and gave them good cover, but water soaked through Ferdy's clothing making him cold and miserable. He kept thinking of Potsy's dry warm cave and his stomach began to rumble. He was sure it was long past lunchtime. Being discreet, he managed to unwrap a corner of the cheese in his pocket and broke off a small chunk.

He was stuffing it into his mouth when his pony stopped, pricked up its ears and stared into the mist. Ferdy saw nothing, but began to have wild imaginings of wrakes and wolves and other nasty creatures.

But it was Snowball who whinnied in greeting as a knight astride a chestnut warhorse emerged from the fog, startling Marta. Frovin reassured her and the rider held a finger to his lips just as another rider appeared on her opposite side. As she saw more riders emerge out of the mist and heard them speak with Artorus and Ikoseer, she relaxed. She realised they had come to escort them to the mountain.

She thought they looked regal with their clinking armour and chain mail. Their red cloaks fell in soft folds down their backs, and spread like blankets across the rumps of the prancing warhorses.

By early afternoon the sun broke through the mist, revealing the Ascension Mountains. Marta had expected to see a large cluster of mountains, and so was surprised when there were only three huge peaks. They were draped in thick mantles of snow and although the highest peak was hidden by white clouds, they were strikingly beautiful—and still some way ahead.

The sun was behind the mountains when they left the valley and began climbing a road that led around the foot of the mountains. Then as the road curved past a jagged rock, there before them in great splendour, rose a massive stone gateway.

Marta gasped. Boris, Ferdy and Frovin stared in awe at the two carved figures set into the gouged-out niches of the pillars on either side of the entrance. A black male figure stood within a white pillar and a white female figure within a black pillar.

With one arm outstretched, the figures held swords that crossed each other to form the arch joining the two pillars. A skull rested in the other hand of the female statue and the male grasped a decorated cross turned on its side to form an X. Beside the sandaled feet of the male were irises, and at the breast of the female was a cabbage rose in full bloom. Although dressed in simple flowing garments, they wore royal crowns, and with heads held high, stared defiantly across the valley.

Ferdy felt uncomfortable as they approached the gateway. He thought the statues were watching him, so looked away as he passed underneath the arch and onto the entrance way.

Several minutes later Ikoseer halted the company. Sliding from Helios, she left the road and called for the others to join her. They entered the royal cemetery. From the gate, the land dipped slightly before flattening into a small lush area covered with moss, heather and alpine flowers. The flowers and plants were a reminder that since crossing the valley they were now in Arctus, the land of snow and ice.

Towering headstones dotted the cemetery. Some were plain with just a single symbol; others were richly decorated, like those of kings and queens. Frovin and Marta stopped to read several stones. It reminded Marta of the graves of her grandmother Maria, and her mother Roselin, in the World of Man. In the years since her mother had died, she had often visited both graves.

But Ferdy stayed close to Boris and gave the headstones a cursory glance as they trotted after Ikoseer. They halted in front of Thrim's headstone. It read:

HERE LIES THRIM OF THE LUX MOUNTAINS

FORGER OF BLADES

MASTER CRAFTSMAN TO THE ISLE OF SPHERES

Apart from a pair of crossed swords carved into the stone beneath the words, there was no other decoration.

They all stood in silence, humbled in such a place. Marta picked a bunch of wild daises and placed them on the grave, prompting Ferdy to join in. Soon white flowers covered the ground in front of the headstone. Boris remained deep in thought.

Ikoseer bent down and whispered in his ear, 'The blade knows its master is near.'

'Thrim *owned* Thrust?'

'Thrust was his personal sword. He lost his life on a battlefield and the blade vanished … until you fell at my feet in Greenwood Forest.'

As Ikoseer and the others headed back, Boris waited for a few more moments, and was about to follow when the swords on the headstone suddenly lifted off and joined to form a single flaming sword. He slapped his hands over his bulging eyes and peered between a slit in his fingers.

Then it was gone. Astonished, he lowered his hands and looked back at the engraving. He frowned. Everything looked normal. It was as if nothing had happened. He shook his head, beginning to doubt himself and spun on his heels. Behind him he could hear the unmistakable sound of clashing swords. Refusing to look back and with the mist beginning to roll in again and the light fading, he hurried to catch up to the others.

Far across the Valley of the Queen at the foot of the Lux Mountains, a lone wrake stood on the ridge above the valley. He had not eaten since leaving Onysius' camp and a faint smell of dwarf and horse hung in the air as he stepped down the embankment. Higher among the pine trees the wolves of Skag were also hungry. The pale yellow eyes of the leader looked keenly down into the mist. With ears pricked, it lifted its head to sniff the wind. Instinct told it that a wrake was on the ridge below. Summoning the rest of the pack, it led them out from the cover of the trees and they padded softly into the swirling mist, eager to make their first kill in days.

# PART 3

# DAWN

# CHAPTER 10

After their escape from the Tangled Woods, Volgor and the soothsayer travelled by moonlight for three nights and by dawn the next morning, exhausted, they reached the Abyss River. Attricus crawled under a hanging rock near the bank of the river, beckoning Volgor to join him.

'Thank goodness we've made it,' he said.

He rested his head on his sack and within minutes was softly snoring against Volgor's muddy feet as he curled up against him. They slept huddled together for several hours before they ventured down to the river's edge and finding a calm pool, slipped into the water to bathe off their grime.

On the other side of the river was the Land of Illingaith. Attricus was excited, but his excitement faded at the sight of the wild water crashing over the boulders littering the river bed.

'Is that Illingaith over there? Is that where we're going?' asked Volgor, as he sat on a rock, dangling his feet in the water.

'Yes, if we can get across the river.'

'I'm hungry,' said Volgor making whirlpools with his feet.

'All I've got left are a few strips of dried meat,' said Attricus.

'And I've just got some figs.' Volgor screwed up his nose. Then he brightened. 'But I can try and catch us a fish, if we can find some shallow rapids.'

Attricus looked downstream. 'Do you think we should we go that way?'

Volgor shrugged. 'I don't know anything about this river. Can't you ask your crystal ball?'

Attricus sighed. 'I don't have it.'

Volgor spun around.

'I lost it in the Tangled Woods. Didn't realise it was gone until this morning.'

'I'm not going back there to find it,' said Volgor as he jumped off the rock.

He picked up a small white pebble, clutched both hands and held them out in front of Attricus.

'You choose. Pebble says we go downstream.'

Attricus pushed his glasses up his nose and touched Volgor's left hand. He opened his fist. 'Downstream it is then.'

Neither of them wanted to walk another step, but the possibility of finding food drove them on for another hour, until they came to a bend in the river.

'Perfect!' Volgor skipped across the rapids with new found energy, and began to search among the rocks. Soon he was squealing and laughing with glee as he clutched at the slippery fish. He moved from pool to pool until he managed to grasp the tail of a huge salmon with both hands, and dragged the wriggling creature over the rocks to the bank. Attricus held it as Volgor drove in his knife and killed it.

Unsure of what to do with it next, Attricus wiped his hands on his tunic saying, 'I'll leave you to it and gather sticks for a fire.'

Volgor sat panting on the river bank before pulling himself up. Although wanting to eat the fish raw, he dragged it back to the water to clean it.

This part of the task was going to be easy. Grasping the head, he slit open the belly, pulled out the innards and put them on a rock beside him. Then beginning at the backbone and working downwards, he scraped the iridescent skin from tail to head on both sides.

He washed the scales off and was about to flick the innards away, when something odd caught his eye. There was a tear in the fish's stomach. He lifted the opening with the tip of his blade.

There, almost hidden by the remains of undigested insects, was a beautiful aqua gemstone. Volgor stared in disbelief.

He had the creepy feeling that he was being watched. He slowly lifted his head and scoured the opposite side of the river, but saw nothing unusual. He turned towards Attricus, who was now blowing on a fire as the first puffs of smoke began to rise.

Volgor looked again at the other side of the river. Fairly certain there was no one watching, he prised the gem from the stomach. Rinsing it in the bloodied water, he held it up to the light for just a moment, scanned the opposite bank again, and slipped it into his pocket, beside the yellow man's coin.

Securing his knife, he stood up and called to Attricus to help him carry the fish to the fire. They cooked the salmon on the open coals and afterwards, with full bellies, lay down to rest. In the early afternoon, they were awoken by the screech of a bird.

Volgor sat up with a start. His eyes flitted around their camp and he patted his pocket, reassuring himself the gem and coin were still there.

Attricus rolled over and rested his head on his hand. 'We could try and cross the river here.'

'No, not here.' Volgor stood up and stretched. 'The other side's too deep and the water's still too fast. And even if we could get across, look at the steep bank we'd have to climb.'

'Perhaps it'll be better further downstream,' said Attricus. 'But we need to get going. I do not want to be in Onysius' dukedom any longer than I have to. I'll be happy when there's a river between us and him.'

'And between us and the wrakes and anomirs,' added Volgor.

Attricus shook his head. 'Borders mean nothing to them. They'll be in Illingaith too.'

Without another word, he stood up, put the rest of the fish in his sack and smothered the remaining coals with dirt. He swung his sack over his shoulder and began heading downstream.

Volgor was left to catch up. 'I hope we don't have to go too much further.'

'So do I.'

It took them longer than they expected, not because of the great distance, but because the trees here were closer to the river bank and there were no tracks. It was hard work pushing through brush, and having to weave around tree trunks that twisted in all directions.

After a while Attricus was exhausted, and sitting on a rock to rest, mopped his brow with his sleeve.

Volgor cocked his head to one side. 'Can you hear that?'

Attricus listened and shook his head. Then he turned his ear to the river, and nodded as a soft lilting voice drifted towards them on the wind. Without waiting, Volgor crept closer to the sound. He lay down and peered out at the river. Attricus followed and lay beside him.

They saw a tall willowy man sitting alone on a patch of sand. He was leaning against a boulder, threading a fish hook and singing.

FISHERMAN, FERRYMAN

WHAT AM I?

SHALL I CATCH A FISH?

OR GRANT YOU A WISH?

WHAT WILL IT COST YOU?

WHAT IS MY FEE?

TO CROSS THE ABYSS AND SET YOU FREE,

I CAST FOR MEN, I CAST FOR FISH,

ALL DEPENDING ON THE WISH,

A FISH FOR A DISH, I THINK TODAY,

AND THEN OF COURSE I'LL BE ON MY WAY,

I ...

The man stopped and looked in their direction. 'Do I have company … gentlemen?'

He stood with his back against the boulder. With his hook threaded, he fastened the braided horse hair line to the end of a thin hazel branch, tested the knot, and then, ignoring them, stepped to the river's edge and cast into the rushing waters.

'He'll never catch fish like that,' whispered Volgor. 'The water's running too fast.'

Attricus sighed. 'He knows we're here, so we may as well go down.'

'We don't have to,' said Volgor. 'It sounds tricky. Him and his little song.'

'But perhaps he is a ferryman and he can get us across the river.'

'So where's his boat?'

'I don't know. Maybe it's here somewhere.'

'And what will it cost us?'

'We don't know what the cost is going to be if we don't ask, do we?' insisted Attricus. 'And anyway, we don't have to agree to anything.'

With that he got up and made his way down to the river's edge.

Volgor started to follow, but something made him hesitate. He reached into his pocket and took out the gem found in the fish. He gave it a brief glance, grabbed a hat from his sack and placed the jewel on top of his head. Then pulling the hat down hard until the band touched his eyebrows, he slid down the bank and joined them.

Attricus turned as Volgor arrived, giving him an odd look.

'Welcome gentlemen,' said the fisherman, as he pulled his empty line ashore before casting again. 'And pray tell me. What brings you to my river?'

'Our travels,' said Attricus.

'Ah … and have you travelled far?'

'Far enough,' said Volgor.

'And in … Asilodor?'

Attricus hesitated. 'Y-e-s … some of the way.'

The man turned and studied them. 'Asilodor is not a safe place to travel in. There is a castle near the Arifer Mountains called Jimpiragh. I wouldn't go near there if you plan to stay in the dukedom … unless of course … you're here to cross the river?' He noticed the slight flicker in Attricus' eyes.

'Yes indeed … I am a ferryman. I can help you cross … if you wish …' He gave a slight wave of his hand.

'We haven't decided,' said Volgor. 'Besides, if you're a ferryman, where's your boat?'

'Ah, I have no boat,' he replied. He cast again.

'So, how can we cross?' challenged Volgor.

'With my rock ponies of course.' He nodded in the direction of a pile of rocks.

Volgor had never heard of such a thing, and was about to say that they should be getting on, when the pile of rocks moved and rose in the form of two sturdy ponies.

They stared in amazement as the ponies stretched and shook their pebbled manes. They walked towards the fisherman then stopped to graze on the small rocks nearby. The fisherman inclined his head at the ponies.

'They can cross the river with you on their backs. But as you can see, I am just a poor fisherman with nothing to my name. Except my ponies and my fishing rod.' He paused. 'And all services come at a cost. Perhaps you have something … useful?'

'A rope,' said Volgor.

'Ah … just a rope? Perhaps I might have use for a rope … But is there nothing else to choose from?' He turned to Attricus.

Attricus felt the intensity of the fisherman's gaze, and thought of the short sword in the secret pocket of his tunic. 'I could have offered you a crystal ball,' he said. 'But now it's gone. I have little else except the clothes I wear. Perhaps I could read your palm …?'

'Ahhh,' said the fisherman. 'A soothsayer …'

He bent from the waist and stared at Volgor with dark, deep-set eyes. His fleshy lips were parted and Volgor saw that most of his teeth had gold fillings.

'They say there swims a big shiny fish in my river … that swallowed a gemstone.'

Volgor's eyes widened. 'I … I wouldn't know,' he blurted, averting his gaze.

'We did eat a fish,' said Attricus. 'But there was no gem. I can assure you of that!'

'Yes there was! I was watching you the whole time.' The fisherman's eyes were fixed on Volgor.

'We found something didn't we? So. What did we find, eh? What did we find in my shiny … fat … fish?'

'It … it wasn't a gem … just a strange coin,' stammered Volgor.

The fisherman narrowed his eyes. 'I saw you hold it up to the light!'

'I just wanted to check that it was solid …'

By now, Attricus was looking at Volgor with surprise. 'Volgor?'

'Ahh … so your fine little friend didn't tell you …'

'Where is it?' snarled the fisherman, grabbing Volgor's arm.

Volgor stepped back as he was grasped by the throat and slammed hard against the boulder. 'It's in my pocket,' he squeaked.

'Which … one …!'

'My … my … my right one.'

'Sneaky little kurr … aren't we? Thinking it could keep what's mine!' said the fisherman, letting go of Volgor's arm and driving deep into his trouser pocket.

When he pulled his hand out it was grasping the coin with the strange symbol. Excited, he unfurled his long knobby fingers. His other hand dropped from Volgor's throat and he began to dance wildly as he stroked it. As Volgor coughed and rubbed his throat Attricus frowned and gave him a questioning look.

'And now I suppose you want to cross, eh? On you get then!'

The fisherman waved his hand at the two ponies, turned his back on them and continued his merry dance, lifting his long scrawny legs high into the air as he stepped over the rocks and cackled to himself.

Volgor hesitated. But Attricus seized the moment, shoved his sandals into his pack, grabbed a handful of pebble mane, and swung himself onto the closest pony. The moment that the pony felt his weight, it broke into a trot towards the river and the other pony followed, almost leaving Volgor behind. Running to catch up, he grabbed at the pony's mane with both hands and hung on until they reached deep water, where he could float onto its back.

The ponies crossed against the flow, before they clambered up a bank and onto a small sandy beach a short distance downstream. Having done their job, they buckled at the knees and with an almighty rattle, collapsed onto the ground, tipping Attricus and Volgor off. Then they got up and plunged back into the raging waters.

Attricus and Volgor lay panting on the sand.

'Thank goodness we made it,' said Attricus as he sat up and stared at the rushing water behind them. He looked at Volgor. 'Why didn't you tell me you'd found a coin?'

Volgor stared up at the swaying trees. 'I was going to.'

'But you didn't.'

'No … I'm sorry.'

'If we're going to be travelling together, you need to tell me these things. It could've been disastrous today because I didn't know.'

'But you didn't tell me when you realised you'd lost your crystal ball,' replied Volgor.

A moment of awkward silence passed between them.

'Yes, you're right … I'm sorry too.'

Attricus paused. 'Where did you find it?'

'Do you remember, after we escaped from the Tangled Woods I asked if you'd seen the yellow man?'

'Yes. So he wasn't an illusion …?'

'No … he wasn't.'

'But I still don't understand. The fisherman said you got it from a fish in his river, not from a yellow man. There's nothing complicated about where you find a coin, Volgor. It's either in one place or another … Unless … you did find a gemstone …?'

Attricus was shocked. The kurr sat up and removed his hat. He reached in, and placed the aquamarine on his opened palm.

Attricus drew in his breath and stared. It was beautiful.

'It was in the belly of the fish,' said Volgor.

'So he saw you catch the fish … and he knew. He waited for us at the river. He knew he'd find us trying to cross the river somewhere.'

'I suppose so.'

'You can't tell anyone about this Volgor … do you hear?'

'Why? What is it?'

'I'm not sure … but don't show or tell anyone … for now, at least. I've some needle and thread and I'll stitch it into the pocket of your jacket tonight … for safety.'

Volgor thought he would never understand humans. First Attricus berated him for not telling him about the gem, and now he was forbidding him to tell anyone else.

'At least we're now in the Land of Illingaith,' said Volgor. He got up and slipped the gem back into his trouser pocket.

Crossing the river had left them saturated and as the light of the afternoon faded they began to shiver.

'We need to get going.' Attricus got to his feet, put on his sandals and slung his sack over his shoulder. 'A long time ago I travelled through this part of Illingaith, and I know of a small cave where we can light a fire and rest.'

The soothsayer led the way, pushing through the thick perimeter of trees, while Volgor glanced at the rushing waters of the Abyss, thinking of all the fish he could've caught. But just as he turned to follow Attricus, a flash of movement on the opposite bank arrested his attention, and there in the last rays of the setting sun sat the yellow man upon a prancing horse of air. Once again he tipped his hat at Volgor, and with a knowing smile, the kurr did the same.

Further upstream, the dancing fisherman looked on in shock as the magic rune stamped on the coin suddenly turned bright red. The metal broke into shards, and as the pieces fell from his hand and clattered among the rocks, the remaining image seared into his palm like a hot iron. Cursing and screaming in pain he ran to the river and plunged his hand deep into the cooling waters.

The strange sound echoed along the river, making Attricus halt and listen.

'What was that?'

'Justice?' suggested Volgor.

# CHAPTER 11

Artorus pulled open the door to a large circular room and stood aside for Ikoseer to enter. In the middle of the room was a round oak table. Around the table were thirteen chairs, one for each knight, with an extra chair for the Sage, placed between Artorus and his second in command, Scithios. Ikoseer stood behind her chair, and invited the knights to join her.

Each knight now unsheathed his sword and placed it lengthwise on the table in front of Ikoseer, pushing it forward until every blade point touched the adjoining points. The Sage murmured an incantation and raised her staff towards the centre of the table. The head of it shone brilliant white as she lowered it to rest on the sword points. Blue bolts of electricity surged along the full length of each blade, and the swords began a low pulsating hum.

'Knights of Power. Take your swords!'

Ikoseer's voice boomed as she raised her staff above her head and stepped back from the table. As one, the knights grasped their swords and keeping the tips pointed towards the centre of the table, raised the swords slowly, creating a widening circle of electric blue fire that arced between the blades.

'May the circle of power protect you all,' intoned Ikoseer.

The knights held their swords in formation until the Sage struck her staff hard on the wooden floor. Again as one, they swung their blades up and over their heads and then to the right until the points touched the floor behind them, breaking the electric field.

With the opening ritual completed, each knight hooked his sword behind his chair and sat down, as Ikoseer rejoined them.

'On behalf of the Knights of Power, welcome,' said Scithios. 'What news from the World of Man?'

Ikoseer clasped her hands. 'The enemy has widened their search for the Lightenstone. They believe that if they follow me, they will find the Stone.'

'Could they be so foolish? To think you would lead them to it?' asked Scithios. 'Even we are not privy to the location.'

'They hold onto that possibility because they know that the Queen will not allow the Isle of Spheres to die and she will act to restore it at some point in time. And they know that I will help her.'

The Sage paused. 'And that day has come, brothers-in-arms. Queen Solara has requested the return of the stones to the Pentark.'

A murmur rippled through the group. All except Artorus were taken aback by the announcement.

'Then we'll protect you on your quest …'

Ikoseer raised her hand. 'It is a generous offer, Scithios, but not necessary. Artorus will remain with me. More knights than that will draw too much attention.'

Scithios leant forward. 'The four outer gemstones are our responsibility. We distributed them for safekeeping and are honour bound to return them. We can hold them here until …'

Ikoseer halted him. 'Much is at stake. The Queen has requested utmost discretion in the gathering of the stones.'

Scithios was taken aback. 'Is our ability in question? It's our duty to help you in whatever way we can …'

'I understand your frustration. But like me, your duty is also to the Queen. I don't know what is before us. When the time comes I shall send for you through the Queen, as I did for our arrival yesterday. She will guide you. I regret that I cannot reveal more to you now.

Scithios nodded.

'Is there any news from the resistance fighters?' asked Ikoseer.

'The enemy taunt us by moving ever closer to Arctus,' continued Scithios. 'They have grown in cunning and bravery over the years. And you also have to contend with boorlings, wolves and anomirs.'

'Anomirs have flown as far as Arctus?'

'The distressed calls of the snow eagles have been heard. Only anomirs would cause such a disturbance. Onysius is desperate. The influence of Lord Mortimer and the power of the Prince of Darkness still have hold over him.'

Patrayus, a young knight sitting opposite Ikoseer, challenged her. 'What I don't understand, is why you have given this important task to a young woman, two dwarves, and a badger. It should have been given to us!'

'Hold your tongue Patrayus!' Scithios stood up and gave the young knight a stern look. Patrayus hung his head. Scithios still glared as he sat back in his seat.

But Ikoseer raised a reassuring hand, and swept her eyes around the table until they rested on Patrayus.

'The skills and courage of the Knights of Power are legendary. But sometimes the greatest challenge must be undertaken by those who are often overlooked. It is true that it will be dangerous, and as you seek counsel from me, I also seek counsel from the Queen.

'As you know, the World of the Soul teeters on the brink of disaster. I have chosen my companions with the hope that they will be able to journey with nothing more than a passing glance from anyone we meet.

'However … an escort from here would be appreciated. Perhaps young Patrayus would like to join us, and then return to you, once we have left the borders of Arctus?'

Surprised, the young knight looked up, meeting the Sage's intense gaze.

'Now, I am yet to speak to the Queen,' continued Ikoseer. 'And I must confess that the success of our quest … is less than certain. We will need a measure of good fortune on our side.'

Turning to Scithios she asked, 'How are King Galway's family? He was unwell when I last visited them.'

'He is much better now. Princess Moira continues to look after her parents but twenty years of exile from Mirraway Castle has not been kind to him or Queen Helena.' Scithios pursed his lips. 'But their son, Prince Mir, left the Ascension Mountains a few weeks ago.'

Ikoseer raised her eyebrows. 'Do you know where he's gone?'

'Nobody knows for sure, but he has since sent a message to the outer gates, to relieve his family from more worry. He took one of the guards' horses and left without warning. I assume it's to try and undo the deeds of the invaders. And who can blame him? He will succeed to the throne of Gorthonomir one day … and if he did nothing … he would be king of nothing.

'He is an excellent rider and swordsman, so we were not concerned when the horse returned without him. We assumed he'd decided to travel by foot making it easier to hide. Besides, most of those outside these mountains wouldn't recognise him after twenty years.'

Scithios paused. 'And he also took Honorex …'

'King Farmir's blade?' cut in Artorus.

'It will draw no attention to the untrained eye,' replied Scithios. 'And even though it hasn't been used since the Battle of the Stones, I wouldn't like it pointed at my heart or against my throat.'

'Well … he is entitled to take it,' conceded Artorus. 'After all, it is the blade of his ancestors. May it come to our aid if we need it.'

The other knights nodded and murmured in agreement.

Ikoseer had been drawing a small spiral pattern on the tabletop with her index finger. Now she looked up.

'I would have liked to visit King Galway and his family before we leave, but it will not be possible. Artorus and I, along with our young companions, must first see Solara, the Queen of the Sun. With her blessing, we want to leave the mountain before Onysius has a chance to cross the valley.'

'Are you certain that he's following you?' interrupted one of the knights.

'No, but he did send a wrake after us and I expect he will follow,' replied Artorus.

Scithios leant forward. 'With your permission Artorus, I'll dispatch four knights out across the valley towards the Lux Mountains. If they come across the wrake they can stop him. Perhaps they may even meet Onysius and his soldiers.'

'As you please Scithios. Just as before, you shall lead in my absence.'

Scithios gave a slight bow of his head.

Ikoseer stood and looked across at Patrayus. 'From here on you must look like a commoner. Like Artorus, wear plain clothes over your plated leather armour. Pack some basic provisions. If all goes well we should be leaving Arctus within a few days, and then you can return.'

Acknowledging that the meeting was over, the knights rose and sheathed their swords. Standing behind their chairs they waited for the Sage to speak.

'Go well, Knights of Power. May your inner light shine and guide you in these darkest of times.'

They bowed their heads replying, 'Ikoseer', as the Sage and Artorus left the room.

✧

Boris, Ferdy, Frovin and Marta were told to wait in a nearby room. It was large and airy with a high ceiling, and the morning light entered through a single window that looked out over the valley they had crossed the day before.

Ferdy stood on tiptoe with elbows on the sill, looking out at the majestic view from this castle that had somehow been carved out of the mountain. As they had approached the three mountains, there had been nothing to suggest that there was a castle on the largest one.

They had just finished a hearty breakfast of oaten porridge, stewed spiced apple, followed by fried buttery mushrooms tossed with caramelised onions, and broken bread dipped in honey. It was all washed down with strong hot tea.

Ferdy was still slurping butter and honey off his fingers when Boris sat down on a foot stool, and pulled a rag from his pocket to polish Thrust. Marta was threading a needle to repair her torn pocket and secure a button on Boris' vest. She had already fixed Ferdy's shirt and now it sported a variety of odd-shaped wooden buttons—he was sure his mother would not have approved. Frovin was watching. Curled up on a soft cushion beside Marta's chair, he was soon fast asleep.

At the far end of the room was a large open bookcase reaching to the ceiling. Ferdy shoved his hands into his pockets and wandered down to take a closer look. The books were packed tightly together and most of them were weighty tomes, with red covers and blank spines. He quickly scanned them, leaning back as far as he could to see the top row. There was a very small book just within reach. Ferdy could read Dwarfish as well as the common language of the Spheres but this book was written in a language he had never seen before. He wondered if it was Elvish.

He flipped to another page and was astonished to see the detailed drawing of a battle scene on one page and a folded map on the other. He tried to read the inscription below the scene. He frowned and looked back at the drawing.

Front and centre upon a craggy outcrop, holding aloft a mighty sword, was a powerful figure on horseback. Standing in front of the rearing steed was a robed woman, appearing to show something to the horseman. The rest of the scene was chaotic, with the twisted grotesque bodies of slain soldiers and other strange creatures pinned to the ground by swords and arrows. An angry dark sky loomed over the horrific scene. Then he noticed, upon a windswept tor to the right of the horseman, a lone figure in a flowing hooded robe and holding a long staff. The figure was standing beside a horse, observing the spectacle.

Ferdy stared at the head of the staff and his eyes widened. He saw no distinguishable features in the face but he recognised the faint pattern down the front of the garment. A sudden shiver ran up his spine.

He opened out the map on the opposite page. It was similar to Potsy's maps, except there was greater detail, and the roads, forests, and villages were all in different places. Ferdy ran his eyes to the bottom and noticed that the Dukedom of Asilodor and Jimpiragh Castle were not marked, but he did see a small village south of the Tangled Woods.

This must be an ancient map of the Isle of Spheres, before the Treaty of Spheres was signed. At the top he found the Ascension Mountains. But it was a single mountain, close to the border of Illingaith and at the start of the Lux Mountains, that fascinated him. He was concentrating hard on a symbol at the foot of the mountain when the door swung open and Artorus walked in, bidding them to come.

Ferdy almost dropped the book in fright and, before Artorus had a chance to see what he was up to, he re-folded the map and closed the book, ready to put it back on the shelf. But he wavered. For some reason he slipped it into the large inner pocket of his jacket instead. Folding his arms, and trying to look innocent, he sauntered up to join the others. He looked away when Artorus gave him a questioning glance, feeling the heat rise up into his chubby cheeks. He was not a thief, he told himself. He was simply borrowing the book, and would return it when he had finished.

Artorus hustled them out of the room, and strode ahead along the corridor towards the throne room. Boris and Ferdy had to trot in order to keep up.

'I cannot stress enough the importance of what is about to take place,' said Artorus as they stood before two huge wooden doors. 'As Ikoseer mentioned before, we are going to see someone with the power to help us locate the stones.' He took a deep breath. 'You are about to meet Solara, the Queen of the Sun.'

He kept his eyes on Boris and Ferdy as they stood with an incredulous look on their faces.

'Very few get to have an audience with Her Majesty, so try not to say anything unnecessary. We seek her counsel. So listen carefully to all she says … and don't forget to bow.'

Ferdy was about to ask where Ikoseer was, but Artorus pushed open the doors and led them in. They had expected the room to be massive and ornate with a huge throne in the centre, but instead they saw a small simple room, with no one but the Sage in it. Bewildered, Boris and Ferdy looked at each other. Marta let out a slow breath. Frovin reached up with a reassuring paw on her right hand. The strong clear voice of the Queen filled the room, making the dwarves jump.

'Welcome my brave young souls. Welcome to my mountain. You come to me at a time of great distress … in the World of the Soul and across the Isle of Spheres. Such a weight has been put on your young shoulders. To help find the stones and return them to the Pentark is not a task for the faint hearted.

'Counsel has been sought and given to Ikoseer. The Isle of Spheres stands upon a knife's edge. It is now up to you. I have looked into your hearts and minds and although you are all troubled, I see great strength in each of you. This strength will carry you through the coming journey. Bring your inner will to the fore, that it may guide your hoping hearts to victory.

'Remember: strength comes from adversity. You will be tested, as we are all tested, for strength of heart and purpose of will. But do not burden your heart with your challenges. They are an opportunity to learn and grow. Difficult it may be, but with gratitude, accept them and release them. Forgiveness and understanding are the greatest gift to yourself and others.'

Suddenly, the room filled with swirling, rainbow coloured lights, accompanied by the most beautiful music Marta had ever heard. Starting from the outer walls, the colours moved inwards, spinning clockwise around the room, gathering speed, and then merging into a white vortex around them. It melted away, and hovering before them was the shimmering, ethereal, Queen of the Sun.

Marta, Frovin, Boris and Ferdy stood in awe at the apparition before them.

The Queen was not dressed as Marta had expected. She wore a flowing, plain white dress that moved in gentle waves, creating the shimmering effect. There appeared to be fine interlocking rings of gold over the garment and Marta likened it to the chain mail she had sometimes seen in armour, but with more open weave.

A tiny spark of light was at the centre of each ring, and as the garment swirled, these sparks were like stars that twinkled in the night sky, changing between gold and ultramarine blue. And upon Solara's head was a plain gold crown with a mysterious seal in the centre.

Ferdy's body tingled all over. 'No one is ever going to believe this.'

Boris jabbed him. When he turned to protest he realised that everyone else was bowing. He dropped his head and stared at the floor until something made him look up. When his eyes met the steady amber gaze of the Queen, hovering in front of him, he was mesmerised. It was as if she looked into the very depths of his soul.

'My two young dwarves ... you carry with you Thrust, made by Thrim the master craftsman to the Isle of Spheres. Keep it safe and use it well, for all its secrets are not yet revealed.'

She paused. 'And should your journeys take you into elven lands, may you find the writings of the elves ... helpful.'

Ferdy started and felt for the book as she moved to Frovin.

'Once the Lightenstone is found, it is your task to protect it until it is returned to the Pentark. Just as your ancestors protected it in aeons past.'

Frovin stared in disbelief.

'Be ever watchful of the darkness, even within yourself. The Stone can bring great power. Do not allow the Dark Ones to whisper their wishes into your mind. Subtle and cunning are their ways. You must protect the Stone, even with your life!'

Frovin swallowed hard.

'And now to you … Marta.'

Marta gazed into the eyes of the Queen, and like Ferdy, was unable to look away. Her heart beat fast.

The Queen held out her hand. 'Your amulet,' she said softly.

As if in a dream, Marta pulled it over her head and placed it into the Queen's palm, expecting it to fall to the floor. But the ghostly fingers closed over it, and it began to glow. Tiny shafts of white and violet light streamed from between Queen Solara's fingers, pulsing into ever lengthening rays until her hand became a single ball of light. Marta was fascinated and frightened at the same time. Why did the Queen want her amulet? It was the first time she had taken it off since her mother died.

The Queen breathed on the ball and the light responded. She opened her fingers and a hot blue flame rose from within the ball, licking the air while tiny stars twinkled around the sphere. Marta noticed the rest of the room had darkened.

The Queen looked back at Marta. 'Now the Lightenstone knows that you are all on your way. I have charged your amulet so when your courage falters, use it to guide you. If you need help, look to the symbols all around you: on the ground, in the water, in the sky, in the trees. Even the animals will help. And above all—trust your heart.'

With that, the Queen opened her hand, the lights faded and the amulet returned to normal. Then Solara placed the necklace over Marta's bent head. Marta clutched the amulet. It still felt warm. In the deep silence that followed, an impulse surged through Ferdy. To Boris' horror, Ferdy drew Thrust from its sheath on Boris' belt and with trembling hands, offered it to the Queen.

'Can you charge Thrust too?' he asked in a faltering voice.

Ferdy's knees began to knock and it felt as if his legs would give way as the Queen's gaze returned to him. Flushed with sudden embarrassment he averted his eyes and stared at the sword. He was about to mumble a hurried apology and withdraw when she breathed along the short blade. His outstretched hands tingled and grew hot. But there were no sparks or balls of light and he shrank back as Boris grabbed Thrust, and glaring at him, returned it to its sheath.

Then all at once, Boris' bravado also left him. Their adventure had become a more dangerous quest than he was prepared for, and he was terrified he would never see his family again. If only he and Ferdy had just continued on their way to their cousins in the Rolling Hills.

'Why do we need to be tested?' he challenged. 'Why do we have to help find the stones? Can't the knights and Ikoseer …'

He felt the quick hand of Artorus on his shoulder. He lifted his worried eyes to meet the Queen's.

'Thrim forged Thrust to serve the Pentark and now that you and Ferdy are bearers of the blade …'

The Queen let her words hang as the twins looked at her, wide eyed. 'So shore up your hearts and go well my young warriors. My blessings will always follow you.'

She reached out her hand and placed it on each of their heads in turn. They all felt a warmth flooding their bodies. And then she was gone.

Ikoseer broke the silence. 'We are to leave now. Pack your things while Artorus and I prepare the horses and ponies. A young knight called Patrayus will be joining us for part of the way.'

She strode to the door and was about to open it when Ferdy tugged on her robe.

'So where are we going?'

The Sage hesitated and half turned. 'South-west.'

# CHAPTER 12

The four knights covered their noses and mouths against the stench as they looked at the savaged body of the wrake. The head was untouched but lay at an odd angle, and already fluid was oozing from the nostrils and mouth of the cadaver, sliding down the protruded, swollen tongue.

'The wolves must have been hungry. It's not their favourite food. The wrake must have found the ancient pass through the Lux Mountains.' Rannoch was surprised, and pointed towards the hidden entry into the valley.

'But there are no fresh tracks,' observed Zagar. 'Onysius and his soldiers haven't followed him.'

'Not through here. But we can't leave anything to chance. Artorus said they charged after him into Greenwood Forest. And they'd heard rumour of a sage. They will come.'

Rannoch pursed his lips and turned to the other two knights.

'Shall we go?'

∽

Onysius and his party crossed the plateau on the trail of the wrake sent after the travellers. He was determined to reach the Valley of the Queen by the quickest route. But light overnight rain had washed away any remaining scent and so they were forced to take the usual route through the Lux Mountains.

They reached the Valley of the Queen by twilight the following day and camped at the end of the mountain pass road. It was a cold uncomfortable night and Onysius woke the next morning in a foul mood. His men rose stiff and tired to prepare their breakfast as the rising sun streamed long rays down the valley towards them, promising warmth.

Stores were lean, but Onysius still ate his fill of rye bread, salt-fish and pottage, and now sat by a warm fire drinking a tankard of ale. His Commander approached him.

'Do you think the wrake found the hidden pass?' asked Onysius, looking up and wiping ale from his beard.

'I don't know, my Lord.'

'If he came through here, then he could be returning this way as we speak.' Onysius tore off a chunk of bread and pointed to the main road.

'It's possible. But if he found the hidden pass then he'd take them back that way, and he'll miss us.'

'You think I don't know that!' spat Onysius, irritated. 'That's why I have to find him.' He stared at the hot coals and kicked a piece of unburned wood into the lazy flames.

'Those dwarves could be valuable and I don't want them dead before I get to interrogate them. So we need to search the whole valley. I'll take the remaining wrakes with me and head north along the edge of the Lux Mountains. Deploy the rest of the men. If the travellers have so far evaded capture, then we might still find them.'

'The remaining wrakes have already been gone about an hour, my Lord. They left on horseback after the arrival of a master wrake and his boorling. Headed towards the Ascension Mountains.'

Caught off guard, Onysius glared. 'The same one you sent—that met me on the Trading Road?'

The Commander nodded.

'Why didn't you stop them? Insolent beast! So, the master wrake wants some of the glory does he? I ordered him to return to Greenwood Forest!' he seethed. His spittle sizzled in the coals. 'Get my warhorse ready.'

'Yes, my Lord.'

Impatient, Onysius was soon beside the huge dappled grey and pushed his Commander aside to buckle the girth, all the while reassuring the fidgeting stallion.

'Give my orders to the men,' he barked gathering the reins and accepting a leg-up into the saddle. 'Remind them they're on the lookout for dwarf travellers on horseback, but they must be wary. The dwarves might be accompanied by a sage or a knight. If so, they are not to approach them, but are to return to the camp and wait for me.'

Onysius hesitated. 'Have two soldiers stay behind; one on day watch, and the other on night.'

'Yes, my Lord.'

Onysius spurred his mount at a thunderous pace to make up for lost time, but although the loose shale littering sections of the path slowed him down, within a few hours he was getting closer to the remains. The creeping mist was now upon him and he disappeared into it, as he led his horse off the path and onto the valley floor.

A cool breeze ruffled the horse's forelock. Onysius remained alert, listening: the shriek of a bird flushed out of the clumped tussock grass growing across the valley; the distant striking of horseshoe on stone; the creaking of leather.

Then the stallion startled. Ears pricked, he tensed and halted, staring into the wall of mist. Loyal to their master, a long low warning growl escaped the throats of the other wrakes slowly closing in. The grey lifted his head higher, flared his nostrils and snorted as he struck the ground with a hoof.

Onysius shortened his reins, drew his sword and stood in his stirrups. His eyes narrowed as he searched the swirling mist. Then a familiar odour filled his nostrils—boorling.

The stallion swung his head and spun as the mounted beast emerged from the mist. Too late—Onysius realised it was a trap.

Spurred on, the sheer bulk of the stallion knocked the boorling off balance and it fell, trapping the rider underneath. As the warhorse began to trample and kick, Onysius jumped off and plunged his sword deep into the chest of the clamouring wrake, his battleaxe now just out of reach.

'Nobody disobeys me!' he roared pulling out his sword and turning to face the others.

By this time, the boorling was battered but not defeated. Onysius reined in the stallion and then yanking on the boorling's reins, raged at it to get up.

'Now, I am your master,' he said, sweeping his eyes defiantly around the other wrakes and their skittish horses.

Then Onysius heard the *whoosh* of an arrow slice through the air, and the dull thud of impact, as it embedded itself deep in the heart of the wrake near him. A strange gurgle escaped as the wrake fell and his horse fled. Then a second arrow found its mark.

As the Knights of Power came into view Onysius gave a shout and a third arrow struck. The remaining wrake grimaced in pain as he tried to pull the feathered shaft out of his thigh, but to no avail. Then he spun his horse round, battleaxe raised high, to strike the bowman. But Zagar came from behind plunging his sword into the wrake, and the last of Onysius' protectors fell among the scattering horses.

Now exposed, Onysius swung onto the boorling and spurred it forward as the knights surrounded him and an arrow glanced off his armour. But it was followed by a blade, which sliced open his face, so that he cried out in pain and swore while the boorling almost unseated him. He tried in vain to stem the blood pouring from the cut and flooding his right eye, as he charged forward. When he was blocked, he swung hard left on the reins to find another gap, holding his sword out in defiance as he disappeared into the mist.

Onysius' stallion lingered nearby. Rannoch approached, admiring the strength and conformation of the destrier as he grabbed the dragging reins. As horse marshal to the King, he recognised it as a valuable warhorse, and he had no intention of leaving it for the hungry wolves of Skag. With ears laid back the stallion snorted and showed the whites of his eyes, then struck out with his near foreleg and lunged at Rannoch, attempting to bite.

Undeterred, Rannoch stepped back, spoke in low tones and then with caution, extended his hand. Slowly, the dappled warhorse responded. The knight gently stroked its nose, the hot fast breath welcome on cold hands. He dipped into a small drawstring bag tied to his belt, produced a lump of sugar and offered it on an open palm. The sugar disappeared and with a smile, Rannoch ran his hand down the stallion's front legs, checking for soundness.

'Come. Now you belong to the Knights of Power.'

'Should we continue after the rest of them?' asked Zagar as the brothers-in-arms regrouped.

'No,' replied Rannoch. 'Onysius is hurt, but our horses are no match for the speed of a boorling. I expect Onysius would have ordered his soldiers and scouts to spread out in small groups across the valley to search for the travellers. It's a vast area to cover. Ikoseer, Artorus and Patrayus will handle them if they happen to meet.

The grey suddenly turned his head and stared intently into the mist. The knights fell silent. They thought they could hear the occasional soft footfall of a lone horse, and the jingle of a bit as it shook its head. Then there was silence.

*Probably one of the wrakes' horses*, thought Rannoch. He waited for a few minutes then indicated with a jerk of his head that it was time to go. Leaving the carnage, they rode back across the valley towards their home.

$\backsim$

The hidden rider had been setting rabbit snares when he saw the wrakes approach from below. He concealed himself among the pine trees and watched them pass, with only a moment of uneasiness when the boorling sniffed the air and looked up the embankment towards him. The rider held his breath and waited until it looked away. Then he set his last trap, giving them time to get away from him. But then not too far behind them was Onysius, riding a huge grey warhorse. So the rider waited a little longer and had been following them for the last hour at a distance. Now downwind, he continued through the trees until he reached a clear bank where he could zigzag down to the valley floor.

He was pleased when the mist rolled in and gave him some cover. His horse was unshod, so as long as no stones were dislodged, he could travel undetected.

But then he heard the sudden clash of swords and shouting. He realised he was closer than he thought, when one of the wrake's terrified horses fled past him. He lunged at the bridle but missed. Then another horse almost crashed into him.

*It must be the Knights of Power!*

He waited, cold and stiff, until he could hear nothing except the sigh and lull of the lifting breeze. Deciding it was safe, he headed towards the bloody scene.

He found the wrakes first, also hoping to find the body of Onysius, the Earl who had destroyed his home and killed his family. Afterwards, the man had joined the resistance fighters and lived a simple life in the mountains. But now even these pristine mountains were succumbing to the creeping darkness.

It was time to fight back.

He dismounted, knelt beside one of the wrakes and checked the protruding arrow head. He spat on his fingers and rubbed away the congealing blood, searching for a small insignia stamped into the steel.

It was unmistakable. The arrow had come from the Knights of Power.

Then he saw the master wrake, easily identified by a small brand seared into his forehead. He smiled as he gazed down at the pitiful sight. He wondered where the boorling was, and it seemed that Onysius was now gone. He knew he would not be alone and so there would be more of his soldiers in the valley. Pondering his next move, he remounted.

He urged his mount to move on and as the horse turned the man noticed something on the ground, bound in black cloth. He dismounted and rolled the object with the toe of his boot. It would fit in the palm of his hand but he was reluctant to pick it up. Instinct told him not to but as a resistance fighter he knew that it might be important. Breaking off a thin stick of nearby heather, he tried to remove the binding, but it was too tight. Then he used a fine trapping strap to secure the object to a ring near the pommel where he could keep an eye on it, and then remounted.

He would be a day early. He had planned to bring fresh rabbit to share, and although he was close to the hidden pass, it would still take him many hours to make it in through the mountain.

But he had important news.

Potsy would be pleased about that, but the resistance fighter wondered what the podgy old dwarf would make of the bound object, now bumping against the chestnut's shoulder.

# CHAPTER 13

After their escape from the ferryman, Attricus and Volgor stayed overnight in the cave near the Abyss River. They ate fish scraps for their supper, sucking the salmon bones clean. Afterwards, Attricus stitched the gem to the inside pocket of the kurr's jacket.

'Where are we going from here?' asked Volgor as Attricus tied off the thread and broke it with his teeth.

'To Elodom Monastery.' Attricus handed the garment back to him. Volgor took it and placed the fish skeleton between his knobby knees.

'Is it far?' he asked sliding his arms into the sleeves and shrugging the jacket over his threadbare shirt.

'Distance is unimportant when you're evading the enemy,' replied Attricus, putting away his needle and thread.

Volgor's shoulders slumped. 'You've been there before?'

Attricus pushed his glasses up the bridge of his nose. 'It's my old home.'

Volgor blinked in surprise. 'Don't monks live in monasteries?'

Attricus nodded.

'Are you really a monk?'

'No, but I was trained to become one. I was left at the main gates when I was just a babe. I was raised there.'

Attricus turned his palms to the fire and stared wistfully into the hot coals. 'It was a good life. I was taught to read, write and count. And I helped the lay brothers in the vineyard and gardens. But I yearned to travel. I wanted to see what was beyond the monastery. So I left before I had to take my vows.'

Volgor frowned. 'What's a vow?'

'A promise to spend the rest of your life praying for the souls of all the people in the Isle of Spheres.'

'Why would anyone want to do that?' Volgor snapped off some bones to chew, then added, 'But wouldn't that be better than living in Jimpiragh?'

'I wasn't living there by choice,' said Attricus, rubbing his hands to warm them. 'I was still at the monastery when Lord Mortimer started the civil war. No one knew anything about the invasion until fleeing families came to the monastery for sanctuary.

'So I joined a band of resistance fighters. That's how I knew about this cave. But I couldn't wield a sword or swing a battleaxe, so I wasn't much help to them. Then one day we came across a caravan of nomads, and I left the fighters to join them instead. An old woman travelling with them taught me how to read palms and scry crystal balls.'

'And that's how you became a soothsayer.'

Attricus nodded.

'And then you were captured by Onysius,' prodded Volgor.

'I was tricked.' Attricus picked up a stick, pushing it deep into the coals.

Volgor stopped chewing on his bones. He waited for Attricus to continue, but the only sound was the spitting of hot sap.

'All Onysius cares about is finding that stupid stone.' Volgor cocked his head at the soothsayer. 'And with a bit of luck he'll find it. And then he'll leave all of us alone.'

Attricus gave him a stern look. 'If he finds it Volgor, things will be worse … not better. He and Mortimer will attempt to use it for nothing but evil …'

'Have you ever seen the Stone?' mumbled Volgor rolling the bones around his mouth, and trying to crunch them with his teeth.

'No. Not even in my crystal ball.' Attricus was anticipating
the next question.

Volgor leant closer as if he expected the cavern walls to be listening. 'Did
you tell Onysius everything you saw in your ball?'

'Of course not.'

Volgor sat bolt upright and stared, his hand on his jacket's inner pocket.

'I didn't find the stone he's looking for, did I …?'

'No, you didn't!'

Volgor looked at him in disbelief. 'Then how do you know it's not the
Stone … if you've never …'

'Because I saw a drawing of it in the monastery's library,' explained
Attricus. 'I had to study the history of the Isle of Spheres as part of my
training. Your aquamarine is the wrong colour and the wrong shape. Until
the Stone was removed it sat in the Pentark on a fell near Mirraway Castle.
It was always guarded by the Knights of Power.'

Volgor shivered at the mention of the Knights of Power. He had seen them
in action. During the civil war the kurrs living along the Bleak River had
fled the fighting. After they realised that no one was interested in them,
they returned to their favourite fishing spots. But Volgor was captured
when he wandered too far from the group and was taken to Jimpiragh. He
could still hear his distraught mother's high-pitched wail when she realised
that he was gone.

He soon understood that Onysius and Mortimer were obsessed with
finding the Stone so that they could rule the Isle of Spheres. Volgor
scratched his nose, swallowed the bones, and opened his mouth to speak.

Attricus peered at him over the top of his glasses.

'And before you ask me again why you shouldn't show the gemstone to
anyone, it's because, even though it's not the Lightenstone, it is still very

important to Onysius. If any of his soldiers know you have it, they'll try to steal it from you—and kill you in the process. That's what the ferryman would have done if you hadn't fooled him with the coin.'

Volgor looked away and stared into the hot coals. As they sat in silence, his mind wandered back to his family. He had never been so far from home, and he felt miserable that he was now probably going to set off in the opposite direction and move even further away.

'How far is the monastery from here?'

'It's quite a way into eastern Magirus. Close to the border with the World of Man. Not far from here there's a massif of the Arifer Mountain range. We can follow an old road along the base until they end and the mountains veer west. But the road continues through the Ageless Forest and we can follow it eastwards to the Intrepid River. At that point Magirus will be just over the river. The monastery is another five days journey from there.'

Volgor groaned and sat on his haunches, cradling his chin in his hands.

Attricus sighed. 'I just hope Onysius' anomirs and wrakes have stopped looking for us by now. But we must leave this cave soon. We're still too close to Jimpiragh.'

'And the ferryman,' Volgor shuddered.

Attricus stood up and stretched his weary body.

'Is there another way we could get to the monastery?' asked Volgor, flicking the fish remnants on the fire.

'We could follow the Abyss River down to the Mother Sea and then trek along the coastline to the Intrepid River. But it'd be a lot further that way and the closest I've been to the coast is a small village called Riverbend on the banks of the Abyss River.'

Attricus stared blankly and appeared to be in a trance as he continued. 'I've read that the sea is a very beautiful place and that the waters are sailed by seafarers on tall wooden ships, their sails taut with the westward winds. They come from the outer islands to a magnificent harbour called Werthyn, and bring spices and fine cloth to trade. A thousand miles to the far east there are white cliffs where a sphere of light guides the ships at night …'

Volgor was amazed. He did not know what a sea was and he had never heard of ships and sails and westward winds but it sounded very grand.

'Why aren't we going that way then? At least I could catch fish in the Abyss River for us to eat. It might be further, but we wouldn't need to go so close to Onysius' men.' Volgor could feel excitement building. 'And then we could get on a ship and live on another island.'

'It won't be that easy. Since the invasion, pirates patrol the coastline around the Isle of Spheres now. So there's no guarantee of freedom or safety that way either.'

'But no one there will know who we are,' Volgor pointed out. He spread his spindly arms, letting them flop.

Attricus shrugged. 'Not unless Onysius has sent word by anomir. We must sleep now and rise before sun-up.'

He turned away and rolled his hessian sack over, trying to make it comfortable as he got back down to rest. 'The fire's almost out—best to bring your things and join me. The night will get cold.'

∽

Volgor did as he was bid, and although pleased for the warmth, he had an uncomfortable night, dreaming of strange wooden buildings floating on sparkling blue water, with tall poles upon which were huge billowing white cloths lashed by ropes.

On one of the floating buildings stood a woman with flaming red hair. She wore a flowing white dress, and her hands were placed on what looked like a cartwheel with short rounded wooden spikes. And on a box behind the cartwheel, sat a weird creature with pointy ears.

Suddenly the woman turned, fixing Volgor with her copper-flecked eyes. She extended her arm and opened the fingers of her right hand to reveal four precious gemstones, one of which looked very like the aquamarine Volgor had cut from the salmon. Then the woman smiled, closed her hand and turned away, commanding her sailors to 'go to starboard'.

Volgor woke up with a start but stayed huddled to Attricus as he stared into the dark. He somehow felt sure that despite the danger the dream meant they should be heading towards the sea.

∽

They rose and made breakfast of their remaining figs and strips of dried meat. Volgor slung his coiled rope over his head and stood at the cave entrance, fidgeting and cold, and anxious to get going. But the dream gnawed at him and he stroked his jacket pocket, feeling the slight bulge of the hidden jewel.

'I had a dream,' he blurted out as the soothsayer joined him. Attricus searched his face, but said nothing.

'There was a woman on a building that floated on blue water, and there was an odd looking creature with her. She held out her hand and showed me four gemstones.'

Volgor looked down at the ground and rolled a small pebble with his big toe. 'One of them looked like the aqua gem I found.'

Attricus was visibly shocked.

'The woman had red hair and copper coloured eyes and was holding onto a cartwheel with rounded wooden spikes … And what does 'starboard' mean?'

Attricus swallowed hard and cleared his throat. It was a profound dream. 'Starboard means the "right side" of a ship.'

Volgor jerked his head up and stared at Attricus. 'The building I saw floating on water … was a … a ship?'

'Yes.'

'So doesn't it mean we must go to the Mother Sea?' Volgor was
excited but he shivered at the thought of walking through the Ageless
Forest and beyond.

Attricus appeared to waver. 'I don't know that part of the island. If we get
into trouble I can't help.'

For the first time since leaving Jimpiragh, Volgor realised that he was not
the only one who was afraid. 'So what do we do?' he asked.

'Your dream is telling us there's a connection between the aquamarine and
the Mother Sea. But I don't know what it is.'

'But we won't have to worry about the pirates if we don't get on a ship, will
we? We can just walk around the coastline like you suggested.'

Attricus exhaled slowly and shook his head. 'It's a risk no matter where we
go. So now you know you must keep the gemstone hidden. Someone will
always want it.'

'Well, they can't have it!' said Volgor feeling braver and patting his knife.

Attricus' eyes smiled gently at Volgor. Then he adjusted his sack
and stepped out of the cave into the cool morning air. With the
kurr close behind, Attricus led the way through the trees beside the
rushing Abyss River.

With her ear tufts up, the bright eyes of a long-eared owl stared at them
as they approached and passed beneath her. She ruffled her feathers and
watched them disappear. Below, a field mouse searching for food sensed
danger and scurried away.

But the owl had news to share. Hidden and silent, Sheen glided from her
perch and rising above the tree canopy, followed the banks of the river
towards the Port of Werthyn.

The aquamarine had been found!

# CHAPTER 14

As the sun began to set, Ikoseer climbed a steep wooded embankment to a granite boulder, and sat looking down at the activity below.

Boris and Ferdy were busy gathering sticks for two fires—one to roast the rabbits they had snared, and another smaller fire to bake the herb and mushroom bread. Artorus and Patrayus were tending the horses, particularly checking their hooves for bruising. After drinking from a nearby stream, the horses were brushed and left to graze on the lush valley grass.

Frovin was nowhere to be seen.

They had been travelling along the Valley of the Queen for almost a week, earlier receiving news of the clash with Onysius. Ferdy grumbled about the constant mist, but it had allowed Ikoseer to steer them safely away from Onysius' patrolling soldiers.

From her seat on the embankment, Ikoseer could see the landmark she was looking for. Directly across the valley and hidden behind two sheer cliffs was a dry creek bed that wended its way through the Lux Mountains and back into Magirus.

Satisfied, she lifted her eyes above the snowy summits and stared into the distance. She focused on one of the clouds that dotted the sky watching it slowly change shape. Her eyes blurred and she fell into a trance. She could hear the reassuring voice of the Queen of the Sun.

'You know what must be done.'

'I do,' responded Ikoseer.

'Help will come. Onysius will double his efforts to find the Lightenstone. The salvation of the Isle of Spheres is in the balance. My nemesis the Prince of Darkness, and Lord Mortimer, are already gathering a great army. May the light of the Stone guide and strengthen those who have been chosen to protect and carry it. The Pentark awaits.'

'And what of the outer gems?'

'Allay your concerns. The aquamarine of Pisces has already been found, and is on its way south-east to Werthyn Harbour. The others will reveal themselves when the time is right. Tell no one of this, except Artorus. You must now gather your strength Ikoseer … for what is to come.'

A twig snapped behind her, breaking her concentration, and the Queen was gone. His presence now announced, Frovin moved from behind a tree and sidled up beside Ikoseer.

'You have come to join me.' Ikoseer turned towards him.

'I didn't mean to disturb you,' mumbled Frovin, embarrassed.

'And if you didn't mean to disturb me, then what *did* you mean to do?'

Frovin shifted awkwardly, saying nothing.

'But now that you're here, I have something to show you.' Ikoseer pointed across the valley. 'Do you see the two tall cliffs to our right?'

'Yes.'

'Hidden behind the thick hawthorn at their base is a dry creek bed that threads through the Lux Mountains south to the Iscador River. The Trading Road through Magirus is on the other side of the river.'

'Is that where we're going tomorrow … back onto the Trading Road?'

'Yes.'

'And if we keep following the Trading Road, will that lead us to Illingaith?'

'Almost. But getting into Illingaith will involve crossing the Intrepid River.'

'And the route we take depends on where we have to go to find the Stone … Yes?'

'It does.'

'So, where do we go to from *there?*' Frovin kept probing.

Ikoseer hesitated. 'We continue on to the Abyss River. Asilodor is on the far side,' she replied softly.

'But that's where Onysius' castle is, isn't it?'

'Yes. Jimpiragh Castle.'

Frovin sucked in his breath. 'So. Is the Lightenstone hidden in Jimpiragh Castle?'

Ikoseer smiled. 'No …'

'Where then?' pressed Frovin.

Ikoseer looked back to the clouds.

'Its actual hiding place remains a secret.'

'But you've just told me where we need to go. Surely you can also tell me …'

'I have already imparted far too much,' interrupted the Sage. 'I am simply pointing you in the right direction.'

'But if we find the Lightenstone, won't we also need to find the outer gems?'

'No. Your destiny is to protect the Lightenstone … the outer gems are not your concern. The burden of protecting the Stone is more than enough for you to carry.'

A moment of uncomfortable silence sat between them. Then Frovin blurted out, 'Some say in the World of the Soul that the Firebird rose from the dead when Lord Mortimer invaded, and hid the Lightenstone.'

'Do they indeed?'

Frovin wavered. 'Makes sense. The Firebird placed all the stones in the Pentark when it was first built. It flew from the sun, bringing the

Lightenstone with it. Took the outer gemstones from the gnomes and then placed them in the Pentark. With its beak. Then the Firebird was burnt to cinders by the Pentark's power.'

'I know the history of the Pentark,' rebuffed the Sage.

Nothing more was forthcoming; Frovin looked across to the cliffs. 'So, is going along the old creek bed and into Magirus the most direct route to Asilodor?'

'It is.'

Ikoseer pulled a map from the leather satchel beside her. She unrolled it, stretched it across her knees and pointed to their current position. As she spoke, her finger began to follow their expected journey to Asilodor.

'Here's the dry creek bed and this is where it comes out from the Lux Mountains. Now, see the Iscador River. To join the Trading Road it is best to cross over these shallow rapids. From there the safest route is to stay on the Trading Road only until the end of the Enthra Pass. Then leave it and follow along the eastern side of the Trading Mountains down to the Intrepid River.'

Frovin looked closely at the map. 'The Intrepid River's huge. How can we possibly cross that, especially with the horses?'

Ikoseer pointed to a narrow bend in the river. 'There is a barge here that was used as a bridge between Illingaith and Magirus. If he is still there, the Hermit of the Living Waters will take you across.'

'But what will we do if the barge or the Hermit isn't there?'

Ikoseer ran her eyes quickly over the map. 'You'll have to swim the horses. The Trading Road does eventually cross the river but that way is much more dangerous.'

She pointed again at the map. 'Do you see? The closer you go to Mirraway Castle the more likely you'll come into contact with Onysius and his men and wrakes.'

'But once we leave the Lux Mountains tomorrow, we'll still be in danger from them anyway, won't we?'

'Yes, you will. However, I know they're already on the other side of the Lux Mountains, and are returning through Magirus towards Mirraway as we speak. I only hope they'll stay ahead of you all the way.'

Frovin suddenly frowned. Looking up at Ikoseer he whispered, 'Oh … You're not coming with us to Asilodor, are you?'

'It is your quest and that of your companions Frovin. I too have my own work to do, but I shall return.'

Frovin looked back at the map and noticed a large single mountain near the junction of the Lux and Gorthwain Mountains. With furrowed brow, he leant closer to read the name.

'White Timber Mountain'.

Frovin suddenly realised that Ikoseer was going home. He wondered if she would leave them before morning. He shivered at the thought of having to head towards Asilodor without her.

There would be no one to open hidden mountain doors with magic words or fully protect them from the savage wrakes. His eyes scanned the map following the expanse of the lands yet to travel.

'Does anyone else know that you are leaving us?'

'Artorus knows.'

'So, why are you also telling me?'

'It is simply a matter of security that one, other than Artorus, must know. Asilodor is heavily patrolled and much is against you. Knowing where you must go allows for you to prepare …'

'And where to once we're in Asilodor? I don't even know what the Lightenstone looks like … so how will I …'

'The Stone will know. When you are close Frovin, the Lightenstone will know …'

The weight of the task settled heavily upon the young badger.

They both fell into an uneasy silence until the aroma of roasted rabbit and baked bread drifted up to them. Ikoseer rolled up her map, slid it back into her leather satchel and stood up. Slinging the satchel over her shoulder she looked fondly at Frovin, knowing there was nothing more she could do to help.

'Dinner smells delicious and I'm hungry. Shall we join the others?' She turned and headed back down through the trees.

Frovin took one last look across the valley to the two tall cliffs and ran his eye down to the impenetrable hawthorn. They would need the pickaxe skills of Boris and Ferdy to help clear a pathway in the morning and he intended to make sure they had full bellies and a good night's sleep ahead of them.

But when the others realised that Ikoseer had abandoned them without so much as a goodbye, and left them to find their own way through this perilous World of the Soul, he hoped there might be a bit of anger to make them swing their axes a little harder.

Only daybreak would tell.

# CHAPTER 15

As he and Ferdy swung their pickaxes hard into the roots of the thick hawthorn at the base of the Lux Mountains, Boris was muttering under his breath.

'So, why would Ikoseer abandon us when we have no idea where we're going? And how can we be expected to find the silly stones without her …'

'But we did agree to help,' offered Ferdy.

'Well, I didn't *mean* to agree. It's magical trickery, that's what it is. I wonder if Father knew that Thrust was forged to serve the Pentark and how much trouble we're in now because of it. And there was no mention of Ikoseer leaving us …'

'But we still have Thrust. And remember that the Queen said it has yet more secrets to reveal to us.'

'And what good is that without a sage to wave her arms about with magic words to open mountain doors, eh? And how can we defend ourselves from the wrakes with a single blade?'

'We're not on our own. Artorus and Patrayus are still here. And perhaps Ikoseer's just gone for a day or two …'

'A day or two? Forever, more like! We don't know where we have to go and how we're going to get there. Likely we'll both end up being roasted by the wrakes after all.'

Ferdy glanced back to the camp site and saw the knights leading the packed horses towards them. Marta and Frovin followed behind.

'Artorus must know where we have to go. He's the one who sent us down here to start clearing the hawthorn.'

'Humph! He's a Knight of Power. He doesn't have to … to … risk his life to find hidden gemstones in rivers and goodness knows where else. Now we're leaving the valley, I suppose Patrayus will return to the Ascension

Mountains. Then if something happens to Artorus, we'll be on our own!' This last thought was hoarsely whispered as the others were fast approaching. The twins fell quiet.

'You are doing well my young dwarves.' Artorus was admiring their quick handiwork.

'We'd do better if we had some help to cut away this brush,' replied Boris, yanking thorns out of his hat.

Artorus smiled. 'Luckily I do have a falchion or two. Just before we left the Ascension Mountains Ikoseer suggested we pack them.

'Humph!' Boris swung his pickaxe harder, breaking another root.

Soon the others joined in with the broad bladed knives, but it was still hard work. It took them some time to clear a path wide enough for them to ride through.

As he waited for Patrayus to hoist him into Aster's saddle, Boris wiped the sweat from his brow. 'I suppose you'll be leaving us now?'

Marta turned towards the handsome young knight and their eyes met briefly.

'No … there has been a change of plans. I'll be coming with you for a while longer.'

'See?' piped Ferdy. 'Nothing to worry about …'

Boris swung around and glared at Ferdy as he scrambled up onto Poppins with Marta's help. But Ferdy seemed not to notice.

Artorus led them through the gap in the hawthorn with Patrayus taking up the rear. For many hours they travelled between the mountain cliffs. Spongy green moss covered most of the cobblestones, making it eerily quiet. And in places the path was so narrow that the packs bumped against the walls as the horses swayed.

At one point the sudden cry of a peregrine falcon made Marta look up, but all she could see was overhanging rocks and deep shadowy corners. The stone walls were cold and uninviting. She pulled her shawl closer and reached for her amulet.

Soon they turned the final corner and the mountains parted, revealing the bright morning sky. Artorus halted the group, dismounted and headed towards the exit into Magirus. He climbed up to a better vantage point on a rocky ledge and lay flat, scanning the plateau that stretched eastwards towards the Trading Road.

Frovin scrambled up to join him. 'Can you see Onysius or his soldiers?'

Artorus looked to the horizon, following the road. 'No, but we're too far away to see clearly.'

'How long will it take us to get to the Iscador River?'

'Maybe two hours.'

Frovin cast his mind back to the map Ikoseer had shown him. 'And once we reach the river, we still have rapids to cross before we can travel along the Trading Road and onto Enthra Pass.'

Artorus nodded. 'Yes, it'll take us until nightfall to reach the Pass.'

'It makes for a long day.'

'We have no choice, Frovin. We have to try and get through Enthra Pass before Onysius deploys more soldiers and wrakes. We must use our time wisely.'

Frovin looked along the escarpment. 'Do you think there are any rogue wrakes still roaming the Lux Mountains?'

'It's possible, along with the wolves of Skag. But the mountains are vast. I hope that neither the wrakes nor the wolves are close by.

'We'll just have to risk travelling in the open by daylight.'

Frovin turned to the knight. 'I'm pleased that you and Patrayus are with us. I haven't a sword to wield against the enemy …'

'Your teeth and claws are more than enough to tear the flesh of any wrake or boorling Frovin. The courage of badgers is legendary across the World of the Soul. Even after Patrayus and I leave you I am sure that you will hold your own in any fight with them.'

'Then I hope that you'll be with us for a while yet.'

Artorus smiled, ruffled Frovin's head and jumped down from the ledge.

'Come, it's already late morning. We'll have a bite to eat before we get going again.'

Frovin looked towards the distant Arifer Mountains, and wondered what was in store for them in the days to come.

They reached the river by mid-afternoon. The sun was still warm but a cool river breeze had picked up, ruffling the horses' manes. Dark clouds, heavy with rain, loomed south of the mountains ahead.

Artorus checked along the riverbank before leading them down into the strong current. He guided Famrod for a short while and then loosened the reins, so that the warhorse could pick his own way through the rocks. Patrayus took up his position between the three ponies and the edge of the rapids that dropped to a deep pool below.

The ponies snorted as they were led down into the river, and they struggled on the slippery rocks against the current as the water slapped against their bellies. Boris and Ferdy were unable to swim and they hung on tight as Aster and Poppins stumbled and swayed beneath them. Snowball stumbled too, and almost threw Marta and Frovin off, but Patrayus reached down and held the pony's rein until it recovered.

They needed to rest after the harrowing crossing and Artorus led them up the far riverbank onto a flat grassy area beneath a clump of trees. They all dismounted and the two knights peered through the trees towards the

Trading Road. But the only movement they could see was a horse-drawn wagon followed by a few travellers on foot.

'Nomads?' asked Patrayus.

'Yes, I think so. Magirus is their spiritual home.'

'I'm surprised they're using the Trading Road. It's very exposed. Wouldn't they be concerned about being captured by enemy soldiers?'

'I suspect Onysius tolerates them, and with good reason. The spy he sent into the World of Man was a nomad. He has a use for them—for now. Whoever they are, if they continue on the road towards Enthra Pass we'll reach them within the hour. And they may have news of Onysius or his men.'

Boris left the group, strode back to the riverbank and plonked himself down on a flat granite rock. He looked across the river to the snow capped peaks of the Lux Mountains, feeling very alone. The noise of rushing water masked the approach of Marta as she walked up behind him and put her hand on his shoulder. He startled at her touch.

'Are you all right?'

'Of course I'm all right.'

'Aren't the mountains beautiful?'

'I suppose so.'

'It's difficult, isn't it?'

'What's difficult?' Boris wished Marta would stop asking questions and go away.

'This quest.' Marta sighed. 'I miss my father so much. Sometimes I just want to go home.'

'Humph … me too.'

'But you're part of my new family now.'

'Am I?'

'Yes. You and Ferdy and Frovin. And the knights. And Ikoseer.' She paused. 'I think our quest must be very important.'

Boris crossed his arms and stared at the river.

'You and Ferdy come from Magirus don't you, near the border with the World of Man?' she continued.

'Yes, we live in Banters Den. But it's a long way from here.'

'Perhaps we'll be going that way and you can see your family again soon.'

'I doubt it. Knowing Ikoseer, we'll be heading in the opposite direction!'

Marta laughed and bent down and gave Boris a quick hug, making him squirm. Then hearing Artorus' footsteps, she turned away.

'Time to go,' he said. 'We need to try and make it to Enthra Pass if we can. The road is clear except for some travellers. We've only a few hours of daylight left.'

But as they set off, Boris had a sudden thought and tugged Artorus' cloak. 'Wait! Is one of the gemstones we're looking for in the Iscador River?'

Artorus halted and held the dwarf's questioning gaze. Boris could see a knowing in his eyes, but then Artorus turned away and continued striding towards the horses, uttering a single command: 'Come.'

Boris hurried along behind but looking down, put his hand on Thrust and felt the now familiar tingling. He frowned. He felt sure that one of the gems must be in the river. As they left the cover of the trees Boris kept his eyes focused on Artorus.

'It's a silly quest,' he muttered to himself. 'What's the point of not looking for the gemstones straight away?'

'What?' Ferdy trotted up beside him on Poppins.

'Oh, nothing.'

Artorus led them south onto the Trading Road and they soon caught up with the travellers that the knights had seen from the trees. The horse and cart halted when they approached, and the small group of nomads walking along behind it gathered together, eyeing them suspiciously.

'We mean you no harm,' said Artorus, dismounting.

'That means nothin' in these parts,' said an old woman as she stepped forward, hands on her ample hips. She scowled at him, and Marta noticed untidy wisps of greying hair poking out from under her colourful headscarf. She wore a long full skirt and big round gold earrings. A smaller gold ring pierced her nose.

'She's right an' all,' added an older man beside her. 'Can't trust no one … 'specially not travellin' this road.'

Just then a grubby boy squeezed between them, staring at the dwarves and badger.

'I agree,' added Artorus. 'But I was wondering if you'd seen others on this road in the last day or so.'

'What others?' another queried.

'Riders. Military men,' replied Patrayus.

The nomads fell silent.

'We are seeking to avoid them,' added Artorus.

'Saw 'em yesterday,' blurted the boy.

In an instant the old woman grabbed his ear, and twisting it, pulled him towards her. His face contorted and a loud cry escaped his lips.

'OW!'

'Hold yer tongue,' she scolded. 'Or you'll be gettin' us all killed.'

'How many?' pressed Patrayus.

'Lots!' blurted the boy again, ducking to avoid the swift hand that came for him.

'Were they heading towards Enthra Pass?' asked Artorus.

'Coulda' been goin' anywhere.' The old woman was staring at the knight. 'An' can't be sure they was soldiers neither.'

Suddenly the group parted as the cart driver came forward. He was a tall, athletic man dressed in peasant garments underneath a long brown cloak. His hand rested on the hilt of a sheathed sword. His tanned face was hidden deep within his hood, and his dark hazel eyes rested on Artorus and his big black steed, Famrod.

'They mean us no harm,' he said to the others in a strong, sure voice. 'We can speak freely with them.'

Artorus immediately recognised the voice, but Patrayus took longer. Marta watched the young knight as he frowned and stared at the man. Then recognition dawned on his face. Sniffing the air, Frovin stretched and rested his paws on Marta's shoulders. Somehow the three men knew each other and there was relief in Patrayus' expression.

Meanwhile the old woman was listening carefully to their conversation.

'Onysius was leading a small band of soldiers,' said the driver with a slight nod of his head towards the road. 'I have no doubt they are returning to Illingaith or Asilodor via Enthra Pass. They rode past us in great haste— with little interest.'

Artorus nodded. 'We've just come from the Valley of the Queen. Onysius and his soldiers and wrakes were in the valley and there was a clash between them and the Knights of Power. It seems the knights were alerted to the Earl during his lethal fight with a master wrake. The knights killed the other three wrakes there with them, but Onysius escaped on the master's boorling.'

'Ah! That explains why he was riding a boorling yesterday. You going far?'

'No, we're only following the road to the end of Enthra Pass.'

'Then I bid you safe travels. But beware. Apart from boorlings, anomirs have been seen through here of late.'

'We're grateful for your warning,' replied Artorus.

Marta, Boris and Frovin were becoming alarmed. 'Ano- …
what?' spluttered Ferdy.

Frovin's heart was beating rapidly but he patted Marta on the shoulder. 'It'll be all right, Marta.'

The old woman looked at the cart driver with a knowing. He had been with them less than a week, entering their camp early one morning. She knew from the start that there was something unusual about him. He had voiced gratitude when they made room for him around their fire.

After offering him a cup of hot broth, she had left to consult her cards. Shuffling the tattered deck, she had asked them who the stranger was, selected a random card, and turned it over: *The Prince of Fire, holding a crown in his hands.* Surprised, she had selected the next card: *The King of Fire, crowned, upon a throne and with subservient peasants looking up at him.*

'Well, well, well … We got a king amongst us.'

With some apprehension, she had then turned the next card—this showed her the future. In the middle of the card was a dancer dressed in a flowing rainbow coloured veil. The dancer was ringed by twelve small circles, which she knew represented the outer gems of the Pentark. There was an image in each corner: an angel, a raptor, a bull and a lion.

She had muttered to herself, all the while running a gnarled finger around the dancing figure. 'Change is a-comin'.' Returning to the group round the fire, she had invited the stranger to stay.

Artorus brought her back to the present: 'Are you also travelling through the pass?'

'Yes, but then we'll follow the Eastward Road before heading south-east towards Elodom Monastery. For the moment our plans are to remain in Magirus. There is much to do here, but times are uncertain …'

As the old woman looked at Artorus and Famrod, she recognised how powerful the stallion was, and she knew from the way Artorus spoke and held himself, that the man standing before them was a Knight of Power. These people were not their enemy, but their friends.

'We could travel together to the end of Enthra Pass if it pleases you,' said the driver.

Artorus considered the invitation. 'We are grateful for your offer but it's safer if we travel separately. As you're currently in favour with Onysius and his soldiers, it would be wise to use this to your advantage. We have no wish to endanger your lives.'

Boris was alarmed and Ferdy leant towards him whispering, 'What did he say? Are our lives in danger again?'

'Sshhh!' replied Boris louder than he intended, prompting the knights to turn and look at them. Both dwarves looked down, embarrassed at the attention.

'Then we shan't hold you up any further,' replied the driver. 'But perhaps we shall meet again.'

'We'd welcome that should it come to pass,' said Artorus. He and Patrayus gave a slight bow of their heads.

Artorus remounted and they set off, soon leaving the nomads way behind. Marta allowed Snowball to fall a little behind the others, and when she was sure they were out of earshot, she turned towards Frovin perched on the pack behind her.

'Who was that man … the cart driver?'

'Do you remember the night we sat around the campfire, and Ikoseer told us the rest of the story about how, when Mortimer invaded Illingaith, the royal family fled from Mirraway Castle? First to the Lux Mountains, and then to the Ascension Mountains. Where they still live in exile?'

'Yes. But we didn't get to meet them when we went to the Ascension Mountains.'

'No, we didn't,' replied Frovin. 'And I don't know this for certain but I think the cart driver might be Prince Mir, the future King of the World of the Soul.'

# CHAPTER 16

On the morning after Ikoseer left Marta and the others in the Valley of the Queen to return to White Timber Mountain, Volgor the kurr woke with a start and rubbed his bleary eyes. He slowly lifted his head and listened, but all he could hear was the running river, and although everything seemed normal, something was not quite right.

He and Attricus were further south-east near the Abyss River. They didn't light a fire, partly from exhaustion, but also because while Volgor was fishing for their supper, Attricus had recognised a footprint along the muddy bank of the river.

'The print's not fresh, but where there's one wrake there are sure to be more,' the soothsayer said as he helped prepare their meal.

They slept tucked up against each other, bunked down close to the river under a stout forest fern with large overhanging fronds. And it was through these that Volgor now squinted. He eased himself onto his haunches and reached for his knife, just as a twig snapped nearby and footfalls could be heard moving closer. He peered frantically through the fronds. Attricus's gentle snoring was obviously guiding the invisible creature, so Volgor shook the soothsayer, hoping to wake him up. The snoring stopped, but Attricus slumbered on.

The footfalls halted. Volgor prepared to spring out. He leant forward, easing himself down onto his scrawny knees, and closer to the fronds. His heart was pounding in his ears and his nose twitched but the only thing he could smell was damp rotting leaves and the earth beneath them.

His mind flooded with the vision of the ferryman they had tricked a few days before. Volgor began to panic. Perhaps he had followed them along the river. He felt for the bulge of the gemstone in his coat, and shook Attricus again, harder this time. He stirred. Volgor adjusted the grip on his knife.

Then came a familiar harsh growl. Volgor froze. It was a wrake!

The footfalls came closer. He could hear the intense sniffing of the beast until it came so close to the fronds that Volgor could see the coarse black hairs sprouting between the scales on its mottled legs. He felt nauseous. Not knowing what else to do, he stabbed the wrake's leg with all his strength, just as it reached down and wrenched him up through the fronds.

The beast howled with rage as the momentum of the lift drew the knife back out of its flesh, splaying it open. Blood spurted out as it flung Volgor against a tree trunk. All the kurr could do now was rasp and cough. Unable to stand, he remained hunched on the ground, clutching his ribs and gasping, watching through watery eyes as the wrake came for him again. He felt around in vain for his knife. Knowing he would not survive against such brute strength without it, he closed his eyes tight.

He felt himself being lifted high above the wrake's head. Strong fingers squeezed his body. Deciding to feign death, Volgor let his body go limp. But suddenly the wrake grunted in surprise, and then bellowed in pain as the blade of Duke Tardor's sword was driven to the hilt near the beast's shoulder blade. Volgor was thumped on the ground as the wrake roared and spun around to confront Attricus, who was trying in vain to retrieve the blade.

Defenceless, Attricus had nowhere to go. All he could do was watch as the wrake reached over its shoulder, attempting to pull the blade out. The thrust must have severed muscle for now its arm hung loose. The wrake took a step towards the soothsayer, grimacing as it attempted to raise a clenched fist.

Attricus knew that he could not outrun the beast. If it caught him, it would break his neck. He picked up a rock and struck the beast in its face.

Undaunted, the fuming wrake pulled an axe from his belt with its uninjured arm. With a menacing snarl, it advanced on Attricus, spinning the axe around his wrist. Terrified, Attricus backed towards a tree. He swerved as the wrake charged.

The first blow struck the trunk, but in one powerful yank the axe was wrenched free. By now, Volgor had recovered sufficiently to leap onto the beast's back. Gripping a leather strap over the wrake's shoulder, the kurr kicked against the blade protruding from its back. A terrible scream escaped from the wrake.

Letting go of one hand, Volgor grabbed the handle. With a see-saw motion, he managed to pull the blade free. The wrake dropped the axe. Its scaly, mottled hand reached for him. In a mad frenzy, Volgor swung out of the way and slashed with the Duke's blade at the beast's neck.

The skin was much thicker here and at first, the wounds only maddened the beast more. Finally Volgor managed to stab a vein sending purple blood gushing down the wrake's scaly back. The beast spun and slammed against the tree trunk. Volgor's feet slipped and he had to let go. He scrambled up the closest tree and watched as the wrake passed below him, swinging his axe menacingly. Then he looked to the north. He saw the gentle sway of the dense understorey ahead, and realised that it must be Attricus.

The wrake suddenly stopped and turned in that direction, lifting its head and sniffing. Volgor was looking for something to throw when a forest raven flew down from the branch above and drove its black beak deep into the open wound on the wrake's back.

With a now even more enraged wrake below, Volgor knew that all he could do was run! *Too risky to follow Attricus*, he thought. *He'll meet me in Riverbend anyway. Won't he?*

He knew that wrakes could not swim so he clambered down the tree, made for the river, and plunged in. As the current swept him away, he scanned the riverbank, hoping against hope that Attricus had also managed to escape. The thought of leaving him was horrifying, and his heart sank. Now he was alone.

As he floated downstream on his back, the water massaged and soothed him, washing him of the stench of the wrake's blood. He felt for the gemstone—it was still there. And so was Duke Tardor's short sword.

With the blade cradled on his chest he gripped the gilt handle, as sunlight glinted off the jewel. He needed a weapon, but not this one. It was incredibly valuable but far too big. How was he going to conceal it for the rest of his journey?

He knew that they were close to Riverbend, the village that Attricus had told him about. And soon enough the river widened and the waters eased. Swimming towards the bank, he was caught in an eddy that swept him around a cluster of boulders. He scrambled into the middle and flopped into a heap.

The sun was overhead when a dragonfly landed on Volgor's nose. He swatted the insect away, stretched and yawned. His tummy rumbled. He had slept for hours. He was fully awakened by the rhythmic sound of oars upstream. He looked over the boulders and saw a small wooden boat.

An old man was rowing with long slow strokes. As Volgor watched the boat approach, he remembered what Attricus had told him. Although the small unfurled sail was limp, he thought this must be the boat that Attricus had described to him. Fish traps were stacked in the flat bottomed hull. From a steel ring on the bow a painter rope dragged in the river. Volgor crept over the boulders and slipped into the water. He grabbed the rope.

The village was not far and before the fisherman moored his craft, Volgor let go of the rope and hid under the jetty. He breathed deeply, salivating at the smell of fresh fish flapping in the woven baskets above his head. Peering between the boards, he watched the old man haggle with a fishmonger and then with a chinking pocket, hobble away.

Volgor pressed the aquamarine concealed in his coat. I should wait for Attricus, he thought, but he is a soothsayer so he should be able to find me, no matter where I am. Making up his mind to keep going, he released the boat. With his back pressed against the hull, he pushed hard against a pile. The boat bobbed at first, knocking against the craft on either side. Using them for leverage, he gave another shove. The boat began to drift, moving slowly towards the current. Just as it reached the flow he clenched the jewelled sword between his teeth, grabbed the gunwale and pulled himself up into the boat, landing on tangled ropes.

Panting, he looked around. The oars were still in their rowlocks, resting against the inside of the hull. He struggled to lift the blade of one oar, but then groaned and let it drop. Collapsing onto the ropes, he put his head in his hands and wept with exhaustion.

The slap of the water against the boat at last soothed him and it was a few minutes before he heard a dull knocking against the hull. He cocked his head, and then dismissed the noise as a floating tree branch. They were common along the river. When he heard it again he realised it was coming from inside the boat. On edge, he gripped the Duke's sword. He stared at the tangled ropes and with his heart thumping, grabbed the closest one and flung it towards the stern.

He collapsed to his knees, his eyes streaming with tears of relief. Then he grabbed the wriggling fish and hugged it lovingly to his chest before biting its head off, savouring the eyes. They were delicious.

As he crunched on the tail, he thought he heard voices shouting in the distance. He assumed it was villagers sent to retrieve the runaway boat, but all he cared about now was his full belly and a safe ride down to Port Werthyn—well deserved considering his valiant fight with that wrake.

There was little in the way of comfort except for a hessian sack he found shoved under the prow. Folding it in half, he sat down again and felt for the gemstone. Holding the short sword close, he leaned back, and watched dappled sunlight filter through the trees. When the boat rocked he could just see over the gunwale.

A family of red deer was drinking at the riverbank. The stag lifted his proud head and stared at the passing boat, his huge antlers spreading like a bony chalice to the sky. Skittish, his doe snatched a final draught before they all disappeared.

Volgor fought to keep his eyelids open but they grew heavy and his head dropped. His body rocked from side to side until it finally slid onto the piled ropes and the kurr slipped into the river of dreams.

# CHAPTER 17

The day after their encounter with the nomads, Marta and the others continued south through Enthra Pass until they reached the junction with the Eastward Road; the road that led to Banters Den, Boris and Ferdy's home. It was early evening by the time they arrived and heeding the warning about boorlings and anomirs, Artorus guided them off the road and into the bordering woods, to a small mossy clearing where they made camp for the night.

As he set a few rabbit traps, Boris kept thinking about Banters Den at the end of the road. When he returned to the camp, Ferdy was sitting alone by the fire. Boris plonked down next to him, his head in his hands.

'Have you thought about leaving here and going home?' he whispered.

'You've been thinking about that too? I do miss home, but remember what the Queen said about Thrim forging Thrust to serve the Pentark. We'd have to leave it with Artorus.'

'Never!' Boris was aghast. 'It's a dwarf blade! Father gave it to us for safekeeping.'

'But leaving here won't be as easy as it sounds,' continued Ferdy. 'While you were away I saw the knights poring over the map. I had a look. From here, Banters Den is miles and miles away. It'd take us weeks to get there without the ponies. What would we do if we were attacked by wrakes or soldiers? We'd have nothing to protect us besides Thrust. And we don't have the oak border of Greenwood Forest to hide in.'

'We can hide just as easily in these woods. Did you notice how far they went?'

'According to the map they border both sides of the Eastward Road and end about half way along.'

'There you go. We'd have protection for quite a way.'

'I don't know. It's dangerous either way. But somehow I feel safer with the knights. Besides, I would miss Marta and Frovin. A part of me wants to stay and a part of me wants to go.'

Boris sighed and stared into the flames. 'I don't know either, but we'll have to decide by morning.'

'If you decide you want to go home, you'll have to be the one to tell Artorus! I'm certainly not going to. And now I'm off to bed.'

He and Ferdy slept late the following morning. It was the knight's preparation of the horses that eventually woke Boris. Feeling cold, stiff and sore he pulled his blanket closer, opened an eye and looked around at the campsite.

The few remaining coals of the evening's fire glowed red through the soft grey ash. Wisps of smoke spiralled lazily upwards into the crisp air. Prompted by hunger, he carefully rolled away from Ferdy and went to check the rabbit traps. Finding an empty sack, he slung it over his shoulder and left the camp. As he walked through the trees he met Marta returning with an armful of wood. Frovin was following behind her, busily sniffing the surroundings.

'Can you smell any wrakes?'

Frovin shook his head.

'What about boorlings?'

'The trees are too close for wrakes to ride in here. They only ride boorlings over open ground.'

'And what about those other things that the nomads warned us about. What were they called? Was it anomirs?'

'I think they fly, so I doubt they'd be here either.'

Boris shivered but narrowed his eyes. *Frovin knows more about anomirs than he's letting on*, he thought.

'Then the sooner we leave this place the better!' continued Boris. 'Perhaps we should stay under the cover of the trees when we travel. Do you know if we're going to follow the Eastward Road?'

'I'm sure Artorus knows where we need to go,' Marta said.

'Humph,' replied Boris. 'Let's hope he does and that we don't get attacked by those nasty creatures. I've had enough adventure to last me for quite a while.'

'Banters Den's at the end of the Eastward Road.' Frovin was watching Boris closely.

'Yes, but that's still a long way from here.' Boris shoved his hands in his pockets, beginning to feel uncomfortable.

'That day we met in Greenwood Forest, where did you say you were going to, the Rolling …?'

'The Rolling Hills.'

'So we've come almost full circle.'

Boris' bottom lip began to tremble. He knew his parents would be thinking that he and Ferdy were safely tucked away with his cousins in the north. But in reality they were in more danger than ever. There was an awkward silence.

'I'm sure you'll make the right decision,' said Frovin.

'I didn't say we're going anywhere. I'm just not sure about things that's all.' Boris wiped his nose on his sleeve. 'Anyway I've got to go and check my rabbit traps.'

'Are they far?' asked Marta.

'No they're not. So I won't be long.'

'Well just be careful,' added Frovin as he and Marta turned towards the camp. 'Apart from wrakes, we don't know what else might be lurking in these woods.'

'Like what?' asked Boris. But they were already moving away and Frovin didn't answer.

Boris found his first snare. It had been sprung with a stick. Annoyed, he removed it and put it in his sack before checking the others, but he soon discovered that all five of his traps were empty. It wasn't unusual to find one of his traps sprung … but all of them? Something was amiss and as he walked back to the camp empty handed, he scanned the surrounding trees warily. But there was only the gentle swaying of boughs and the rustling of leaves.

He got back to find Ferdy awake and standing at the restored fire, blowing onto his cold hands and rubbing them together furiously before holding them out to the flames. Ferdy groaned at the sight of the empty sack that Boris threw on the ground. He wondered what he was going to eat for breakfast.

'No rabbits?' asked Patrayus.

'Not a one. All my traps were sprung deliberately!'

'And what makes you think that?' Artorus had just joined them.

'Because there was a stick poking out of every trap!'

'Well, we are just inside the Norfolk Woods.'

Boris and Ferdy turned and stared at him, horrified.

'These are the *Norfolk* Woods—the *elven* woods?' Ferdy cried.

'Why didn't you say so?' asked Boris. 'Our parents have warned us about these woods! Don't you know that elves and dwarves don't like each other?'

Artorus smiled. 'Well, I suppose we could have camped beside the road in full view of the wrakes. But I thought you'd rather be surprised by an elf than a wrake.'

Boris knitted his brows into a deep frown and caught Ferdy's eye. They both now realised that if they left, they would not be able to use the woods for protection. They would be exposed to danger all the way to Banters Den.

'Why do elves and dwarves dislike each other?' asked Marta.

'They just do!' said Boris.

'Perhaps they could help us.'

'I doubt it! An elf helping a dwarf? That'd be a historical event!'

'Well, perhaps history is the problem,' said Frovin.

Boris turned and glared at him.

'It's not right that we should take their rabbits, Boris,' offered Ferdy. 'We wouldn't like it if they took ours.'

'I didn't know I was setting my traps in elven woods, did I?' Boris gave Artorus a dark stare.

After an awkward silence, Artorus spoke. 'You shouldn't doubt that the elves will help. Doubts inhibit us and can lead to pride. And pride prevents guidance. Have confidence Boris. It may be your only companion in the coming days.'

'And we should be grateful for a safe night,' added Patrayus. 'We have flour and a few herbs left. Marta and I will make the bread. Did you see any mushrooms when you went to check your traps?'

'No, but I wasn't looking for mushrooms!'

'Then we'll eat what we have and look out for berries and mushrooms on the way.'

'And the elves probably won't like that either,' mumbled Boris as he turned away to roll his scant bedding. Reluctantly he handed it to Artorus to tie behind Aster's saddle.

After their meagre breakfast, Artorus led them back to the edge of the woods. Through the trees, he scanned the Trading Road as it continued west through a gap in the mountains towards the bridge in Illingaith. The roadway was clear.

'Where are we going?' asked Ferdy, frowning.

'To the Intrepid River,' replied Artorus.

Ferdy was shocked. 'What? The border between Magirus and Illingaith?'

'Yes.'

'But how long will that take?'

'I expect to reach the river within a few days … provided there
is no opposition.'

Ferdy wished that Ikoseer was still with them. Marta tensed at the thought of being attacked. They had been lucky so far. A vision of her mother suddenly arose in her mind and she reached for her amulet.

'Are we going to keep following the Trading Road?' probed Ferdy.

'No, it's too dangerous,' said Artorus. 'We'll follow the tree line of
the Norfolk Woods, and reach the Intrepid River from this side of
the Trading Mountains.'

'Wouldn't it be safer to travel away from the mountains and follow the Eastward Road instead?' asked Boris. 'The way the nomads are going?'

'Perhaps it would be safer. But it'd add several days to our journey.
And we'd still have to skirt the eastern border of the woods south to
reach the river.'

Artorus smiled at the feisty young dwarf. He knew that, despite the fact that Banters Den was still a few weeks' journey away, Boris would be having doubts about continuing on the quest. 'This way will save us several days riding, Boris. Time is running out.'

Boris and Ferdy looked at each other, abandoning their forlorn hope to at least catch a glimpse of their parents before going on.

Meanwhile Marta was wondering, *What's that supposed to mean … time is running out?*

'Artorus, how close to the river do the Norfolk Woods go?' she said aloud.

'They finish to within a half day's ride. We can follow the woods most of the way, but our movements can still be detected by anomirs, so we mustn't think …'

'But I still don't know what anomirs are!' interrupted Boris.

'Yes, I don't know either,' added Ferdy.

Patrayus turned to the dwarves.

'They are scaly vulture-like scavengers with razor sharp claws. They were created by the Prince of Darkness, bred by Lord Mortimer and are large enough to carry goblins into battle. With goblin riders aboard dwarves are perfect pickings. And like all raptors, anomirs can detect movement from a great distance.'

The dwarves shivered. Ferdy squeaked, frantically looking skyward through the trees. 'Then we haven't a hope of getting to the Intrepid River, what with soldiers, wrakes, boorlings, and *now* anomirs.'

'Sometimes, hope is all you have,' replied Artorus. He pushed Famrod out onto open ground and headed the warhorse south to follow the woodland border.

Patrayus took his place at the rear of the party, and with a knight either end, they travelled uneventfully until late afternoon the following day, when the incessant chatter and squawk of woodland birds began. A tingling sensation spread up Marta's spine and down her arms, prompting her to scan the summit of the mountain range.

Frovin leant forward. 'What is it?'

'I don't know … but something just gave me the shivers.'

Frovin followed her gaze. 'It's probably nothing. We're all a bit tense.'

Famrod halted and swung his proud head, firstly towards the mountains, and then back along the tree line in front of them. With ears pricked and nostrils flared he snorted and struck the ground hard with a front hoof. As the other horses stopped, the Knights of Power drew their swords.

'Into the trees. Now!' yelled Artorus.

But it was too late. Two anomirs with their goblin riders appeared from above and behind them, and with a single blood chilling scream, attacked with full fury. With talons outstretched, the anomirs dived into the chaos of terrified ponies and their riders. With readied swords, Artorus and Patrayus spun their brave warhorses to face the anomirs. Artorus swung and sliced deep into the scaly flesh of the first one, sending the mounted goblin to the ground.

Frovin jumped down from Snowball and sank his teeth deep into the goblin's throat, tearing it apart as it tried to get up. The creature shrieked and tried to haul the badger off, but the savagery of Frovin's attack sapped the strength from the goblin. Death was quick.

Standing in the stirrups, Patrayus charged the other anomir, but it wheeled just out of his sword's reach, and rose up ready for another attack.

As Frovin went to help Marta, he saw the terrified faces of Boris and Ferdy as they clung to their ponies, now bolting into the woods. As he began towards them, a cloaked man burst from the trees. Wielding his sword, he put himself between Marta, Snowball and the remaining attacker.

'Don't be afraid! Hold your pony as best you can!' he urged. 'Honorex will stay the attack. The enemy will think better of it next time.'

As the second anomir turned and sped towards them, the man stepped forward and readied himself. Unafraid, the anomir focused on this new opponent, and extended its talons to strike him. But something about the thrust of the sword made it hesitate. At the last moment it veered away towards the mountains.

As its goblin rider failed to force it around to attack again, the war lust on the goblin's face turned to disbelief. How could he be forced to leave the battle in this way? What was it about this man and his sword that gave them such power?

'Thank goodness! We beat them! But the dwarves' ponies have fled into the woods!' Marta was frantic as Frovin rejoined her. 'I tried to stop them! Snowball was too much of a handful.'

'I know. I saw the ponies bolting too, but don't worry. The trees are thick. I'm sure they've not gone far.' Frovin tried to calm her.

As Artorus and Patrayus joined them, the stranger pulled back his hood to reveal a strong tanned face framed by soft ringlets of long black hair. His dark hazel eyes rested on Frovin and Marta and they recognised him as the cart driver they had met several days earlier on the Trading Road.

'Greetings again, my brave knights,' said the nomad.

Artorus and Patrayus lightly bowed their heads.

'It seems that two of your companions and their mounts are missing.'

'Yes,' said Artorus sheathing his sword. 'But we can look for them now the anomirs have fled.'

'The anomirs might come back,' said Marta.

Artorus scanned the mountains. 'Not today. But I expect there'll be more attacks from now on. I'm sure Onysius will hear of this scuffle soon enough and send more of his henchmen.'

Marta shivered at the thought and looked at the nomad. 'I haven't thanked you for saving my life … and Snowball's life too.'

'You're welcome. And what is your name?'

'Of course … I'm so sorry.' Patrayus was embarrassed. 'Marta and Frovin this is …'

'Yoska.' The nomad extended his hand to Marta.

Marta returned his greeting. 'Why did you follow us?'

'Marta, don't speak like that to … ' began Patrayus.

But Yoska held up his hand and smiled. 'Remember the old woman who berated the knights for asking too many questions? She is a card reader. She told me you were all in grave danger. I wanted to assure myself that you were safe, so once we reached the Eastward Road, I left the others to continue on to Elodom Monastery without me.'

'Then, we are indebted to you,' said Patrayus.

'Not at all. If the Isle of Spheres is to survive, we must all do what we can to defeat the enemy.'

'May I ask of your plans?' asked Artorus.

'I have no plans.'

'Then you're most welcome to travel with us from here. If you so wish,' said Artorus. 'We would be grateful for an extra sword to stay the enemy.'

Yoska hesitated. 'Then I accept your invitation.'

'Can I offer you Famrod to ride?'

'Thank you. He is a stunning animal. But I'd prefer to walk.'

'As you wish.'

'We need to look for Boris and Ferdy. I'm worried it will be dark soon.' Marta was anxious.

Yoska smiled and gently placed his arm around her shoulders. 'Then, let's see if we can find them. Perhaps they're not too far away.'

But Marta was not comforted by his words. And her fear that something had befallen them was confirmed during the following hours of fruitless searching. Along with their ponies, Boris and Ferdy were nowhere to be found. Marta felt it most heavily in her heart. She had become very fond of both of them and she wept tears of utter hopelessness and grief at the thought of perhaps having to leave them behind. Frovin did his best to ease her pain, but they both had a sleepless night.

The following morning Patrayus handed Marta some hot gruel that Yoska had made. 'Come Marta, you must eat.'

Marta was worried. 'Ferdy and Boris must be starving by now.'

'They know how to look after themselves. They were doing that when I first met them in Greenwood Forest,' reminded Frovin.

'But they're in the elven woods now—here they're not welcome.'

'I'm sure they'll survive. They might not even meet the elves. And if they make it onto the Eastward Road they could head home to Banters Den.'

'But they're part of us now, and even the Queen of the Sun said …'

'Sometimes plans change,' Patrayus reminded her.

But Marta did not want to think about never seeing them again. Fresh tears welled in her eyes.

Frovin watched Yoska groom Famrod. 'How do you know the nomad, Patrayus?'

'Artorus and I know him from the Valley of the Queen.'

'The horses like him. He's very regal for a nomad.' Frovin turned his focus to Patrayus. 'In fact, he's not much like a nomad at all.'

'No. Perhaps not,' replied the knight, stirring his gruel. 'But I don't know him that well.'

'And there was something about his sword that turned the anomir away when it attacked. It was most strange.' Frovin was probing.

But Patrayus would not be drawn into the badger's conversation, and said nothing as Artorus and Yoska joined them for breakfast. After their meal Marta and Frovin doused the campfire, while the others packed. Within the hour they were ready to leave.

Marta scanned the trees as they set off, on high alert for the slightest sign of Boris and Ferdy or their ponies. But the forest gave up nothing and she finally realised that they would have to continue on to the Intrepid River without them. Deep in thought, Marta wondered about the nomad walking ahead of them along the tree line.

Then she remembered something he'd said. 'His sword had a name.'

'What?' Frovin leaned forward.

'When the nomad stood in front of me to face the anomir, he called his sword something.'

'What did he say?'

'I can't be certain. But it sounded something like Honor
… perhaps Honorex?'

Frovin whispered, 'So, I was right after all. That's the famous sword wielded by King Farmir in the Battle of the Stones. I bet that's why the anomir fled … He *is* Prince Mir, the future King of the World of the Soul.

Marta started. 'Are you sure? Why would he want to travel with us?'

'Oh, I think I know why he's here, Marta. He's come to help us find the Lightenstone and return it to its place in the centre of the Pentark.'

# CHAPTER 18

After the anomirs attacked and their ponies bolted into the Norfolk Woods, Boris and Ferdy became hopelessly lost. Somehow, they managed to stay upright as the ponies swerved madly around trees and crashed through the undergrowth. But finally they all became entangled in thicket. With Aster jammed behind Poppins, the dwarves slumped along the ponies' necks. Boris took stock of their predicament.

'Now look what's happened.' He was panting. 'We should've just gone home to Banters Den!'

'We both knew it was too dangerous. Besides, it would've taken us weeks to get there,' Ferdy reminded him.

'We're in danger now anyway. Considering what's happened, perhaps we should've still gone home. It's going to take us weeks to get out of these woods now—'specially if we get captured by the elves!'

'I wasn't to know this was going to happen!' Ferdy retorted, close to tears and looking anxiously at the thicket that entangled them. 'It's not my fault the anomirs attacked. Besides, the others will come looking for us, won't they?'

Boris sat up straight. 'For all we know they could be badly hurt. Or dead. And if we're the only ones that have survived, we'll be expected to find the hidden gemstones on our own.'

Ferdy realised his brother was right. He shuddered. 'Well that quest is the last thing I'm interested in at the moment. I'm hungry and tired. Why don't you try to back Aster out of this mess? I'm getting off.'

'And how do you plan to get back on Poppins again?' asked Boris.

'Don't know. I'll find a stump somewhere.'

'A stump? You know that trees are sacred to the elves, so there won't be …'

'Then I'll fell a tree.'

'Have you lost your mind? One swing of your axe and we'll be surrounded by elves.'

'He is right you know,' said a deep voice.

'Who said that?' Boris drew Thrust as Ferdy scrambled for his axe.

A light wind rustled the leaves and the boughs sighed.

'I said, "Who said that?", repeated Boris, as they scoured the surrounding trees.

'Who said that? That said, "Who said that?"'

'Stop mocking me! Show yourself now!' demanded Boris.

'And who are you that wants to know who I am?

'I'm … I'm not at liberty to say!' stammered Boris, trying to pinpoint the voice.

'Don't you have a name?'

'Of course I do. I … I just don't …'

'Dwarves don't ride ponies.' The voice interrupted, changing the subject.

'That's a matter of opinion. *We* do!' Boris was indignant.

'So I see. I hear you're on a quest looking for hidden … err … gemstones.'

'That's none of your business. Anyway it's rude to listen to other peoples' conversations.'

'Times are dark. You could be the enemy of my people, the elves.'

'All we want to do is get out of here,' piped Ferdy, vividly remembering his encounter with the menacing trees of Greenwood Forest. 'Perhaps you could point us in the right direction?'

'Ah, what a pleasant little fellow you are. Unlike your brother …'

'And who said we were brothers?' fired Boris.

'I am the Guardian Elf of the Norfolk Woods. I know many things.

*What's a guardian elf?*

The abrupt sound of moaning startled them as an elf suddenly shot up from the woodland floor nearby. The twins had never seen a real elf before but they immediately recognised it as one, although its fingers and hair looked just like Norfolk twigs. Their jaws dropped and their eyes widened as the elf grew and flexed, stretching its arms and legs until it reached full height, towering over them.

In disbelief, their eyes scaled its height, unable to see its head.

'W … what's going on?' stammered Boris, swallowing hard.

'I am the spiritual elf of the elves of Magirus and of the Isle of Spheres.'

'Is that so? I … I have never heard of you. I know the Norfolk Woods belong to the elves. I know they believe their trees are sacred. But … but … I've never known of such a thing as a spiritual elf. That can just sprout from … nothing?'

For some reason, the elf found Boris funny and it began to guffaw loudly, jerking its arms, sending showers of sticky pine needles and prickly cones from its fingers and hair.

'Do you mind?' said Boris. 'The whole blessed forest will know we're here!'

'What a feisty little fellow you are and both of you descendants of Thrim, master craftsman to the Isle of Spheres.'

The dwarves gasped.

'How do you know that?' cried Boris, as the elf reached down and playfully jabbed him in the ribs.

'Stop it!' he shouted.

Swinging Thrust and flapping his stubby legs he pulled back on Aster's reins. But it was no use. Both ponies found the thicket to their liking and refused to move, picking delicious young leaves and flowers that were magically sprouting from among the thorns. Exasperated, Boris was at a loss for what to do when the massive elf vanished in a spontaneous burst of tiny showering sparks.

'Good grief! What's happening now? Where did the elf go?' Ferdy was frantic as the falling sparks made his body tingle.

'We need to get out of here. Now!' yelled Boris. But something strange began to happen. The ponies were startled as the thicket they were munching on evaporated, and a clear winding path formed and stretched out before them.

Ferdy's heart thumped and he began to tremble. 'The Norfolk Woods are just like Greenwood Forest! The trees are alive. What are we going to do?'

There was nothing they could do but follow the path. Although they were now free from entanglement, a new thicket formed on each side of the enchanted path ahead. It was impossible to do anything but move forward.

Ferdy looked behind him bouncing wildly as the ponies started to trot at a faster pace. 'We're trapped!'

He could see that the thickets were advancing with them. But the ponies seemed to have a new lease of life and soon broke into a canter, ignoring the desperate efforts of the dwarves to pull them up.

After several miles a magical dreaminess overcame the twins. Their bodies felt heavy and they lost their will to fight. They slumped onto the ponies' necks and fell into a deep slumber as Aster and Poppins cantered on. They continued on the ever stretching path from late afternoon until midnight, when they were stopped by the heavily guarded gates of Alfura, the enclave of the elves. The twins were hauled off their mounts and were searched before being carried to a prison cell. They were aware of strange faraway voices but were too weak to fight their enemy.

It was the rattle of keys and the delivery of breakfast the next morning that eventually woke them. They sat up, yawned and rubbed their bleary eyes. A slim, well dressed guard with swept back ears and an elegant face, laid a platter of food just inside the door. It was laden with fruits, breads and nuts that neither of them had ever seen before, and there was a jug of water and two goblets. With a cursory nod and saying something they could not understand, the guard relocked the door and left them to it. Ferdy jumped off his bed and started towards the food.

'Wait!' said Boris following. 'It could be poisonous for all we know!'

'I don't care. I'm starving.' Ferdy grabbed a piece of fruit and bit into it cautiously. The juice spurted out, spilling down his beard. 'Ooooh … it's very juicy—bit like a particularly luscious apricot. Here, try some.'

He poked a hole in some bread and filled it with nuts and jammed it in his mouth. He filled the two goblets and handed one to Boris.

'What do you think, eh? Better than bread and mushrooms!' Ferdy spluttered through a mouthful.

'We're prisoners of the elves, Ferdy!' Boris downed his water in one gulp.

'So why are they feeding us? And look at our lodgings. Ever seen such a nice prison cell?'

Boris had to admit Ferdy was right. Their cell had comfortable beds, natural light, two stools and a mat made of woven leaves.

'Not like the prison cells from home,' continued Ferdy. 'Remember old toffee-nosed Bartelby Finch threatening to throw us in one of the local cells 'cos we always stole his walnuts for Mother?'

The memory brought a faint smile to Boris' lips. As children they used to play near the small prison house on the outskirts of Banters Den. Built of stone and without light, it looked cold and unforgiving.

Boris snapped out of his daydream. 'But we're still prisoners. Don't forget, they have Aster and Poppins too. And I'm trying to remember what happened to us when we got here. Can you remember anything?'

'Um … I think they searched us …?'

'Uh? Where's Thrust?' Boris sprang to his feet realising that his belt was missing. His eyes swept the room. Then he saw the belt coiled on top of one of the wooden stools in a corner of the cell.

'Oh, no! This is worse than I imagined. They've stolen Thrust. How dare they!'

He began banging on the thick wooden door. 'Guards! Open the door now!' But his shouting was ignored and he gave up. He picked up his belt and put it on before slumping on the stool.

Not being one to waste good food, Ferdy finished off what Boris left. He patted his satisfied tummy and downed another goblet of water before returning to his bed. He stared at the ceiling. Then something tweaked his memory and a cold shiver ran over his body. Humming, he checked to make sure that Boris was not watching, and then undid his jacket and slid his right hand through the opening to the inner pocket.

The book was still there!

He had not forgotten about it entirely. But ever since he had stolen it from the library on the day they went to see the Queen of the Sun, he had tried to ignore it. And he'd got so used to feeling it against his ribs that it had become a part of his clothing. Then he remembered the words of the Queen.

*'And should your journeys take you into elven lands, may you find the writings of the elves … helpful.'*

Ferdy wavered, wondering if he should tell Boris about the book now. But he knew his brother would not be very happy about not being privy to his secret. He decided not to. And if the elves had not taken the book when they searched him, then maybe it was not that important anyway. In fact, perhaps it was not even written in Elvish. His mind wandered back and forth with all manner of possibilities until he was in quite a state.

He was interrupted by the sudden arrival of guards who bundled them both outside and marched them along a street with very unusual paving stones. The twins sneaked a quick look at their captors. The elven guard who delivered their breakfast was the first real elf they had ever met. They heard stories about elves when they were children, but they had not expected them to have such fine features.

'Dreadfully grotesque,' said one aunt, pursing her lips and screwing up her stubby nose in disgust.

'Never trust an elf! They flit everywhere, mostly unseen. They dress in tatty clothes and think they're better than us hard working dwarves. They wouldn't have a day's work in them,' their father said knowingly.

Boris and Ferdy had no intention of trusting them now and had no idea whether or not they were hard working. But from what they could see the elves were not ugly and certainly were not dressed in tatty clothes. They were slim and elegant with pale smooth skin, almond-shaped eyes, and ears that curved to a point. Their hair colour varied from blonde to dark brown and they were taller than the dwarves by more than half a body height; some were even taller.

And these guards were wearing light green fitted jackets with a belt and buckled leather boots, and from their green felt hats swept a bright red feather held fast by a crested clasp. A single bow and quiver of arrows hung from their shoulders. As they walked, the dwarves heard a trumpeting sound that seemed to be the cue for a mass exodus of curious elven folk from their elegant houses to follow, point and stare at them.

Boris and Ferdy were embarrassed to realise they must be an unprepossessing sight to the elves who had never seen a dwarf before. They were dirty and unkempt from weeks of travel, with tangled hair poking out from under their hats, and beards now reaching down to their midriffs. Boris suspected that they also probably smelled a lot like their ponies.

As they rounded a corner, Boris and Ferdy were awed by the beauty of a building that came into view. The whole front wall of the building was sculpted from sandstone overlaid with interwoven waves of turquoise and clear glass, spilling from large suspended rings like water and moulding into the sweeping patterns carved into the sandstone. It reminded them of a waterfall and the dwarves wondered at its beauty.

They gaped as they were led up several stone steps, along a stone portico supported by clear glass columns, through double oak doors and then along a short corridor and down more steps. A final set of glass doors opened into a light-filled room where five distinguished-looking elves sat behind an exquisitely carved pine table. Boris and Ferdy were surprised when the elves stood upon their arrival, then nodded before returning to their seats. The guards pushed the dwarves towards the table and unbound them before bowing and leaving the room.

The elves spoke briefly among themselves in a language which neither of the dwarves understood. Ferdy felt sick and wished he he'd not eaten so much. Boris gritted his teeth and clenched his fists, trying his best to look brave.

The elf furthest to the left was assisting the one beside him to open a large red leather-bound book. When it was open he hesitated for a moment before dipping his quill into a glass jar of royal blue ink and writing with a flourish. Meanwhile the two elves on the other side clasped their hands and stared at Boris and Ferdy, making them squirm. These two were distinguishable by their identical upswept hats, one orange and the other yellow.

The elf in the middle was taller and older. His long, straight, white hair sparkled with gossamer threads. He wore a rich purple mantle trimmed with white and his strange mitred hat was the same colour. He peered at the dwarves over gold-rimmed spectacles. After clearing his throat, he greeted them with an elegant spread of his hands and began to speak in the language of the Isle of Spheres.

'Welcome to the court of Alfura, the enclave of the elves of the Norfolk Woods. 'Please state your names.'

'I'm Boris.'

'And I'm Ferdy.'

'I am Elvendor and these are my elven Fellows.' Elvendor then turned to address his colleagues.

'Today we have before us two trespassers. Word has come from the woodland border guards of a breach by dwarves near the Eastward Road. Attempted poaching of rabbits is the charge.'

'Now just a minute here …, ' said Boris.

The old elf leant forward. 'Are you denying that you set traps to catch rabbits in the Norfolk Woods?'

'I didn't set the traps … he did,' blurted Ferdy trying to be helpful. 'But … but … we were hungry. We didn't know we were in the Norfolk Woods.'

'How could you *not* know? As dwarves, you surely know that the Norfolk Woods belong to us. Yes?' Elvendor raised an eyebrow at Ferdy.

'Yes we do. From our parents and other folk. But we've never been here before. The woods weren't named on the map …' Boris jabbed him with his elbow.

'Dwarves with a map? What's this? Surely the Norfolk Woods would have been named on your map? If you *had* a map …'

Ferdy began to sweat. He shuffled from foot to foot and looked down at his boots.

'So! A map you say? And where is this map now?' asked the scribe as his nib flew across the pages.

'We … we … don't have it anymore. Must have lost it.' Boris was getting agitated. 'Or perhaps the guards took it!'

The elves conferred in their native tongue. The one in the orange hat shook his head.

Elvendor continued. 'What brought you to our gates? And at midnight—it's a long way from the Eastward Road.'

'We had no choice! We were attacked and got lost!'

'Who attacked you?' asked the scribe's assistant.

'Horrible flying things.' Boris realised he'd already said too much.

'Anomirs?'

'Yes. Yes, that's them. Our terrified ponies bolted straight into your woods. Didn't stop until we were tangled in a thicket. And then we were confronted by a huge elf. Called itself the Guardian Elf of the Norfolk Woods,' scoffed Boris. 'And where's my sword? It's not yours to have. I want it back!'

The elves were visibly taken aback by Boris' outburst. The room fell silent.

'So, where were you going when you were attacked? I presume you must have come from Banters Den.'

Ferdy gulped and then nodded.

'You're very young to be in such dangerous territory. Are you on your own?' Elvendor looked from one to the other.

'Just us and our ponies,' said Boris, a little too quickly.

'And you didn't say where you were going.'

'Nowhere in particular.' Boris crossed his arms.

'Hmmm.' Elvendor pursed his lips. 'Now tell me about this guardian elf you say you saw.'

'It was enormous! Sprang up right in front of us.' This time it was Ferdy who answered, trying to copy the elf's voice. 'It said, "I am the spiritual elf of the elves of Magirus and of the Isle of Spheres".'

His attempt made Elvendor smile.

'And then the thicket opened up to form a path that ended at your gates. So we had no choice but to follow it,' Boris broke in again.

'A visit from the guardian warrants closer attention, don't you think?'

The other elves nodded and murmured.

'Are you implying that the guardian elf brought you to us … *deliberately*?' asked the elf in the orange hat.

The elf in the yellow hat added, 'and why would it do such a thing?'

'I can assure you we wouldn't be here unless we'd been forced to come!' Boris shot back.

'Well, can *you* think of any reason why you were led straight to our gates?' Elvendor eyeballed Ferdy.

'Uh-uh.' Ferdy shook his head, rubbed his nose and looked away.

'Perhaps you have something that belongs to us?' insisted Elvendor.

'I … I wouldn't know.' Ferdy stammered, feeling clammy and wanting to take his jacket off.

'Huh? You can't mean Thrust!' Boris exploded, putting his hands on his hips. 'I'll have you know my sword was forged by Thrim our ancestor, master craftsman to the Isle of Spheres. You can't have it!'

Elvendor looked thoughtfully at them. He took Thrust from his lap and placed it, still sheathed, at the front of the table.

'It is not the sword we are enquiring about, Boris. It clearly doesn't belong to us. We have been attempting to remove it from its sheath since the guards confiscated it but have not been able to do so. And now I know why. Thrust can only be wielded by a direct descendant of Thrim. It is only in your hands that it has any power … unless it happens to fall into the hands of a sage …'

Ferdy's eyes widened.

'Please take it.'

Wasting no time, Boris grabbed it and fastened it to his belt.

'But the guardian doesn't just bring any ordinary folk to our gates. So you must have something for us.'

'We have nothing save our ponies and what's in our packs. And I'm sure you've searched those too,' said Boris defensively.

'Ferdy?' asked Elvendor.

Ferdy gulped. With a long sigh he undid the buttons of his jacket and pulled out the book. With trembling hands, he stepped forward and placed it gently on the table.

Boris stared at him, open-mouthed. 'Ferdy??'

Elvendor reached for the book and carefully opened it. The other elves watched fascinated. With great reverence, the old elf began to read aloud. Although Boris and Ferdy could not understand a word, the language of the elves was very beautiful, and its melodic lilting sounds seemed to calm them. After reading the first page, Elvendor stopped and closed the book.

'How did you come by this?' he asked.

'I … I found it. In a library.' Ferdy's voice was barely audible.

Boris was astonished. He frowned.

'And tell me, where would I find this library?'

'I … in … in a mountain.'

'There are many mountains in the Isle of Spheres.
Which mountain, exactly?'

Ferdy felt sick. 'The Ascension Mountains,' he murmured, eyes downcast.

The elves raised their eyebrows. Boris was flabbergasted. *Ferdy's had this
book since we were in the Ascension Mountains and hasn't told me?*

As Elvendor rose and stood behind his seat, Ferdy looked up. The old elf
was watching them closely. 'The Ascension Mountains are the home of the
Knights of Power. You said you had come from Banters Den. So … what
sort of conundrum have you two got yourselves into?'

Suddenly it was all too much for Ferdy. He began to sniffle as tears ran
down his cheeks and into his beard.

'It all started when I found an apple. In Greenwood Forest,' he sobbed.
'And we ended up in a cave … with a sage and a knight. And now we're on
a quest. To find some precious gemstones.'

Despite the fact that he had revealed their quest to the arch enemy of
dwarves, Ferdy felt a huge weight lift from his shoulders. But Boris was
horrified that their plans had now been exposed—they could all be
in mortal danger.

'What was the name of the sage?' asked the scribe, his nib hovering.

'Umm. Iko … something,' said Boris taking over, trying to
rescue the situation.

'You met Ikoseer? The Sage of White Timber Mountain?' Elvendor's
eyebrows shot up in surprise. The other elves fidgeted.

'Um, her name might have been something like that.' Boris
was deliberately vague.

The old elf peered over the top of his gold rims and rested his palms on the
table. He tapped his fingers, thinking.

'And a knight too, you said? What was his name? Or don't you remember that either?'

Boris's face reddened. He wondered if he should give any more names. But it was of no use. To tell a lie at this stage would only bring more trouble. He felt defeated.

'Artorus,' he said in a flat voice.

'Ah! Then you have not come here without reason. I may be able to help you.'

'Huh?'

'When Ikoseer was a guest of mine quite some time ago, we spoke at length of the future of the Isle of Spheres. She indicated to me that soon the time would come to make a final stand. She asked for my help. Her wish—and that of the Queen of the Sun—was to restore the Pentark. To eliminate the scourge of Onysius and Lord Mortimer from our lands.'

'You already knew?' Boris was confused.

Elvendor nodded. 'I knew some things. But I didn't know that the Queen had given her orders. That Ikoseer had already begun the quest.'

'When the anomirs attacked … We don't know if the others survived,' exclaimed Ferdy. Boris turned and glared at him.

Elvendor smiled. 'The others? Well, well. You are full of surprises. Don't you think that if my scouts found your traps, that they might not also find your companions?'

'You were spying on us the whole time?'

'We were *observing* you.'

Ferdy brightened. 'So … You know what happened to the others then?'

'It seems that they may have survived. Our scouts didn't see the attack of the anomirs. However, word has come just this morning of a small camp

along our western border. There are two horses and a white pony, three
men, and a young woman.'

Ferdy got excited. 'They're all right!'

But Boris was frowning. *Three men? But there should only be two.*

'And a badger?' added Ferdy, his eyes bright with hope.

'There was no report of a badger.'

'Oh.' Ferdy was downcast, remembering his blurry vision of Frovin
attacking the fallen goblin. Fresh tears welled up and his nose began
to run again.

'Should your friend the badger have passed, then his death would have
been an honourable one,' said Elvendor with compassion. 'But now you
both need to rest—for a few days at least. Anyone who is a friend of
Ikoseer and the Knights of Power, is a guest of the elves of Alfura. Come,
wipe your tears Ferdy. Let me reunite you both with your ponies. They too
are having a well-earned rest.'

With that, the court of the enclave of Alfura was concluded with the final
flourish of a nib. To the surprise of Boris and Ferdy, the other elves stood
and bowed as Elvendor led them out, first to the stables, and then onto
their new lodgings.

Clutching the book that Ferdy had returned, Elvendor was pondering
deeply on the two scruffy dwarves behind him and their possible
connection to the air sign Gemini, the twins in the zodiac. The gemstone
of that sign had been held in trust at his palace since the invasion. It
belonged in the Pentark and it must be returned.

But how? he wondered.

# CHAPTER 19

Snowball ground her teeth as Marta breathed in the crisp morning air and looked across the expanse of grassland towards the Intrepid River. The rising breeze caressed the tips of the long grass, moving them like ripples in a vast green river. It reminded Marta of home. She used to love running her hands across the ears of the oats in spring, knowing that the sun would soon be ripening the grain for harvest.

She recalled the village men saying that food was short in the World of the Soul, and much of the ground they had travelled over so far was barren. The plants were stunted, struggling to survive.

'Why is the grassland so lush here?'

'We're close to a ley line,' answered Artorus, watching her.

When she frowned, he continued. 'Do you remember your mother telling you about the three light spheres on the coastline of the Isle and how they are connected to the Pentark at Mirraway?'

Marta nodded.

'A direct ley line of energy is created between each of the spheres and the Pentark. And each ley line radiates out on either side, enriching everything nearby.'

'But some of the Pentark's stones are missing now …'

'Yes, but there is still a little magic.' Artorus continued. 'They call this Calligan's Plain. Nomadic tribes used to graze their animals here, but they left after the invasion of Illingaith.'

Marta opened her mouth to speak and then stopped.

'What is it?' he asked.

'If we cross the plain now, we'll leave an easy trail through the grass for the anomirs to find. Shouldn't we wait until dark?'

'Anomirs can't see as well in the dark, but they fly then, too. And wrakes and boorlings know no rest.'

Marta lowered her eyes, her lids brimming with the sting of fresh tears. Then she felt a slight brush as Patrayus pushed his horse beside Snowball.

'We have to take the risk, Marta, and cross while we have the chance. We should reach the river by late afternoon. We can hide under the tree canopy there.'

Marta nodded.

'Do you think Onysius has heard from his rider goblins about their attack on us yesterday?' asked Yoska.

Artorus looked towards Asilodor. 'Yes, he'd know by now. The goblins would've driven their anomirs without rest to tell him.'

Artorus urged his stallion from the cover of the trees and led them down a small slope and onto the plain. As Snowball fell in behind Famrod, Marta looked to the clouds for some kind of reassurance that all was well. But she saw nothing unusual. A heaviness settled within her. She took one last glance over Frovin's shoulder at the Norfolk Woods, hoping to see Boris and Ferdy bursting madly through the trees on their ponies. But in her heart she knew that they were leaving them further and further behind. As she wiped away her tears, an elven spy leapt from a treetop, glanced at the departing riders and headed back to Alfura with his news.

The lush grassland of Calligan's Plain was dotted with sharp rocky outcrops and small clumps of trees. Although they travelled free from aerial attack, by early afternoon the clouds gathered and darkened. Wild winds swept up, creating a dust storm that came all the way from the dry baked earth of Asilodor.

'Thank you,' said Marta gratefully as Patrayus handed her a scarf to protect her face. He gave her a blanket to shield herself and Frovin from the stinging dust.

The horses' heads hung low in the long grass, letting their rumps bear the force of the fierce winds. They struggled on until they reached the protective belt of trees along the Intrepid River. As they slipped under the canopy, the winds dropped to a light breeze.

Marta saw the look between Artorus and Frovin.

'What is it?' she asked Frovin as she dismounted. 'Why did the winds die as soon as we were under the trees?'

'I don't know. The storm just finished.'

'Has it got something to do with our search for the Lightenstone?'

'Shhhhh! It's not safe to mention the Stone now that we are getting closer to Asilodor. Apart from the anomirs, you don't know who or what else might be looking or listening for us.'

'Was the storm trying to stop us from reaching the river?'

He hesitated. 'Yes. I think so.'

'So does the wind also know we're looking for the Stone?'

'No, but the Prince of Darkness will try and manipulate the elementals— the sylphs of the air, the gnomes of the earth. The undines of the water and the salamanders …'

' … of the Fire,' she finished. Her skin crawled at the mention of his name. She felt for her amulet. 'Does the Prince of Darkness know we're here?'

'I … I don't know,' admitted Frovin. 'But there are powerful forces trying to stop us from finding the Stone before they do. They'll use any means possible, heedless of how they do it. And who they use for their own ends. And because it's my job to protect the Stone I have to be wary of more things now.'

She held his gaze. 'Do you know where we're going to tomorrow?'

'We must try to cross the river into the Land of Illingaith. There's an old barge on a narrow bend in the river. It connects the two Lands, and we'll be able to use it if we can find the Hermit of the Living Waters.'

Marta stared at him. 'How do you know all this?'

'Ikoseer told me the night before she left us.'

'So why wasn't I told too?'

He shrugged. 'I can only obey Ikoseer's orders.'

That response was not going to stop Marta's questions. 'So did Ikoseer also tell you where the Stone is?'

'Good heavens, no! I'm not privy to *that* information, but we must be getting closer to it. Artorus must know where it is, surely?'

'And what about the outer gems? Does Artorus also know where they are? There might be one in this river. Boris and Ferdy are gone so they can't help …'

'We don't have to worry about the outer gems. For now. The Lightenstone is the most important one.'

Marta studied him closely. She wondered what else he was not telling her. She crossed her arms. 'And what will we do if we can't find the Hermit?'

Artorus approached them, drawn by Marta's angry questions. 'There'll be no need for us to search for the Hermit. I expect that he already knows we are here. But if he's not at the river bank by morning, then we'll attempt to swim the horses across.'

'But we can't do that! Onysius' soldiers must patrol the river—they'll attack us as soon as we've crossed into Illingaith.'

'Yes, but it's unlikely they're anywhere near this area. The Hermit has never allowed the invaders to use his barge.'

'How can he refuse them?'

'You will see. But now we have to make camp and hope that we'll have use of the barge tomorrow.'

As Artorus left them, Marta lifted Frovin off Snowball's rump and pulled wildly at the pack straps, causing them to tangle.

'I still don't understand why I'm needed to help find the Stone. You're the one who has to protect it.'

'I think it has something to do with your amulet. Once the Queen of the Sun held it she told us that the Stone knew we were coming. I suppose I could ask you to give me your amulet to take with me, but I doubt you'd part with it.'

'Of course I won't. It belonged to my mother.'

'Then we'll have to keep together.'

Marta set her face and swung the packs to the ground, lifted the saddle flap and released the girth.

'I miss Boris and Ferdy. I hope they're safe …'

'We've all left loved ones behind,' Frovin reminded her. 'And they could already be on their way home.'

'You're right. I'm sorry. I sometimes forget that I am not the only one feeling pain.' She looked at Frovin, managing a weak smile as he squeezed her hand.

'Come on then,' he said. 'We need to help make camp. I seem to remember Yoska putting cornmeal into Famrod's saddle pack, so we just might get some hot corn bread for supper.'

He paused for a moment. 'And even if you did let me have your amulet—without arms and hands—how would I carry it?'

Marta grinned at him and dropped the reins. 'Snowball needs a drink first. Can you take her down to the river, please?'

Frovin rolled his eyes but grabbed the end of the reins in his teeth and tugged until Snowball plodded after him. Finding a small embankment he jumped down to the river's edge and pulled the pony after him, keeping a wary eye on the river. Artorus soon joined them and filled their water skins as the horses drank.

Frovin looked to the far side of the river. 'I hope the river isn't as wide as this at the crossing. If the barge isn't there tomorrow I wouldn't like to see poor old Snowball made to swim that far.'

'You needn't worry. The crossing is narrower but I didn't think you cared much about the horses.'

'Well I don't. But Snowball's carried me safely for most of our journey. And I'm getting used to her company—in spite of myself.'

The pony lifted her head, nickered and dripped water all over him.

Artorus chuckled. 'I think Snowball likes you too.'

Frovin shook the water off. 'And I don't think Marta would be very happy either if anything happened to her pony.'

'But remember—Snowball isn't her pony. Although free to do as she pleases, Snowball's true home is in Arctus with Helios and Ikoseer.'

'I know,' conceded Frovin watching the river flow.

'So there's no need for you to worry. She can swim the river if she has to.'

'Once we've crossed the river into Illingaith, what direction do we take to reach Asilodor?'

Artorus looked at him sharply. He glanced over his shoulder to make sure that they were alone.

'I want to try and make it to the Ageless Forest. The shortest route is to go due south from here. But it will take us three days. We can follow an old road part of the way and then, using the forest as cover we'll continue south for another week towards Jimpiragh and the Abyss River, the border with Asilodor.'

Frovin's resolve strengthened. 'Will we be exposed at all on the way?'

'Not until we reach the farm lands. So be on your guard then. The Dark Ones are increasing in strength. You saw how fast the dust storm rose up.'

Frovin sighed. 'I worry about Marta's safety.'

'She has greater protection than you realise.'

'Oh?'

Frovin waited until Artorus had secured the last water skin. 'Is it far to the barge?'

'Just a short way upstream.'

'Do you think the Hermit will be there tomorrow?'

'Don't know.'

Artorus led his horses back to the camp. As Frovin tugged on Snowball's reins, she halted, pricked up her ears and turned her head towards the middle of the river. He followed her stare and shivered as he noticed dark ripples appear on the surface.

'Come on Snowball. Protective magic or not, there's something in that river. Let's hope the Hermit decides to come out of his hidey hole tomorrow and we don't have to swim.'

∽

The following morning they packed up their camp and Artorus led the party upstream until the trees thinned and they were within sight of the crossing. But the barge was nowhere to be seen. Frovin groaned.

As the two knights explored further, Marta noticed a delicate whirlpool in the river. 'Look!'

'Huh?'

They watched the water accelerate and expand before leaping upwards, transforming into a beautiful creature.

'What is it?' whispered Marta.

'I don't know. But I think it's an undine.'

The creature glided towards them, her translucent body sparkling in the early morning light. Then raising her arms, she cupped her hands to create a shimmering goblet and filled it with aqua blue water from her mouth. Snowball snorted as the undine stopped at the river's edge and held out her offering. As Snowball gingerly reached out, Frovin grabbed Marta's shoulders with his sharp front claws and pulled himself up.

'No! Wait!'

But Snowball ignored him. A warm tingling sensation swept through Marta's body as the pony drank from the vessel.

'Who are you?' demanded Frovin. 'We're looking for the Hermit of the Living Waters. Where is his barge!'

The undine smiled and waited for Snowball to finish, then dropped her hands. 'I am the guardian of the Intrepid River. If you seek the Hermit then you must express your wish to cross my river.'

'I ... I ...'

Suddenly Famrod was beside them. Artorus bowed his head.

'In the name of the King of the World of the Soul, of the Queen of the Sun and of Ikoseer the Sage of White Timber Mountain, we seek safe passage across the Intrepid River.'

Without warning, the undine collapsed back into the river. Her place was taken by a watery little old man.

'Then I, the Hermit of the Living Waters, grant you permission.' He bowed in return. 'I will do my best, but it has been a very long time …'

With that, the Hermit laboured and sloshed his way into deeper water. With a pulsing, whooshing sound, he drove his hands into the river, working them in ever widening circles, creating ripples that became large whirlpools. Then he reversed his hands, and from the chaos emerged a barge of translucent and—somehow, solid—water, which he pushed towards them.

'Get ready!' warned Patrayus.

'Hurry!' The Hermit yelled as he grasped the barge and pushed it into the river bank.

The knights' horses snorted and shied as uprooted debris fell from the watery structure and splashed back into the river. Marta urged Snowball with her legs and the pony jumped and skidded onto the watery deck. Then the other horses followed. A watergate shut fast behind them.

The Hermit groaned as he struggled to manoeuvre the laden barge and as they neared the middle of the river, a fierce wind whipped up waves that slapped against them. There was barely enough room on the barge for the large horses, and the men struggled to control them. Famrod struck out at the strange wall of water in front of them and white lather foamed on his black coat. Marta looked through the translucent deck to the river flowing beneath them. She silently prayed that the Hermit could hold on until they reached the other side.

The horses began to prance as they neared the end and Snowball stamped her hooves. The waves continued to batter the barge until the Hermit, using the last of his strength, ran it into the sandy bank. It lurched as the watergate in front fell and dropped and the horses jumped off together into the Land of Illingaith.

Then as the Hermit dropped his hands, the barge collapsed and he stood spent and unsteady as the river swept around him. With great effort he lifted his head.

'Go well young warriors of the light. May the true King of the Isle of Spheres soon reign once more.'

Yoska bowed his head slightly but the Hermit had already sunk back into the river. Marta saw a brief patch of aqua blue as he disappeared beneath the water. She draped herself over Snowball's neck and gave her a big hug while Frovin patted her on the rump.

As Artorus reached down and pulled Yoska up to sit behind him, Patrayus rode up beside Marta.

'Are you ready? We must be on our way.'

They scrambled up the bank into the trees and Artorus headed Famrod south.

Marta whispered over her shoulder. 'Do you know where we're going?'

'No.'

'Do you think the Stone's in Illingaith?'

'Don't know.'

'Well, I hope it's not in Asilodor. That would be terrifying. I don't want to go there.'

∽

At the same time that the Hermit was plunging his hands deep into the Intrepid River, Ikoseer was holding out her staff and lighting her way through a maze of passages to the inner sanctum of White Timber Mountain.

After placing the staff in a ringed holder by the mantelpiece she built a fire between two decorated iron dogs, expanding and contracting her hands to adjust the flame. Initially, she made the fire roar. She wanted to warm the room and she needed hot coals to cook the small loaf of herb bread that she was now mixing. She also wanted to warm a pot of sweet spicy mead.

When the coals were ready, she reduced the flames, placed the dough into a shallow-sided cast iron pan, put a lid on top and nestled it in the coals at the edge of the fire. She put the pot of mead on the other side. She sat down at a sturdy oak table and broke some sharp vintage cheese, and from a ceramic jar she took three slices of dried apple. The smell of the baking bread was somehow comforting. It reminded her of the others and the difficult task that they had been set. Ikoseer turned to look at the owl waiting in the darkest corner of the room.

Sheen ruffled her feathers and stared back with big orange eyes. Then she flew silently across the table and perched on the back of a chair opposite the Sage. Ikoseer placed three dead mice on the table in front of the owl. Sheen gobbled them down thankfully.

'I dreamt of you, Wise One, and flew here as fast as I could. I was in the snowfields in the far reaches of Arctus. It is bitterly cold there at any time of year, even now, in late summer …'

Ikoseer nodded and smiled at her feathered friend. 'I knew you would arrive in good time. I assume that you were flying as an eagle?'

'I admit I used a little magic …' Sheen said playfully. 'I bring news from the banks of the Abyss River. Attricus, the soothsayer and his companion, Volgor are on their way to Port Werthyn. The kurr has found the aquamarine of Pisces in the river.'

'You confirm what the Queen told me, and now who found the gemstone. Have you alerted our contact in Port Werthyn?'

'I have. He is expecting them in due course.'

Ikoseer nodded thoughtfully and stood up. From the warming pot, she ladled sweet spicy mead into a wooden cup and after removing the bread from the pan, set both down on the table. After breaking the bread, she drank a mouthful of the warm mead and began to eat.

They continued chatting but once Ikoseer had taken the last draught of the mead her mood changed. She slowly placed her cup on the table.

'I know you have not come all this way for nothing,' said Sheen.

'No, I haven't.' Ikoseer's tone was now grave. 'I have to prepare for the coming war.'

'All because of the Prince of Darkness.'

The Sage nodded. 'He and his allies continue to destroy our world. Diplomacy has not worked. You already know the Queen has set in motion a plan to restore the Pentark. From now on, I need greater help from you. Apart from the outer gemstones, the safe return of the Lightenstone is imperative. I'm leaving you in charge of the animals.'

Sheen ruffled her feathers. 'You know that I and the other animal helpers will do whatever is asked.'

'It also brings great peril,' added Ikoseer solemnly, thinking of those left behind at the Lux Mountains.

'Our survival is dependent on the successful outcome of the restoration too.'

Ikoseer took a deep breath. 'Thank you. I can't do this on my own.'

The room became still. All that could be heard was the crackling of the fire. Ikoseer finished her meal and with a nod rose and retired to her bed. She knew she would not sleep well. Her mind drifted back to the last time the Lightenstone was restored to the Pentark, two hundred years earlier. She had succeeded then, but the forces of darkness were much more powerful now.

# PART 2

# AWAKEN

# CHAPTER 20

After leaving the Hermit of the Living Waters and the banks of the Intrepid River behind, Artorus led the small band south along a winding tree-lined road. By midday they reached the point where the trees began to thin and Artorus led them off the road to rest and eat.

'Where does this road go?' asked Marta.

'The Ageless Forest,' replied Artorus, holding a stirrup iron for Yoska to dismount.

'How long will it take to get there?'

'Three days.'

'I saw tracks on the road.'

'Yes, the enemy is closer than I thought. But there's nothing to worry about. The tracks aren't fresh and they veer off towards Mirraway. Those soldiers are looking for resistance fighters and deserters.'

'Why wouldn't they be looking for us?' asked Marta.

'Only goblins on anomirs will be searching for us. Onysius would've sent more of them to scour Illingaith once he heard about the attack at the Norfolk Woods.'

'But what if his soldiers see us anyway?'

'Leave them to me. We're just travellers crossing to the Ageless Forest. Nothing more. These soldiers wouldn't know about us yet.'

'Won't they think it strange? The only travellers we've seen so far are the nomads.'

'Marta's right.' Patrayus had been listening closely and now spoke up.

'We can expect to see more people from now on,' replied Artorus. 'The Kingdom of Gorthonomir is vast. Small communities of displaced families

have hidden for years in the mountains and the forests. They're waiting—
for action and the day of reckoning.

'Unfortunately, there were also many who agreed to become messengers
and spies for the enemy. They travel these roads too. But don't judge them.
It was a difficult choice to make—and they made it out of fear for their
families. Even among them, there are still some we can trust.'

'How will you know who you can trust?' Marta was dismayed.

'The families in exile will respond to the ensign of their king. The
others—I admit they'll be much more difficult.'

'What does the ensign look like?' asked Marta looking straight at Yoska.

Their eyes met and he understood. She had guessed who he was.

'I shall draw it for you,' he said. He reached for a stick and scribed a
circle in the dirt. Within the circle and touching the circumference, he
drew a 'W' overlaid by an 'M'. Then he marked a dot in the middle.
Marta studied it.

'What do the symbols mean?'

'The circle with the dot is the sun that the Pentark absorbs. The 'M'
represents the mountains. The 'W' is the water that rushes from the
mountains to the Mother Sea. The diamond shapes created by the two
letters symbolise the Queen of the Sun, a crown. They also represent the

original name of the Isle of Spheres: Magi Mundi, which translates to the Magic World.

Marta nodded at his explanation, but her heart skipped a beat. She had seen this pattern on a brooch in her mother's drawer, with another symbol on the underside: a white arum lily. She gave a shiver and wondered: *How would my mother come to have a brooch with these symbols on it?*

Ever since crossing the Intrepid River, Marta had been aware that something had changed in her. She recalled the tingling sensation she had when Snowball drank from the undine's goblet. Suddenly she felt frightened. She sensed that Artorus was watching her closely. He seemed to be aware of her discomfort. She looked away, staring into the trees.

As they continued through to late afternoon, the road remained deserted and the skies clear of anomirs. The trees first thinned and then gave way to smaller denuded clumps and what had been a level road began rise and fall as it made its way between undulating hills and valleys of abandoned farm land.

From one rise, Marta could see once fertile hillsides, now lined with rows of struggling vines. Paddocks below were devoid of animals, the untended fences fallen into disrepair, the crops gone. A stone farmhouse and barn were snuggled into the hill below them. Artorus dismounted, leaving Famrod with Yoska and went down to check that it was safe. Eventually, he called them to join him.

The barn was large enough for each horse to have a stall. Yoska found a well nearby and although the staves in the bucket were shrunken from lack of use, he was able to draw enough water for them all.

Meanwhile Marta and Frovin stepped through the broken doorway of the farmhouse. Their eyes swept the room. Pots, pans and cutlery were scattered about the room. Clear rings were marked in the dust where they once stood. The mattress on a single bed had been slashed, the stuffing of feathers and wool strewn about and the warm overlaid skins were gone. Valuable iron fittings had been ripped from the fireplace.

Beneath a stout table with three crude chairs was a small child's toy, a carved wooden unicorn. Marta picked it up, brushing off the dust. Underneath was a button with blue threads still attached and she immediately thought of the buttons she had sewn onto Ferdy's shirt. She smiled as she recalled his indignant look when she handed the shirt back, now with mismatched buttons.

'The family left in a hurry,' said Frovin.

'Yes, the poor child must have been terrified.' As she put the pieces in her pocket Marta thought of her own escape from Brechin.

'We'll sleep in the barn with the horses.' Artorus came through the door behind them. 'Yoska is …'

' … really King Mir, isn't he …?' She turned slowly to face him. She reddened at her boldness, and her heart pounded. She forced herself to hold the knight's gaze. 'I deserve to know the truth.' She expected him to be dismissive, and was surprised by his slight smile.

'You do,' he agreed quietly, resting a hand on the pommel of his sword.

Marta felt the comforting push of Frovin's sharp claws and rough pads into the palm of her hand.

'Yoska is still a prince,' said Artorus. 'He won't become king until after the death of his father, King Galway, who is in exile in the Ascension Mountains.'

Marta's eyes widened. 'The King was in the mountains when we were there?'

'Yes. Along with Yoska's mother Queen Helena and his sister, Princess Moira. His grandfather King Gordir, and his grandmother Queen Eleanor, were both murdered during the invasion.'

'How awful.' Marta remembered how she felt when her mother died.

Artorus nodded. 'So yes, Yoska is Prince Mir. But you must continue to use his nomadic name,' he warned. 'His life depends on it, and the longer the enemy thinks he's still with his family, the better.'

'He's fighting for the return of his family's kingdom.' Marta frowned as she began to understand.

'His mission is to reclaim his home, Mirraway Castle and the Kingdom of Gorthonomir. But also to help save the Isle of Spheres from any more desecration.'

'Then he must know all about the Pentark. Is he taking us to where the Lightenstone is?'

She watched as Artorus wavered. 'I deserve to know about that too, don't I?'

'Now is not the time.'

Marta stared at him. 'You never tell me anything. Unless I force you to. The time will never be right.'

Tears smarted as she pushed past him and made for the barn. Unsure of what to do, Frovin rolled his eyes at Artorus and followed her.

'I didn't ask to be here,' she said to Frovin. She gave Snowball's mane a vigorous brush.

'We discussed this yesterday,' he reminded her gently. 'You wouldn't be here at all if Artorus hadn't saved your life. And he continues to protect you.'

'And my debt to him grows every day! I'll be in the World of the Soul forever trying to repay it. I'll never feel able to go home.'

'You must trust Artorus. Don't be afraid.'

'Of course I'm afraid, aren't you?' She sniffed, giving him an aggrieved look as she tugged on a knot.

But Frovin was thinking. 'There's more to it than that.'

'What do you mean?'

'Do you remember the storm yesterday? How I told you that the Dark Ones will use any means possible to stop us and retain their power?'

'Yes, but what …'

'Don't you see? The enemy wants you to be afraid …' Frovin let the words hang. As if to agree with him Snowball reached down and much to his annoyance, nuzzled his head.

'They want to break up our team,' he continued.

Marta stopped. 'Is that what happened with Boris and Ferdy?'

Frovin shook his head. 'To be honest, I don't know.'

Marta thought for a moment. 'If Yoska's going to be the king he must know where the Lightenstone is.'

'I'm not sure that he does. It's all very secretive. All I know is that the Queen of the Sun asked me to protect the Stone with my life, and I intend to do that—once it's found.'

Frovin felt for Marta's hand again. 'And what about Ikoseer and all the innocent people who've suffered? They deserve our help, don't you think? And we can't help them without Artorus. So fighting against him isn't helpful.'

There was an awkward silence between them. Marta raked her fingers through Snowball's mane, mulling over what Frovin had said.

'I still don't see how the enemy can deliberately separate us. That's our choice,' insisted Marta.

'But who influences the choice?' Frovin stood his ground.

'Battles are fought on all levels. Even in the mind,' he continued. 'I vividly remember the Queen's warning to me, "Do not allow the Dark Ones to whisper their wishes into your mind. Subtle and cunning are their ways".'

'My mind is my own,' said Marta stubbornly. 'I can think what I like.'

'Exactly,' replied Frovin. 'So make sure you have your inner sword ready and choose the right thoughts.'

Immediately a thought entered her mind. *He doesn't know what he's talking about!*

Surprised by the force of it she tried to banish the thought but it refused to move. She tried again, harder this time, but confusion and anger against Frovin rose up in her. Horrified, she put all her energy into pushing it down. She was grateful when Yoska called for them to eat and the anger dissipated.

A new battle over the Lightenstone had begun.

# CHAPTER 21

After an early breakfast, the group left the abandoned farm the next morning. Artorus kept on the road towards the Ageless Forest until it changed direction, stretching westward towards Mirraway Castle.

'We leave the road here and continue south,' he said, guiding Famrod onto a faint track.

The terrain slowly changed from rolling hills and farmland to flat scrubby ground with jutting rocky outcrops. It reminded Marta of crossing the plateau to the Lux Mountains, except that there were a lot more crags. Clad in red, the iron-rich pillars stood to attention like soldiers ready for battle. As they passed through the outcrops, Marta looked for places to hide if they were attacked.

The afternoon sun now hung low and Marta became aware of an increasing stillness as they rode through a cramped corridor of towering spires. Snowball's shoe struck a rock and the sound echoed loudly off the sheer walls. There was no birdsong and the air thickened. Tightness gathered in her throat. She sensed danger and her hands began to tremble. She felt for the comfort of her amulet.

Artorus seemed aware of the danger too because he looked around Yoska to check on her. From his seat on the saddlebag behind Marta, Frovin saw Patrayus draw his sword and scan their surroundings.

High above them, a goblin gloated over his success, even though the party below him was not exactly what he had been sent to find. He had been ordered to look out for a fat soothsayer and a scrawny kurr. Lengthening shadows were helping him and his anomir stay camouflaged against the rocks. They were not meant to attack anything, just observe and report back. This time, Onysius wanted his prey alive, not crushed to death or torn to shreds.

The anomir became impatient and the goblin muttered for it to keep still. He was an amateur rider, snatched from his family. Not long ago

he had been dragged from near starvation in the kitchens of Jimpiragh
and trained to fly anomirs. He was tempted to attack, just for fun, but
he knew it would be foolish. He had no backup and there was something
about the riders that made him baulk. Since he felt no real allegiance to
Onysius, he felt no impulse to hurry back. Instead, he decided to wait,
watch and follow.

As he squinted at the rock face Yoska noticed the slight movement of
the anomir. Not wanting to give his observation away, he whispered to
Artorus, who nodded and pushed Famrod on, much to Marta's distress.
Urging the horses into a trot, he found a gap between the spires and led
them through the rocky labyrinth. The setting sun soon plunged them
into darkness. Snowball bumped into Famrod's legs as he slowed through a
narrow point, but the way then opened into a large hidden grotto.

Marta was surprised to see people gathered around a campfire, cooking
and warming themselves. She realised that Artorus must have been in
this cave before, and guessed that these people were some of the refugees
the knight had spoken about. Frightened children were hurrying to their
mothers and the men were grabbing weapons. It was a tense moment. In
her peripheral vision, Marta saw an older grey-haired man step from the
shadows into the firelight, his bow and arrow aimed straight at Artorus.

Marta knew that they must have been an imposing sight. The flames
flickered against Famrod's proud magnificence and she saw looks
of awe and bewilderment on the children's faces. One child peeked
around his mother at Snowball, pointing to Frovin perched on the
saddlebags behind her.

'Identify yourselves,' demanded the archer, drawing his bow home.

Artorus held up his hand. 'From the Ascension Mountains and in the
name of King Gordir, we come in peace. We bring news from Solara, the
Queen of the Sun.'

'We know that King Gordir is dead. They are empty words these days,' the
man replied, lifting his chin.

'They are, but if you will allow me?' Artorus adjusted his cloak slightly to reveal the hidden Crest of Power clasped at his shoulder.

The archer moved closer, lowering his bow to look.

'That and your horse could be stolen.'

'Then perhaps I can convince you.' Yoska slid off Famrod's rump.

The man stepped back and raised his bow again.

Marta watched as Yoska pulled back his hood and released his cloak, letting it drop. He pulled the front of his nomad shirt to one side. Although she could not see what he revealed, she could see the shock on the archer's face. He immediately lowered his weapon and with head bowed, sank to his knees.

'Your Highness … I … I didn't know,' he stammered as recognition crossed his face.

There was a collective gasp. *He must be a former soldier to King Gordir, Yoska's grandfather*, Marta thought. Yoska would have been about her age when Mortimer invaded.

'No need to apologise.' Yoska stepped out of his cloak and extended his hands to the man, bidding him to rise. 'You were wise to question us.'

Realising that they were safe, the refugees fussed about, helping with the horses and treating them all as royal guests as they shared a meal around their campfire. They soaked up Artorus' news. Excited children wanted to groom and sit on Snowball, or have Frovin on their laps. They jostled with each other to pat him and—much to his annoyance—tugged on his tail to get his attention.

Once the children were asleep, Artorus, Yoska and Patrayus gathered the adults around the fire to warn them about the anomir they had seen, and to tell them about Solara's decree to restore the Pentark. Buoyed by the news, the refugees produced tattered maps, excitedly poring over them and discussing war strategies.

'But we need to gather our allied countrymen and women into a fighting army and prepare them for the coming war,' said Artorus finally, looking around the group. 'Time is running out and I ask if one of you is willing to take charge of that.'

His words carried a heavy responsibility. Marta watched the firelight dance across their faces as comprehension dawned. She noticed that the woman beside the archer put a hand on his shoulder.

The old archer nodded and gently squeezed her hand. 'I'll do it,' he said, looking at Artorus. 'I offer my life in service to Galway, the new King of Gorthonomir.'

Yoska stood and faced him. 'King Galway will be eternally grateful. Kneel before me.'

With a puzzled expression, the archer obeyed. Yoska drew Honorex. With the flat of the blade he gently touched the top of the archer's shoulders.

'By the power of this sword and in the stead of the exiled King, Galway of Illingaith, I bestow upon you the rank of Knight of Illingaith. May those here present bear witness on this day.'

Tears glistened along the archer's eyelids as the woman hugged him and his comrades shook his hand.

'Does that mean I have to call you Sir Henry now?' asked one, slapping him heartily on the back. They all laughed.

Before dawn the following morning, the children crowded around Marta as she saddled Snowball. Frovin gave her a pained look as a child grabbed him and struggled to lift him onto the saddlebags.

Marta overheard Artorus giving the archer his final instructions. 'We'll reach the Ageless Forest by the end of today.'

'And from there?' he enquired.

'Nothing has been decided.' Artorus was guarded in his reply. 'The future depends on many things,' he continued, as Yoska was given a leg-up to sit behind Famrod's saddle.

The archer nodded his understanding. With a final farewell he stood back as Artorus guided the group out of the grotto and into the dawn.

Further south and high above, a sudden movement of the anomir woke the dozing goblin, prompting him to stand up on its feathered back. The anomir stretched its neck and focused on the narrow gap below. High up in the shadow of one side of the pillars, they watched the first rays of sun paint with burnt orange the tops of the pillars opposite.

'Can you see horses coming this way?' whispered the goblin, peering over the scaly head. A high-pitched whine began low in the anomir's throat.

'Quiet!' The goblin growled as the raptor grew restless. But the whine began again, louder this time as the anomir stretched its wings wide.

The goblin teetered on its back and slapped its neck. 'Shut up and keep still.'

The anomir reached round and clamped the goblin's leg with its curved beak. Pulling back hard, it sliced it open. Cursing and gnashing his teeth, the goblin grabbed his leg as blood spurted, soaking into the anomir's feathers.

Suddenly it tipped the goblin onto the rocks beside him. Now free of the rider, the anomir dropped silently from the ledge into full flight. Marta was the first to see the darkened shadow sweep down the rock face.

'Anomir!' she screamed, pointing ahead of them.

'Marta! Beside me!' Artorus yelled as Yoska slid from Famrod. All three men drew their swords.

Patrayus moved his horse to the other side of Snowball, shielding Marta and Frovin between the two warhorses.

'Quick! Help me up. I can't see anything from here,' said Frovin. Marta shoved him hurriedly onto Patrayus' warhorse.

Furiously fast and with talons extended, the raptor attempted to grab Famrod's head but the horse reared and struck out, clipping the anomir's chest with a front hoof. The anomir faltered, then regained balance. Emitting a high-pitched scream, it wheeled around to attack again.

'Where's the rider?' yelled Frovin scanning the ground around him.

From between the jostling warhorses Marta caught a glimpse of Yoska as he strode away from them, holding Honorex ready, taunting the anomir. He braced himself as the raptor quickly changed direction and homed in on him.

Marta's heart leapt recalling how Honorex had repelled an anomir when Boris and Ferdy were still with them. But Yoska was still in shadow and this anomir kept coming. Marta urged Snowball forward.

'Get back, Marta!' bellowed Artorus.

But she seemed deaf to his warning and watched horrified as the anomir was almost within striking distance.

Suddenly, Snowball leapt into the open. Jolted forwards, Marta grabbed a handful of the mane and gripped her legs tight around the pony. Marta glimpsed the fear in the anomir's eyes as Snowball spun and twisted, kicking hard with both back hooves.

The force of the pony's legs flung the anomir onto its back and pushed it along the ground. Flapping madly, it scrambled to right itself as Yoska ran forward and swiftly drove the huge sword deep into its breast.

'Hah! Serves you right!' sneered the goblin, who was watching from high above. The anomir's wings flopped to the earth and stilled. But now the reality of his situation was clear. Injured and stranded, he would need to climb back down the cliff face. But then what? He was sent to search for the soothsayer and his scrawny friend to the east from Jimpiragh as far as Elodom Monastery. And the monastery, a haven for refugees and deserters, was still far away in Westwood Forest, near the border with the World of Man.

He had no desire to face Onysius and explain the death of his anomir. And he knew that he could not keep up with the horses. He decided that his best plan was to return to his family in Hammerlock, the goblin enclave in the World of the Dark Night, even though that too was far away. As the rising sun brightened the shadows, he gritted his teeth and watched the horses pass below him. The rider on the brave white pony looked up at the ledge he was peering over. He shrank back from view.

Shaken by the attack and with everyone on high alert, Marta noticed the slight movement. 'Why didn't this anomir have a rider?' she asked Artorus as he followed her line of sight.

'Sometimes they fly without them,' he replied mildly, looking back at her. 'Anomirs are raw creatures, bred for scavenging. Carrion is scarcer now, so they have become opportunistic killers. It must have attacked us because it was hungry. It was after the horses, but if desperate enough, they will even eat human beings. Onysius uses goblin riders now to control them, to direct attacks and to bring him news from the air.'

'Then it's hopeless. With anomirs flying above us all the time, Onysius will know our every move.'

'But not this time.' Frovin placed a paw on her shoulder. 'This one was alone.'

'I hope they don't fly across the border into the World of Man looking for food.'

'For the moment, your world is safe from anomirs.' Artorus was reassuring but Marta shuddered at the thought of them terrifying her world.

They pushed further south towards the Ageless Forest, leaving the bleeding goblin far behind.

# CHAPTER 22

A few days after their encounter with Elvendor and the court of Alfura, Boris and Ferdy were just finishing a delicious lunch when an official-looking envelope was slipped under their door.

'What does it say?' Ferdy asked, wiping wine off his beard with his sleeve.

'If I knew that, I wouldn't have to open it.'

Boris slid Thrust's blade under the flap. He unfolded the enclosed letter and frowned at the Elvish seal. It was written in the common language of the Isle of Spheres.

'It's an invitation!' said Ferdy excitedly. It says, 'You are invited to a feast and dance festival this evening and …'

Boris flipped the letter wanting to read it himself. ' … and a place will be set for you at the main table.'

'I love to dance. It'll be fun and imagine all the food.' Ferdy was rubbing his already expanding tummy.

Boris held up his hand. 'We also request that you present yourselves on the sundown hour before the feast for counsel with Elvendor.'

'Why would he want to see us before the feast?' Ferdy took the invitation from him.

'I'll bet it has something to do with the quest … seeing as they know all about it now!'

'I didn't mean to tell them.' Ferdy peered over the top of the letter.

'I get the feeling that this'll be our last night here.'
Boris looked thoughtful.

'Why do you think that?'

Boris stroked his beard. 'Last night I dreamt that the Queen of the Sun was standing in front of me with a Pentark gemstone in her hand. We can't go home Ferdy. She's reminding us that we still have to look for the gemstone.'

'What makes you think it was a Pentark gemstone?'

'What else could it be?'

'We've never seen one of them. The dream might not mean that at all.'

'She also said it was time for us to leave.'

Ferdy slowly put down the invitation. 'But where will we go?'

'I don't know. But we won't find the gemstone if we stay here.'

'You mean we have to cross the Intrepid River? Try to catch up to the others?'

Boris shook his head. 'I don't think that's possible. They're days ahead of us.'

'And what if Marta and the others find it before we do?' Ferdy crossed his arms.

'I expect they're only looking for the Lightenstone.'

'How could you possibly know that?'

'I can't. But in the dream the Queen held out a purple gem.'

'And how do you know that the Lightenstone isn't purple?' Ferdy raised his bushy eyebrows.

The hairs on Boris' neck bristled. He glared. 'I expect that the Lightenstone is *lighter* in colour than the outer gems are!'

'Ikoseer said that there are four outer gems,' Ferdy reminded him.

'I know that. But I was only shown one in the dream.'

'Then I hope it means we're not expected to find the rest of them,' said Ferdy spreading his hands. 'That would be an impossible task. You heard Artorus. Two gems in the four great rivers. And he didn't reveal which rivers they're in. And so far I've only seen three rivers marked on any of the maps. Goodness knows where the Rubicon River is. For all we know it probably doesn't even exist! And what if the gemstone you dreamt about is in the Iscador River? We just crossed it a week ago. We should've searched for it then!'

'Exactly,' said Boris. 'But when I asked Artorus if one of the gems was in that river, he just gave me the strangest look.'

Ferdy brightened. 'So does that mean that there isn't a gemstone in the Iscador?'

'I don't know. Maybe we don't need to go looking for the gemstones. Perhaps they'll just find us.'

'That's a silly idea. How could a Pentark stone find us?'

'Through Thrust.' As he spoke, Boris picked up the blade and walked to the window overlooking the courtyard below, where three brightly coloured elves were practising a dance. The hilt of the sword felt hot in his hand and suddenly the sound of a single note broke upon his ear. He wondered where it was coming from and looked for the musician.

He turned as Ferdy joined him. 'Can you hear that?'

'Hear what?'

'A musical note.'

Ferdy leaned out of the opened window. 'There's no music being played. Not yet anyway.'

As the note faded Boris knew that what he had heard was real. Puzzled, he sheathed the blade and made for the door, hesitating at the top of the stairs.

'I'm going to visit the stables. You coming?'

'No thank you! I don't wish to smell like a horse again until I absolutely have to. My poor backside is just beginning to recover. Think I'll sleep off my lunch and get ready for this evening.'

'So I'll give Poppins a pat on your behalf then?'

'Please do,' said Ferdy.

He was determined to make the most of his comfy bed, especially if Boris's dream was right and they were to be leaving anytime soon. As he laid his head on his feather pillow and stared at the ceiling, he wondered how he could possibly get out of traipsing the length and breadth of the World of the Soul, blindly looking for a coloured gemstone in some unknown river. And looking for gemstones was dangerous work; the thought of being attacked by wrakes, boorlings and anomirs made him shudder. In fact, the new expectations placed upon his shoulders, none of his own doing, began to make him baulk at the whole idea.

Then a thought struck him. As the bearer of a most valuable elven book, he might be in a position to extend his stay with the elves. It was Boris who'd had the dream and as he carried Thrust, it must be Boris who's meant to find the gemstone. Satisfied, Ferdy closed his eyes, determined to ask Elvendor if he could stay a little while longer. He felt confident that the old elf would oblige him.

As Ferdy drifted off to sleep, Boris strode through the large barn doors, grabbed an armful of hay, and headed to the ponies' stall. On his approach, he heard the pure, ethereal sound of an elf singing. He expected it was the stablehand that he had seen there the previous day.

Boris crept the last few yards and peered under the stall door. He could see an extra pair of legs between the ponies, but the elf's head was obscured from view by the angle of the door. Then Aster nickered, sensing someone familiar. The singing stopped. Boris slid under the door and moved quickly between the ponies. It was hard to say who got the greatest shock.

Boris didn't know what to say and stood with his mouth open, staring at the most beautiful and delicate creature he had ever seen. Her long auburn hair was tucked behind ears that were gently upswept, not exaggerated like those of her kin. She returned his stare with the bluest almond-shaped eyes, wide in surprise at seeing a dwarf.

'Ah … ah … Oh dear. I'm terribly sorry if I startled you.' Boris mumbled, embarrassed by his boisterous entrance. 'Um … I thought you were their stablehand.' Unbothered, Aster and Poppins went on happily pulling at the hay in his arms.

As he saw the initial shock fade from her eyes, he dropped the hay and took a step towards her between the ponies. He held out his hand.

'I'm Boris of Banters Den.'

She leant forward and shook his hand firmly. Boris had never felt such soft skin.

'My name is Yahdra,' she said in a gently lilting voice. 'I thought my father had sent someone to look for me and I didn't want to be found. There is a festival tonight and I am expected to get ready soon, but I would much rather groom your ponies.'

He smiled. 'Well I'm sure that Poppins and Aster are very grateful. They were sorely in need of a rest. Your folks have looked after them very well since we arrived.' Boris glanced down at their trimmed and polished hooves.

'My brother Ferdy and I have received an invitation to the festival too. We're to sit at the main table.'

Yahdra raised an eyebrow.

'Do you know what the festival is for?' He cocked his head to one side.

'No. But my father requested it.'

'Oh? And who is your father?'

'Elvendor.'

Boris froze.

'He's the King of Alfura. But I expect you already know that.'

'Elvendor is a *king*?'

'Of course. You met him the morning you arrived at our gates, didn't you? I heard my father talking about two wayward dwarves. It's not often that we have such unusual guests. The last one we had was a sage.'

'But I … I thought Elvendor was just a court official,' spluttered Boris.

She began to giggle. 'How amusing. My father as a court official?'

'It's not funny.'

'I think it is. I wonder what he would say about that if I told him.'

'No! You mustn't! You can't.'

She pouted. 'I can do what I like.'

'I suppose you can but I didn't mean to be disrespectful. It's just that nobody bothered to tell us he was a king. And he didn't say that he was one either.'

'The sage who visited us knew that he was a king.'

'Yes, but sages do know these and many other things.' Boris was now quite flustered.

'I overheard my father say that you know the Sage called Ikoseer, and that you have travelled with her in the World of the Soul. She was the one who visited us.'

'You shouldn't listen in on …'

'Perhaps I shouldn't,' she interrupted. 'But do you have any idea what it's like to be a princess following this and that rule? Having to always be on my best behaviour …'

'Hardly …' blurted Boris.

Yahdra laughed and he joined in the laughter. Then she looked at him seriously. 'Do you know that I haven't travelled outside the Norfolk Woods since the invasion by Lord Mortimer? Father's worried I'll be captured. I hate being cloistered up here, but he says it's too dangerous for me to leave the woods anymore.'

'He's right. It is dangerous. The Norfolk Woods are still unaffected by the darkness and so they hold their magic. For the moment, at least. But the land beyond is slowly dying. Many foul creatures now roam the barren landscape looking for …' Boris trailed off.

'Looking for … what?'

'Oh, nothing. It doesn't matter.' Boris shifted uncomfortably. He could feel her blue eyes questioning him.

'Does it have something to do with the Pentark above Mirraway Castle?'

'Ah … I …,' started Boris, making a funny little cough. He stepped back to scratch Aster behind her ears as she rubbed her forehead hard against his chest and nickered softly, as if answering the question for him.

Yahdra studied him for a moment. 'I do know some things, you know.'

'Like what?'

'I know about the Treaty of Spheres. In fact, my father was part of the council that agreed upon the divisions of the Isle of Spheres.'

Boris was shocked. 'Good heavens. But that was two hundred years ago, after the Battle of the Stones. No wonder Elvendor has such white hair. He must be ancient!'

Yahdra grinned. 'Like dwarves, elves can live a very long time.'

Boris nodded, but wondered if he would ever make it to old age.

Then she suddenly grew pensive.

'I know that something is seriously wrong again now. After the Sage came to visit us, my father changed. It's as if he's preparing us for war. Our army, the Arrowsmiths, are often sent to patrol our border. That's how they found your travelling group. And I know that the army is sometimes sent beyond that, deeper into Magirus. Perhaps even further.'

Boris felt a tingling sensation down his arm. He touched the hilt of his sword. 'How do you know about the army's movements? Have you been spying on them too?'

She smiled coyly. 'Perhaps. But I do have friends in many places.'

'And yet you don't know why we are having a festival tonight?'

'No, I don't. But why is that so important? We have many festivals.'

He shrugged. 'Maybe it isn't.'

She frowned. 'We did have a festival for Ikoseer. And if you've been invited to sit at the main table then maybe this celebration is for you and Ferdy. Are you planning to leave us? Is that what this is about?'

'No. No. Not at all. No one has mentioned anything about us leaving.' Boris could feel his face turn bright red. 'Although, we must not out-stay our welcome. I'm sure we'll be moving on soon enough.'

Boris saw that she was thinking hard and her stare made him feel weak and vulnerable. He wondered what was going on.

She paused for a moment then spoke slowly. 'You and Ferdy are on a quest with Ikoseer the Sage, aren't you?'

'Uh … no … no we're not. Well, we were when we started out … but we aren't anymore. In fact, Ikoseer left us overnight. She didn't even say a word, but that's sages for you. She was gone, just like that!' said Boris, indicating her exit with a dismissive flourish.

Yahdra suddenly stepped towards him. Boris gulped and leant back as she leant forward, her eyes locked with his.

'Then you must tell me of your adventures … the ones before Ikoseer left you. I will ask my father to seat you beside me at the festival table, shall I?'

Boris nodded weakly and within a flash she was gone. To revive himself he drove his flushed face deep into the ponies' water pail and blew raspberries before taking a long, cool draught.

'That's better.' He wiped his face dry with his sleeves, and then noticed that Aster and Poppins were watching him.

'And what are you two looking at, eh? Anyone would think you'd never seen a princess elf before. And I'll grant you that she's lovely to look at, but she knows too much for my liking. Besides, I expect we'll be leaving here by the morrow so that'll be the end of that. And I know that you won't understand, but elves and dwarves don't … *can't* … be on friendly terms. If you get my meaning. So I'd get a good night's sleep if I were you. Make the most of your comfortable stall.'

Feeling strangely sentimental, Boris gave them both a big hug. *I must be going mad! Fancy talking to the ponies as if they understand what's going on.*

He left the barn and walked back to their lodgings with his head bowed and still dripping water.

'Must be elven magic,' he muttered. 'It's all because of this quest. Now we have to leave here and somehow find this gemstone for the Queen. And then I s'pose, try and return it to the Pentark. And do all that without being killed or getting captured.'

At sundown two guards came to escort Boris and Ferdy to Elvendor's castle.

Ferdy noticed a change in Boris since he had been to see the ponies. He seemed to be preoccupied with something and had said little since he came back, apart from telling Ferdy the shocking news that Elvendor was a king. He thought that Boris' eyes had a funny faraway look—he wondered if an elf had put a spell on him.

None of the buildings looked anything like a castle so they had no idea where they were being taken. They passed by the festival where young elves were busy arranging tables and chairs and hanging brightly coloured lanterns from the branches. Musicians were practising on flutes and fiddles and the smell of cooking food drifted on the air, making Ferdy salivate. He couldn't wait for the festival to start.

They were taken through a long avenue of trees that led to stone steps ascending around what they thought was a massive column of rock. A short but steep climb took them to a portico before the grand entrance. Boris ran his hands over the striated rock and realised that the castle was an ancient petrified pine—they were standing on the lowest branch. Before he could look up at the canopy a guard opened the door. He pushed them into a small circular room with a domed ceiling, closed the door after them, then left.

They gaped at the beauty of the room and Boris wondered if Yahdra was secretly watching them. Behind the main room was a larger identical room. This room encircled a large sweeping staircase made of a living fig tree that disappeared from sight. Boris' eyes swept around the walls, taking in the stone carvings and the elegant flowing patterns that adorned them.

Curiosity got the better of Ferdy and he wandered over to get a closer look.

'Come back!' whispered Boris fiercely. Ferdy ignored him. 'Look! This carving's just like the picture in the book.'

Boris followed.

'See? That's what I saw. No wonder Elvendor wanted his book back.'

Boris frowned as Ferdy pointed to a hooded figure standing on a tor. 'I'll bet that's Ikoseer. Look at her staff and the pattern down the front of her garment.'

Boris screwed up his nose, concentrating. 'I doubt it's her.'

Ferdy seemed not to hear him. 'What if it's a scene from the Battle of the Stones?'

Recalling his conversation with Yahdra, Boris looked for Elvendor but couldn't see him. 'I don't think it is,' he said, 'but if that's Ikoseer, then who are the other two? One looks like a knight.'

'I don't know. Does it matter?'

Boris focused on a tangled pile of fallen bodies. He caught his breath as he noticed that the shape of two of the battle shields among the bodies looked just like eyes—eyes that were staring back at him. He felt for Thrust and forced himself to look away. He grabbed Ferdy, but he had already turned away and was now looking up at the main ceiling.

'That's the same map too!' Ferdy said, pointing a finger.

Boris tried to remember the map Ikoseer had scribed in the sand, but this looked different.

'Can you see that mountain over there close to the border of Illingaith? I think that's …'

'White Timber Mountain.' The elven reply behind them made them both jump.

'The history of the Isle of Spheres is carved on my castle walls and ceilings. Do you recognise any of the pictures, Ferdy?'

'Yes and I'm so sorry I … borrowed your book, but I'm very pleased that it's returned to its rightful place now.'

Ferdy saw Boris' warning glance, but chose to ignore it.

'And we are most grateful for all you have done for us, Elvendor. Perhaps we could return the favour? As you know we are miners by trade, but beer brewing is a specialty too and Banters Den Ale is famous throughout …'

Elvendor held up his hand. 'Elves are not beer drinkers and we have no need for mining.'

'Oh, then I'm sure we could easily do something else. Building maybe?'

'We have the finest architects … unless you have seen something that needs improvement?'

'No, of course not,' spluttered Ferdy. Um, cooking?'

'I thought you might be more interested in why I have requested your presence again?'

'I … we are …' stumbled Ferdy.

But he was cut short as Elvendor made his way to the stairs. The twins hurried after him.

Boris felt the eyes of the elven figures perched on the top of the newel posts watch them as they crossed the floor to the bottom step. As he passed he gave a sideways glance at one with its stony stare guarding the entrance doors.

Despite his misgivings, Boris marvelled at the stairs. He didn't know if it was made of one fig tree or many. The entire structure was a mass of tamed roots and branches. There was no railing to hold onto but the evenly spaced balusters hung like living ropes from the high ceiling, suspending the structure in mid-air.

Elvendor stood by a doorway on the first landing and with a flourish ushered them in. It was a small bare room furnished with a circle of ten elegant wooden chairs, upholstered in the finest red brocade. In the middle of the circle was a low round table, with a plain round box on it.

Elvendor indicated for the dwarves to take a seat and sat down opposite them. The chairs were intimidating for the dwarves. Their feet dangled above the floor and the wings of the chairs were like those of a satisfied raptor that had caught its prey and driven it to the ground. They both wished they were somewhere else.

'I have been giving some thought to your quest,' began Elvendor. 'And I have made a difficult decision.'

All manner of thoughts flooded the dwarves. Their hearts raced.

Elvendor pointed at the box. 'I have been keeping something for Ikoseer.' He looked at Boris. 'Do you know what it is?'

'A gemstone?' offered Boris swallowing hard.

'What kind of gemstone?'

He hesitated. 'A Pentark one?'

The room was deathly silent. Elvendor was slowly wringing his hands as if he was unsure about what he was doing. He reached for the box in the middle of the table and pushed it towards the dwarves.

'Ferdy, would you like to open the box?'

Startled, Boris looked between the two. He opened his mouth to object, but Elvendor silenced him. Ferdy slid off the chair in disbelief and flipped the lid as if it was going to bite him.

It was the purple gemstone that Boris had dreamt about.

'Boris is correct,' continued Elvendor. 'This agate is one of the four outer Pentark gems. It was brought to me for safekeeping. War is coming to the Isle of Spheres and my people need me, yet I am also duty bound to fulfil my pledge to Ikoseer and the Queen of the Sun—to return the gem to the Pentark near Mirraway Castle in Illingaith. But time is running out. I cannot be in two places at once. I question whether, against my better judgement, I am wise to entrust the gem's return to two wayward dwarves.'

'Wayward?' protested Boris, sliding off his chair and standing beside Ferdy. 'Ikoseer said that we turned up to help her at just the right time,

and because we're bearers of Thrust it's our task to help find the gems
and return them.'

'Ah, so that's what you were really up to when you were attacked by the
anomirs.' Elvendor was tapping his fingers on the arm of the chair.

Boris looked down at the gem thinking how wonderful it would be to
own it. Watching him, Elvendor cleared his throat. Their eyes locked.
Boris mumbled something incoherent and jammed his hands in
his trouser pockets.

'So. I've made a decision,' said the King. 'As Boris has Thrust, I am
entrusting the gem to you, Ferdy.'

Ferdy was befuddled. 'Me?' Thoughts of staying with the elves dissipated.

'I'm not sure I want it. And what if I lose it, or get eaten by a wrake, or
attacked by an anomir?' He was getting hot and flustered. 'And I don't
understand why Boris can't have both of them.'

'What do you think, Boris?' asked the King. 'Should I entrust the gem
to your brother?'

Boris felt as if his soul was being laid bare. 'Umm … He did once lose a
handkerchief Mother gave him …' he offered feebly.

'But he did safely carry and return the most valuable elven book …'

*Only because we were captured and you asked for it*, thought Boris.

'But how will I carry the gem? In my jacket pocket?' Ferdy wished Marta
was there to reassure him.

Elvendor smiled. 'It can be carried in a common waterskin, stamped with
the seal of the Isle of Spheres. Wear the waterskin over your shoulder. If
you must take it off, keep it close.'

Elvendor reached inside his kingly garments and pulled out two items:
a small wide-necked waterskin and a cylindrical leather case threaded
to a strap. The twins watched fascinated as the King removed the gem

from the box. He placed it carefully in the skin and from a jug beside his chair poured some water in after it. Dipping two fingers in the liquid he wet the seams on either side of the skin, pressed them together and waited. Satisfied, he plugged the neck and sealed it. Holding the skin with both hands he uttered an Elvish incantation. Then much to Ferdy's consternation, he leant over the table, slipped the skin over the dwarf's hat, under his stubby arm and across his expanding midriff.

Elvendor placed the now empty box under the table. Then he unbuckled the round leather case, pulled out a roll of parchment and spread it across the table.

A familiar realisation of the quest settled on the twins. The map was almost the same as Ikoseer's. Boris had resigned himself to their task, but knew that once they left the protection of the Norfolk Woods, they and their ponies would be easy pickings for the enemy.

'Expecting us to carry this gem without any protection and return it to the Pentark is …'

'What is Thrust, if it's not protection?' interrupted the King, scanning the map.

Boris knew he was right. Apart from the connection between Thrust and the Pentark, he had almost forgotten the parting words of his father; "*it may see you out of a fix yet*".

Elvendor tapped the map. 'Here is Banter's Den.'

The twins squinted at the tiny dot then drew in their breath—the map was written in Elvish.

'We can't read this.' Boris swept his hand dismissively across the parchment.

'You don't need to,' replied the King. 'All you need is the topography.'

'But we won't know which road, river or mountain is which,' squeaked Ferdy pressing the point.

'This is Alfura, and here is the Pentark,' continued Elvendor, indicating the points on the map. 'Once you leave the Norfolk Woods, head westward until you find the corridor between this side of the Intrepid River and the Trading Mountains. Follow the river upstream until you reach the gap between the end of the Trading Mountains and the start of the Gorthwain Mountains. There is a bridge here.' He paused for a moment, to make sure that the dwarves were keeping up. 'Cross the river and turn right onto the Lake Road. This road will take you past Mirraway Lake and up to the castle.'

'Then it's about half the distance we've already travelled.' Ferdy scanned their old route and felt relieved.

'The distance might be shorter, but the enemy is thick on the ground. Therefore you must also travel in disguise.'

'What sort of disguise?' asked Ferdy.

'That has been arranged. As in earlier times, you will deliver a gift, a cart loaded with elven goods, to Mirraway Castle.'

Ferdy opened his mouth to speak but the King interrupted. 'You can even pretend that you stole it from us. That may put you in good stead and help you to become a small but useful asset to the enemy.'

'Asset? We don't want anything to do with them!' Ferdy shuddered.

'But it will put you very close to the Pentark,' insisted the King.

'Are Poppins and Aster going to pull the cart, then?' This was getting all too much for Ferdy to think about.

'No. I'm lending you a bullock called Ranger, along with a driver. The driver will look after Ranger and teach you how to drive him. Just in case. The ponies will be tied to the back of the cart and there are provisions for all of you.'

'Wouldn't it be easier to escape the enemy if we rode the ponies?' asked Boris.

'You are meant to be delivering a gift to the enemy, not running from them.' Elvendor looked down at the pair over the top of his glasses. 'Once you leave the Norfolk Woods, it will be more believable if you are sitting on the cart and holding Ranger's reins.'

The twins looked at him doubtfully. Raw memories of the anomirs' attack surfaced. Elvendor rolled up the map and returned it to the leather case. He made for the door.

'Are we going to the festival now?' asked Ferdy running into the back of the King as he paused.

Elvendor peered down. 'I'm afraid not. Plans have changed. But perhaps you could take a few more figs on the way down the stairs to stay your hunger,' he suggested.

Flaming torches threw a soft glow upon the steps as guards opened the entrance doors, and the dwarves wound their way back down to the waiting party below.

Boris descended with a heavy tread. He had been right about the gemstone. It did find them and his dream had come true too. A part of him was relieved that at least one of the gems was found and he wondered if Ikoseer would somehow know that. He grasped Thrust's hilt, the comforting heat reassuring him, and then heard the same musical note again. He started and glanced over the balustrade, but there was nothing there. And then his thoughts turned to Yahdra. He had promised to tell her about his adventures and he was annoyed at his forced departure. He focused on the shadows as they crossed the bottom step, and wondered if she was there.

They found the ponies, unsaddled and tied loosely to the cart. Aster and Poppins nickered a soft greeting to the dwarves as they went to pat them. Distracted by the drifting aroma of festival food, Ferdy was puzzled by the attention he got until he felt their soft noses nuzzling his pockets, looking for figs.

Elvendor introduced Ranger the bullock, and his driver Tom who held a long-handled whip with an equally long switch. Tom nodded acknowledgment. The twins thought he looked comical, disguised as a dwarf. He was far too tall and thin, although he tried his best to hide his upswept ears under a hat, made in Banters Den style. The separate band added to the rim and folded up did not quite do the trick.

Ranger was a huge beast. With their hats off, Boris and Ferdy could almost walk under his belly. Standing proud and calm in his halter and harness, glossy strings of slobber dripped as he chewed his cud. He turned to look at them, reached out and sniffed. Slobber stuck to their hats and he slid his tongue into his nostrils to clean them. The twins screwed up their faces in disgust and stepped back as his broad horns loomed above them, sweeping out and up to the cosmos.

Elvendor grasped Boris's shoulders and turned him around. 'I almost forgot. You might need this.' He slipped the leather case with enclosed map over Boris's neck and under his arm.

'Thank you.' Boris knew the King had not really forgotten.

'Go well young warriors. May the Pentark guide you both.' With that, Elvendor turned away and headed towards the festival.

Checking the waterskin, Ferdy suddenly realised he had forgotten to ask Elvendor how he was supposed to get the agate out of the skin and into the Pentark. But it was too late: King Elvendor was gone.

The twins hauled themselves up onto the cart and sat together on the wooden seat. Tom handed the reins to Boris from where he stood beside the bullock, and commanded, 'Get up, Ranger.'

Pulling against the upturned collar, Ranger headed purposefully into the night, with Tom walking beside him. Stars twinkled above them, and the rocking of the cart and familiar dull thud of the ponies' hooves following behind comforted the dwarves. Eventually, sleep overcame them and they leant back against the load, their bodies rolling to the rhythm as they snored and dreamt.

Boris dreamt that Ferdy had invited friends around to eat big mouthfuls of spiced honey coated walnuts washed down with draughts of frothy beer. And Boris was sitting by a winter fire toasting his toes and reading his favourite book, 'The Adventurous Tales of Yew'.

But when Boris opened the book expecting to see a sketch of his favourite hero, instead he saw Yahdra staring back at him with her mesmerising eyes, whispering that she had to fight for her kin and go to war. Boris felt his arms reach out to try and stop her, but it was useless. Holding his gaze, she pushed something into his hand, and then kissed him.

Confused, Boris' eyes shot open. He scrambled for Thrust as a brief flash of green dropped from the side of the cart. At once, he realised that Yahdra really had been there. He spun and stood on the seat, desperately scanning the trees behind them, but it was too dark to see. She was gone. When he looked down, clutched in his other hand was a lock of auburn hair.

Boris rubbed his eyes and slumped back with a leaden heart, knowing he would probably never see her again. He carefully coiled her glossy auburn lock around his fingers, brought it briefly to his lips and tucked it into an inside pocket. Ferdy was still snoring beside him, with the precious waterskin cradled on his tummy. Boris wondered again if the quest was worth it.

Pretending he'd had a nightmare, Boris leant against Ferdy again. With one eye shut and the other squeezed into a tiny slit, he watched Tom for a moment but it seemed that the elf had not noticed anything unusual. Once he was satisfied that no one had seen Yahdra, he relaxed as Ranger plodded on, heading west towards Mirraway Castle.

# CHAPTER 23

While Marta and her companions were heading south through the Ageless Forest, Volgor was peering over the gunwale as his boat rushed through the mouth of the Abyss River into Werthyn Harbour. Although the wharf of Port Werthyn was hidden from his view it was close, and the onshore winds carried the unfamiliar sounds of a working port to him.

He was in awe at the number of small fishing boats bobbing on the water. Strong-armed men were hauling in the longest nets he had ever seen, and when he saw that they were bulging with fish madly trying to escape, he began to salivate. There were also bigger boats with elongated woven traps stacked on their stern. He wondered what strange fish they caught from the sea.

Everything about the harbour excited him: the freshness of the salty air, the sparkling blue water, the strange sounds of wheeling seabirds, and the unmistakable whiff of fish. He was relieved to have made it to the port alive and now he just needed to find his way around the coastline to the monastery Attricus had told him about. He still pined for his companion and wished that he was there to see the amazing spectacle.

Unable to steer the boat and at the mercy of the water flow, Volgor finally dropped from the gunwale and squeezed behind the ropes heaped in front of the covered prow. He waited. It was not long before he heard voices shouting about the wayward craft. Then came the dull clunk of a rescue boat knocking against the hull. Soon, following bellowed instructions, an adolescent boy grabbed the painter, tied it to his dinghy and begun to row.

The sounds from the wharf grew louder and Volgor cautiously poked his head out from under the prow. The wooden structure was similar to the wharf at Riverbend, but was huge by comparison and bustled with sailors, fishmongers and hawkers.

Berthed at the wharf were three tall ships, just like the ones Attricus described. As they came near the first one, Volgor was shocked by the sheer wall of a wooden hull towering over them. Cautious, he leant out and tilted his head up to take in the full height to the crow's nest. Yes, there were the tall poles that he had dreamt about in the cave. They looked like huge trees growing out of the ship, but denuded of bark and foliage. He had never seen so many ropes and guessed they were to tie the poles down. Attached at right angles to each pole were several straight branches, each one shorter than the one below, and each with a roll of cloth roped to it except for one pole, which had an unfurled sheet of cloth tied to its lowest branch and a man inspecting it. *They must be the sails that fill with the westward winds*, thought Volgor. He watched the man release and re-lash it.

As they passed the three ships, he saw painted figurehead carvings jutting defiantly from each prow. The face of the middle one looked like the woman in his dream, with flaming red hair and a white dress with a gold trim that swept down to the waterline. Upon her head was a golden crown adorned with a blue star. Startled, Volgor felt for the aquamarine and King Tardor's short sword. He stared at her until she disappeared from view.

Carved across the stern and high up on the bow of each ship were their names: *Arcadia, Sirius* and *Sancta Maria*.

Taking care not to be seen by his rescuer, yet full of curiosity, Volgor looked further ahead and saw smaller boats being run ashore to unload their catch. Hitched to drays, teams of draught horses and oxen waited, with some teams already hauling full loads of what looked like pilchards towards the long row of sturdy buildings set back from the wharf.

Volgor put the sword between his teeth and waited. As soon as the boy turned away to steer the dinghy, the kurr grabbed the gunwale and scrambled over the side. He made a bigger splash than he intended, but kept close to the hull, hoping it would hide him for a few oar strokes. He saw the rower stand up and frown, scanning the water either side of the boat.

Although kurrs were good river fishers, Volgor hated getting water in his ears, but he had no choice. Holding onto the sword and taking a big gulp of air, he checked to see where the wharf was. Then as the boat pulled away, he dived.

He had never experienced such clear deep water and as he flapped his feet and swam, his eyes began to sting and he got his first taste of salty water. He hastily rose to the surface and drew water up his nostrils. Coughing and spluttering, he swam towards the bow of the *Sancta Maria*, hoping that nobody had seen him.

He worked his way along the hull to the stern, bobbing up and down until he could see the white carved dress of *Sirius'* figurehead draping gracefully into the water. Almost afraid, Volgor floated on his back and looked up at her.

He thought her long red hair looked as if the westward winds were blowing a gale. Her locks were full and wild, and the hair on the top of her head was the only part tamed by her starry crown. He didn't see her copper coloured eyes, but he thought she was beautiful. Even though her arm was not extended as it was in his dream, he was by now convinced that the aquamarine stitched in the pocket of his sodden jacket was connected to her and this ship.

He righted himself and watched the hustle and bustle of the wharf above. Having only Attricus's description of ships bringing spices and fine cloth to trade, Volgor did not really know what to look for. But there seemed to be nothing amiss, and he felt that that this part of the Isle of Spheres might still be safe from Onysius and Lord Mortimer.

Then he was distracted. A scrawny dishevelled child who had apparently been hiding behind a large wooden bollard, suddenly swung out on a thick rope and after dangling for a moment, shimmied to the *Sirius* and disappeared onto the deck.

Volgor glanced at the wharf then glided between the two ships until he reached the bow of the *Sirius*. Using the carved folds of the figurehead's dress, he worked his way along to where it blended into the hull. Now almost within reach of the wharf's piles, he realised that they were enormous. They were also encrusted with strange white shells. He swam over and ran his finger over a small cluster, pulling it back quickly as the sharp edges drew blood. There seemed no way that he could scale the piles. There were no ladders and a mat of green slime was growing between the shells.

There was no choice but to swim between the piles towards the shore, hoping that the shells would thin out to a point where he could climb onto the wharf unseen. From there he could observe the comings and goings on the *Sirius*. The piles were three deep under the wharf and he thought they would be easy to navigate, but as the sea rose and fell, with a strong current running through, he was pulled willy-nilly.

In his frustration, he clenched the Duke's sword between his teeth and began to swim overarm, unconcerned about any splashing sounds he might make.

But below him, a sea monster awoke. Releasing itself from a nearby pile it propelled itself gracefully towards Volgor as he swam above. It extended a tentacle and jabbed at his flapping feet. And when Volgor stopped and looked around, the sight of the short jewelled sword between his teeth made the monster tremble with excitement.

Volgor had no time to react. The octopus was on him in a flash. With eight tentacles wrapped around him, Volgor could not use his arms or legs, but, nearly out of air and not wanting to let the precious sword go, he struggled violently against his captor. He pushed his head down towards his hands and curling his body inwards was able to put the sword within reach. The current spun them round, and they began to tumble, hitting the rocky bottom in turn.

Volgor's lungs were on fire. He looked up at the daylight streaming through the blue-green water and unable to hold his breath any longer, let the sword go. As the last bubble escaped from his lungs he felt the tentacles loosen and his last thought before losing consciousness was that the sea monster must have been after the sword when it attacked him.

He came to, it seemed only minutes later, lying face down on the wharf with someone jumping on his back. It felt as if his ribs were going to explode with each blow. He vomited sea water, gagged and tried to breathe in—all at once.

Meanwhile there was a furious argument going on above him.

'He's mine.'

'No he's not. It was my hook that snagged 'im.'

'And it was me that hauled 'im in.'

'Only 'cause I was away getting sumthin' fer us to eat.'

'Yer always hungry.'

'Am not.'

'Are too.'

Still woozy, Volgor heard the sudden scuffle of boots and assumed the two above had decided to settle their argument with a wrestle. He tried to move his arms but they were tied to his sides. He twisted his hand hoping to feel the slight bulge of the aquamarine still in his pocket. His jacket was missing and the gemstone was gone! He thought the sea monster must have that too.

Then he saw his jacket crumpled beside a fishing rod nearby. He tried to lift his head, looking for the ship, but his head swam and he slumped again. Other people began to mill around as the fight evolved into a boxing match. He decided to wriggle to his jacket and get away.

'So … what 'ave we got here, lads?' There was a deep snarl from someone breaking up the fight by dragging one of them by the ear towards Volgor.

'OW! We were goin' to tell you we found 'im.'

There was a moment of silence and Volgor felt the crush of a large boot on his back.

'Yeah … we were going to,' said the other voice.

'Didn't know what 'e was though,' said the first voice.

'Never seen nothing like it,' confirmed the other.

'He's a kurr.' The boot pushed harder into Volgor's back, making him groan.

'Could put 'im in your auction. Sell 'im to the soldiers.'

Volgor froze. Soldiers?

Someone gave him a kick. 'Sale's on the morrow, so we won't even 'ave to feed him. Skinny thing though in't 'e?'

Volgor winced as pain shot up his leg.

'So you two, what's all this saying he belongs to one of you, and you're going to sell him?' demanded the man with the menacing boot.

'Ah … 'e's all yours master, but we did hook 'im.'

The boot eased off his back. 'You'll get your reward. I'm taking him to the shop and locking him in the storeroom.'

'What about 'is jacket? Might be worth sumthin' …'

The man with the boot noticed it for the first time. He walked over and picked it up, all sodden and soiled. He rolled it in his hands, inspecting the stitching. There was a tear where the fish hook had snagged it but despite its shabby appearance, it looked tailor-made and he suspected that his prisoner had stolen it.

'Throw it on the pile inside the wash door. We'll sell that too.'

Then the man threw Volgor's body over his shoulder and headed to the ground-floor shop set back from the wharf while the lads gathered his jacket and their fishing rods. With the blood rushing to his head, Volgor turned to check if anything was happening around the *Sirius*. Even upside down he could see that there was a lot of activity, and he worried that it was being prepared for sail.

But it happened that the same scrawny child shimmying along the ship's rope from the wharf was secretly watching as Volgor was carried through the shop's doorway. After they had all gone inside, the child returned to the *Sirius* and reported to his Captain.

Volgor was uncomfortable. They had dumped him in the storeroom, his clothes were damp, and he felt ill. His only joy was finding the knife that he had stolen from Onysius's kitchen, still tucked under his belt. It was a miracle that it survived the sea monster's attack, and his rescuers had been so preoccupied with fighting that they did not bother to search him. He was able to cut the ropes that tied him, but he heard them close the storeroom door with a crossbeam, and he knew that he would need the element of surprise if he was going to escape.

The storeroom was a small windowless room with a cobbled floor, filled with empty wooden boxes and old fishing nets. The walls and door were timber and if he put his ear to the door, he could hear muffled voices. He attempted to slide the blade between the wallboards to lever them apart, but he did not have the strength and his knife was too small. The only available light came from under the door and once night fell he would be in complete darkness.

Volgor knew he had to hide behind the opening door when he heard his escort coming for him. He hoped it would be the two bumbling lads who had saved him from drowning. He didn't want to hurt them, but they and their master were only interested in selling him to the highest bidder. His greatest worry was retrieving his jacket. He shuddered at the vision of the sea monster stealing Duke Tardor's sword. If he ever made it home to his family he would have the most amazing stories to tell them.

He was still thinking about the loss of the sword to the eight-armed beast, when he heard footsteps outside the door. As the crossbeam slid up he moved into position, his knife ready. The door was heavy and opened slowly. He watched as his two rescuers peered into the gloom. They pushed the door wider, frantically searching the boxes, flinging them aside one by one. Finally one of them spied the cut ropes. He spun round just as Volgor slipped through the door behind them.

There was a momentary delay before one of them yelled, 'Get the slimy little git.'

Volgor had no idea which way was out or where his jacket was, but he had to find it!

The shop was incredibly untidy. There seemed to be all manner of goods piled high: woven baskets, chainmail, old soldiers' uniforms, hats, pewter jugs like the one Onysius used to throw at him, pots and pans, broken chairs, books, candle holders, a dented gauntlet. Many other items Volgor didn't recognise. He needed more time. He hid by crawling under a table jammed with goods, but in his hurry his big toe caught the handle of a cup that clattered to the floor.

His captors were onto him. With one on either side of the table they were trying to grab him when the shop door opened and their master walked in. He bellowed when he realised that his prisoner was at large, scruffing one of the two by the collar and dragging him out of his way. Volgor saw a huge hairy hand reach for him and stabbed it. A roar filled the room as the man's bloodied hand flew to his mouth and he hit his head hard on the underside of the table. Amid the swearing and cursing Volgor jumped out and made for the open front door.

He squinted against the glare of the overcast day as he ran towards the *Sirius*, shoving the bloodied blade under his belt. But as he weaved his way through the crowd his heart sank. He knew he had to return for the jacket. He ducked beneath an ox cart and leant against the inside of the wheel. As he caught his breath, he peered between the spokes. The crowd was all heading in one direction—to stand outside the very shop he had just escaped from.

At first he did not see the large outdoor display of secondhand items ready for sale but then he spotted the jacket—it might be easier to steal than he had thought. Buoyed by this, he looked around for some sort of disguise. He grabbed a straw hat and a shawl that had been thrown onto the seat of the cart. Both were far too big, but he put them on anyway.

So, with the wobbling hat sitting just below his eyebrows and the shawl dragging behind him he made his way around the gathered crowd and headed towards one side of the store façade, avoiding the large group of soldiers milling on the other side. Once there, he gathered up the shawl and holding onto his hat, manoeuvered among the crowd's legs. Most people tolerated him but some took exception and he couldn't avoid being jostled and even trodden on. He stood one row back from the front and watched as the sale proceeded. He had never been to an auction before and he watched several sales before he understood how it worked: The person offering the most money got the goods. But Volgor had no money so he had no choice but to steal his jacket as soon as possible.

Peering between the legs of the crowd he got his first real glimpse of the seller, the man he had stabbed in the hand. He looked just like the ruffians in Jimpiragh, and Volgor grinned with satisfaction whenever he moved his bandaged hand and grimaced with pain.

But as he was working his way further to the right he stopped dead. A chill ran through him. On a box at the front and centre of the first row, sat the strange pointy-eared creature from his dream of the port. Beside it on the box rested a three cornered pirate's hat decorated with three large white feathers. Fascinated, Volgor moved closer.

Using the box as cover, Volgor stood right behind him, realising that the pirate creature was a purchaser too when the next item was held up for sale. The bidding began. It was his jacket! Aghast, all Volgor could do was watch.

It still looked old and drab although the seller went to great lengths to point out that the garment had once graced the halls of a king. It was held up high, but nobody stepped forward to confirm such a wild declaration. The first bid came from the box in front of him. Judging by the murmur that ran through the crowd, Volgor concluded that the bid must have been quite high, but apparently it was not enough for the auctioneer, so he created a higher one by pointing to someone in the back of the crowd.

The price rose considerably. The soldiers craned their necks to see who it was. The creature upped the bid. The ghost at the back matched it.

The creature purred smoothly. 'Before I make another bid I would like to see the stitching you have so beautifully described.'

The auctioneer hesitated but then came forward. Perhaps without its owner selling it, the garment might achieve a better price.

'My eyes are not what they used to be,' crooned the creature. 'Would you mind bringing it a little closer? Please?'

The crowd moved back a little, leaving Volgor partly exposed. His heart thumped as the jacket was almost within reach. He dared not look up but just then the mood changed. A woman pointed at him and shrieked, 'That's my hat!'

As everyone turned to stare, the creature snatched at the jacket, but it dropped to the ground. Unable to believe his luck, Volgor seized it, tossed off the hat and shawl and pushed his way hurriedly through the legs of the crowd towards the ships. The auctioneer roared and the horde erupted into pandemonium.

The cocked hat creature chased after Volgor, gaining on him with every bound. He was almost trampled as he sprinted under a team of draught horses waiting near the *Sirius* for salted pilchards to be unloaded.

But this gave him an idea. He stumbled on two empty fish baskets, jumped in one and pulled the other after him. He waited for the uproar to subside. Panting heavily, he felt for the aquamarine in the jacket pocket. It was still there!

Volgor hugged his jacket, keeping his knife at the ready. He could hear folks along the wharf looking for him but eventually they left empty handed. Exhausted after all the excitement, he fell into a deep sleep.

It was cold and dark when he finally woke. His legs were cramping and he knew that he needed to stretch. Disorientated by hunger and dehydration, he sensed that the wharf was moving. He tipped the fish basket over, pushed the inner one out with his feet and rolled out after it.

He was rubbing his bleary eyes and swaying on his feet when he suddenly realised that he was on the deck of a tall ship. He could see the wharf some distance off to the port side but the sails were still lashed.

'*Sirius* is at anchor,' said a voice behind him.

Volgor spun and reached for his knife but it was still in the basket. It was the same weird creature with the cocked hat.

'What are you?' Volgor demanded, looking up at him perched on a wooden cover. The creature was watching with a haughty expression.

'I am a cat. My name is Tibbs and I am Captain of this ship,' it replied, slowly grooming its whiskers with unsheathed claws.

'Are you a pirate?' Volgor remembered Attricus's warning about Mortimer's pirates patrolling the outer islands.

'That depends on your point of view.' The cat studied him. 'I've been waiting a fortnight for you and your friend to turn up.'

Volgor was dumbfounded. So they had been spied on.

'Where is your companion, Attricus? It appears he didn't make it. What happened?' The cat licked its paws and washed its face.

'We were attacked by a wrake. Attricus stabbed it with Duke Tar-' Volgor sniffed, wiping away tears. He halted.

The cat stopped and stared at him. 'You had the Duke's sword when you arrived. So where is it now?'

'Under the wharf. Stolen by a … a …' Volgor flapped his arms wildly, trying to demonstrate what he saw.

'Ah yes! An octopus,' finished the cat, turning to glare in the direction of the wharf. The fluffy ginger tail swished irritably.

'I almost drowned!'

'But you didn't. And here you are, just as you were meant to arrive.'

The cat looked around to make sure that they were alone.

'Do you still have the *other* item?'

Volgor's eyes widened. The cat knew about the aquamarine. And when he nodded his understanding, the Captain appeared to smile at him.

'You must be hungry. You need a drink and a soft warm bed. Get your knife and follow me.'

Overwhelmed, Volgor obeyed. As he was about to enter the bowels of the ship, he thought of Attricus again. He looked to the east, remembering the white cliffs and the sphere of light that guided the ships at night. Instinctively he touched the gemstone in his pocket and could have sworn that he felt it pulsate.

# CHAPTER 24

Far away, in the Ageless Forest Marta and Frovin were sitting in front of a fire while the badger ate a mound of roasted acorns. It was a week since the anomir's attack on their group, and from looking at Artorus's map, Marta knew that the forest stretched three hundred and fifty miles from the Intrepid River in the east, to the Arifer Mountains in the west.

Marta knew that they were heading south and getting closer to Jimpiragh Castle and danger. She felt very safe as they rode through the forest, sensing that the oaks protected them, and Snowball seemed unharmed after bravely attacking the anomir. Marta had a newfound respect for the pony.

And Frovin seemed to be content to change his nocturnal ways, happy to be foraging for worms and acorns on the forest floor as they rode along. He spent most nights curled around his bloated tummy, snoring.

It was the happiest Marta had been since being forced to leave her father, but as she sat by the fire, thinking, she realised just how fleeting this time of joy and rest was.

'Did you know that my family's sett in Greenwood Forest is underneath a small grove of golden oaks?' Frovin suddenly asked her. 'I took Boris through there on the way to find Ferdy. During the rescue, Boris let go of the rope securing Ferdy too quickly, and his poor brother plunged headfirst into a prickly thicket. You should have seen it!'

Frovin started to guffaw. He rolled around, holding his heaving tummy, making Marta smile. But his talk of the twins also started her wondering what had happened to them since the anomirs attacked them in the Norfolk Woods.

'How did you meet Boris?'

'He stepped on me as I slept under a pile of leaf litter.'

Marta noted his tone of indignation and grinned, imagining Frovin's swift retaliation.

'Why weren't you sleeping in your sett?'

'I was on my way there. But I was a little … indisposed. I was feeling unwell and decided to rest awhile.'

Marta looked at him askance. 'You mustn't have been too sick to look for Ferdy though.'

'I wasn't. Once I was awake, I soon rallied. As my dear mother always said, "Badgers have a strong constitution".'

Marta saw his sheepish look and wondered what he had really been up to.

'I was actually on my way back from your world when that happened.' He was watching her.

Marta stared at him. 'But how did you cross through the Arkfeld?'

'I walked through it. Anything from the World of the Soul can pass through an Arkfeld.'

Her initial look of doubt suddenly brightened.

'Now I understand how my mother and other refugees were able to cross the border during the invasion. I was always told the Arkfelds were there to protect and keep the three worlds separate. And were impossible to cross.'

'Now you know differently.'

'But now it seems that anyone or anything can cross now.'

Frovin tried to reassure her. 'Remember that Ikoseer said there's still some magic left. And didn't you feel resistance when Artorus pushed Famrod through it?'

'But it's still not strong enough to keep the enemy out,' she insisted. 'And how did Lord Mortimer manage to breach their border and attack Illingaith all those years ago?'

'The Prince of Darkness used sorcery to breach the other Arkfeld between his world and this one.'

'Why didn't the Queen stop him?'

Frovin shrugged. 'I don't know, but I expect he used some sort of awful magical trickery.'

'If he can fool the Queen then what hope do we have against him?'

'We do it by trying to look as unimportant and ordinary as we can. Why do you think Ikoseer left us?'

Deep in thought, they both stared at the flickering flames.

'How did you open the Arkfeld?'

Frovin crunched another acorn. 'I stood in front of it, waited for a portal to open and then stepped right through it.'

'That's not what I meant,' she chided, giving him a glowering look.

'Purity of the heart opens it.'

'So why aren't the hearts of the people in my world good enough to open it too?'

'They have to awaken to the spirit magic that's around them first.'

'They can't do that if there's no magic in the World of Man.'

'No magic? Then perhaps they haven't looked hard enough.'

Marta pursed her lips but said nothing. She picked up a fallen leaf, tracing the indented lines along the leaf's crisp brown fingers. The pattern reminded her of the creeks and rivers on the map, and the veins in her hands.

'Is there something special about the border of oaks between my world and yours?' Marta asked.

'I'm sure there is. Local badgers call those particular oaks the 'waking trees'.'

'Why?'

He shrugged. 'That's what we've always called them.'

'Are they part of my world or yours?'

'Although they're between the Arkfeld and your border, they still belong to the World of the Soul.'

After a pause Frovin added, 'And don't forget that this whole quest started along that border. Boris and Ferdy were heading north through it to the Rolling Hills when they found your apple, and that's where Boris found me too. I was sleeping there beside the old Greening Road when you and Artorus must have passed me.'

He paused. 'Had you realised that?'

Marta shook her head.

'And then Boris needed my help to find Ferdy. Oak trees are magical. Can you feel them in this forest?' he asked.

'Yes. They must be very strong. The darkness hasn't affected them at all. I saw a drawing of an oak tree in a book that belonged to my mother. The tree looked so old and wise with its lowest branches resting on the ground. And now I come to think of it, to the right of the tree was the faint outline of a building. There was a name on the building ...' Marta shook her head, 'but I can't remember what it said.'

Frovin stopped eating. 'Was that in the same book where you saw the drawing of the Pentark?'

Marta nodded.

'Do you remember what else was drawn in it?' he prodded,
watching her closely.

Marta shrugged. 'There were other sketches but I was quite young.
I don't remember them all, but I do remember a two-page sketch of
a flaming bird.'

'That's the revered Firebird! Historically it flew from the sun, bringing
the Lightenstone with it. Took the outer gemstones from the gnomes and
then placed them in the Pentark with its beak. Afterwards the Firebird was
burnt to cinders by the Pentark's power.'

Frovin paused. 'Statues of the Firebird are relatively common in the World
of the Soul. You would have seen some in the Ascension Mountains.'

'Yes, but I had no idea that the Lightenstone originally came
from the sun.'

'That's why Lord Mortimer wants it.'

'What a pity the Firebird couldn't help us with the Lightenstone now,'
she said wistfully.

Frovin grunted in agreement. 'Do you still have your mother's book?'

'I looked for it after she died, but I never saw it again.'

'Something might trigger your memories about the other sketches. I'm
grateful for any snippet of information about the Lightenstone that
could assist me.'

The next morning, Marta was woken by the crunch of leaves under boots
as Patrayus approached with a hot drink. The filtered light through the
trees played across his handsome youthful face. Green hazel-flecked eyes
met hers as he squatted down to pass the cup. Marta looked away. Most of
the time, he distanced himself from her, only speaking to her in a non-
committal tone. He was clearly ambitious. She envisaged him in Artorus'
position one day, but something seemed to have changed in him since they
had been in the Ageless Forest.

Warming her hands round the cup, she asked, 'Where's Artorus taking us?'

'He's the only one that can reveal that. My task is to protect the group.' He gave her a gentle smile.

'We aren't going to the Abyss River, are we?' she probed. He shrugged.

'But I don't want to leave the Forest. I feel safe here.'

Patrayus gave an understanding nod but said, 'You have to come with us Marta. We can't leave you here on your own.'

'Why not? Frovin's the one who needs to protect the Lightenstone. Can't you take him to retrieve it and then return to the Forest? I could stay here with Snowball and then rejoin you.'

'Snowball must come with us too. She's proven that she will attack anomirs. We need her.'

Then he said: 'Wasn't your amulet charged by the Queen of the Sun? So that when your courage faltered …' Patrayus let his question fade.

Marta's cheeks reddened. 'Who told you about that?'

'Very few are given the Queen's blessing,' he reminded her. He stood and left her to her thoughts.

Angry tears welled. Putting her cup down she felt for her amulet and stared into the trees. 'If you expect me to continue on this quest Solara— send me a sign.'

There was a long silence and Marta wondered if anyone had heard her plea. Then a soft white feather floated lazily from the branch above and landed gently at her feet. Startled, she looked up. The striking orange eyes of Sheen, Ikoseer's owl, returned her stare.

Marta stood and picked up the feather. Then she stepped back as a group of forest animals suddenly appeared from behind the nearby trees. She saw the larger animals first: a brown bear, red and roe deer, a wild boar, and then moving in front of them came otters, beavers, stoat, lynx, hare, red squirrel, field mice and lastly grouse, ducks and woodcock. Together, as if on an unheard signal, they bowed their heads.

Marta realised that before the invasion they had roamed free throughout Illingaith, Magirus and Arctus, and the Ageless Forest must be their last sanctuary. Until the Lightenstone was returned to the Pentark, they would be forced to remain in this forest. Wanting to share this special moment with Frovin, she looked towards the camp, but he and the others seemed to have seen nothing.

She turned back just as the animals melted into the trees. In their place and to their left, a huge grey wolf emerged, standing tall and stiff legged. Distinctive scars ran across its nose and under one eye. With ears erect and hackles up, it bared its teeth. Marta started, and shrinking back, glanced quickly towards the camp. After a brief stare, the wolf disappeared.

Remembering Ikoseer's warning about the wolves of Skag, she knew it was an ominous sign. She hurriedly tucked the feather into her pocket and made for the campsite. Behind her, Sheen flew silently up through the canopy, transforming into an eagle, soaring beyond the reach of the anomirs, then turning northwards towards White Timber Mountain.

After breaking camp, Artorus immediately headed south towards the Abyss River. Marta did not reveal what she had seen, but the experience remained vivid and she kept looking for the animals as they wended their way through the trees. Snowball seemed aware of them too, because she often pricked up her ears, nickered and tossed her head.

Artorus halted them at midday on a ridge along the southern border of the forest. Marta noticed that between them and the river was a mostly barren plain.

Artorus explained, 'This is called Sarsen Plain. It might be difficult to see from up here, but between us and the river is a circle of ancient Sarsen stones, a large outer ring and a smaller inner. Until the invasion, they were used for sun festivals.'

Fascinated, Marta could just make out the megalith. Then it triggered a memory: there was a partial sketch of tall stones in her mother's book. Some distance away and to their far right she noticed a small group of mountains.

'They're a massif of the Arifer mountain range but are more jagged and prominent,' Artorus said as they dismounted. 'There's a road on the far side, leading north to Mirraway Castle and west to Jimpiragh.'

Pointing back across the plain he added, 'The river is only a few hours away but we'll stay here until after dark.'

Marta's anxiety rose. She remembered Ikoseer saying that the wolves of Skag hunted at night.

'Are you taking us all the way to the Abyss River?'

'Yes.'

'And where to after that?'

Artorus hesitated. 'We're going to cross it.'

Marta felt ill. 'Into Asilodor? But that's where Onysius lives.'

She gave Frovin a questioning look. Despite his attempt to appear innocent, she was sure that this information was not news to him.

Yoska came forward. 'We didn't want to frighten you Marta, but you know that we have to go where the Lightenstone is.'

Her eyes widened. So, the Lightenstone must be in Asilodor!

'We'll cross the river into the dukedom at daybreak tomorrow,' said Artorus.

'Is there a bridge or barge there?' asked Frovin.

'Not this time. The horses will have to swim across.'

As Snowball nuzzled Marta's hand she thought again about all the forest animals she had seen.

Artorus noticed her pensive mood. 'We don't want to go deeper into enemy territory Marta, but take some comfort from the fact that Onysius doesn't know that the Lightenstone is hidden in his dukedom.'

Her stomach churned and she shivered. 'Is the Stone in Jimpiragh Castle?'

'No. But it is in Asilodor.'

She sighed with some relief, but then with a flash of anger asked, 'Why didn't you tell me any of this earlier?'

'If I had, wouldn't you have tried to return to the World of Man?'

Marta looked down at her feet. He was right.

'It's a matter of judgement. As it is, I didn't intend to tell you until after we'd crossed the Abyss tomorrow.' Artorus spoke gently and as if reading her thoughts he added, 'I changed my mind because from here, the land will be swarming with soldiers, wrakes and boorlings. So …' He paused a moment. 'If there is a clash with them, we ask for an act of service from you.'

She looked from the knights to Yoska and back again. 'What do you mean?'

'If they attack us you must escape and take Frovin to the Lightenstone without us.'

Marta's heart thumped. 'How can you expect me to do that if I don't know where to go?'

'It's too dangerous to reveal the Stone's hiding place just yet. Use your amulet as a guide. Snowball and Frovin will be with you. If we're separated, we'll rejoin you as soon as we can.'

Marta looked at Frovin and the pony in dismay. 'But … Snowball can't outrun wolves,' she blurted.

Artorus raised his eyebrows. 'Wolves?'

'Don't the wolves of Skag come from around here too?'

'I've seen no wolves.' Artorus looked at her quizzically. 'But Snowball has proven that she can hold her own.'

'We're travelling by night and we have the advantage of surprise. I'm hoping the enemy won't notice Snowball leave us if we're attacked,' explained Yoska in a soothing tone.

'Of course they'll notice her! It's not long after the full moon— and she's white!'

There was an awkward silence as Marta gently stroked the pony's neck.

Artorus was insistent. 'I have to obey Ikoseer's instructions. Each of us has our part to play. I gave my word to her that I'd assist Frovin to fulfil the Queen's decree.'

Marta helped prepare their meagre lunch with fearful emotions. Afterwards she unsaddled Snowball and gave her a longer brush than usual. She tried to sleep until nightfall, but the vision of the huge grey wolf kept pushing into her mind.

The moon was still rising when Artorus led them down the ridge and onto the plain, towards the Abyss River. Once they were on level ground the warhorses flanked Snowball, giving her some protection.

Marta felt drawn to look back at the Ageless Forest, but whenever she resisted the urge, the vision of the wolf rose again. She shivered and clasped her mother's amulet, silently praying for safe passage.

Frovin had a better vantage point riding on the warhorse's rump again. Although his night vision was not good, his sense of smell was, and he spent most of his time sniffing the air.

'I expect we'll arrive at the river after midnight,' said Artorus.

Marta cringed at the thought of having to swim across the cold river at dawn. She turned her thoughts to the Sarsen rings. But as they got closer, the cool night breeze carried the sounds of gathered men and they could see the faint glow of firelight against the huge stones.

Artorus led them away from the megaliths and almost onto the path of a battalion of foot soldiers. A warning caught in Frovin's throat as the first of them emerged suddenly from behind a crag. They had no armour and the sound of their tramping feet was smothered by the sandy plain. The knights backed away into the darkness, their horses close around Snowball. Marta held her breath as the men marched past.

It was the first time they had seen the scale of the enemy's forces, but Artorus could see that these men were battle weary. Their heads drooped, their shoulders sagged, and for some, their rhythmic march was more of a tired shuffle. It seemed to take an age for them to pass but there was some cloud cover and if any of the soldiers saw the horses, none sounded the alarm. Perhaps they did not have the strength to care.

They remained on alert and the rest of the crossing was uneventful, but Marta's sense of fear increased as they approached the trees bordering the Abyss. The wind picked up and the closer they got, the more violently the branches tossed and swayed. It took her straight back to Greenwood Forest: she felt that someone or some thing was watching them.

Artorus appeared to notice it too. He halted Famrod, and drew his sword, staring into the trees. Yoska slid off Famrod's rump and stepped away, thrusting Honorex forward. Patrayus lifted Frovin back onto Snowball and readied his blade. Famrod snorted, striking out with a front hoof, and with ears erect and head lifted high, Patrayus' horse pranced, white foam forming under his breastplate.

Marta was sure that she saw a fleeting movement as the first wolf of Skag emerged from the shadows. Her mind whirled. She recognised his scars. *He's the wolf I saw in the Ageless Forest. I should have told the others what I saw!* she thought.

The pale yellow eyes stared at her as the pack followed him into the moonlight. Sniffing, with heads down, the pack encircled them.

The three horses jostled into position, and with rumps together, turned outwards to face their enemy. Yoska stood between Snowball and Famrod. When the scarred male attacked, Snowball leapt. Striking with her front hooves she bared her teeth and grabbed him, holding on as the wolf snapped at her windpipe.

'Look out!' Marta yelled as the next wolf attempted to grab Snowball's back leg. The pony kicked hard and the animal yelped in pain. But he got up again waiting for another chance. Another wolf joined them.

Frovin jumped down into the fray, savagely grabbing the rear of the closest animal, and tearing its soft underside. As it bled and tried to retaliate, Frovin was bitten on his back by another. He spun with ferocity and attacked again, this time at the throat.

The screaming of the horses and the yipping of the frenzied wolves and the war cries of the men brought a huge shadow into the moonlight to watch. Some of the wolves sensed it. They slowly backed away, snarling. With its head down, the charging silhouette was upon the wolves. It was too late for the scarred male. Impaled on the animal's horns he was tossed aside.

Marta had never seen such a massive bull. As he spun to charge again, his shoulder muscles rippled, his pitch-black hide glistened. More wolves were repelled as Yoska and the knights raced to drive their swords deep into the gored enemy.

Artorus bellowed: 'GO, MARTA!'

As Marta looked frantically for Frovin, Patrayus threw him back up onto Snowball behind her, and then slapped the pony's rump. Marta met the knight's gaze for a brief moment before they fled into the trees and towards the Abyss River.

As if irritated by their sudden presence, the boughs whipped low, lashing Marta's face. And the slap of the leaves stung. Then, just as in Greenwood

Forest, the roots came slithering along the ground, twisting and snatching at Snowball's hooves. But the valiant pony met every challenge, nimbly jumping over branches that kept falling before them, constantly changing direction. Until they finally made it to the river's edge.

Without hesitation, the brave little pony plunged into the cold dark waters of the Abyss and began to swim.

# CHAPTER 25

Marta picked crusty sleep from her eyelids and rubbed her face hard, wincing at the scratches and bruises made by the lashing branches the night before. Standing up, she pulled her shawl closer and stamped her boots on the ground. She glanced at Frovin curled up against Snowball's belly and saw him watching her through a half-closed eye. He immediately roused himself, yawned and stretched his stiff back.

'We need to get going,' he said. Snowball stood up and shook herself.

'Shouldn't we wait for the others?' Marta was scanning the far bank of the river.

'If they were going to follow us, they'd be here by now,' replied Frovin.

She watched the rushing waters. 'So, what do we do?'

'We have to look for the Stone without them.'

'But where?'

'You saw Artorus' map. Can you remember any strange symbols marked in Asilodor?'

She shrugged. 'No. The only thing we know is that it's not in Jimpiragh Castle.'

'Then all we have to guide us now is your amulet.'

'How, though?' asked Marta. 'All the Queen said was that the Stone knows we're on our way.'

'Perhaps you need to take it off and see what happens,' he suggested.

Snowball took a few steps and nudged her.

'When I stood by my mother's grave I promised her that I'd never remove it.' Marta was holding the amulet close. It felt hot in her hand.

'You took it off for the Queen,' he reminded her. 'Or perhaps we could just wander aimlessly throughout Asilodor until the others eventually find us.'

Marta glared at him.

'It's just us now Marta. There's no one else here to help us.'

Snowball rubbed her face hard against Marta's back and pushed her forward.

She looked back at the pony. As Snowball nickered, a lump caught in Marta's throat. She lifted the necklace over her head and squatted down so Frovin could see. In the shadow of the river trees, they stared at the four-pointed charm. Snowball pricked up her ears, resting her muzzle on Marta's shoulder.

'See? It's not doing anything.'

'Patience. Wait.' Frovin reached out his paw and gently touched it.

Marta gasped. 'The tips are moving around.'

When the amulet stopped, the point now facing south-west began to glow royal blue.

'Now turn your hand west towards Jimpiragh.' Frovin leant closer.

As Marta turned her hand, the amulet moved until the blue point again faced south-west.

'Now turn your hand in the opposite direction, towards the Intrepid River.'

'It's showing us which way to go,' he blurted excitedly as the blue point again moved to face south-west. 'We have to follow it to the south-west.'

Marta stood up crossly, tucking the amulet out of sight.

'I don't care where we go as long as we get away from these trees.'

'We'll be out of here soon enough. But in the meantime, they do keep us hidden from the anomirs. The enemy will be on alert once they find the dead wolves, and don't forget that the ones that retreated when the bull charged, will by now have formed a new pack.'

Marta shivered as she remembered the image of the impaled wolf.

'Did you know about the bull?' she asked him as she saddled Snowball.

Frovin nodded. 'He's in our folklore. I know the story of Toros, the Bull of the Abyss. The Abyss in the story isn't a river but a dark fathomless gap beside a temple! The bull appears when the next novice is ready to grasp his horns and ride him across the gap.'

As if reading Marta's thoughts he then added, 'You can't cross unless you've conquered your lower emotions.'

Marta frowned. 'What's on the other side of that Abyss?'

'According to the story, you have to cross to know.'

'The World of the Soul is a very strange place. I wonder if my mother knew about Toros.'

'I'm sure she did. There are stories about other animals too.'

Marta's stomach grumbled, reminding her how hungry she was.

'We haven't got any food. It's with the others,' she said, changing the subject.

'We have acorns,' said Frovin eyeing off the slight bulge in one of the saddlebags. 'Would you … er … like some?'

Marta screwed up her nose. 'No thank you, they're too bitter.'

She scratched Snowball's forelock while looking in vain for some juicy grass. 'There's nothing here for Snowball either.'

'I'm sure we'll find something for her on the way, but we can't worry about food now. We have to keep going.'

They finished packing and headed away from the river to the south-west, both wondering where the amulet was leading them, and what would happen when they got there. Marta checked several times that they were going in the right direction, and within an hour they emerged from the river trees.

In front of them stretched an expanse of semi-vegetated sand dunes. Unknown to them, and several days away to the west, were the hills which Volgor and Attricus crossed to escape from Jimpiragh Castle. Some of the dunes were held together with clumps of long dry grass, but most were bare, the gusting wind sweeping sand high into the air. Marta noticed that the branches of a nearby copse of haggard trees had been forced into almost horizontal positions.

They both felt uneasy and Frovin leaned over Marta's shoulder. 'Artorus did warn me about something.'

'He said the terrain in Asilodor was unstable ground, and that it constantly changes. We don't want to get lost out there. The only thing we can trust for direction through here is your amulet.'

'But only the bare dunes would shift, wouldn't they?' she asked, feeling his warm breath on her cheek.

He hesitated. 'I hope so.'

They skirted around the base of the dunes where they could, but sometimes they needed to climb between or over them. When Snowball began to struggle in what seemed to be ever deepening sand, Marta dismounted to walk beside her.

Initially, she looked back to familiarise herself with any unusual landmarks, but one dune blended into another, closing behind them like the falling pages of a book. Sand worked its way into her boots and the blustering winds whipped the grains across her face, stinging her sore cheeks, and drying her lips. She remembered the scarf that Patrayus had given her when they were crossing Calligan's Plain. She found it in the bottom of a saddlebag and gratefully wrapped it around her head.

The hot dry sand squeaked beneath her boots as they trudged on and she yearned for the cool river waters far behind them. Frovin was uncomfortable too, but his spirits lifted when he spotted a thicket of straggly trees.

'Look!' he said.

Tugging on the reins, Snowball pulled Marta along, making for the shade. After lifting Frovin down, Marta unsaddled Snowball and drank a little from the waterskin. Then cupping a hand, she carefully poured water for Frovin and Snowball. She unwound the scarf and slumped down, leaning against the closest trunk. Shielding her eyes, she squinted against the glare of the sun off the pale dunes.

'You should check your amulet again. That should be south-west,' said Frovin, pointing.

'It's too hot and I'm too tired to go on now,' replied Marta. 'We should stay here until dusk.'

'I just want to know if I still have my bearings right.'

With a deep sigh Marta wiped off the beading sweat and pulled out the amulet. As she looked down at it Frovin noticed her mouth open slightly, as if to say something.

'What is it?' he asked, moving closer.

The amulet began to transform. Now, all the tips changed into a dull translucent blue. They both stared at it.

'We must be almost there,' said Frovin stepping back.

'Why? What's happening?'

Frovin spoke softly. 'The Lightenstone does know that we're on our way to it. Because the Queen charged your amulet, it's guiding us straight there. The closer we get …'

Marta stared at him.

'So, Ikoseer must have known about it the whole time. And Artorus, he must have killed the gambler and taken me from the market. Because I had my mother's amulet?

'I feel as if I've been tricked,' she added with rising anger. She wondered if Patrayus knew about it too. She glared at Frovin, her eyes blazing. 'Did you know?'

He held his paws up in defence. 'No, but don't forget that I did offer to carry it for you when we were at the Intrepid River. It would've been impossible of course. But what you should be asking is why did your mother have it. She came from the World of the Soul, didn't she?'

There was a brief silence. Frovin spoke first. 'After the invasion, she must've taken it with her into the World of Man. And now you have it. Perhaps it's just meant to be returned to this world.'

'Then why didn't Artorus, Ikoseer or the Queen explain that and ask for it back?'

The same question had flitted through Frovin's mind. He shook his head.

'I don't know why but I'm sure that the Lightenstone must be close by, and once we find it we can get out of this horrid place.'

'But the amulet's all one colour now, so it can't direct us anymore.' Marta was staring at it, moving it around.

'True,' conceded Frovin, 'but that doesn't matter. The Stone can't be far from here.'

'Wait,' she whispered, peering closer and shielding the amulet with her hand.

Frovin leant forward and saw it too. The blue tip that pointed south-west was now a pulsing fleck of red light. Wide eyed, they stared at each other.

'We have our compass back,' said Frovin.

'Kraa! Kraa!'

They were startled by the sudden sound of a forest raven. Marta hid the amulet and stood up. Frovin fluffed his fur, sniffed, and then emitted a deep growl. The raven hopped casually through the branches and stopped in front of Marta. With head cocked, it leant so close that she could see the detail of his beady brown eyes.

'Be careful,' warned Frovin. 'We're in Asilodor now and we don't know how long that bird's been listening to us.'

'But it might be a messenger, like the one that spoke to Ikoseer in the Lux Mountains,' she said.

'Or it could be a spy sent by the enemy,' Frovin insisted. Marta felt Snowball nudging her again.

Unsure if the nudge was a warning, she stepped aside. But Snowball stretched out her neck and after beak touched muzzle, the excited raven began to hop, bow and flap, making low gurgling sounds that ended with a shrill alarm. As Snowball nickered, the raven gave her a cheeky peck on the nose, making her pull back sharply. Screeching 'Kraa! Kraa!' the messenger flew away, disappearing over the dunes.

'What did the raven say?'

Frovin gave Marta a blank look. 'I don't know,' he said.

'Don't all the animals in the World of the Soul speak the same language?'

'Mostly, but I find ravens too hard to understand ... it was the same when the raven came to Ikoseer in the Lux Mountains.'

'So, apart from Ikoseer, Snowball must have understood the raven then too.'

'I expect she did,' said Frovin.

'Can't you just ask Snowball what the raven said?'

Frovin was indignant. 'I've already done that. We animals often use our minds to communicate with each other, but Snowball's keeping this information to herself. I'm assuming that Ikoseer sent the raven to find her and also to check up on us.'

Marta touched her amulet, thinking about the nudge that Snowball had given her to take the charm off.

'How could I be so ignorant?' she said. 'She's understood everything we've said to each other too.'

She studied Frovin. 'But you already knew that.'

'Not at first,' he replied defensively. 'Only some animals are born with the gift of understanding human speech. It wasn't until I was a teenager and overheard humans speaking for the first time that I knew I had the gift too.'

Then leaning closer he added, 'But Snowball's true home is in Arctus with Ikoseer.'

He saw Marta's shocked reaction.

'I suppose deep down, I already knew that,' she said quietly. 'She was stalled beside Helios and the other ponies when I arrived with Artorus at the Wayfarers' Cave. I guess Aster and Poppins live with Ikoseer too.'

'I'm not so sure,' he replied. 'Those two remind me of the scruffy moor ponies from Magirus. Herds of them used to forage in Greenwood Forest before it was tainted by Lord Mortimer's lot.'

Marta patted sweat from her face and looked out at the monotonous dunes.

'So, why doesn't Snowball talk to me like you do?'

'The World of the Soul works in strange and mysterious ways,' replied Frovin.

'You sound just like …'

' … Ikoseer!' finished Frovin with a chuckle.

'You don't know why, do you?' she challenged.

'No, I don't,' he admitted, 'and I'm not going to ask her why because anything to do with sages is always a mystery. Besides, she speaks to me in symbolic riddles anyway.'

'Oh?' Marta was running a hand gently down Snowball's face. 'If you told me what she said perhaps I could …'

'Animal riddles are different to human riddles.' Frovin averted his eyes. 'And as protector of the Stone, Snowball's riddles are for me,' he insisted, despite a quick nip suggesting otherwise.

'So, if Ikoseer's sent a message to Snowball, then we should let her decide when it's the right time to leave here,' said Marta.

'Agreed,' said Frovin. But Marta noted a reluctant tone.

Snowball didn't attempt to move so Frovin curled up to sleep. Marta leant back against the tree trunk and closed her eyes, pondering the pony's secrets.

It was several hours before Snowball nudged Marta awake. Frovin roused himself and sniffing the air, looked out at the dunes while she saddled up. Although the heat of the day had waned, Marta still felt faint from the lack of food and water and her stomach was grumbling. She lifted Frovin onto Snowball's rump and grabbed the reins. She kept checking her amulet as Snowball headed directly south-west.

The sun was almost below the horizon when jutting rocks became visible just ahead. Marta threw the reins over Snowball's head. Now with greater freedom, the pony's steps quickened as she led them up through a narrow gap between two large rocks, and then onto a rubble path that zigzagged down the other side.

Marta started as her eyes feasted on the sight below. Surrounded partly by pale cliffs and bare dunes was a small elongated oasis. Tall trees with large spiky fronds bursting from the crown grew around the water's edge, and beside the oasis was a stone building.

They rushed to the water to drink. After a long cool draught, Snowball playfully splashed about as Marta replenished the waterskin. Then she wet Patrayus' scarf and used it to clean her face and neck. She enjoyed the coolness as she washed her hair and Frovin ventured in for a brief but joyful swim.

Marta stood up and wrapped the dripping cloth around her neck. She relieved Snowball of her saddle and bridle, leaning the saddle against the trunk of the closest tree. She threw the bridle on top.

'What do you think that building's for?' she asked. Without waiting for an answer she left the others to take a closer look. She was closer now and the building was much larger than she had first thought. It was a plain structure made of large square blocks of granite, with the craftsmen's tool marks still visible on the surface. Three deep but narrow stone steps led to a plain arched wooden door, with a keyhole but no handle. She squinted at the faint word engraved in the stone above the doorway.

## ARAMARK

'Be careful!' warned Frovin, quickly coming up behind her as she took a step towards the door.

'Do you think the Lighten- …'

'Shhh!' Frovin hissed and looked around as she glanced down at her amulet. Marta's breath caught in her throat. She whispered and pointed towards the door. 'Oh, my goodness. I think it must be in there.'

'Don't go any further! Show me.'

But Marta ignored him and with her eyes fixed on the amulet, she took another step.

'Marta, stop!' Frovin growled.

'It's changing with each step!'

'What?' Frovin was straining to hear her and clinging to her trouser leg. Dragging him with her, Marta took one last step. Without thinking, she knocked.

'What are you doing?' Frovin was nearly fainting in shock when the door trembled and in a tenor voice asked, 'Who's knocking?'

Frovin managed to say, 'Don't answer!'

'Who is before me?' insisted the door.

Horrified, Frovin tugged hard on her trouser leg. 'Marta, we have to go.' Then realising what he'd said, he clamped his paw over his mouth.

'Ma … r … t … aa,' responded the door.

'Roselin … Ma … r … t … aa,' the voice continued, as if it was thinking.

'No, no,' she corrected. 'I'm Marta. My mother was Roselin.'

'Maria. Roselin. Marta.' The door was now quivering.

Her eyes widened. 'How could you know that? Maria was my grandmother's name.'

'I have been expecting you.'

Marta's heart thumped loud in her ears and she grasped the amulet. All four tips were now sharp points, each one glowing blood red against the pulsing royal blue centre.

'I … I … I've got … Frovin here too.' She felt for his reassuring paw, giving him a brief glance.

'Indeed. You have. But the amulet carrier must enter alone.'

'No! Why?'

'And your entry comes with a warning,' continued the door. 'You must gaze into the Well of Forgetfulness.'

Frovin began to jabber, his paws flapping in exasperation. 'No. *No!* It's impossible. There must be another way. You can't go in there Marta. If you can't conquer the Well of Forgetfulness … you'll … you'll be in there … forever! And I won't be able to save you! Even Snowball won't be able to help—maybe not even Ikoseer!'

Just then a small white feather floated down and settled against the bottom of the door.

*The Queen is with me*, she thought.

As she tightened her grip on the amulet, the sharp points dug into her palm. Marta stepped forward, placed her right hand over the keyhole and pushed her whole weight against the door. Frovin screamed.

The door gaped wide and swallowed her up. Her garbled words sounded from somewhere inside. 'We have no choice, Frovin.'

And in reply the door echoed, 'She has no choice, Frovin.'

In anguish, the badger raked his long claws down the ancient door and attacked the keyhole savagely with his teeth. But he knew it was pointless. He soon gave up and slumped against the door, whimpering. Frovin had overheard Artorus talk about this place to Yoska. This was Aramark, the discarded and forgotten spirit temple of the World of the Soul. Within it was the Well of Forgetfulness: the perfect place to hide the Lightenstone.

Dark ominous clouds gathered and Frovin looked south towards the World of the Dark Night. A sudden bolt of lightning struck so close that he jumped in fright. The electrical charge stood his hair on end. In that moment, he knew that the Prince of Darkness' attention was now on them.

Lightning was soon cracking all across the sky, and the badger looked frantically for Snowball in the fading light. He saw that she too had turned to face south, her head erect and her ears pricked up. With a final glance at the door, he bounded down the steps and settled between the pony's front legs. They could watch the storm together.

'Toil,' said Snowball aloud as the first heavy raindrops splashed in the dry sand.

Frovin had no idea what she meant. But he knew that all they could do was wait.

# PART 5

# STRIVE

# CHAPTER 26

'Whoa, Ranger,' said Tom, in his soft elven brogue, halting the bullock on a high bank beside the Intrepid River. It had taken Tom, Boris and Ferdy a fortnight to travel from Alfura in the Norfolk Woods to the main bridge between the Land of Magirus and the Land of Illingaith. Staying out of sight, the three of them watched the bridge below. It was busy, with enemy soldiers and an assortment of travellers all waiting to cross.

'Are they the Gorthwain Mountains?' Boris pointed to the range running on their side of the Intrepid River and stretching into West Arctus.

'Yes,' said Tom. 'Their snowy peaks march on until they plunge into the Mother Sea. They separate Arctus from Illingaith.'

The elf pointed across the river. 'And that mountain range is called The Veils.'

With a sweep of his hand southward, he explained. 'They continue almost to the border of Illingaith and Asilodor. We're too far away to see much, but through the gap in that mountain range is Mirraway Castle. The castle has ten silvery white spires—some of the spire tips are visible from here.'

Boris and Ferdy frowned and blinked, but couldn't see them.

'On Way Fell, further up and to the right of Mirraway Castle is the Pentark. It doesn't have spires, but twelve small liths.'

Ferdy shuddered, clutching the waterskin that held the Pentark's agate. He remembered Ikoseer saying that there were twelve outer gems and immediately envisioned having to climb one of the Pentark's liths to put the agate back. But which lith? And he hated heights. It always made him dizzy when he looked down.

Tom was becoming fond of the twins. Although they began by travelling on the cart from Alfura, within two days the dwarves abandoned it altogether and, with Tom's help, were riding Aster and Poppins again.

Despite Elvendor's instructions, Tom had long given up trying to teach Boris and Ferdy how to drive Ranger. Boris's temper was too short and the bullock's response to his demands was to turn and stare, which only made Boris curse and blow more. And, although Ferdy showed potential, Ranger either refused to move or became unsettled. Once he even deliberately trod on his foot when he got too close, and Tom had to push Ranger off when Ferdy's painful yelling seemed to echo for miles.

'Another day's ride to Mirraway then?' Boris estimated the distance from Elvendor's map.

'Bit more than a day, I should think.' Tom nodded at the bridge. 'And judging by the swarm of soldiers coming and going, you're likely to be searched and given an escort.'

'I didn't know the bridge would be so beautiful,' murmured Ferdy.

'It's called the Lake Bridge because the road on the other side is called the Lake Road,' said Tom. 'You can't see it from here, but there's a large lake on the plateau below Mirraway Castle.'

'Yes, Elvendor told us about it.' Boris patted the rolled leather case with the enclosed map, then said, 'I can't read Elvish, but …'

'We elves believe that this bridge holds the stars in place and was built by our ancestors, the celestial light weavers.' Tom gestured to the sky. 'And every elf has a light thread connecting them to the weavers.'

Boris gave Tom a sceptical glance. There was no thread of light coming out of Tom or any other elf he had seen. But he did agree that the bridge was beautiful. Milky white and graceful, it arched high over the mighty Intrepid River.

'I don't want to go down there just yet,' said Ferdy watching the activity below. 'I'd rather we waited for nightfall.'

'It won't make any difference when you go. You'll still be stopped and searched by the soldiers,' said Tom.

'Better that it's dark.' Ferdy was twiddling the tassel around the neck of the waterskin.

Boris suddenly turned to Tom, his eyes narrowing. 'You are coming with us, aren't you?'

Tom stared into the distance.

'Tom?' Ferdy sat up in his saddle.

'I wasn't intending to go any further,' he admitted. 'King Elvendor ordered me to return to Alfura once we'd reached the bridge.'

Ferdy began to splutter in his native Dwarf, which only Boris could understand.

Boris replied. 'See? Elves can't be trusted! First, we were deserted by Ikoseer, and now by Tom.'

'But how can we deliver the gifts to Mirraway?' squeaked Ferdy, turning towards the elf. 'We can't pull the cart without Ranger!'

'I know,' he said, idly scratching the bullock between the horns as Ranger tilted his head in blissful response.

Ferdy brightened. 'So, that means you'll come with us then?'

'Yes. But because our plans have changed, I must dress properly. And I agree with you that it's best we wait until dark,' said Tom, leaving the bullock, to change from his ill-fitting dwarf disguise to his elven clothes.

To ease Ferdy's anxiety, Tom sent the dwarves to search for mushrooms and herbs among the trees. An hour later, and using their turned-up vests as makeshift baskets, they headed back to the cart. But despite Tom's warning, as Ferdy passed a hawthorn bush, he just could not resist the urge to push his way through it to spy on the bridge.

'Alright, I'm coming!' he muttered moments later, as he felt the jab on his taut breeches.

He backed slowly, being careful to avoid the thorns, but was suddenly scruffed by his jacket and jerked out. Mushrooms and borage spilled everywhere. Ferdy was utterly confused. His captor let go of him and then, grasping the back of his belt, pulled him up and suspended him at waist height.

'Spying on us, were you?' asked a gruff voice, his arm straining under Ferdy's weight as the dwarf wriggled and kicked.

'N … No, just picking mushrooms.' Ferdy was thinking furiously.

'Doubt it,' said the soldier. 'Who did you think I was when I poked you just now?'

'N … No one.' Ferdy was trying to lift his head as the waterskin was perilously close to slipping off his neck. From the corner of his eye he saw another pair of legs arrive.

'Look what I found,' said the first soldier. 'Haven't seen a dwarf since we invaded Banters Den, near the World of Man.'

The other soldier grunted in agreement. Ferdy jammed his mouth shut, adding to their suspicions about him.

'Mushroom picking or not, you're coming with us.'

Dropping him roughly to the ground, they bound his hands and marched him down the bank and towards the bridge. Ferdy frantically searched for Boris among the trees, but couldn't see him.

By this time Boris realised that Ferdy was not with him. He retraced his steps until he found Ferdy's scattered mushrooms and herbs. He rushed back to Tom, with bright red cheeks and almost out of breath.

'It's happened again!' Boris fumed, dumping his mushrooms, and stomping on the ground, his arms wide and his fists clenched.

Tom waited for him to finish.

'It's just like in Greenwood Forest when Ferdy was taken by the soldiers and wrakes,' puffed Boris. 'Frovin helped me to find him then, before the wrakes could eat him. But who's going to rescue him this time!'

'It's not as bad as you think,' said Tom calmly, holding up his hand.

'What do you mean? Do you realise what he's carrying? I tried to tell Elvendor.' Boris shook his head.

'The soldiers will take Ferdy to their leader first,' insisted Tom.

Boris glared at the elf. 'They'll drag him before Onysius!' He was now on the verge of tears.

'Perhaps not.' Tom tried to reassure him. 'Onysius lives in Jimpiragh Castle and it's a long journey from there.'

'What are you suggesting then?'

'We continue as planned, except that you hide in the cart. Once we've crossed the bridge, you can escape and look for Ferdy … but we'll have to free the ponies before we leave.'

Tom saw the pain in Boris's eyes. 'That way they'll have a better chance of survival. If they stay with us they'll be butchered and fed to the wrakes, and you wouldn't want that to happen, would you? If they can make their own way back to the Norfolk Woods, they'll be safe.'

'What about Ranger? Won't they eat him too?' asked Boris.

'They have a superstition about killing oxen. It comes from the story about a bull called Toros.'

Boris nodded, although dwarves were too practical to be interested in such things. He stared at Aster. He had come to love the ponies, and quiet tears trickled into his beard as he helped Tom unsaddle and groom them for the last time. He cleaned their feet as Marta had shown him, told them they must return to Alfura immediately and, cutting a lock of his hair with Thrust, he plaited it into Aster's mane.

Boris stayed with Aster and Poppins until twilight. Then he gave them a final drink and an apple each from the cart. He hugged them and kissed their soft noses, all the while singing quietly in the language of the dwarves. They dropped their heads so he could reach to take off their bridles and nickered when he stood waiting for them to go, but wanting them to stay. Aster reached out and nuzzled his face, her whiskers tickling him and her lips smearing apple juice, sticky and sweet, on his skin.

'Boris?' Tom broke the magic.

'I know,' he said, trying to keep the quiver out of his voice. 'All right, you two, keep out of trouble and behave yourselves for once in your lives.'

The ponies tossed their heads and spun round, kicking up their hooves and galloping away, back along the Intrepid River towards the Norfolk Woods. Boris sniffed, wiped his nose with his sleeve and threw the bridles into the back of the cart. With a leg-up, he got in.

'Get up, Ranger.' Tom was now resplendent in elf green and driving the bullock from the cart seat.

Hidden beneath juicy red apples in a large wicker basket, Boris swayed and bumped to the cart's rhythm, pulled along by the steady and surefooted Ranger. It reminded Boris of the day he and Ferdy had wagged school to hide under the hops in their neighbour's cart at beer brewing time.

Their mother had been furious. 'You're lucky you weren't thrown in with the wort and drowned,' she'd scolded, wagging a finger and threatening all manner of punishments. Their father, on the other hand, had been secretly proud of his spirited sons.

Boris heard Tom command, 'Come here, Ranger,' and knew they must be turning left onto the Trading Road, the main road to the bridge. He felt the cart turn, heard the rumble of the wheels on the new surface, and soon after that came the surprised shouts of soldiers and sentries. Boris swallowed a giggle as he thought of them suddenly catching sight of Ranger, with his massive horns and shoulders taller than the soldiers' heads, moving towards them from out of the dark. That would have startled them enough without the sight of the small elf in charge of such a beast.

As the cart was stopped by soldiers near the bridge entrance, he strained to make sense of the muffled voices. Then someone lifted up the rear of the cover to see what was underneath.

'Bring me a torch,' a voice barked. 'Hold the cover up.'

Boris peered through slits in the wicker basket, just able to see the sweeping flame.

'What've the elves sent?' asked another voice.

'Food!' said the torch bearer. 'Calabash, turnips, dried herbs, figs, onions, apples, fresh mushrooms …'

'Ah. And elven wine.' Someone was dragging a large earthen demijohn closer and exposing the ponies tack behind it.

Boris tensed when a bridle moved and the bit rattled.

'Why bring us horse tack? Even the saddles are too small for anything except ponies.'

A long pause followed. Boris imagined that the three soldiers must have looked at each other.

'Show me the bit,' said the torch bearer. 'This grass is fresh, so where are the ponies now?'

A chill spread through Boris at the ensuing grunts. He felt for Thrust as he saw one soldier grab a handful of the fresh mushrooms wrapped in a cloth. 'And what about that dwarf we caught earlier. He'd been picking mushrooms too.'

'Bring me a wrake!' barked the torch bearer suddenly, sweeping the flame further in.

Boris knew he must act fast. But as he carefully released Thrust and jostled to get his feet beneath him, he dislodged a few apples. Assuming that the soldiers must have seen them drop, he exploded from the basket. Blindly grabbing a turnip, he threw it wildly. It hit the closest soldier hard across the bridge of his nose.

The soldier's hands flew to his smarting eyes as the torch bearer roared, 'Get him!'

But as the third soldier lunged for him, Boris, aided by the element of surprise, trampled and slashed past them all, jumped from the cart, sprinted through a gap of confused sentries and disappeared into the night. He did not slow down until the shouts of his pursuers had faded. Finding a fallen log, he collapsed behind it into a heaving heap. Now bereft and alone, he buried his head in his hands and wept, ruing the day he had crossed with Ferdy to the Lux Mountains, and everything that followed.

Early the following morning, Ferdy, with his hands still bound, was tied to a steel ring on the back of the cart, next to Tom. The elf whispered that the ponies had been set free, and added how relieved he was to see that Ferdy still had Elvendor's waterskin. But Ferdy was more worried about Boris. He constantly looked out for his brother, hoping that he was coming to rescue him.

Meanwhile the soldier was attempting to make Ranger pull the cart away from the bridge entrance, where he was blocking the traffic. But the bullock casually went on chewing his cud and refused to shift.

Eventually, the soldier realised that he would have to release Tom if he wanted the cart moved. Tom commanded, with the lightest touch of his whip, 'Get up Ranger,' and the cart rattled across the bridge under escort from Magirus into the Land of Illingaith.

Walking behind the cart, Ferdy was awed by the bridge. It reminded him of the architecture in Alfura, grand, upswept and elegant. And now that he was closer, he noticed that the ropes securing it were a complex plait of honey coloured and milky-white strands. Somehow, the weave reminded him of the crown hugging Ikoseer's head.

He didn't mind being made to walk behind the cart. He was able to take in his new surroundings and soon realised that there were more travellers between Magirus and Illingaith than he had expected. Although the soldiers had been rough with him, it was the wrakes he kept his eye on, particularly as one of the soldiers rode a wrake horse, a boorling. It was the first time he had seen one. As he thought what an ugly creature it was, he remembered Ikoseer's warning: *'Try not to get tangled up with one if you can help it'.*

But Ferdy did not think that they were in danger yet. He had overheard the soldiers' chatter and knew that they intended to take them all to Mirraway Castle first.

*They must think we know something.*

After crossing the bridge, Tom said 'Gee off, Ranger,' and as the bullock obeyed by turning right onto the Lake Road, Ferdy was tantalised by the pungent aroma of fresh mushroom and wild herbs in the cart.

They continued west along the Lake Road, which ran parallel to the Intrepid River. By late morning they were close enough for Ferdy to snatch glimpses of the tips of some of the spires of Mirraway Castle, rising behind the mountain peaks that swept in front. Soon the whole castle was revealed, bit by bit.

It had obviously been built within a part of The Veils that formed an almost complete circle around it, except for the gap that Tom pointed out. Ferdy immediately thought of the slumbering rock giants who, according to Ikoseer, created the Isle of Spheres. He wondered if they had also created the rocky fastness in order to protect the castle.

Now completely visible through the gap, Mirraway Castle, breathtaking in its silvery white beauty, rose up like two giant hands, joined at the wrists with the palms turned out. And the ten elegant spires were like long fingers pointing to the heavens.

*It looks like a giant chalice,* thought Ferdy. *If the stars or moon fell, it could catch them.*

Ferdy couldn't stop staring. He wanted to look for the Pentark but the cart blocked part of his view. He also did not want to raise the suspicion of his minders.

They camped by the lake. Ferdy was given bread and water for his supper, and left tied to the cart. He made a feeble attempt to climb into the back to find some more food but the rope was too short. So he slept underneath on the rocky bed, cradling his precious cargo. He was woken the following morning by a fresh chill in the air and the sound of Tom re-hitching Ranger. And, most of all, by growing hunger pangs.

The winding road from the lake up to the castle took another two hours. By the time they reached the main entrance Ferdy was feeling sick to the pit of his stomach. He looked furtively at the guards. They stepped aside for Ranger to pass through the barbican and then ordered the wrakes to put their weight to the winch and raise the portcullis.

He felt numb as he was untied from the cart and forced through the curious crowd that was gathering, all gawking, poking or jeering at him. And as he was brought before his inquisitor, any remaining vestige of bravery deserted him completely.

Ferdy was unbound. He rubbed his wrists vigorously as he was taken to a large room with a star pattern inlaid in the centre of the stone floor. There he was told to stand in the middle of the star, facing the throne. He was alone. Looking down through an arched window and to his right was a portly middle-aged man displaying what Ferdy recognised as the rank of Commander. It was several minutes before he turned around. Ferdy recognised the man and looked away.

The Commander was leaning on the sill, studying him. 'We've met before.'

'Have we?' Ferdy attempted to sound nonchalant.

'You look like the dwarf that the scouts and I found dangling from a tree branch in Greenwood Forest. Although if it is you, your beard and belly have grown somewhat since then.'

'It wasn't me you saw. There are lots of dwarves in Greenwood Forest.'

'Not anymore there aren't,' shot the Commander, easing away from the sill. 'So, what's your name, dwarf?'

'F … Ferdy.'

'So, Ferdy, do you know Ikoseer the Sage?'

'Everybody's heard of her.' Ferdy swallowed hard as the knee-high boots slowly circled him.

'When was the last time you saw her?'

'Never seen her.' Ferdy could feel his face flush.

'Mmmm …' The Commander stopped and rested a hand on the pommel of his sword. 'So, if you weren't the dwarf I saw in Greenwood Forest, then you must be the dwarf that crossed the plateau to the Lux Mountains.'

Ferdy started. 'No … no … That wasn't me either.'

The Commander locked his fingers and cracked his knuckles.

'By the reckoning of one of Onysius' wrakes, two horses and two ponies accompanied by dwarves and humans, left the Trading Road and crossed to the Lux Mountains. That same wrake was sent to find them.'

'I don't even like horses. Why would I be doing that?'

'That's what I'm trying to find out.' The Commander was watching Ferdy intently. 'But dwarves keep appearing out of nowhere. The dwarf up the tree escaped from my camp, rescued, according to the wrakes, by another dwarf. Dwarves crossed with humans to the Lux Mountains. Goblins reported that two dwarves on ponies fled from an anomir attack at the Norfolk Woods. And yesterday, you, Ferdy, were caught gathering mushrooms near the Lake Bridge, while another dwarf escaped from the elf cart that brought you here this morning. In the cart there were fresh mushrooms and tack belonging to two ponies—yet not a pony in sight.'

The Commander paused, then bending from the waist, he levelled his face with Ferdy's. 'Not that it matters … but a wrake on a boorling was sent to track the ponies down.'

The Commander noted a slight flicker in Ferdy's eyes. 'Now why would a dwarf travel with an elf anyway? Are they not natural enemies?'

Ferdy assumed the Commander was referring to Boris, escaping from Tom's cart. 'Perhaps the elf didn't know he was in the cart.'

'Hhmmm … maybe. I'm sure the elf will tell me. What's his name? Tom?'

Ferdy shrugged, tightened his grip on the waterskin and looked down at the star.

The Commander turned and slumped on the throne. He hooked a leg over an armrest and slowly rubbed his hands together. 'Where's the Lightenstone, Ferdy?'

Ferdy's mouth dropped a little. He was trying not to give anything away.

'Come Ferdy, dwarves are miners. Stones are your specialty. What did the Queen do with it? Did she hide it down the mines of Banters Den?'

'I don't know. D … d … don't the dwarves of Banters Den mine for metal? Not stones?'

'So they do,' he mocked. He beckoned for him to come closer.

Ferdy's mouth felt dry and his tongue thick.

'Hurry up!'

Ferdy shuffled to the tip of the star, keeping just out of reach of the Commander's arms.

'You have an unusual waterskin. It's quite small.' The Commander leant forward, gesturing for Ferdy to take it off and hand it over. 'Where did you get it?' he asked, turning it slowly in his hands.

'I stole it … from the elves,' said Ferdy haltingly.

The Commander raised his eyebrows, rubbing his thumb over the seal stamped into the leather and furrowed his brow.

'From Tom?'

Ferdy nodded.

'Then you're just a common thief.'

'Or … an opportunist?' suggested Ferdy, staring hard at the wall behind the throne.

'Why steal a waterskin? One is much the same as another, except that this one has the seal of the Isle of Spheres.'

'I was thirsty.'

'You were close to a river full of water.'

Ferdy thought it prudent not to comment.

The Commander shook the skin, listening to the water slosh. 'But there's still something unusual about it.'

As he began to study the sealed top Ferdy coughed and ventured, 'Anything elvish is strange.'

'So, have you ever been in the Norfolk Woods?'

Ferdy shook his head vigorously. 'I wouldn't dare go there.'

The Commander suddenly sat up, scowled, and twisting the tassel tight around a finger, barked, 'So, what were you doing spying on the Lake Bridge then?'

Ferdy took a step back. 'I was lost,' he said hurriedly. 'I was supposed to be going to the Rolling Hills but then I lost my map and …'

Ferdy could see the veins in the Commander's neck begin to bulge.

'Here, I'll show you.' Ferdy was desperately searching his pockets until he found what he wanted. He pulled it out, dirty, tattered and squashed. Holding it by one corner, he gingerly offered it to the Commander.

The Commander put the waterskin beside him and took the grubby object.

Ferdy held his breath. It was the introductory letter his mother had written. The twins were supposed to give it to their cousins in the far north when they arrived after leaving Banters Den. Unfortunately, it was written in Dwarf, except for two words, 'Rolling Hills'.

Ferdy watched the Commander run his tongue around the inside of his mouth and pout as he scanned the message.

'And I didn't pick the mushrooms or herbs either,' offered Ferdy. 'I was so hungry I stole those from the cart too.'

The Commander looked up from the letter, considering his prisoner.

'Hmmm. I could make use of a thief,' he said returning the letter to Ferdy who gratefully stuffed it back in a pocket.

Reaching down beside the throne, the Commander picked up a royal goblet Ferdy hadn't noticed before and held it out to him.

'Take it,' he said.

Ferdy moved cautiously forward and wrapped his chubby fingers round the stem of the goblet. His eyes bulged and he almost retched as the Commander somehow popped the stopper on the waterskin, tipped it up, and poured the water into the goblet.

*How did he do that? Elvendor sealed the top with an incantation!*

The Commander leaned back into the throne. 'Let's drink.'

Ferdy looked into the water, brought the goblet to his lips and sipped. It was the most delicious water that he had ever tasted. He tipped the goblet up and drank the lot before the Commander could stop him.

Grabbing the arms of the throne, the Commander slid to the edge of his seat, his smouldering eyes bursting into flame.

'And you are a greedy little thief too,' he snapped. Jamming the stopper in the waterskin he threw it back at Ferdy's feet.

Forcing himself to keep eye contact, Ferdy put the goblet down and slowly picked up the skin, hoping that the precious gemstone was still inside. He carefully slipped the skin back over his head, reminding himself that the agate was the reason he'd been sent by Elvendor to Mirraway Castle. But now he had just swallowed the water, the stopper was loose and the agate was literally within reach of the enemy.

The Commander began tapping his fingernails on the carved lion's heads on the arms of the throne. It reminded Ferdy of when Elvendor appeared to waver about whether he would entrust the agate to him and Boris.

Suddenly the Commander asked, 'Do you know who Onysius is?'

Ferdy managed to nod.

'And you know that he's looking for the Lightenstone?'

Another nod, but this time a chill of foreboding began to creep into Ferdy's bones.

'Onysius has put me in charge of the search. Our intelligence points to a quickening. Goblins on anomirs have found dead wolves near the Abyss River, some gored, some stabbed. There were bovine, warhorse and pony prints around. So something is afoot.'

Ferdy shrugged and shuffled a little, attempting to appear ignorant of this pleasing news. But the Commander was not so easily fooled.

He leant forward. 'Ferdy, when I find out where the Lightenstone is, you're going to steal it for me.'

Ferdy began to splutter in Dwarf.

'Or I could feed you to the wrakes instead?'

Ferdy hung his head as Elvendor's warning about becoming a *small but useful asset to the enemy*, echoed in his ears.

'You can sweat in the scullery until I want you. I wouldn't advise you to try and escape from the castle. And you are forbidden to go beyond the barbican. Do you understand?'

Ferdy nodded.

'Guards!' The doors to the throne room opened. 'Escort the prisoner to the scullery and put him to work. He can sleep with the servants in the kitchen.'

Holding the waterskin close, Ferdy turned his back on the goblet and flanked by the two guards, trod heavily back through the tall gilt doors. As the doors closed, the Commander mulled over a recent memory that niggled at him.

Although he could not read Dwarf, there was a Dwarf word in Ferdy's letter that he had seen before. It was something that Onysius showed him. And then he remembered. The same word was embroidered in red on a small white handkerchief found by a wrake beside the Trading Road. Ferdy or someone he knew had crossed to the Lux Mountains!

'He's a liar as well as a thief,' he said to himself, but then smiled in grudging appreciation of the dwarf's audacity.

∽

Boris had not stayed hidden behind his log for long. He soon rallied and worked his way back to the bridge later that same night.

Early the next morning, he took off his hat and squeezing between two boulders, watched as Ferdy and Tom crossed the bridge under guard. He followed the travelling party by sight until Ranger's head was just a bobbing black dot on the road to Mirraway Castle.

He dismissed the thought of trying to cross the Intrepid River, in any other way than by bridge. Fearless and force fed by the melting snow of the Gorthwain Mountains, the raging torrent thundered past. As he watched the rush of water, the image of the purple agate suddenly came into his mind. Artorus had said that two of the outer gems were cast into a river. *I wonder if they're in this one?*

Acting purely on instinct, Boris twisted round, feeling for Thrust. He managed to work the blade free and dragging it up against the boulder, held it out in front, pointing the blade at the river.

'Is there a Pentark gem in the Intrepid River?'

Boris stared at the blade for a moment, and then grabbed the hilt tight with both hands. 'Is Ferdy carrying the agate from Elvendor?'

Thrust reacted so swiftly that it almost pulled out of Boris' grip. The blade shot upwards in the opposite direction, sending a shiver up his spine.

*The Queen was right*, thought Boris. *Thrust does have more secrets to reveal.*

So was it possible? Two of the outer gems the dwarves needed to find were in one of the rivers: the Iscador, the Abyss or the Rubicon River.

'Well, we're not going back to look for them. We don't have the time and we're too close to the Pentark,' he told Thrust. 'For now, Ikoseer will just have to be satisfied with the agate that Elvendor gave Ferdy.'

He gave Thrust a respectful pat, and slid it inside the front of his vest. After a few moments of reflection he began to study the elaborate girders of the bridge, and decided that if he could climb up to them from the river bank he might be able to work his way across the river, undetected beneath the bridge.

There was nothing more he could do before dark, so he snored gently in his rocky bed until the early autumn sun was replaced by flaming torches, and the reassuringly faint new moon. He wriggled out from the boulders and jammed on his shabby hat. He gripped Thrust and inched his way down the ridge, peering through the dark and taking care not to dislodge any stones.

The excitement of the previous night seemed to have waned. There were fewer soldiers now and the wrakes and boorlings were gone, but Boris kept downwind just in case and gradually edged closer to the roaring water that would blanket any noise. Whenever the light from a torch beamed from the sentry gate he crouched down to mimic a rock. When he was close enough to the huge pylons rammed into the riverbank, he estimated their height and cursed that his rope was still in the cart. But, as Thrust suddenly began to pulse in his hand, he smelled something familiar; he froze as a whiff of sweet smoke drifted towards him. He climbed up behind the closest pylon and crept along. He hugged the bank until he saw a hooded figure in the shadows below, standing on a flat rock and leaning back against the bank, as if waiting for someone. He seemed unaware of his presence. Boris crouched down again to watch.

The burning glow of 'baccy', as dwarves called it, rose and fell in the bowl of a pipe. Only a few wisps of smoke escaped from the figure, somehow forming into a ball shape in the air. Each puff increased the size of the ball, until, as Boris watched in fascination, the smoker held the pipe away from their body and with short bursts of breath here and there, started to sculpt the wisps.

Slowly Boris realised that the ball of smoke was beginning to look just like him. His mouth fell open as the figure turned, and his own smoky reflection followed, still hovering in the air. Instinct told him to run, but his legs felt as if they were set in stone. The figure blew again. As the smoke disappeared Boris' eyes widened. Forgetting about the soldiers, he scrambled down the bank and in his enthusiasm, almost toppled both of them into the water.

'What are you doing here, Yahdra?'

'I found the ponies in the Trading Mountains. When I saw your hair plaited into Aster's mane and realised that Tom wasn't on his way home, I thought I should come and see what you were up to.' Her cheeky grin disarmed him.

'Surely you haven't been following us since we left the Norfolk Woods?' said Boris, hurriedly sheathing Thrust. 'You're meant to be in Alfura. Your father must be furious with you. How are the ponies?'

'Safe for now. But they did have a wrake and boorling after them.'

Boris gaped. 'Oh, no! What happened?'

'Don't worry. The wrake and boorling are dead. Killed by elven arrows.'

Although relieved, Boris scratched his head. 'Are there elves nearby?

'Well, I'm an elf and I'm nearby.' Yahdra gave a mischievous giggle. 'So, what are you doing down here besides trying to evade the enemy?' Her blue eyes looked at him quizzically.

'Ferdy's been captured and taken to Mirraway Castle. Tom's under guard as well. So I have to try and cross this river into Illingaith and rescue them,' said Boris.

'Then you'll need a rope.' Yahdra was looking up at the pylons.

'I know that! But I left mine in the cart.'

'Like to borrow mine?' She reached inside her cape and pulled out an elven rope.

'Dwarves can't use elven ropes,' he said doubtfully, noting how thin it was.

'If I can smoke dwarf baccy, then you can use an elf's rope.' Yahdra tapped him playfully on the nose with the stem of her pipe. Boris wondered how she had got it. In Banters Den, only dwarves who had lived for a hundred and fifty years or more were permitted to smoke. And when he and Ferdy, hiding among the vines at a beer festival, coughed and spluttered their way through a plug of baccy, they were ill for days afterwards.

Now, as Boris was checking the pylon and realising that the first strut was higher than he thought, Yahdra fastened the end of the rope to an arrow and sent it on its way. As soon as the arrowhead stuck fast, she bounded up the bank and Boris scrambled up behind her. She tugged hard on the rope and then handed it to him.

'Once you make it to the top, drop the arrow and keep my rope. But you must be careful when you cross. You don't want to fall into the river.'

Boris' face fell. 'You're not coming with me?'

'I am always with you Boris. You have a lock of my hair and now my rope. War is coming to the Isle of Spheres. I have to help my kin.'

'Yes, just like I have to help Ferdy—again!'

'But you want to save your brother because you love him.' She gently lifted his chin and kissed him on the lips.

The shock of it made his whole body tingle, down to the tips of his toes. It felt as if his boots were on fire. His bottom lip began to quiver as he hugged Yahdra tight. Then he turned away and, after testing the rope, pulled himself up the pylon. He hesitated for a last look into the blue eyes below before dropping the arrow for her to catch. He coiled the elven rope, and slung it over his head and across his chest, looking along the girders for the safest route.

As the mighty Intrepid River surged and rushed beneath him, Yahdra melted into the shadows. She knew that somewhere in the Trading Mountains, a secret group of Arrowsmith elves were gathering intelligence on the enemy. It was their arrows that had killed the wrake and boorling and saved the ponies.

She set off, determined to find them.

# CHAPTER 27

At first, it was too dark for Marta to see anything inside Aramark Temple. After leaving Frovin and pushing through the door, she stood, waiting for her eyes to adjust before deciding what to do next.

She took off her amulet and held it out in front of her. It was now giving off just enough red and blue light to see by. She moved forward slowly. Marta expected the Well of Forgetfulness to be in the middle of the room, but she reached the opposite wall without any sign of it. When she held the amulet up to the wall, all she could see was another door, again with no handle.

But this door had a large snow capped mountain carved into it, with a geometric symbol in the centre. It reminded Marta of the King's ensign that Yoska had drawn in the dirt with a stick, but this symbol was more complex. Marta stared at it, thinking. She knew that from the outside, the temple seemed too small to have another room. *This door must exit the back of the temple.*

She turned away from the door. Holding the amulet high, she ran her fingertips along the smooth granite walls, all the while peering into the dark centre of the room and counting the corners as she went.

One. Two. Two and a half ... *This is where the entrance door should be.*

But there was no door. She kept walking ... three corners, four ... Here was the second door again ... and the room was empty!

She stared at the second door. Her heart beat faster as she recalled Ikoseer's words: *'All mountains are a door but not all mountains have a door. The bearer must earn the key to open the door. Until then, the door remains a mystery.'*

Frowning, she looked at the symbol again. With her index finger, she traced, first the circles, then the pentagon, the four-pointed diamond, the cross. Last of all, she touched the central dot.

Marta felt the dot quiver, so she repeated the sequence, pushing the dot harder. Nothing. She frowned. She tried running her finger over the symbols in different orders, but always ending with the dot. She knocked but unlike the entrance door, this door did not speak and it had no keyhole. Marta clutched the amulet in one hand and spread the other over the whole geometric symbol. Then she swapped hands. Still nothing.

Then, out of frustration and still holding the amulet, she pressed it onto the diamond shape in the centre of the symbol. Suddenly the pentagon snapped from the outer circle, and grabbed her right hand.

She recoiled in shock but her hand was now stuck fast. She pulled hard, but it was no use.

As she attempted to prise up the points of the pentagon with her free hand, she noticed that the amulet began to pulse, emitting a sapphire blue glow beneath her fingers. Instinctively, Marta placed her free hand on top of her trapped one and pushed hard. The entire middle section of the door abruptly dissolved. She would have fallen through, except that the gap was a thick force field, similar to the one between the Arkfeld and the World of the Soul.

Thankfully, there were no menacing trees here, but instead, a circular room. It was faintly lit with a soft glow like that of a candle, but there was no obvious light source. In the centre was a well hewn out of stone, not level with the floor as they sometimes were, but built up a few feet. *At last,* she thought, *the Well of Forgetfulness.*

Marta put the glowing amulet back over her head and keeping her eyes closed, she moved closer, halting every few steps. She stopped only when her boots touched against the base of the surrounding stonework. Her hand rested on the flat surface of the rim that was as wide as the span of her hand, and feeling bumps and hollows, she guessed that the zodiac signs must be carved into it.

Not knowing what to expect and blindly tracing the indentations with one finger, she decided to work her way around the circular well. When she was back where she had started her thoughts were vacillating wildly. *What am I supposed to do now?* Marta felt that she was being sorely tested.

Then the wise words of the Queen came into her mind.

*'Remember that strength comes from adversity. You will be tested … as we are all tested … for strength of heart and purpose of will. But do not burden your heart with your challenges. They are an opportunity to learn and grow …'*

With that, Marta opened her eyes and gasped. A wizened female face stared back at her from the blue-green water and their eyes met. Marta perceived that the face knew all about her, who she was, where she had come from. And why she was there.

The wizened mouth opened wide, and continually changing images flowed out and hung in the air. The writing around the rim of the well was now lit in blue and gold, and explained the images.

Marta was seeing molten rock giants that rose out of the Mother Sea, giving birth to the Isle of Spheres. As the giants' bodies cooled, mountains and valleys formed and now she understood that the tunnels and caves within the Lux and Ascension Mountains were really the veins and inner cavities of the giants. Snow settled on the mountainous peaks of hardened knees, elbows and noses. Melting snow fed rivers that fed plants, and then from other islands in the archipelago, humans and animals arrived.

But there was something different about these humans. Marta saw goodness in them. They seemed connected to the land, in harmony with the nature spirits around them. She saw the building of the powerful Pentark and the three light spheres on the headlands which gave the island its name. She watched the gnomes with their huge intelligent heads and small lumbering bodies, as they found, extracted and cut the precious gemstones. Then she saw the Firebird holding the Lightenstone in its beak.

The island flourished for a time, but then something changed.

Cracks began to appear across the moving pictures, and as the cracks widened, greedy, sword-wielding warlords broke through them, stabbing the good of heart till their blood flowed, seeping into the earthy pores of the rock giants. Marta did not want to keep watching the devastation, but somehow she could not pull her gaze away.

Next came the Battle of the Stones. Although she found it hard to believe, Ikoseer was wielding her staff against the enemy. Then, holding Thrust before him, a strong but battle-weary dwarf, burst through a crack. *That must be Thrim*, thought Marta as he turned to face the fearsome fighter behind him. The enemy swung a spiked battle-flail, and with great precision and force swept Thrim aside and flung Thrust high into the air.

Taken back to the Pentark, Marta started as a slight, shrouded figure stretched across it to remove the Lightenstone. Ikoseer. She was there too, removing the four outer gems. Everything was being done in great haste.

Marta could see that the enemy were on their way, and that several Knights of Power were charging on their war horses to meet them. Helios was waiting, ready, with his golden head up and ears pricked. Ikoseer and her companion slid onto his back straight from the Pentark. Then Ikoseer turned Helios off the roadway, urged him off the top of the fell, down the steep escarpment, and away from Mirraway Castle.

Marta momentarily held her breath as she watched them disappear into the rocky fastness. When she saw them again in the presence of the Queen of the Sun, she watched in fascination as the Queen took the Lightenstone and placed it into the open beak of a huge phoenix perched beside her. As the phoenix spread its fiery wings and left, Marta realised that the Firebird still exists and it must have taken the Stone to Aramark Temple. Then the Queen handed something back to Ikoseer's companion, who turned and looked up at Marta.

Marta stared. Although she could barely remember Maria, her grandmother, she recognised her now, and in her hand was the same tarnished amulet that Marta had worn ever since her mother, Roselin, had died.

Marta was dumbfounded. *My grandmother removed the Lightenstone? And the Queen gave her this amulet? That I now wear?*

'I … I'm so sorry grandma.' Marta found her voice, 'but I didn't know how important the amulet was. Why didn't Ikoseer just tell me that it would guide me to this temple and then open its door? If I'd known that, I would have given it back to her so she could return it.'

As the pictures and writing faded, the wizened face returned.

'The enemy knows that Ikoseer was instrumental in the removal of the Stones from the Pentark, so it was safer if the amulet could be carried here by a stranger. If she had told you the truth, you might have unknowingly confided in the enemy. She could not take that risk. But like your grandmother and mother, you too have a connection to the Lightenstone. As do all females of the royal ancestral lineage of the Rose.'

'What do you mean? I'm not royalty. I don't know anything about roses.' Marta watched in amazement as the face was replaced by a ring of nine beautiful red roses encircling a larger single rose. The petals of the central rose gently opened, revealing the face of her mother.

'How can it be …?' whispered Marta as tears of joy ran down her face. 'Oh, Mother. My heart is going to break. I miss you so much. I didn't know anything about the amulet. But I will find the Stone and give it to Frovin. Then I can go home to Father. But how will I remember what I have to do if this is the Well of Forgetfulness? I don't want to forget you. Or Father. Or all my new friends …'

'Shhhhh, Marta,' her mother murmured. 'Nothing is ever forgotten. From the beginning of time every deed and every utterance, whether good or bad, is recorded. Haven't you just been shown the birth of the Isle? This well is called the Well of Forgetfulness because it remembers what people have long forgotten. It doesn't mean that you will forget what you already know. The old adepts of this temple used to call it the Well of Akasa. The Akasa remembers the Isle's history.'

Marta felt a great weight lift from her body. 'So, is the Lightenstone hidden in the well?'

'Yes, it is.'

'Can you help me find it?'

'I can.'

Marta's lip quivered. 'I would rather stay. What does it matter if the Pentark waits?'

'I know and see your pain, Marta, but time is running out for the Isle of Spheres. The Pentark has already waited far too long. Think of those who have protected you and sacrificed so much to get you here.'

For a moment Marta held her mother's gaze and then through brimming tears, gave a weak nod.

'If you take off your amulet, you will find the Lightenstone,' said her mother. In an instant, she and the roses were gone.

As Marta removed the charm, a ruby red stone suddenly rose up through the blue-green water, stopping just below the surface. Marta gasped as a cold shiver ran through her. In the middle of the stone was a diamond-shaped cavity. Her amulet was not just a guide and a key to a door, but also the centre of the Lightenstone itself.

*No wonder the Queen said that the Lightenstone knew that we were on our way,* she thought. *My grandmother must have taken the amulet from its centre into the World of Man. She passed it on to my mother, who then passed it onto me.*

Her hand shook as she held her charm over the ruby red stone. The water swirled into a vortex, pulling the stone into the lowest central point. With the amulet's spikes digging into her palm, she cautiously lowered her hand towards the water.

The Lightenstone responded. It changed to a dark opal, shimmering with all the colours of the rainbow, and then back to ruby red. Marta heard the inhalation of air as the stone appeared to expand. Then came an exhalation as a shaft of blue light pierced the cavity. A single musical note filled the room.

The water became turbulent, bringing the stone briefly to the surface before sinking it again. Then it slowly rose out of the vortex and a tremendous bolt of electricity shot up Marta's arm as the stone flew through the air, locking like a magnet onto her amulet. Energy surged through her whole body before it ran up her spine and out through the crown of her head. In that instant, Marta felt as if her whole body was on fire.

As the energy and sound abated, Marta grabbed the side of the well and held the re-formed Lightenstone to her heart. *I must get it to Frovin. We must get going.*

Suddenly the voice of the Queen filled the room.

'It is Frovin's destiny to protect the Lightenstone. Your destiny is to carry it, like your grandmother and mother before you. Stay alert, Marta. And take care on your journey home to the Pentark.'

Bewildered, Marta shook her head. *How can any of that be true?* For the first time, she dared to study the beautiful stone in her hand, now coloured dark violet. She slipped it over her head, hiding it under her doublet as best she could and wrapping Patrayus' scarf around her neck. A sudden pang of hunger brought her back to reality. *I have to get back to Frovin. He must be frantic with worry.*

She turned away from the well and headed towards the door. Then the realisation hit her.

'Roselin ... the ancestral line of the Rose.'

# CHAPTER 28

When Marta walked back into the main room of the temple, the wall ahead was still blank, but at each step towards the entrance, the door slowly re-formed. Greatly relieved, she pressed the bulge of the Lightenstone under her doublet. Marta noticed that this time there was a handle on the door. She turned it and pushed, thankful once more that the door remained solid.

Holding the door ajar as she waited for her eyes to adjust to the coming dawn, she looked eagerly for any sign of Snowball and Frovin. The only sound she could hear was the quiet lapping of water at the edge of the oasis.

Marta looked west and was startled when the clouds parted momentarily and she saw the first sliver of light from the new moon dipping below the horizon.

*I must have been in the temple for several days, not hours! No wonder I'm famished.*

She took a deep breath and stepped through the door, wincing when it clicked shut behind her. Frovin woke immediately, easing himself away from the warmth of Snowball's belly. He peered from behind a date palm, but saw only a vague shape moving down the temple steps.

Snowball stood and pricked up her ears. Frovin sniffed. 'Wait here. I won't be long.'

The pair had almost given up hope of seeing Marta again. It was the seventh day since she had left them, and the small amount of food had dwindled. The water was a luxury they would miss, but they agreed that this would be their last night. They planned to leave and look for help.

With the surrounding palm trees for cover, Frovin skirted the building, gradually working his way to the base of the back wall. He had initially tried to dig his way under the temple to get in and help Marta—the mounds of sand from his frantic efforts were still there. To gain some height near a corner, he climbed the biggest mound, and was alarmed by a familiar drifting smell.

He scurried down the mound. Around the corner he came face to face with a pitiful wretched creature, backed against the granite wall. Behind him was Marta. It was hard to say who got the greatest shock.

'I should kill you right now,' growled Frovin. 'I've killed goblins before.'

The goblin snarled and bared his sharp teeth. He shuffled towards Marta.

The badger closed in. 'Stay where you are.'

'Thank goodness you're here, Frovin.' Marta spoke softly.
She sounded weak.

'Who sent you here, Onysius or Lord Mortimer?' demanded Frovin, feeling even braver.

The goblin scoffed.

'Where's your anomir?'

'Dead,' spat the goblin.

Frovin narrowed his eyes. 'I suppose more of your lot are waiting nearby.'

'Just me.'

'So, what are you doing here … all by yourself?'

'Going home … to Hammerlock.'

They had seen the goblin enclave marked on Artorus' map. Hammerlock was on the far west coast of the World of the Dark Night: bordered on one side by sheer sea cliffs and separated from the Land of Illingaith by the Raven Mountains. Artorus had told them of his last visit there to see the goblin King in order to negotiate with him on behalf of the Queen. But it had been too late. King Hord had already sanctioned Lord Mortimer's unfettered use of his army to ride Mortimer's anomirs.

'You're closer to Jimpiragh than Hammerlock.' Frovin assumed that's where the goblin had come from. 'Why not return to the castle and get yourself another beast to ride?'

The goblin gave Frovin a disdainful look.

*Perhaps even primal creatures like these miss their homes too,* thought Frovin.

'Besides, why travel through the desert?' he continued. 'There's quicker and easier ways to get to Hammerlock.'

The goblin sneered, then suddenly grimaced and grabbed his lower leg.

'Are you hurt?' Marta leant towards him.

'Don't touch him!' warned Frovin. He could smell the faint odour of putrefied flesh. 'You've seen how ruthless the goblin riders are when they attack. If he dies, that's one less enemy to worry about.'

'I was sent to spy, not attack,' snapped the goblin.

'So! You *were* spying on us?'

'No!'

'Who were you spying on, then?'

The goblin wavered. 'Two escaped from Jimpiragh Castle. I was ordered to track them down. Take them back to Onysius.'

'Why not just kill them?'

The goblin curled his lip. 'The one called Attricus is a soothsayer. Rumour has it Onysius was expecting him to locate the Lightenstone. My comrades think he must've escaped. Seen something in his crystal ball. Didn't want to share it.'

Frovin glanced at Marta. 'And the other escapee?' he asked.

'Bah! Only a kurr. You'd think Onysius'd just grab another one from the Bleak River.'

'Describe them,' demanded Frovin.

'What? Never seen a kurr?' The goblin sneered, but then gave
a basic description.

'So, are they hiding somewhere in this desert?'

The goblin shrugged. 'Don't know where they are. And I don't care
anymore. I'm going home.'

'If Onysius finds out you've deserted him …'

'As if you're going to tell him,' he fired back.

Marta stepped back. 'If you're returning home, then we should let you get
on your way. But you're hurt …'

'I'll survive,' he muttered. He hobbled past.

'What happened to your leg?' she asked, following him.

'Anomir.'

'Perhaps we can help you somehow.'

The goblin scoffed again, but he wanted to rest near the temple steps.
Frovin was keen to leave the creature to his fate but Marta insisted on
checking his leg first. As she touched it, the goblin shrieked and then
backed away as Snowball appeared and nickered a greeting.

'Oh, Snowball's just a pony. She won't hurt you,' said Marta, giving
Snowball a joyful hug.

Frovin's eyes widened and he stared at the goblin. 'Was your anomir killed
in a rocky gorge?'

The goblin's coarse hair stuck out in front like a verandah, shielding his
dark eyes, but Marta saw fear in his face. *He must be the missing rider of the
anomir that attacked us near the grotto.*

'I'm sorry, but we had to protect ourselves.' Marta flinched at the memory.

'I'm not sorry,' growled the goblin, shifting the weight off his throbbing leg. 'Served the anomir right. Wouldn't obey me. It wasn't supposed to attack you.'

'How strange that you've found your way here. But we aren't going to hurt you … are we, Frovin?' Marta ruffled the top of the badger's striped head.

Frovin muttered something incoherent as Marta studied the pitiful creature, noting the small shiny knobs all over his swarthy skin.

'What's your name?' she asked.

'Rhyll.'

'If you come over to the oasis you can bathe your wound. It'll help,' she encouraged.

Marta saw his doubtful expression and waited for him to move. Then as he grudgingly limped to the water, she and Snowball followed. Frovin held back.

*We have to leave now,* Frovin was thinking. *Our quest is far more important than helping an enemy goblin and I want to find out what happened in the temple. If Marta has the Lightenstone, I need to take it back to the Pentark.*

When Rhyll stood ankle deep in the water and Marta squatted in front of him, they were at eye level. So she could now see an unusual brand seared high up on one cheekbone. She supposed that it was a clan symbol and wondered what it meant. As she leant over to splash water on his wounded leg, Marta held one hand over the Stone under her doublet.

*I don't know if this will work, but we can try*

Rhyll's relief was plain. The pain eased and his putrid flesh began to heal almost immediately.

Although she was sure that the goblin was cured, she felt his wound and hoped he had not noticed anything unusual. As she stood up and stepped back, she caught his curious stare. Rhyll seemed unsure of what to do next.

He patted his wiry leg and put his full weight on it. He gave it a funny little flexing movement and then waded back to the water's edge where Snowball and Frovin were waiting.

Frovin's jaw dropped. *He's been cured? How? Marta must have the Lightenstone!*

Marta joined them as they watched Rhyll straighten his tattered uniform.

'I hope you find your way home safely,' she said.

Rhyll knew that he should say thank you for the healing, but it was such a foreign thing for goblins to do. They usually caused fear wherever they went, and even at home it was every goblin for himself. So he blurted out the closest thing to 'thank you' in goblin speak, expecting no one to understand. As he slunk into the trees he reminded himself to look out for the missing humans and their warhorses.

Once he was out of sight, Marta went straight to the water's edge to drink.

Frovin followed her, anxious to hear her news. 'Thank goodness he's gone. Snowball and I have been so worried about you. Do you have it?'

Marta just nodded and briefly touched her chest. Frovin could barely contain himself.

'I'm so hungry, is there anything to eat?' She wiped the water from her mouth with the back of her hand.

'There's fruit growing on these trees.' Frovin moved away to show her. 'As soon as you went through the temple door there was a terrible storm. A few branches blew down.'

Marta started at the news of the storm but followed Frovin to the closest trunk. Ripened by the hot desert sun, a piece of soft brown fruit hung from the end of each broken branch. Marta pulled off a piece and tried it. It was delicious.

'We need to take as many of these with us as we can,' she said, savouring the sweetness.

'Tell us what happened in the temple,' demanded Frovin.

Snowball stood quietly and Frovin listened wide eyed while Marta ate, relating most of what she had seen. As she neared the end, she briefly showed them the Lightenstone before secreting it away again. Frovin stared, awed by its beauty.

'You know you can't keep it,' he reminded her. 'The Queen said I have to protect it.'

Marta hesitated, taking a deep breath. 'You're right. You do have to protect the Lightenstone. And I'm sorry Frovin, but the face in the well said that I have to carry it, not you.'

As if in agreement, Snowball nudged him.

Frovin's jaw dropped. He looked incredulous. 'But I don't understand. How can that be? It was me that worked out how to use your amulet to get us here.'

'I know you did. I wasn't expecting this change either.'

He looked deflated and she watched him struggle with the news.

'But I can't do this alone,' continued Marta. 'I still need you and Snowball to help me return it to the Pentark.'

Snowball nuzzled the top of Frovin's head and nickered softly.

'We have to go.' The badger abruptly brushed Snowball off. Turning away, he began to tear fruit from the nearest branch, dropping them onto the ground.

Marta sighed and went to find Snowball's gear. After giving her a quick brush and tacking up, she re-checked their waterskins, and then joined Frovin. She squatted beside him to gather up as much fruit as she could.

'I'm truly sorry,' she ventured, 'but just remember: of all the badgers in the Isle of Spheres, the Sun Queen chose you to protect the Stone. You should be honoured. Don't let this come between us—if it does, then the enemy have already won.'

As Marta's words sank in, Frovin remembered the Queen's warning: *'Be ever watchful of the darkness ... even within yourself. The Stone can bring great power. Do not allow the Dark Ones to whisper their wishes into your mind. Subtle and cunning are their ways.'*

Frovin hung his head. 'It's just that I was so focused ...'

Marta put an arm around him and pulled him close.

'I wouldn't have made it here without help from you and Snowball. And I must thank you both for waiting so long for me to come out of the temple. And then being ready to protect me from the goblin.'

Snowball tossed her head, making her bit jingle.

'You didn't seem to need—or want—my protection,' shot Frovin.

Marta shrugged. 'Rhyll was alone. And he knew better than to challenge you.' She gave the badger a gentle squeeze. 'But he did need our help, and trying to heal him seemed the right thing to do. Do you remember Ikoseer telling Ferdy that she wouldn't kill a wrake unless she had to? And that wrakes can't help being born wrakes? Just like us, wrakes and goblins have the instinct to survive.'

'Then let's hope he doesn't go blabbing to other goblins about us.'

'I don't think he will.' Marta looked to where the goblin had disappeared.

Frovin grunted. He was doubtful. 'We need to get going anyway. We should go back the same way we came. At least we know that's safe.'

'Perhaps we should let Snowball decide again?'

Frovin nodded slowly. 'Alright.' He looked towards the World of the Dark Night, sniffing the air.

'Do you think the enemy knows that I have the Stone now?' asked Marta.

'Hope not,' said Frovin, 'but when you went through the temple door, it did seem to start that storm. I'm sure Lord Mortimer knows something unusual has happened. Perhaps even Onysius by now. And what with soothsayers and spying goblins, we'll have to be extra careful. Onysius will replace Rhyll soon enough.'

Frovin thought for a moment. 'If the Stone can heal a goblin then surely it can protect us.'

'I don't know what it can do,' said Marta lifting him onto Snowball's rump. 'I just want to return it to the Pentark as quickly as I can. I only hope I have the strength to carry it.'

Frovin saw her pensive expression as she put the reins over Snowball's head. As they waited for Snowball to move, Frovin realised that something seemed different about the pony too. Was it the carriage of her head or the added look of determination in her eye?

*She's such a mystery. It's no wonder I get frustrated sometimes.*

And Frovin was right—something was very different. First, instead of leading them back the way they came, Snowball skirted the oasis, and headed due north towards the pale cliffs they had seen from the top of the ridge.

As they approached, Marta forced herself to look into the shadowy holes pocketing the rock face. *Everyone is relying on me, she thought. What if I fail the Queen and Ikoseer? What if the Stone falls into the hands of the enemy?*

Then she remembered how when Boris was doubting the elves would help him, and Artorus warned him to remain confident. But she doubted and worried, none the less. So she was amazed when, instead of clambering up the escarpment, Snowball led them through a hidden cleft in the rock face and along a short parallel wall. Then, she suddenly turned again, completed an 'S' shape, and brought them into a narrow chasm.

And Marta spun round in shock as the rocks re-joined behind them with a low grating sound.

'Rock giants,' said Frovin, following her gaze.

Remembering how she had seen the rock giants giving birth to the Isle of Spheres and then cooling to form its mountains and valleys, Marta ran her hand over the rough wall. 'Thank you for helping us.'

Frovin whispered and nodded to the Lightenstone. 'They're protecting their own.'

The moment he spoke, the ground began to tremble as the tangled bodies of smaller giants broke through on either side of them, creating parallel walls and the path between. The slumbering rocks of a larger giant groaned at his abrupt awakening and waterfalls of dry sand flowed from the rising shards. Then a head suddenly broke through the surface. It yawned, snorting pebbles and gravel from his nostrils. As columns of basalt hair were shaken free, loose shards flew out, clattering along the walls. Then with a deep sigh, this giant rested his chin on the ground and opened his mouth.

*His hair reminds me of steps and stairs,* thought Marta as she watched the basalt columns settle and re-set again.

Without hesitation, Snowball made her way forward. When they reached the giant's head, she climbed onto his tessellated chin, and led them into the gaping cavern of his mouth. Marta jumped when the mouth snapped shut, plunging them into blackness. She felt for Snowball and holding onto a handful of mane, pulled the Lightenstone out of her doublet. The stone was so bright she left it hanging round her neck, and shielded it with her hand until her eyes adjusted.

The inside of the giant's mouth reminded Marta of the refugees' grotto, except that this was a much smaller cave. With nowhere else to go, Snowball made towards the throat.

They passed under two stalactites. 'Don't touch those!' said Frovin. 'I don't want to be spewed out of here.'

Marta was amused. 'Where do you think this passageway will take us?'

'Don't know. With any luck it's all the way to the Abyss River or beyond.'

'I hope the others are still there.'

Frovin shook his head. 'It'll be safer without the knights and Yoska, at least until we get closer to Mirraway Castle.'

'Boris and Ferdy keep coming into my mind too,' continued Marta. 'I wonder if they're safe. I get a horrible feeling that something's happened to them.'

'Don't worry about them.' Frovin dismissed her concern. 'They can look after themselves. Whatever they're up to, I'll bet nothing good will come of it. Trouble, that's what they are.'

'I'm sure they're helping somehow,' she insisted.

'If they had any sense, they would've returned to Banter's Den to brew beer and mine ore.'

'You know they can't,' Marta reminded him. 'Thrust was made to serve the Pentark and Ikoseer gave them the task of helping to find the outer gems.'

Frovin rolled his eyes at the cavern walls. *But my task is far more important.*

Snowball seemed to know her way through the labyrinth of passageways and openings. All around them, different minerals in a myriad of colours and crystal formations glittered in the reflected light. Some crystals were so delicate that they splintered into elongated fragments at Marta's touch.

But they were not alone underground.

Snowball was the first to notice. There were gnomes all around them. Encumbered by oversized heads and inadequate bodies, they initially stole furtive glances at them from the dark recesses ahead. But by the time the trio reached the gnomes' hiding places, they had already melted back into the walls—all they could see were eyeballs of polished black and white onyx, keeping constant watch.

As the hours passed more eyeballs appeared, and when they approached the central crossroad of four passages, Marta and Frovin were startled by a large gnome suddenly lumbering into view. With a long walking stick clutched in each hand to support his body, the gnome stopped in front of them. He studied them with keen intelligent eyes. Marta noticed, perched on the back of his head, a very small crown that would have remained hidden if he stood up straight.

Frovin was already wary but when he saw what seemed like hundreds more gnomes step out from the walls and crowd around them, blocking the passageways, he was concerned for their safety.

'On whose authority do you carry the Lightenstone?' The gnome's speech sounded as if he had several glass marbles rolling around in his mouth.

As Marta stepped forward, she recognised him from the historical images that she had seen in the Well of Forgetfulness. Suspecting that he already knew the answer, she said, 'On the Lightenstone's authority.'

'How did it come to you?'

'From the temple,' said Marta, cautiously.

'Mmmm. How do you know that what you carry is the Lightenstone?'

'I saw it held in the Firebird's beak. I was also shown how the gnomes cut the outer gemstones. And I saw your face in the images.' Marta paused. 'If the Lightenstone is false, then so are you.'

A hushed whispering spread throughout the passageways.

'And what if I, King Jigs, were to ask for it?'

'Then come and take it.' Marta removed the necklace and held it out for him.

Frovin froze in horror and there was a collective gasp and rattle of walking sticks as the gnomes jostled to watch their King's reaction.

'Who sent you to find it?' he asked.

'Those who need it most.' Marta placed the necklace back around her neck.

The King changed the subject. 'The rock giants and the roots of plants tell us that they feel the advancing march of many feet. War is coming from the World of the Dark Night. Time is running out.'

'We know,' piped Frovin, fluffing up his coat and moving forward onto the saddle. 'Which is why we shouldn't be wasting any more time discussing it.'

The gnomes shrank back. They had never heard an animal speak before.

'Will the gnomes and rock giants help us when the war comes?' asked Marta.

'If we're asked to,' replied the King.

'Then on behalf of Ikoseer and the Queen of the Sun, I ask for your help. The Isle of Spheres needs you all.' Looking around at the gnomes, Frovin doubted that such clumsy earth elementals could possibly help in a war raging far above them.

King Jigs stared at Marta briefly. Then seeming to make up his mind about something, he moved clumsily aside to let them pass.

Snowball again took the lead and as they passed King Jigs, Marta was able to study his crown. Attached to the top of a small, slim circle of gold, was an even-armed cross set on a horizontal plane. The arms of the cross extended past the rim, with one jewel set at the end of each of the four points. The jewels reminded Marta of the Lightenstone. They were similar in shape and colour, but quite small.

'If you keep straight ahead, the rock giants will guide you to another cave close to the Abyss River,' he said.

Marta patted Snowball's shoulder. 'She already knows the way.'

'How could any animal possibly know as much as a gnome?' he asked as the others shook their heads and murmured in agreement.

'Oh, she knows quite a bit,' said Marta. Snowball snorted at the King.

Quiet tittering spread throughout the passage and Frovin suppressed a smile. 'Something must be getting up her nose.'

King Jigs glowered at him as tiny droplets of pony snot sparkled on his bald head and the tittering grew louder.

'How will you know when to come?' asked Marta, referring to the looming war.

'The jewels on my crown will glow hot and I will probably get a headache.' He put emphasis on the words 'probably' and 'headache'.

'Then we should leave you to your work.' Marta gave King Jigs a cursory nod and moved past him.

Some of the gnomes fell in behind them for a few steps, pressing against Snowball's legs and rump. They had never touched a real pony, or a badger—let alone a human being—before. When they grabbed at her tail Snowball turned her head and gave one of them a short, sharp kick when she caught him reaching into a saddlebag.

As the gnome teetered and fell, those around him stepped away. Once he was down, they scrambled onto his bulbous head as he melted back into the rocks.

Leaving the clamour of gnomes behind, Snowball's only focus now was to make it safely to the Abyss River where she knew that help would come.

# CHAPTER 29

Volgor had been on the *Sirius* for ten days, and although the sailors spoke to each other in a strange language, he was fascinated by the daily working of the ship. The young lad Volgor had seen shimmy along a rope from the wharf had been assigned to look after him. 'Name's Nipper,' he'd said in introduction.

Nipper explained that his name came from his job. He was in charge of tying and untying the ropes of the anchor and the capstan whenever the anchor was raised. Although slightly taller than Volgor, Nipper was just as scrawny, his unkempt, salt-stiffened hair contrasting with his smooth olive complexion and curious grey-blue eyes. He spoke to the sailors in their seafaring tongue and they seemed to keep an affectionate eye out for him.

Usually accompanied by Nipper, Volgor spent the first two days exploring the ship. The first discovery was that each mast, rope and sail had a special name.

With his three-pointed hat tilted so that one ginger ear was free, Captain Tibbs roared to the quartermaster from a raised wooden box near the middle of the deck.

"Clew up the mainsail!"

"Hoist outer jib!"

"Brace round forward!"

Sometimes he paced back and forth on the gunwale, swishing his tail and leaping onto the deck to attack a bare leg to hurry a sailor along.

And below deck there was also a lot to see. Volgor was particularly curious to see Captain Tibbs' cabin, accessible from the main deck at the stern of the ship.

'Cap'n's cabin's there in the aftcastle. An' that's the poop deck above it,' Nipper told him.

As they passed the doorway Volgor stopped and studied the painted coat of arms carved into the wood. There was a wide white 'V' on a copper coloured shield and three anchors on the 'V' and a cocked hat resting on top of the shield. Finally, on a wavy sea blue ribbon above the 'V', was his surname Tibbs—carved in the shape of cat's claws.

The latch was attached to the door jamb at cat height and secured with a heavy lock, similar to those used by Onysius in Jimpiragh's dungeon.

As their eyes met, Nipper warned him, 'If you're caught breakin' in there, you'll be forced to walk the plank, wiv' your 'ands tied behind your back.' He gave Volgor an animated demonstration.

*That won't happen. You don't know what I've got.* Volgor felt for the aquamarine in his jacket.

Throughout this tour of the ship, Nipper kept thinking that something was awry. It was not unusual for the Captain to send him to spy on someone, but this was the first time he had seen the Captain let a stranger have relative freedom on board the *Sirius*. What's more, he had expected the ship to sail across the harbour as usual and back through the Berthing Gates to the Mother Sea, but instead, here they were, going the opposite way, heading towards the mighty Intrepid River.

While the *Sirius* was at full sail in the harbour, Volgor's favourite spot was near the bowsprit. He loved to lean over the bulwark and look down on the crowned figurehead carved beneath it, watching her plunge and part the waves as the ship pitched. The white water from the oncoming sea slapped hard against her long white dress, making it sparkle as the bow lifted high, and the salt spray drifted onto Volgor's face.

In fact, since the mouth of the Intrepid River was many miles wide, it took a day or two for Volgor to realise that they had left Werthyn Harbour and were in the river. By then, the wind dropped somewhat and the river narrowed, giving him glimpses of the banks.

And it was then that the Captain ordered that the flag of the *Sirius*, an indigo-blue background marked with the stars of that constellation, and the ensign of the Isle of Spheres, be replaced with the skull and crossbones, the Jolly Roger. Nipper explained that this was a pirate flag.

'So, is the *Sirius* a pirate ship?'

'No, just pretendin'.' Nipper puffed out his chest. 'The *Sirius* will be whatever Cap'n wants her to be.'

Later, where the salt water met the fresh, they passed small fishing boats. The fishermen were wide eyed, and some of them had to pull in their salmon nets and row out of the ship's way. In their village that night, the fishermen sat around the fire, relaying all that they had seen.

'The *Sirius*, you say?' asked an elder.

'Oh, aye.' The fishermen nodded their heads in the flickering firelight. Soon after, the elder left in a hurry to spread his sacred fish bones for a reading.

On the morning of the sixth day, Volgor approached Captain Tibbs.

'Where are we going?'

Captain Tibbs stopped washing his face with his paws and gave Volgor a blank look.

'Into danger,' he replied.

Volgor started. 'Has it got something to do with the gem?'

'Silence!' hissed the Captain springing up, one paw ready to strike. Volgor blinked and stepped back.

'I will summon you when my ship is at anchor.'

From then on, Volgor often stood beside a sailor named Slacker, watching him throw a sounding lead over the side to measure the depth of the water in the river.

'Can't be havin' the *Sirius* run aground, now can we?' explained Slacker.

On the tenth day the Intrepid River had narrowed to the point where it was only traversable by row boat. With her sails lashed and the ship becalmed, the quartermaster yelled, 'Let go the bower anchor.' The rope slithered across the deck, the plunging anchor sank to the riverbed and the *Sirius* drifted slightly downstream until the rope grew taut. From his elevated box, Captain Tibbs surveyed it all with his steely gaze.

Below deck and before sunrise the following morning, Nipper shook Volgor awake. 'Shake a leg. Cap'n wants you in his cabin.'

Half asleep, Volgor rolled out of his hammock and rubbed his eyes and followed Nipper up the steps to the deck. Nipper knocked on the cabin door. They waited. The decorated door seemed to swing in by itself, but only just enough for Volgor to squeeze through. Nipper closed the door after him.

In the dimly lit cabin was a large table strewn with nautical charts. Square-shanked nails secured each table leg to the floor. On a bench under one of several cabin windows a large plush cushion was also roughly nailed in place—Volgor decided it must the Captain's bed. The centre of the cushion had been compacted into a neat circle and there was a fine layer of ginger fur stuck to the royal blue cover. Two wooden bowls were beside the cushion, one filled with fresh water. The other had a few dried pilchards, making Volgor's nose twitch and his mouth water. He looked around but couldn't see the Captain anywhere.

He shuffled closer to the table, noting that one corner of the Captain's hat poked out from under the charts. A small inkhorn rested beside the hat but he didn't see any goose quills for writing.

He turned to a wide wooden dresser topped with an open bookcase. The crowded books, secured halfway by a thin rail, made him think of the soothsayer and he felt a pang of sorrow, wondering what could have happened to him.

High up and in front of the biggest tomes was what appeared to be a carved sandstone cat, its head obscured by the fretwork on the corner. Volgor stared at it for a few seconds and then forced himself to focus again on the room.

With growing impatience, he slid past the table to the windows and stretching on tiptoe, looked down. Moving between the windows, he spent some minutes watching the water flow steadily towards the mouth of the river, and remembering his long trip down the Abyss.

Then a strange lurch in the pit of his stomach made him turn abruptly. Although nothing appeared to have changed, he noticed for the first time the neatly folded square black envelope beside the inkhorn. He had never seen fish leather before, but he knew about it. He also recognised the black and silver-grey pattern of his favourite fish: salmon.

Still wary because of that carved cat, and, keeping the ornament in the corner of his eye, he bowed his head slightly and tiptoed to the table. He stretched out a long bony finger and slid the envelope towards him. Wrinkling his hooked nose, he took a deep breath, and with a fingernail, prised open the envelope. He stepped back, rubbing his chin.

At first he thought it was empty but as he peered closer he could see very fine writing on the pale inside of the skin. Then he noticed three unusual quills lying beside the inkhorn: white cat whiskers, their sharp tips blackened with ink.

*I can't read. So what's the point of looking at the envelope any closer?*

But Volgor could not help himself. He spread the envelope out and saw that it was a map, marked with several diagrams. He leant forward, squinting at it and pursing his fleshy lips. A sudden dull thud of something dropping to the floor made him jump. He looked up: The sandstone cat was nowhere to be seen!

Horrified, he stepped back just as a cat leapt effortlessly onto the table. Holding Volgor's gaze, Captain Tibbs sauntered across the table and sat down in front of the envelope. The end of his tail began to swish.

'I see that you've found the map,' he said. He placed one paw on a corner of the map and with the other he indicated a long line and then two symbols. 'This is the Intrepid River. Here is Mirraway Castle. And nearby, the Pentark.'

Volgor leant forward. 'What does this have to do with my gemstone?' He assumed that that was why he had been dragged out of bed.

'Didn't Attricus tell you? The aquamarine must be returned to the Pentark.' The Captain seemed surprised.

Volgor's eyes bulged even more and he spread his hands in disbelief. 'H … he said it wasn't the Lightenstone.'

'It isn't. But it still belongs in the Pentark. It's one of the four missing outer gems.'

'The *Sirius* is here.' Captain Tibbs tapped the map, expecting the now rattled Volgor to take notice. 'I have brought you as far as I can. You must continue to follow the river bank upstream until you come to the white bridge. Here.' He placed a claw on another symbol. 'Cross the bridge and follow the Lake Road. You can't miss Mirraway Castle. On the fell close by it is …'

' … the Pentark,' said Volgor. His shoulders slumped and he looked down at his calloused feet.

Flicking his tail, Captain Tibbs studied him for a moment. 'Nobody will take much notice of a wandering kurr.'

'Oh yes, they will. I come from the Bleak River. It's likely my kin have never been seen in those parts.'

'But Onysius keeps kurrs. And he visits Mirraway Castle from time to time.'

A cold tingling spread throughout Volgor's body. *How does Captain Tibbs know that?*

'He might have left you behind on one of those visits?' The Captain was eyeing off his breakfast and licking his mouth.

Volgor swallowed hard. 'You don't know Onysius like I do. And it's especially dangerous for me now that I have the aquamarine. If I'm captured, he'll find it.'

'No, no. Don't worry. He'll be too busy plotting with Lord Mortimer to worry about you. Now, Nipper has made up a sack for you with a few days' provisions and the boatswain is waiting to row you across to Magirus. It'll be safer travelling on that side of the river. And don't forget the map.'

Avoiding the Captain's gaze, he reached out to take it, but the Captain kept one paw firmly on the map, forcing Volgor to look at him. The Captain began to blink slowly and make a strange whirring sound. And as Volgor pulled the map towards him, it moved in small jerks as the Captain's claws extended and retracted in a kind of rhythm, grabbing the map and then letting it go.

*What a weird animal. Here I am, about to risk my life, and the Captain seems somehow pleased.*

He re-folded the map and was shoving it in his pocket when the door opened. It was the boatswain. 'Ready about. Shake a leg now, will ye.'

With a quick look back, Volgor slipped through the doorway onto the deck. Nipper was waiting for him beside the starboard bulwark. He handed Volgor a small hessian bag secured with a leather strap and Volgor slung it over his shoulder. Worry lines furrowed Nipper's brow.

'Goin' to miss you.' His bottom lip quivered a little as he searched Volgor's eyes, looking for answers.

'I'll miss you too.'

Nipper handed him a rope and asked where he was going.

'To a castle.' Volgor grabbed the rope, and then climbing over the gunwale, steadied his feet against the hull, ready to drop.

'Is it far?'

'Hope not,' said Volgor as a shout to hurry up came from below.

'Then wishin' ye a fair wind and calm seas,' yelled Nipper as Volgor shimmied down the rope and disappeared.

It did not take long for the boatswain to row to the riverbank. Before he stepped out, Volgor tried to get more information.

'Do you know how far it is from here to Mirraway Castle?'

'Oh, aye.' The boatswain nodded. 'About two hundred miles.'

Volgor's mouth fell open. 'Two hundred miles!'

'Oh aye, that's as the crow flies.'

Volgor scrambled angrily out of the boat and wobbled up the riverbank, feeling the land beneath him move like the deck of the ship. He glared back at the ship, but Captain Tibbs was now interested in the new visitor tapping on his window. Volgor turned his attention to the river bank ahead.

'Welcome Sheen, my dear friend,' purred the Captain. 'Tell Ikoseer that Volgor the kurr is on his way with the aquamarine. The *Sirius* will return to the Mother Sea.'

Sheen ruffled her feathers. 'Ikoseer will be pleased for the confirmation. She sends her regards, thanks you for your service. And she implores you to take great care, Mr Tibbs. She warns of impending war, on the land and also on the sea.'

'My ship and crew are ready. Ikoseer can be assured that word has spread among the other islands. More folk will come to our aid. I'm certain of that.'

'Then I hope you are right. The Isle of Spheres is treated with suspicion by most from the archipelago.'

'But they too are concerned about Lord Mortimer's plans. His pirates have pillaged, destroyed and captured many of the ships that sail between the Isle of Spheres and the outer islands. Trading with us has almost stopped.'

He groomed his whiskers, before moving closer and whispering, 'What news of the Lightenstone?'

'In the Dukedom of Asilodor, some of the rock giants have woken.'

The cat's eyes flared. 'Are you saying it was hidden in Asilodor all these years?' Sheen bobbed her head.

'There is a quickening now, then?'

'Indeed, Mr Tibbs, there is. And because of it, I have much more to do.'

The Captain inclined his ginger head towards the riverbank. 'Will you keep an eye on our scrawny little messenger?'

'If I am able. But I have spread word amongst the other animals to watch out for him too.'

She paused. 'Did you see the aquamarine?'

'I did. It's still secure. In the inside pocket of Volgor's jacket.'

Sheen bobbed her head in satisfaction. 'Then I must leave you now Mr Tibbs, to your beautiful ship and worthy sailors.'

'Before you go, I have a fresh gift.'

The cat pulled a dead mouse from under his cushion, holding it up by the tail. Sheen gobbled it down gratefully. After a courteous nod between them, she soared into the early morning sky.

Volgor was already trudging along the river bank. But his legs still felt strange and he found it hard to keep his balance. He stopped to take one last look at the *Sirius*. He was loath to leave her and the enchanting figurehead behind. Soon he saw sailors come onto the deck and heard the familiar cry: 'Weigh anchor!' Without thinking, he raised his hand as he watched Nipper spring to his post at the anchor rope.

'Two hundred miles,' he muttered. He adjusted the sack and then decided to check his provisions. He was hungry and beginning to salivate at the smell of dried fish. When he opened the hessian bag, dried pilchards were all he could see.

*The enemy will smell me before they see me.* He rummaged through the pilchards to the bottom of the bag. But there he felt something quite different. He peered in and pushed the fish aside. A shiver ran up his spine. Volgor gaped at Duke Tardor's sword: smelly, oily and covered in salt. Last seen when he was forced to drop it under the harbour wharf in his battle with the sea monster.

# CHAPTER 30

It took a full day for Snowball to negotiate the rock giants' arteries to a cave near the banks of the Abyss River. The entrance was blocked by a mass of rambling vines through which Marta could just see some nearby trees.

'It's twilight. We should sleep for a bit before we leave,' she said. Frovin jumped onto a ledge and sniffed the air.

Marta looked at him and frowned. 'Can you smell wolves?'

He shook his head. 'No … just river water.'

'I hope this isn't the same place we crossed after the wolves attacked us.'

Frovin shrugged. 'Surely the rock giants have brought us closer to Mirraway than that.'

'Can you remember where the source of this river is?' Marta was absent-mindedly scratching Snowball's forehead.

'I think it starts in the Arifer Mountains.' He was trying to recall Artorus' map.

'Yes, that's the mountain range I saw from the Sarsen Plains,' said Marta. 'Artorus said there's a road to Mirraway on the far side of the range. If we follow the river upstream we should be able to find the road. But I don't want us to stay in Asilodor any longer than we have to. We'll need to cross the river back into Illingaith first.'

'I'm sure that there are shorter routes to Mirraway,' Frovin pointed out rather tersely. 'Besides, that road is also the main road between Mirraway and Jimpiragh. It'll be heavily patrolled by goblins on anomirs. Anyway, I thought you wanted Snowball to guide us now.'

As Snowball began to grind her teeth, Marta pursed her lips and stared at the cavern walls.

'Given the chance, she might take us in a different direction.' Frovin's frustration was growing.

'Regardless, it's still too dangerous to stay in Asilodor.'

Frovin lowered his voice. 'It's dangerous everywhere, now that you have the Lightenstone.'

Marta sighed. 'Somehow, it doesn't seem fair for me to expect Snowball to decide these things. Returning the Stone to the Pentark is my burden, not hers.'

Frovin looked at her crossly. 'Yesterday you were grateful that we were helping you. And don't forget that I have to protect the Stone. With my life.'

As their eyes met, tears welled. Marta turned away and mumbled, 'Sorry.'

She slumped to the sandy floor, and buried her head in her elbow. When Snowball's head dropped, Frovin curled up on the ledge to sleep.

A few hours later, all three were roused by the hooting of an owl. Perched on a branch at the cave entrance, the bird was bobbing its head. Its bright orange eyes peered at them through the mass of vines. Snowball nickered a greeting as the bird squeezed through into the darkened cave. Frovin looked alarmed. Marta was at the back of the cave.

'My name is Sheen,' said the owl. 'I bring greetings from Ikoseer and have come to warn you. The ageing Earl Onysius and Lord Mortimer are now leading an exodus of enemy soldiers, wrakes and other despicable creatures from the Lord's castle, Mawdark, in the World of the Dark Night. They are heading towards Mirraway.

Sheen paused. 'Something seems to have roused the Prince of Darkness into action.'

A chill ran up Marta's spine. She got up quickly, placing her hand over the hidden Lightenstone. For the first time, she felt a surge of energy in her palm, and when she dropped her arm, the energy seemed to expand into the cave.

Marta replied, coming to stand beside Snowball. 'The gnomes and others have already warned us about the impending war.'

'Except that now it's a reality.' Sheen ruffled her feathers.

'How did you find us so easily?'

Snowball extended her nose and touched Sheen's beak.
Marta's eyes widened.

'I was returning home to White Timber Mountain when Snowball asked me to fly over Asilodor to check on the enemy. That was when I saw the army.'

Frovin gave Sheen a very sceptical look. 'You must have wings of magic. The World of the Dark Night is two hundred miles from here.'

'I didn't have to fly all the way to that world and I'm not always an owl. Sometimes, I am an eagle.'

'Is the enemy close, then?' asked Marta, hurriedly
covering Frovin's discomfort.

Sheen hesitated. 'Relatively. They are already camped at the turnoff to Jimpiragh Castle. It will take the main army about another three weeks to reach Mirraway Castle, but the wrakes could arrive within five days. If they're riding boorlings, they could be there in half that time.'

Marta felt ill and looked at Frovin. 'Then we have to reach Mirraway Castle before Mortimer's army does.'

'The wrakes and boorlings are your greatest threat,' said Sheen. 'Although they are indiscriminate killers, they both have a particular taste for young dwarves, ponies … and badgers.'

Frovin moved forward on the saddle in another attempt at bravado. 'I'm one of Ikoseer's helpers too. I've already killed a goblin rider. And a wolf … and Snowball has …'

Sheen interrupted him. 'I know who you are. But it was Toros the bull that saved you from the wolves of Skag, remember? The safest and quickest route to Mirraway is back across the river and through the Ageless Forest. Snowball knows the way.'

Marta suddenly remembered the owl in the Ageless Forest; a soft white feather had floated to her feet, and now she felt for it in her pocket.

*Sheen was with us even then.*

'Do you know the dwarves, Boris and Ferdy? Have you seen them too?' she asked eagerly. A sudden gust of wind rustled the leaves of the vines across the cave entrance.

'They seem to have disappeared.' Sheen tipped her head to the side.

Marta's face fell. 'What about … Patrayus? Artorus and Yoska?'

Sheen lowered her voice. 'They've almost made it to the Gorthwain Mountains to join the other Knights of Power.'

Marta's dismay was turning to anger. 'So, Artorus expects us to return to Mirraway without him—even now, with the enemy so close?'

'Ikoseer had sent for the knights. Besides, their gathering in the Gorthwain Mountains will draw the enemy away from you. In their stead, the animals in the Ageless Forest will help you.'

Now Marta's words of protest came tumbling out, her anger rising.

'But you say that we have to re-cross the Abyss River, and then the Sarsen Plain. And apart from the wolves, that's where we saw a troop of soldiers before. And we've already been attacked by anomirs. Twice! After their attack on us at the Norfolk Woods, the rider goblins would have told Onysius about us. And now Lord Mortimer will know too.'

Suddenly looking at Frovin she added, 'We won't be able to travel as if we're unimportant and ordinary any more.'

'Yes, you can,' soothed Sheen. 'Everyone looks on the Knights of Power as the traditional guardians of the Pentark.'

'But we've been travelling with them …' Marta's voice trailed off.

'Try to stop worrying. Your thoughts are creating an energy that is drawing the enemy to you.'

Sheen twisted her head to look behind her, and back again. 'Help is already here. Toros is waiting to take you across the Abyss River and into Illingaith. I, however, must return to White Timber Mountain.' Bright orange eyes stared into deep blue. 'Ikoseer will want to know …'

Marta put her hand over the Lightenstone and Sheen bobbed her head in understanding. Snowball nodded goodbye and with a final hoot, Sheen left the cave, transforming into an eagle before flying swiftly towards Arctus.

Marta hugged Snowball's neck. 'I don't know how you contacted Sheen, but thank you.'

Snowball nickered and Frovin said knowingly, 'I expect she used the air element.'

Suddenly, a black mass completely blocked the cave entrance.

'Toros!' Frovin whispered fiercely as Snowball pricked up her ears and backed away. Marta went with her.

They stood back as Toros began tossing his head from side to side, slashing the vines with his horns in the same way as he had impaled the male wolf before tossing him aside, before they escaped across the Abyss River. The bull worked quickly, steam rising from his nostrils into the cooling night air as his hooves trampled the tangled mess. Then, letting out a long, deep bellow, he turned towards the river.

Snowball followed close behind with Frovin now on her back but as they left the cave Marta heard the familiar grating sound behind her. She turned briefly to see that the rock giants had already closed the cave's entrance. With menacing shadows now flickering through the trees ahead, Marta focused on the steady movement of the massive rump and bobbing horns in front of her.

As soon as they reached the riverbank, Toros lowered himself onto his knees and waited. Marta gave Frovin a bewildered look.

'I think he expects you to get onto his back,' he said.

Marta hesitated. Even on his knees Toros towered over her. She had to jump to scramble up onto his back. Sitting just behind his shoulders, she squeezed her legs tight while he stood up and lifted his head, tilting his horns towards her. She leant forward and grasped the tips of his horns. The moment Toros stepped into the river, a charge shot through Marta's hands and down into the bull's body. And as she stared at the flowing water beneath them it suddenly disappeared. She was looking into a fathomless black pit.

'Look ahead,' bellowed Toros as he crossed the void.

Marta obeyed, feeling his power moving beneath her. Her hands felt as if they were on fire. Toros began to change colour from jet black to grey and finally to pure white as he strode up the riverbank into the Land of Illingaith. Marta was astounded. Exhausted and heaving, he dropped his head, sliding his horns out of Marta's grip. She pushed herself back along his spine, and turned to peer over his rump just as Snowball joined them. His mouth agape, Frovin stared at the mighty bull. Toros was now as white as the snow eagles of the Lux Mountains.

*So, what I thought was folklore is actually true.*

Within minutes, Toros regained his strength and so they continued on until they emerged from the tree line onto the Sarsen Plain. It was too dark to see much, but when the clouds parted Marta glimpsed the faint outline of the Sarsen stones in the distance.

She pointed towards the megaliths and whispered, 'The rock giants have brought us back to the same place. There are the standing stones.'

Frovin could not see them but he nodded nonetheless. He was sniffing furiously for wolves and now—wrakes.

'Is that where we're going?' he whispered back.

'Snowball?' Marta was about to swing her leg over Toros' back and slide off.

'Stay where you are, Marta. I will take you to the Ageless Forest,' said Toros in his slow bass voice.

Marta pulled her shawl close, grateful for the warmth of the bull's body. And then, as if issuing an invitation, a sliver of moonlight caressed the tops of the stones and Marta knew that Toros was taking them there first.

They reached the ring of stones by midnight, and Marta craned her neck to see the top of the outer stones. She counted twelve as Toros walked around the circumference. Pausing between two of the outer stones, each marked with the sun symbol, he dropped his head briefly, as if in reverence. Then, as if some unheard permission had been granted, he entered, but now turned to walk in the opposite direction, between the larger outer stones and an inner ring of twelve smaller ones. He came full circle, then walked between two of the smaller stones into the inner sanctum and scribed another circle, again in the opposite direction.

The Lightenstone become hotter with every turn and now it pulsed to Marta's heartbeat. She was pressing her hand to her chest when Toros said, 'You are safe here now, Marta. Please take it out.'

Reluctant, Marta pulled the Lightenstone out of her doublet. Shielding her eyes, she looked around her as Toros led them to a central stone table. Marta noticed the twelve signs of the zodiac carved around its circumference. In the centre were four images: a bull, a lion, a raptor and an angel.

Six female dancers suddenly appeared from between the inner and outer rings and began to weave patterns around Marta, Frovin and Toros. Their garments reminded Marta of the Queen's: a plain white gown, long sleeved and gathered gently at the waist, then a rose-gold gossamer veil over the gown. As the dancers moved, their veils flowed as if the air around them was alive.

Seven more dancers joined them, with white veils flying and each clad in a gown of a different colour: red, orange, yellow, green, blue, indigo and violet. Like floating flames, the red, orange and yellow dancers merged and transformed into a creature that Marta suddenly remembered seeing in that strange book of her mother's.

By now Frovin's hackles were up. He kept a vigilant eye as the creature, proud and fearless, circled them.

'My name is Mafasat. I am the Sun Lion.' His magnificent mane flamed and his body moved like liquid gold. 'Welcome to the Sun circle. Come. Eat and drink.'

And the four remaining colourful dancers set down hay and milk thistle for Toros and Snowball; nuts and berries for Frovin; corn, olives, apples, and red grapes for Marta; a wooden bowl of spring water for each animal, and the same in a goblet for Marta. The dancers backed away, leaving the four visitors all eating quietly.

'Thank you,' said Marta. She was ravenous and thirsty, savouring the flavours that reminded her of home. 'Where did all this food come from?'

'The elementals,' replied Mafasat.

Alarmed, Marta and Frovin looked at each other.

'The Prince of Darkness can manipulate ...' began Marta.

'The Sarsen stones are sacred. The Prince of Darkness has no power here,' Mafasat assured them. 'Toros brought you here because you are all sorely in need of nourishment. This is also the birthplace of the Pentark stones.'

Marta looked doubtful. 'But the gnomes mined and cut the gemstones underground,' she said, recalling the pictures from the Well of Forgetfulness.

'That is true,' acknowledged Mafasat, 'but afterwards, they brought them here. There is still a slight depression underneath the table where the gnomes emerged from their tunnel. It was the first time that the sun charged the gemstones. Then the Firebird came with the Lightenstone. With the twelve smaller gemstones hidden under its feathers and the Lightenstone in its beak, it flew them to the Pentark. Afterwards, it was consumed by the power of the Pentark. Once the gnomes were relieved of their responsibility, they returned to the earth. Then this became a sacred place.'

Marta nodded, now understanding why King Jigs had been so defensive.

'So, that's why the zodiac is on this table.' Marta was staring at the carved signs. 'And four of the symbols are repeated in the centre. An angel, a raptor, a lion and a bull.'

'Yes. They represent the four elements.' Mafasat gave Marta a knowing look, and began to pace back and forth.

'If the Firebird was here it could return the Lightenstone again.' Frovin echoed Marta's previous sentiments.

'It's not that simple. I understand your reasoning, but you are in the World of the Soul,' he reminded them. 'If the hierarchy of the Isle of Spheres were to do everything for you, then your soul will never be tested and will never expand to higher levels.'

If you say so, thought Frovin, rolling his eyes. By now the first six dancers had also gone.

Emboldened, Marta approached Mafasat. 'I've seen a drawing of you and some of the Sarsen Stones in my mother's book.'

Berry juice squirted from Frovin's mouth as he bit down hard.

Marta continued, feeling a little bolder. 'And like the symbols in the middle of the table, we were told that the outer gems removed from the Pentark also belong to the four elements.'

The lion appeared to smile and his flaming eyes softened. 'Your mother and grandmother came here just before the invasion.'

'I thought the invasion was unexpected.'

'Deep down, your grandmother knew that something was wrong, so she came to seek wisdom from the standing stones. From then on, she and your mother stayed close to the Pentark.'

He paused, watching her face as she thought about what he said. 'If you leave now, there is still time to reach the Ageless Forest by sunrise.'

Marta tucked the Lightenstone away and thought of Patrayus as she re-wrapped his scarf around her neck. Frovin jumped off the table onto Snowball and then Marta used it too to slide onto Toros' back. Once they were ready, Mafasat led them back through the megalith, stopping short of the outer entrance.

As they passed through it, he said, 'We are all with you, Marta.' She opened her mouth to say goodbye but Mafasat had already gone.

She pulled her shawl close and found comfort in the twinkling stars. After they cleared the megalith she looked behind her, first south towards the World of the Dark Night and then west towards Jimpiragh Castle where the stars were hidden by darkening clouds. Ahead of them, the animals in the Ageless Forest were stirring.

The Sarsen Plain, thirsty and dry, was eerily quiet. The only sound was the creak of leather and the occasional jingle of Snowball's bit.

# CHAPTER 31

After they were greeted by the waiting animals of the Ageless Forest, Marta, Frovin and Snowball parted from Toros and headed north-west through the forest.

Marta felt safe and very much at home among the stately trees and she wondered if her grandmother had also travelled thorough the Ageless Forest on her way to the Sarsen stones. Frovin gorged on worms and acorns again and Snowball savoured patches of sweet grass. Red squirrels left little piles of nuts wherever the trio camped, and a brown bear found wild honeycomb, delivering it to them dripping with sweetness, balanced between the tusks of a wild boar. There were late berries to eat and they drank from spring water streams. The animals protected them, gathering around the little band every night while Frovin entertained Marta with stories about each of them.

They made good progress through the forest and by late afternoon of the sixth day they reached the furthest point.

'I don't really want to leave here,' said Marta.

'All of the forests in the World of the Soul were like this before the Lightenstone was removed … even Greenwood Forest near Brechin Village.' Frovin was watching her. 'And it can be like that again,' he added.

'But what if we're attacked or …'

'If you can survive the Well of Forgetfulness and ride a white bull across the Abyss River … well …' Frovin made a face at her and spread his paws wide.

She gave him a faint smile. 'Where to from here, then?'

Frovin closed his eyes, trying to visualise Artorus' map.

'Snowball might have other ideas but I think we have two choices. We can follow the main road to Mirraway and hope to blend in with other travellers. Or we can cross the plain to The Veils and then skirt that mountain range to the castle. I expect it's a similar distance.'

Marta pursed her lips, thinking. 'I wonder where Mortimer's army is by now.'

Frovin cracked an acorn. 'Hopefully still behind us. But remember—the wrakes, boorlings and anomirs are what we have to watch out for most. We should wait until dark before we leave.'

The forest animals stood guard while they rested and slept. Marta hugged each animal goodbye and watched them drift back into the forest then saddled Snowball and lifted Frovin up before swinging into the saddle herself. They waited for a moment just behind the tree line and Frovin put his paws on Marta's shoulders. They looked south towards Jimpiragh. The road appeared to be deserted but it was hard to tell, for clouds kept drifting across the waxing moon.

An unpleasant odour wafted towards them. Frovin jerked his head north and froze as he heard the faint rattle of pebbles. They had been dislodged by the long black claws of the approaching boorling that had just come into view. Frovin noted that the master wrake was riding the beast on a loose rein and seemed to be half asleep. Snowball stepped back as the boorling stopped and stared into the trees. The wrake swore and kicked but the boorling refused to move.

Frovin was very familiar with wrakes and boorlings, but Marta was now glimpsing their worst enemies for the first time. The darkness hid their finer features but Frovin had already described the scaly wrakes to her and she remembered Ikoseer's warning that boorlings were 'vile, savage creatures'.

The wrake dismounted, battleaxe ready, and drew closer. The boughs of the trees began to whip back and forth, but the wrake stopped only when a huge brown bear emerged. There was a brief stand-off. The wrake gave the bear a surly look and the wrake slowly returned to the road. The boorling was by this time drooling at the scent of pony and badger and began to emit a high-pitched moan. But the wrake remounted and screamed in frustration, knowing that without re-enforcements, the bear could seriously maim them. The bear roared back as the wrake spurred his mount south towards Mortimer's advancing army.

Marta was not sure why, but she felt comforted by the bear's presence. Once the road was clear, the bear stood on the crown and guarded it, only returning to the forest after the trio had crossed safely and disappeared from sight, heading towards The Veils. Marta was reminded of the constellation of the Great Bear in the northern sky, and of the last time she had searched for it. It was when they had left the Trading Road and crossed the plateau to the Lux Mountains. Now, she looked for the constellation again, and wondered if she would see a falling star this time as well. But not on this night.

She shivered, hoping it was not a bad omen.

The journey to the base of The Veils took a further two nights. Marta loosened the reins, giving Snowball her head, and the pony instinctively seemed to find rocky outcrops to hide among during the day. The land was undulating and reminded Marta of home and her father with Wallace, their faithful wolfhound. Sometimes they passed clumps of weathered trees and a few abandoned farm houses at the bottom of a dip. The houses were small, mostly constructed of wattle and daub, and common enough in the World of Man. Snowball did not avoid the houses—but she did not stop at them either.

On the last night they passed a larger farmhouse. Here there were empty stock pens and a barn, similar to the barn they stayed in after crossing the Intrepid River. It triggered another memory for Marta and she searched in the bottom of a pocket until she found the tiny carved unicorn, and the button with blue threads.

'I'd forgotten about those,' said Frovin as Marta cupped them in her palm.

'Me too.' Marta put the button back in her pocket and rubbed the unicorn thoughtfully between her fingertips. 'Do unicorns exist in the World of the Soul?'

'No, but they are mentioned in folklore.'

' … like Toros?' Marta glanced at the badger.

Frovin shrugged. 'Yes, but bulls naturally have horns. And horses don't. So … if anyone owned a unicorn, it would have to be Ikoseer.' Then, realising what he was suggesting, he peered around Marta to Snowball's bobbing head.

'But that's not possible, of course,' he added quickly, shaking his head. 'And just imagine trying to cover up something like that!' He was visualising a pointed horn in the middle of Snowball's forehead.

But the possibility played on his mind. After reaching the base of The Veils at sunrise, while he scratched out his bed, Frovin stole a glance at Snowball's forelock. When Marta removed the bridle and ran her hand down Snowball's face, she did feel a hard lump under the whorled crown on her forehead. She put her hand to the Lightenstone and wondered if Frovin had guessed the truth. Snowball's forelock still covered the lump but Marta now realised there were other changes in the pony. While they had been in the forest, she needed to loosen Snowball's girth strap and lengthen her bridle. And when she cleaned her hooves the previous day, they somehow seemed wider.

The mournful cry of a peregrine falcon woke Marta mid-morning of the following day. She propped herself on her forearms and looked up at the lofty peaks, shrouded with the misty clouds that gave them their name. Snowball was already standing and greeted Marta with a soft nicker. Marta smiled but when she went to brush her, she realised that Snowball had grown taller overnight. And the long hair on the backs of her legs and belly was almost gone, replaced with a finer, whiter coat. Her mane and tail had grown too.

So much for Sheen's reassurance that we can travel as unimportant and ordinary, thought Marta. But Sheen had been right in most respects. The lump under Snowball's forelock was not changing, but the pony slowly was.

Hugging the base of The Veils, they headed towards Mirraway, but the rough terrain meant that this part of the journey was much slower. Frovin did not notice the changes in Snowball until the next morning when he looked down at Marta from his seat on the saddlebags. 'I don't know what's going on but Snowball's getting taller. If I fall from here, I could be seriously hurt.'

'Yes, I think she's gradually becoming a horse.'

'It must be because of …' Frovin inclined his head to indicate the hidden Lightenstone. 'But I hope it doesn't make me grow too, because if it does then I'll never fit down a badger's sett again.'

Marta grinned. 'There was a time when you asked me to put you high up onto the rump of a warhorse so that you could see further.'

Frovin could not argue that point. 'But then we were being attacked by an anomir! And I didn't have sharp rocks beneath me. Besides, when Snowball's going over rough ground like this I get swayed from side to side. Same as when I've had too many fermented app- ….'

Marta raised her eyebrows and gave him a curious look. He tried to cover up what he had said by feigning interest in the way ahead until she lifted him back onto the ground.

A ridge of gentle hills running parallel to the base of the mountains helped to hide the trio for the next two days. Left to his own devices, Frovin now trotted ahead with his nose constantly to the ground. Occasionally he would wait for them to catch up and once guided Marta and Snowball to a bubbling spring. The Veils reminded Marta of the Lux Mountains, except that here, basalt columns sometimes rose straight up out of scree slopes. Clumps of heather grew among the scree and Marta scrambled up to break off branches of coarse leaves for Snowball to eat.

By mid-morning of the following day the protective hills petered out into the once lush plains, so Marta kept a keener eye out for anomirs. The constant vigilance was stressful and whether Snowball sensed danger or not, as the sun dropped and the full moon began to rise, she suddenly trotted between two rock walls onto a partly formed pathway. Frovin panicked when he couldn't see them.

He caught up as Marta was unsaddling Snowball under an overhanging rock. 'Don't do that to me again!'

'You were too far away. It wasn't safe to call you back.'

Snowball reached around and gave him a quick nip on his rear stretching his loose skin as she pulled back. Now Frovin was furious. He spun around, baring his teeth, as Snowball let go and Marta stifled a giggle.

'Snowball's testing her growing teeth,' she teased.

'Not on me, she isn't.' Frovin was warily eyeing off Snowball's wider hooves and deepening girth.

The next day Snowball led them further into The Veils. After many years of disuse, the path was mostly overgrown by moss, ferns and low dense shrubs. Then, on a clear morning, they rose onto a crest and Marta could see for miles before the path dropped again to a small river at the bottom of a ravine. She quickly looked for Mortimer's army and saw a huge cloud of slow moving dust in the distance.

They kept following the ravine but crossed the river over and back wherever it was shallow, attempting to confuse any following enemy. Frovin hated swimming or even getting wet unless he had to, so he very reluctantly let Marta hold him in front of the saddle each time they crossed.

'We must be getting close to Mirraway Castle by now,' he said as she put him back down for the umpteenth time. 'If we climb to the top of that ridge we might be able to see something useful.'

Marta followed his gaze and as he made off up the slope she left Snowball to forage and scrambled after him. By the time she caught up, he was already engrossed by what he saw.

Marta stared, her hand over the Lightenstone. 'I never imagined that it would be so beautiful,' she whispered.

The silvery white spires of the castle rose proud and stark inside the protective circle of mountains surrounding it. Below and between, a glen gradually widened as it snaked west.

'That's called Glen Bain.' Frovin swept his eyes along the valley.

The glen was different from other valleys that Marta had seen: it was narrower and the floor swept up gracefully, covering the rock giants on either side with a verdant blanket. Behind them was Jimpiragh. Ahead of them Arctus. And to the east, home and the World of Man. Marta looked eagerly for a glimpse of the Pentark, but in vain.

'So, how do we get to the Pentark?' Frovin asked, frowning in concentration. 'Mirraway looks impenetrable. The only access seems to be from the far side, close to the Intrepid River.'

'There must be another way.' Marta was remembering the image she'd seen in the Well of Forgetfulness: Ikoseer propelling Helios off the top of the fell near the Pentark, down a steep escarpment, and away from Mirraway Castle.

She did not know how Ikoseer had reached the Ascension Mountains from there but the niggling memory of a lilting ballad her mother used to sing to her father came into her mind.

> *O'er the way of the glen*
>
> *On the lush slopes by a fen*
>
> *A rose afore me, is the path to thee*
>
> *O Light of my mind, O Light of my heart*
>
> *May we never be apart …*

Marta scanned the glen and as waterbirds took flight in the distance she saw a brief sparkle as the sinking sun caught a ripple of water. She started.

*The song wasn't about the love of my mother for my father: it's
about the Lightenstone!*

'I think there's another entrance.' She suddenly pointed across the glen.

Frovin noted the excitement in her voice but gave her a
sceptical look nonetheless.

'Where?' he asked, sweeping his eyes along the base of the mountains
again, but by then, Marta had already left the top of the ridge. He
scampered after her, catching up as she part ran, part slid, back
down the slope.

'If we rest now we can use the moon to help us cross the glen tonight.' She
was already removing Snowball's tack.

'But she'll shine like a beacon,' he protested. 'I swear that she's almost as
tall as Helios now,' he added, running his eye from hoof to wither.

Marta stroked her glossy neck, nodding in agreement. 'But that's to our
advantage. The boorlings, wrakes and henchmen will be on the lookout
for a pony.'

'Regardless. They'll be hungry, no matter what she looks like.'

Marta faced him. 'You saw what she did to that anomir near the grotto.
Who knows what she's capable of now that she's bigger. I don't want
this anymore than you do, but we'll have to cross the glen regardless of
which way we go and I'm leaving Snowball's tack behind. It's too small for
her now anyway.'

'What about our food?' Frovin was pushing his nose into a saddle bag.

'We'll take that but leave anything unnecessary.'

Marta was already putting the saddle blanket aside and unbuckling the
bags from the back of the saddle. She spread their contents onto a flat
rock. One bag had been taken up by cooking utensils, horse brushes, a

crude hoof pick and a rope. Their leftover food and waterskins had been in the other bag.

'The rope might come in handy but we'll leave these.' Marta placed the utensils and brushes on top of the saddle and bridle and hid them nearby.

'What's this?' Frovin pushed his snout into the coiled rope and was now pulling something out with his teeth.

Marta frowned and gently taking it from him, traced a finger over the metallic symbol and admired the craftsmanship. It looked like two "X's" joined side by side.

'Ikoseer must have put it in there,' she said softly.

Frovin shook his head. 'If she had, we would've found it before now.'

He suddenly brightened. 'It must have been the gnomes. They live in the mountains. They cut gemstones and forge things. Snowball did kick one of them for getting too close, and it does look a bit like a mountain in front of a ravine.'

'Hmm, I don't know,' replied Marta. I also see two letter M's mirror imaged, she thought as she turned the object over in her palm and studied it. Then she remembered the king's ensign that Yoska had drawn for her in the dirt. It was similar except that it was not scribed by a circle; and then there was her mother's brooch …

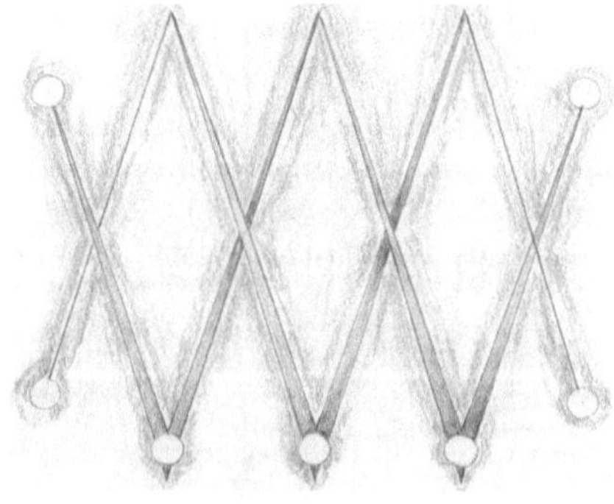

Before slipping it into an inner pocket she wondered, *I think it's another key. Is that how the gnomes are helping us?*

Marta repacked the saddlebags, then wrapping Snowball's saddle blanket around her shoulders, she looked for a place to rest.

Frovin had a fitful sleep. In a dream he was tormented by the gnomes' bulging black and white eyes peering at him from the tunnel walls. Unsettled, he left the others and returned to the ridge. He looked eastward and his thoughts wandered to his family's sett, dug beneath a protective stand of golden oaks in Greenwood Forest. He tried to visualise each of his siblings and recall his past adventurous forays into the World of Man with his favourite cousin; and then, as Ikoseer's helper, the seemingly serendipitous circumstances that had brought him to within reach of the Pentark.

*If Boris hadn't stepped on me when I was sleeping under that pile of leaves, I wouldn't be here; and if I manage to survive this quest, I'll be able to tell stories for decades.*

As he stared across the glen at the spires of Mirraway Castle, the heavy drifting clouds seemed to turn the eye of the moon on and off. It seemed to him too that tension was building in the air—perhaps because Mortimer's army is bringing all their hatred and greed with them, he thought.

Frovin's pondering was interrupted by the rattle of stones below him. He had heard it earlier, fearing it might be another boorling, but dismissed it as being the shaggy long-horned mountain goats he had seen precariously balanced on the highest slopes of The Veils. He froze and focused on the direction of the sound. He decided that the steadily increasing puffing interspersed with restful silence was someone steadily climbing up towards him.

He cautiously moved closer to the edge and sniffed. Then, instead of heading back to warn the others, he hid behind a scraggly shrub and readied himself to attack, expecting to see an enemy soldier dressed in leather armour clamber over the rise. But this man was wearing a dark cowl over a loose-fitting habit, and he slumped down where Frovin had just been, heaving from over-exertion and resting his head in his hands. Once his breathing slowed, he also looked towards the spires of Mirraway Castle and, of more concern to Frovin, appeared to be searching for the Pentark.

Suddenly the man looked in Frovin's direction and whispered, 'Is someone there?'

Frovin was reassured by a slight tremor in the man's voice. *I wonder if he's escaped from Mortimer's army?*

Although the man's face was mostly in shadow, his sagging jowls and haggard appearance suggested that he had been hungry for some time. The stranger took off his sandals and gently massaged his feet. It was then that Frovin decided he was harmless. None the less, he might know something about Mirraway.

The man stiffened when he caught sight of Frovin but apparently decided that he was just a badger. 'I wasn't expecting to see a badger in these mountains. You want to be careful around here. You might end up being eaten.'

The man inclined his head back in the direction of Mortimer's army and then, as if pleased to have someone to talk to (even if it couldn't talk back), he asked with a touch of casual amusement, 'I don't suppose you know a Sage called Ikoseer.'

'I know of her,' replied Frovin carefully.

Startled, the man stopped rubbing his feet. 'You have the gift!'

'I do,' said Frovin, with a tinge of pride.

The man seemed to waver and then re-strapping his sandals, asked, 'Would you recognise Ikoseer if you saw her?'

Frovin shook his head. To avoid eye contact, he began to scratch himself vigorously.

'Hmmm.' The man paused and then casually picked up several white pebbles beside him, rolling them between his palms.

'I was hoping the Sage might be here somewhere, especially with Onysius and Mortimer's army so close to Mirraway.' The man inclined his head towards the army again.

'I saw you looking at the castle,' ventured Frovin, now sitting up and changing the subject. 'Have you ever been there?'

The man gave him a curious glance. 'Yes, a long time ago. But why would a badger like you be interested in that?'

'I've never been there,' said Frovin indifferently. 'Just wondering where the entrance was.'

The man threw his pebbles in front of Frovin and began to read them. Frovin started. This man was a magician!

The man slowly looked up: 'So what are you really doing up here?'

Frovin stepped back. His hackles rose. He had no idea what the man could see in the pattern of pebbles, but it made him very uncomfortable. And now he wished that he had gone back to warn the others.

'Just like you,' replied Frovin quickly. 'I'm looking for someone.'

'In the castle?' The man peered at Frovin, furrowing his brow and seeming to suddenly realise something.

'I've seen a badger with face markings like yours before—but in a book.'

Frovin's markings were slightly different from other badgers. He had the usual black and white stripes, but there was also a fine white ring of hair around each eye.

'I'm sure that there are many badgers with markings just like mine.' Frovin took a further step back.

The man leant towards him, lowering his voice. 'I was taught that only badger protectors of the Lightenstone have that marking.'

'I don't know what you're talking about.' Frovin was now alarmed and turned to go.

'Wait! If you want to know how to get into the castle, I can help you.' The man shifted position and grimaced. 'I'm looking for the Sage for a reason. It's to do with the Lightenstone too.'

'I just want to know where the entrance is.'

'I wouldn't go anywhere near Mirraway if I were you … not with the army down there on the plain. They will be at the main gate of the castle within days. And by tomorrow Mortimer and Onysius will be sitting and brooding on the thrones of the rightful King and Queen.'

He almost spat the last sentence out.

'I have no choice,' revealed Frovin.

The man nodded slowly. 'The main gate is on the far side, near the Intrepid River. But I've heard that there's another entrance, built by the gnomes.'

The moon suddenly broke though the inky clouds, revealing a spark of interest on Frovin's face.

'Do you know where it is?'

'Over there somewhere.' The man looked across the glen and then back at Frovin. 'But even if you did find the other entrance, there's sure to be some sort of ancient door that you won't be able to open.'

*Where's Boris when you need him?* Frovin remembered how Ikoseer had told Boris how to use Thrust to open the Lux Mountains door.

The man looked back at his pebbles, frowned and then stared at Frovin who had just remembered the object he had found when Marta emptied the saddlebags.

'Ah. That's what this means … you already have a key …'

'I have no such thing,' said Frovin, horrified.

And he became even more so when Marta suddenly appeared, halting when she saw them. There was an awkward silence as she gave Frovin a questioning glare.

Suddenly, the piercing screams of hunting anomirs echoed along the glen.

'Hurry!' The man groaned as he rolled over. He got up stiffly, gesturing for Marta to lead them off the ridge.

She was thinking furiously as they headed back to where Snowball was waiting. *It's time for the three of us to get going, and we can't have this dishevelled stranger tagging along.*

Snowball was waiting in full view at the bottom of the ridge. With ears erect and head high, she greeted them all with a nicker. The man offered a flattened hand for Snowball to nuzzle and Marta took the opportunity to size him up.

The man turned to Marta. 'As you can see, I've already met your badger friend. But I haven't properly introduced myself.' He pushed his crooked glasses up the bridge of his nose and glanced at Frovin.

He offered his hand to Marta. 'My name is Attricus. I am seeking Ikoseer the Sage.'

The pair stared at him. Frovin broke the silence. 'You're the soothsayer Onysius is looking for. He sent a goblin on an anomir to capture you— and the kurr that escaped with you.'

Attricus swallowed hard. 'The K-k-kurr's gone.'

Frovin bristled again and bared his sharp teeth. 'Do you work for Onysius?'

'No longer. I was his soothsayer in Jimpiragh Castle but I escaped with the kurr. His name is Volgor.'

Frovin was unimpressed. 'Explain yourself.'

Attricus haltingly recounted his time in Jimpiragh Castle and some of what he and Volgor had gone through after their escape.

'So, what did you tell Onysius about the Lightenstone?' pressed Frovin.

'Nothing really. Sometimes I used to make things up, just to placate him. I did study the Pentark in Elodom Monastery. But the last time I looked into my crystal ball all I saw was a dead gambler, killed by a Knight of Power. And there was also a young woman, an apple seller.'

'Did you tell Onysius that?' Frovin was now very alert.

'Most of it. But he dismissed it as useless information, although he did reveal the gambler was probably one of his spies.'

Marta caught her breath.

'Did you see the young woman's face?' asked Frovin anxiously.

Attricus glanced at Marta but shook his head. 'She had her back to me.'

Marta released her breath slowly. 'Is that what you want to tell Ikoseer about?'

'Yes,' he said. Marta and Frovin suspected that there was more, but Snowball nudged Marta's elbow and taking it as a sign to trust the man, she reluctantly finished the introductions.

'Frovin tells me that he's looking for the main gate to Mirraway Castle but I've warned him about using the main entrance. I wouldn't go anywhere near the castle unless it's absolutely vital.' Attricus was now more relaxed, and recounted what he knew about Mortimer's army, and the gnomes' supposedly secret door.

'Alas! It seems I'll have to skirt this glen to get into Arctus and trek to White Timber Mountain to find the Sage.' His shoulders slumped at the thought of the arduous journey and coming winter snow.

'You should already know where Ikoseer is,' shot Frovin. 'Surely, you just need to throw a few pebbles, or look into your crystal ball to find that out.'

'Soothsaying is a matter of interpretation.' With a dismissive wave of his hand Attricus added, 'My ball is long gone. Lost it in the Tangled Woods over a month ago. That's why I've resorted to pebbles. But all I ever see now is the Lightenstone, or something connected to it.'

'What do you see?' asked Marta.

Attricus chose his words carefully. 'It seems as if something's changed. This is probably why Mortimer's army has suddenly come here. I sense that the Lightenstone's been moved, that somehow Lord Mortimer knows about it. The Prince of Darkness does have his eager ear. He is bound to him by the Prince's necklace, Toil.'

I've never heard of Toil, thought Marta but Frovin's mouth dropped. *So that's what Snowball meant*, he thought.

Frovin recalled her saying that word, 'Toil', when the storm started after Marta had disappeared through the door into Aramark Temple.

Attricus dipped his head slightly and spread his hands. 'Maybe Ikoseer already knows this. Maybe I'm wasting my time looking for her.'

A thought crossed Frovin's mind. 'Have you ever seen the outer gems in your readings?'

Attricus considered what he had instinctively gleaned from the precocious badger. Taking a risk he whispered, 'I know about one of them.'
They were shocked.

*So that's the real reason he wants to find Ikoseer.* He moved closer. 'Do you have one of the outer gems?'

'No … no … NO!' Attricus flapped his hands in the dark.

'Aah, but you know who does?' guessed Frovin.

Attricus shuffled, ill at ease. 'Yes.'

And then he told them: About the attack of the wrake and how Volgor found the aquamarine in the belly of the fish that he caught in the Abyss River, and how they were heading to Werthyn Harbour when they were separated.

'I don't know what happened to Volgor,' he continued softly, 'but if he was captured and the gemstone was found, it will eventually end up in Lord Mortimer's hands. I know it's not the same as possessing the Lightenstone, but the outer gems are important too. Without them, the Pentark or light spheres won't have full power.'

*So, Ikoseer was right, thought Frovin. We don't have to worry about the outer gems and now we know that the aquamarine from the Abyss River has been found.*

Attricus' distress made Marta realise how so many in the World of the Soul were being sorely tested. *I've been so focused on returning the Lightenstone that I've forgotten that others are also suffering and fighting to restore the Pentark. Together we are one,* she thought.

When Snowball nudged her to get moving, Marta said, 'I'm sorry for the loss of your companion, and I'm grateful for your information and warnings. But despite that, we must get to Mirraway Castle. If you still want to find Ikoseer then you can travel with us across the glen on your way to Arctus.'

Frovin bristled and gave Marta a disapproving look but she had already thrown the blanket onto Snowball's back and was reaching for the saddlebags.

Meanwhile Attricus was running his fingers through the ends of the frayed rope hanging under his belly. He was already exhausted and he shivered at the thought of the hunting anomirs. He knew it was safer for him to travel alone, but there was something about this trio that niggled at him, something to do with the Lightenstone.

'Thank you,' he said. 'But if we're to make it by morning, we'll have to hurry.'

# PART 6

# FIRE

# CHAPTER 32

The Veils was a vast mountain range. It stretched from Mirraway Castle almost to the border of Illingaith and Asilodor. The castle was nestled in front of the belly of a slumbering rock giant, lying on his side. The giant's head and knees seemed drawn together, protectively encircling the fortress.

Dividing this range was Glen Bain, the narrow valley that Marta and Frovin had seen from the ridge. It was past midnight when they rounded the most northern point on their side of the glen.

'We shouldn't cross yet.' Attricus nodded towards Arctus. 'The further we are from Mortimer's army, the better.'

'We usually let Snowball decide that,' countered Frovin, looking up at her.

Attricus shrugged. Snowball tossed her head at the soothsayer, and nickering in agreement, led them west along the upswept base of Glen Bain. She snatched mouthfuls of lush grass as they went. Frovin raced ahead, nose to the ground, often coming back, anxious that they hurry up. Attricus struggled, much to Frovin's annoyance, but they all waited for him to catch up.

After several miles Snowball turned abruptly and headed across the glen towards Mirraway Castle. The wind continued to pick up until it was a roaring gale but Snowball put her head down and pushed on, taking the brunt of the buffeting easterly force, as the others sheltered on her lee side.

The flying tips of Snowball's mane stung Marta's face. She wrapped Patrayus' scarf around her head, keeping a slit for her eyes and with one hand on the Lightenstone she offered her other hand to Attricus, hoping that the Stone would strengthen him.

Snowball seemed to keep to a straight path. Frovin was puzzled by Marta's painstaking focus. She berated him if he wandered too far from her. 'You must stay beside me now,' she demanded telepathically. Frovin begrudgingly obeyed.

As Attricus scoured the night sky, a bolt of lightning shot from the inky ceiling, striking the ground ahead. Against the brilliant flash he saw the mass of hunting anomirs. *They must have seen us*, he thought.

He tugged on Marta's hand and pointed up. She nodded in understanding, loudly whispering a warning to Frovin. Snowball seemed undeterred and kept steadily on.

The lightning struck again, closer this time and the loud crack made Attricus jump and let go of Marta's hand.

'Grab my shawl,' she yelled as he moved behind her, now at Snowball's flank.

She looked up at the angry sky to see one of the anomirs, guided by its attentive goblin rider, dropping away from the others and gliding towards them. Even in the dark, the goblin's eyes glistened with madness at the tempting feast ahead. His mount's piercing scream rallied the circling horde to join them.

Marta clutched the Lightenstone at her breast and prayed for help. Terrified, Attricus pushed against Snowball. Frovin bared his teeth and readied himself to attack.

'We must keep to the ley line,' Snowball told Frovin, and now he understood. She was following the energy line that ran between the Pentark and the light sphere on the headland of the World of the Dark Night.

As another flash of electric blue lit the sky and thunder pealed along the glen, the mare lifted her head high in defiance, taunting the anomirs to come closer. Her long mane and tail whipped wildly, streaks of silver now running through the white. Suddenly, she reared and with ears flattened, charged forward with the anomirs giving chase. Her blanket and saddlebags slid to the ground behind her. A gust of wind pushed Attricus to his knees, and bracing herself, Marta pulled him up and made a grab for the saddlebags.

'Leave them,' he shouted. She let them drop.

Frovin tugged on her trouser leg yelling, 'Stay on the ley line. Follow me!'

Squinting against the swirling debris Marta thought she could see mounted boorlings coming towards them through the glen; Snowball, now far ahead, sped like the wind towards the far side of the glen, her whole coat transformed silvery white under the waning moon. High above and spurred on by their riders, the ravenous anomirs jostled for the best position. Snowball stayed true to the ley line, galloping, faster and faster.

Eventually the rhythmic drumming of her hooves on the hardened ground stirred a slumbering rock giant resting with his head low on the valley floor. He lazily opened an eye and taking in the pursuit, at once began to open his grass-covered lips. The ground rumbled, reverberating down the ley line and out on either side, knocking Marta and Attricus over as it spread.

Suddenly, a small fissure appeared as the giant cleared his throat and sharp rocks were blasted high into the air. In the dark, the goblins baulked and tried to pull their confused mounts up and away through the debris, but many were struck and fell to their deaths.

Meanwhile Snowball had bolted into the giant's mouth. And now it closed after her. Marta, Frovin and Attricus were left clinging to the ground, waiting for it to stop shaking.

Attricus placed his hand on Marta's back and shouted above the buffeting wind. 'You alright?' Heavy raindrops began to fall.

'What happened to Snowball?' she shouted back.

'Don't know. But the anomirs are gone. For now.'

'But what about the mounted boorlings? They were after her.'

Attricus gingerly raised his head, adjusted his glasses and squinted into the dark.

'Can't see them. Perhaps they've gone.'

'Doubt it!' Frovin moved out from the huddle and sniffed the air. 'We can't stay here. We have to find Snowball.'

They raced on towards the castle, but without the mare's protection they all felt vulnerable.

Boorlings are generally ridden by master wrakes, and Attricus was remembering the fight with the wrake near the Abyss River. His last sight of Volgor was when he was slashing the neck of the beast with Duke Tardor's short sword. Attricus had managed to escape that time. But now, he had no weapon. He wished that he had continued on towards Arctus alone.

All animals in the World of the Soul are naturally tuned into the three ley lines that radiate from the Pentark and power their respective light spheres on the headland, but Frovin had never consciously followed one. Now, calling on all his senses, he weaved from side to side, at times deliberately moving off the line until he could feel the magnetic ley line pull him back. And when he checked on Attricus and Marta behind him he could see that the Lightenstone was guiding her too. He thought that they had a few more miles to go and was anxious to get there as quickly as possible, for a cold rain was now falling steadily.

At that moment, out of sight of anyone on the ground, another goblin was circling his anomir high above. He spotted the five mounted boorlings as they advanced ever closer to the fleeing trio. The goblin bade his anomir pull in her wings and drop steadily behind the charging boorlings. Rain pelted his face and he held on tight as the scales of his mount became slippery.

When they were close enough, she opened her talons on his signal, driving them deep into the back of the closest wrake and snatching him off his mount as the goblin wheeled her away. As she flung the wrake high into the air, the goblin circled her again, preparing to home in on the next one.

But the momentum of the attack caused the tumbling boorling to clip the back legs of the one in front of him, bringing it and its rider down heavily. After a quick look behind them, the other riders kept on going.

In sudden dismay, the goblin turned his anomir away. He recognised the rider on the leading boorling: It was his Jimpiragh master, the ageing Earl Onysius. This goblin was Rhyll, the one Marta healed at the Aramark Temple. Although he was as yet unaware of it, the healing had caused a shift in his consciousness.

On his return to Hammerlock, several days after his encounter with Marta, Rhyll found a female anomir on the ground, flapping madly and trying to free herself from a trap set by resistance fighters. He initially intended to leave her to her fate but, on reflection, decided to free her. He realised that he could use her to help him scour the Kingdom of Gorthonomir, looking for Marta and her companions.

He eventually found them, hiding among the rocks on their journey across the plains to The Veils. Camouflaging his mount high among the cliffs of The Veils, Rhyll saw the amazing transformation of Snowball into a fine boned horse. And now he also recognised the bedraggled man with them: Attricus, his initial quarry. Rhyll thought the badger might survive the coming attack by Onysius and his troop, but Marta and Attricus had little hope against them.

The anomir felt her rider's grip tighten. He had been kind to her and, although it was unprecedented for an anomir to attack a boorling or wrake, she would repay him with unwavering obedience. And so, feeling strangely strengthened, she readied her talons again.

Rhyll decided to change his angle of attack. He steered alongside the three remaining boorlings, and timed his anomir's strike so that she grabbed the last wrake by the head and with a flick, broke his neck. Then she swung the dangling body around, letting it go so that it slammed into the next wrake, sending its boorling into a tangled heap.

Finally the rider of the remaining boorling, Onysius, looked up and realised that their attacker was Rhyll. He stood in his stirrups and drew his battle sword as his mount galloped on.

'How dare you?' he roared, spitting and shaking his sword against Rhyll and his anomir, heedless of the pelting rain and battering winds. As he yanked his mount hard left into a wide arc, he saw the third boorling pass him, without a rider. It was almost upon Marta and her companions, huddled below, watching in horror.

Leaving his master raging, Rhyll gripped tighter. In the pre-dawn light he watched his brave anomir grab the riderless boorling, lift it high, and then drop it so that it fell awkwardly. As it attempted to get up, Frovin raced in and through the leathery folds of its neck, tore at the jugular vein and windpipe. The furious boorling staggered, and after a final desperate lurch, slumped and died.

'Keep going!' Now retreating and bloodied, Frovin shouted to the goblin to save them from the old boorling rider. Frovin had never seen him before, but he recognised the large crest of the World of the Dark Night beaten into his chest armour. He sensed an arrogant air of privilege about him.

Against the first glow of the rising sun, Marta grasped the Lightenstone, and braced for impact.

'I am so sorry, Mother. I have failed you,' she whispered in anguish.

Frovin screamed. 'Take it out! Now!' In desperation, Marta reached inside her doublet.

But they didn't notice the goblin's anomir, who now crossed low overhead and grabbed at Onysius, who had no choice but to force his mount east, followed by the emboldened Rhyll.

Rhyll's anomir was tiring and the storm was abating, so he was satisfied to taunt the Earl with one final pass and then return to the others. He slowed his anomir to land on the dead boorling. Frovin approached with his teeth bared but undeterred, Rhyll slid off his mount's back. Leaving her to feast, he shuffled cautiously towards the badger.

'It's me. Rhyll.'

Marta was standing beside Attricus, watching them. She wiped wet strands of hair from her face. Frovin moved closer, noting the brand seared high up on one of the goblin's cheekbones: The same brand as on the goblin from Aramark Temple, he thought.

'See?' The goblin stuck his leg out. Frovin checked the scar and then nodded to Marta.

Without invitation, Rhyll trotted past Frovin's distrustful gaze and stared at Attricus. Pushing up his long fringe, he leant in for a closer look and grunted.

'You're the soothsayer I was supposed to find. And good riddance to Onysius.'

Marta and Frovin both started, then recovering quickly, Marta said, 'Thank you for helping us today. You saved our lives.'

Rhyll shrugged and looked at his mount. 'She saved your lives.'

'I thought you were going home to Hammerlock,' growled Frovin.

'I was.' Rhyll then relayed most of what had happened since his healing at Aramark Temple before asking, 'Are you going to Mirraway?'

'None of your business,' hissed Frovin.

'Did you see a galloping white horse?' asked Marta hopefully. She gave Frovin a warning glance.

'I saw a silvery white horse disappearing into the mouth of a rock giant. But I thought you'd be looking for your white pony. Haven't seen her anywhere.'

'She's not with us anymore,' said Frovin, perhaps a little too quickly.

For a moment, Rhyll studied Frovin with his dark beady eyes. 'Well, you can't stay here. The other anomirs will find you. Then Onysius will be back with reinforcements. But if you like, we could fly you somewhere.' He pointed to his anomir and then waved his wiry arm in the general direction of Mirraway.

'There is a fen.' Marta pointed west across the glen.

'I've seen it.' Ignoring Frovin he trotted back to his mount. The anomir looked up at him as her powerful beak kept pulling the dead boorling's sinews until they broke and she gulped them down.

Rhyll patted her scaly neck and stroked her wet feathers. 'We can come back,' he told her. With a gentle tug, he led her towards the others. With her wings held out for balance she rocked awkwardly on her talons: her enormous size was intimidating.

Rhyll pushed the front of the anomir's body down so that they could climb onto her back. Attricus climbed up first, offered his hand to Marta, and then with a push from Rhyll, Frovin scrambled up.

Rhyll spoke to the anomir in his goblin language and as she lifted her head and wings, he swung up and sat with his legs astride her neck. He faced her south-west and with another command she began to move, rather awkwardly under the extra load.

'Lie down and hide under her feathers as best you can,' he instructed as she spread her wings wide and catching the air, climbed slowly, leaving the lush glen far below.

When Rhyll flew them back towards their crossing point, Frovin at first thought that the goblin was taking them to the World of the Dark Night or Hammerlock, but then they turned due west towards Arctus. In a sweeping curve, they re-crossed the glen again towards Mirraway, approaching the fen from the west. By taking this circuitous route Rhyll avoided the other anomirs and Frovin, impressed by the anomir's speed, finally acknowledged that this was quicker and safer than walking.

Against the rising sun, the view from the air was spectacular. They could see Mirraway Castle nestled within her rocky fastness, her ten spires like giant silvery-white sentinels. Built entirely from marble, Mirraway was breathtaking and Marta immediately recognised the much smaller Pentark near to it.

It's just as I saw it in the Well of Forgetfulness, she thought, then searched for Ikoseer and Helios' escape route. But steep mountains blocked her view and her heart sank at what still lay ahead of them.

Suddenly, her mother's voice seemed to echo in her head. *You are exhausted, my dear, but you're almost there. Tell the goblin to fly you straight to the Pentark.*

*I can't,* she answered. *You know that I must be tested.*

*You have already been tested,* pressed the voice, now with a smooth mesmerising undertone. *And you have passed brilliantly!*

But the Lightenstone began to judder. Marta took this as a warning: *I will go as I am meant to go.*

*Then I will stop you,* hissed the voice, *and the Lightenstone will be mine!*

Marta pressed the Stone against her beating heart, trying to draw strength from it. *Someone else knows that I have seen the Pentark—and also carry the Lightenstone. Where are you, Ikoseer? I need you.*

By now they were flying over the fen and the castle dipped from view as the anomir dropped in ever-decreasing circles. Rhyll kept checking with Marta until she pointed out a spring that fed the fen. It was trickling from the centre of a faintly outlined rose pattern that appeared to be formed by rock fissures.

As waterbirds took flight below, the anomir tilted her massive wings, dragging them through the air to slow down, and then landed close by on the lush green slope.

Rhyll jumped down. 'Stay under her wings. The sun's rising fast. You'll have to hide soon.'

'Look for a keyhole. A symbol carved into a rock,' said Attricus.

No doors out here, thought Rhyll, scouring the slope.

'Stay here,' said Frovin, as Marta got up to help.

Rhyll didn't know what to look for but he joined Frovin as the badger scampered from rock to rock. He was using his long claws to scratch rubble and moss away, while he scoured the wet ground, pushing and prodding with his feet.

Frovin stopped abruptly and stared. 'Over here!'

Rhyll knelt beside him as Marta and Attricus joined them on the soggy slope.

'That's it?' asked Rhyll.

Marta studied the three dots, with two dashes between.

●——————●——————●

Her body tingled. 'Yes, I think it is.'

'But you'll still need a key to open it.' Frovin bristled.

Marta reached into her pocket and took out the metallic object that Frovin had found in the coiled rope. Rhyll's eyes widened, but his glee was overshadowed by a warning from his anomir. Glancing towards the east he saw several mounted anomirs scouring the ground and gradually coming closer.

He gestured to his anomir. 'Come.'

Soon all five of them were bent over the symbol, the anomir with her wings still shielding them as Marta pressed the three points of the key onto the three dots.

She pushed hard.

The ground shuddered and gave way. Water was now gushing from the opening. In an instant the anomir grabbed Rhyll with her beak as, forced off balance by the sudden rush of water, both tumbled backwards down the slope.

Meanwhile the others had fallen into the now revealed cavern, shocked by the icy water but cushioned by thick layers of moss and a strange creeping fern that grew on either side of the stream. Bruised and shivering, Marta sat up and looked around, returning the key to her pocket. Attricus groaned and rubbed his head as Frovin shook water from his coat and scampered over to them. But Rhyll and his anomir were gone and Marta was downhearted. She hoped that Rhyll had survived, but was also wishing he was still here to help her.

'I was expecting some kind of passageway.' She looked up to where a thin shaft of light from the rising sun was brightening parts of the cave wall. Marta pointed to it. 'We should see if we can get out that way.'

'No, we should stay in the mountain.' Attricus grabbed Marta's hand. 'This isn't the entrance I was expecting, but since the key opened it, there must be a passageway here somewhere.'

Marta searched his pallid face. 'We should drink.' She crouched down and as he joined her and leant forward, he glimpsed the chain around her neck and the soft glow coming from under her doublet.

'What do you know about the passageways?' she asked.

Attricus wiped his mouth. 'All I know is that there are tunnels under Mirraway Castle. I don't know where they go. I can only imagine that if you find the right one, you could follow it to the heart of the castle.'

'Oh! That makes sense. The castle must have been built over the heart of a rock giant. So we just have to find …'

'There will be a labyrinth of tunnels, Marta.' Attricus felt dispirited, remembering the blueprints of the castle he had studied at Elodom Monastery.

'Then we should stay outside,' said Frovin firmly. 'At least we might be able to see the castle's spires to guide us. And anyway, you're on your way to Arctus to look for Ikoseer.'

Marta rebuked him. 'We'll look for the passageway and Attricus is welcome to come with us. He knows more about Mirraway than either of us.'

Their spirits were weighed down by the cold and the hunger rumbling in their bellies, by the weight of expectation, by doubt and the never-ending questions, with answers that never really resolved them.

As Marta helped Attricus up and Frovin searched for a way into the mountain, curious goblins were circling their mounts overhead. But when the leading goblin swept low over Rhyll and his prostrate mount, he assumed they were dead and wheeled towards Mirraway Castle. There Lord Mortimer brooded and paced, with the increasing weight of the necklace, Toil, digging into his fleshy neck.

In the scullery below the throne room, Ferdy was keeping his wits about him. Since the Commander had relegated him there until he was deemed useful, Ferdy had kept his head down. He soon discovered that being a scullion was hot, hard work. It was just as well he was an opportunistic thief—if he was more like Boris he would have starved.

He knew that something was happening when there were suddenly far too many plates to scrape, more bread to break, more goblets to fill. Strange soldiers appeared, bringing war gossip to his ears. And when he heard that Lord Mortimer had arrived and the Lightenstone was mentioned in the same conversation, Ferdy became fraught with worry. He vowed to escape.

There was also the matter of the agate that King Elvendor had entrusted to him to return to the Pentark. It was still in the waterskin hugging his midriff. He made general enquiries about Tom and Ranger, but everyone knew that the odd trio had arrived together and all he got was suspicious stares.

'I've slaved every day for almost three weeks,' muttered Ferdy, furiously scrubbing another pot, 'so where's Boris? Surely he's coming to rescue me.'

He was right thinking that Boris would be coming to rescue him. But it was dangerous work. Since his escape from the bullock cart, the soldiers and wrakes had been on the lookout for Boris, and he had already gleaned from other travellers what happened to Ferdy, Tom and Ranger. It seemed that their arrival at Mirraway Castle loaded with elven goods had created quite a stir.

'C'mmander's got the fat little dwarf workin' in the scullery,' laughed a gangly young lad that Boris had cautiously befriended after he claimed to know everything about Mirraway.

'What happened to the elf and the bullock?'

'I 'aven't seen the driver. But I know they let the bullock loose an' kept the cart.' Then he added with an air of mystery, 'They think the bullock's magical—seein' it belongs to the elves.'

Boris' opportunistic friendship initially paid off. The lad eked out a living by running messages between the Lake Bridge and Mirraway Castle and revelled in tittle-tattle, boasting that he had been in every room and walkway in the castle. It was this knowledge that got Boris through a discreet entrance in the outer wall, the bailey. But it seemed that the lad was more cunning than he looked. After often admiring Thrust and supposedly leading Boris close to the scullery, he demanded Thrust as payment for his services.

'If you can remove my blade from its sheath, then you can have
it,' offered Boris.

Greed lit the lad's face as he grabbed the handle, but then yelped in pain
and flung his arm as an electric bolt shot up his arm. A scuffle ensued
when the lad made another attempt, so Boris stabbed the lad's hand,
making him squeal. It was only then that he discovered that he was
nowhere near the scullery, but was actually close to the dungeons—and to
a group of now alerted soldiers and wrakes.

'The dwarf went that way!' cried the lad.

Boris held Thrust out as he ran, seemingly blindly at first, but soon he
realised that the blade was guiding him through the maze of passages.
And when it suddenly pulled him sideways and lodged itself into a thick
wooden door, he wrenched the blade out, opened the door and shut
it behind him.

But as he leant against the door to catch his breath he was overcome by
a strong stench. He immediately realised that Thrust had led him to a
garderobe, a lavatory. Screwing up his face, and pinching his nose he
looked around, cursing Thrust for taking him to such a place.

Then he heard sniffing outside the door. Gagging, he moved away, sure
that he would soon vomit. He could see hay and dried moss in a basket for
wiping backsides and an unlit candle in a holder, but what surprised him
was the clothing hanging from the wooden pegs embedded in the walls
either side of the door.

He was hiding between the longest garments when the door was opened
by a wrake and then slammed shut again. He desperately wanted to leave
but could still hear the animated voices of soldiers and the sound of their
hobnailed boots on the flagstones. He burrowed deeper into the garments
until his back was hard against the wall.

Then Boris heard a soft padded sound and wondered if Ferdy had
somehow escaped and was hiding in the lavatory with him. Thrust
suddenly felt hot in his hand and the sound of a single note fell upon his

ear, the same musical note that he had heard in Alfura, the elven enclave. He had forgotten all about it. He still did not know what it meant, but the last time he had heard it was before meeting Yahdra and when King Elvendor gave Ferdy the agate. Now Boris assumed that Thrust wanted to alert him to the presence of Ferdy and the agate.

Excited by his newfound belief, he pushed his way back through the garments and with his nose still pinched and his eyes stinging, whispered, 'Ferdy?'

Thrust suddenly began to vibrate and pull him across the room. Wide eyed, Boris tried to control Thrust. Then his eyes grew even wider, matching those of a creature unknown to him. The creature was also being dragged—from the hanging garments on the opposite wall—but by a different blade, a jewelled blade with a gilt handle.

Boris tried with all his might to control Thrust, but it was no use. The creature coming towards him looked terrified as his blade flew from his long bony fingers. Boris ducked and again tried to wield Thrust against the attack, but Thrust refused to obey and then also ripped from his grip.

The two blades clashed.

Boris stared dumbfounded as the blades twisted around each other, spinning faster and faster until they became a single flaming sword, hovering in the foul air between Boris and the creature.

Boris immediately remembered the flaming sword and crossed blades engraved on Thrim's headstone in the cemetery near the Ascension Mountains. Thrust is really TWO blades, not one!

The creature made for the door. But so did Thrust. And as the blade hovered in front of the creature it backed away, eyeing Boris warily.

Boris held out his right hand, his fingers spread wide, and as Thrust returned to him, the flames died. But now, the bone handle shimmered and its grip felt very different. Strength seemed to surge through him and he bore down on the creature.

'Where's my brother, Ferdy? What have you done with him?'

'N … nothing,' spluttered the creature. 'I … I don't know any dwarves called Ferdy. And you can have the short sword. I'm glad to be rid of it.'

'Now that you mention the sword—where did you get it?'

'I … I knew someone who found it.'

'I doubt it was found. I expect it was stolen,' said Boris. 'And it's obviously a dwarf sword. So what were you doing with it?'

'It's not a dwarf sword. Had the Royal Crest of the Isle of Spheres on it. It's a duke's short sword.'

Boris' eyes narrowed. 'Duke? Which Duke?'

'A … a dead one.'

Boris immediately thought of Thrim's grave.

'Did you get it from the cemetery near the Ascension Mountains?'

'No! No. *No!*' The creature was pointing and waving a bony arm at the outer wall as if Boris should know where he meant. When Boris gave him a blank look he said, 'From Jimpiragh.'

All manner of possibilities ran through Boris' mind. 'Did you come here with Lord Mortimer's army?'

Boris saw fear in the bulging grey eyes as the creature took another step back, shaking his head vigorously. 'So, why are you here then?'

Then Thrust sounded the note again, except this time it was sharper and clearer. Shocked, Boris finally understood.

*Thrust must sound the note when one of the gemstones is near.*

'You're here because you've got one of the Pentark gemstones, haven't you?' he breathed.

The creature looked down at his filthy feet. Staring at the unlikely courier, Boris lowered Thrust. *I was right*, he thought, *the outer gemstones really are finding us.*

'Where'd you find it?'

'The Abyss.' The answer was barely audible.

Boris leant closer. 'Which gem?'

'Aquamarine,' mouthed the fleshy lips.

Boris wondered where the creature had hidden it.

'You must stay close to me from now on,' he told him. 'First, I have to rescue my brother, Ferdy. He's supposed to be in the scullery. Then we have to get to the Pentark.'

As Boris cracked open the door, a rush of cool air relieved their eyes and nostrils. The passageway was silent. Boris poked his head out for a quick look and then back again.

'You ready …?' He paused, realising he did not know the creature's name, so raised his eyebrows.

'Name's Volgor.'

'Boris of Banters Den.' He gave a curt nod and then opened the door wider.

'Wait!' Volgor was quickly rummaging through a basket of hats near the door. Grabbing two, he passed one to Boris. They were liripipes, simple hooded hats with a tail. Stitched to the base of the hoods was a cape to cover their shoulders, but since Volgor's head was level with Boris' shoulder, his cape reached past his hips and the tail of the hat almost touched the ground.

Boris roughly jammed the new hat over his own and after another quick check, slipped into the passageway.

Bewildered, Volgor squeezed the hidden gemstone for reassurance and reluctantly trotted after the feisty dwarf and his magical blade, Thrust. He was pleased to be rid of Duke Tardor's short sword but the last place he wanted to go was a scullery. All he could think of was the banging of pots and the stench of hungry trolls cooking soothsayers in Jimpiragh Castle. And of course, this reminded him of Attricus.

*I've got to get the aquamarine to the Pentark. And what if Onysius is here?*

The mention of Lord Mortimer made him cringe. He worried, as Thrust hurried them up a set of steep steps and into another maze of passages.

# CHAPTER 33

The rising sun was gently bathing Glen Bain's slopes as Earl Onysius charged on his boorling to find Lord Mortimer, and Frovin led Marta and Attricus through the cold, dark tunnel leading from the cave she opened using the gnomes' key. While it was easy for Frovin to find his way in the dark, Attricus and Marta were struggling behind him. After a short while Attricus stopped. Leaning against the tunnel walls, he suddenly made a suggestion.

'I've noticed a glow coming from under your doublet. Why don't you take the lead—use that light to see where we're going?'

Alarmed, Frovin looked back at the two of them. Marta hesitated for a moment and then turning away from Attricus, she lifted the Lightenstone from her doublet so that it just lit the tunnel. She moved ahead of Frovin and they all set off again.

Frovin was thinking it looked just like the tunnel near Aramark Temple, then remembering that Marta had asked the Gnome King to help them, he reluctantly searched the walls for the gnomes' googly black and white eyes.

They went on walking for hours and whenever Marta's tummy rumbled, she thought longingly of the food in the saddlebags abandoned while crossing Glen Bain, and of the elementals that had fed them at the Sarsen stones. She wondered if they would be able to help them again, and decided to try visualising a plate full of food floating in front of her. Keeping the vision steady in the air and ignoring other flittering thoughts, she noticed her peripheral vision slowly blurring. Tiny cracks were beginning to run along the walls.

'Huh? The tunnel's about to collapse!' shouted Attricus. He made a grab to pull her back.

'No! Wait!' said Frovin. 'Don't you see what's happening?'

Dozens of gnome hands were pushing young plants through the widening fissures and into the tunnel, sending shards of rubble clattering to the floor. They stopped and stared as the foliage grew and Marta instinctively focused the Lightenstone along each wall. Suddenly the plants blossomed, and then the fruiting and ripening began.

'The light from your amulet has attracted the gnomes, Marta,' Frovin said in an attempt to distract Attricus.

But it was too late to do that. I think more than gnomes are helping us, thought Attricus, reaching for a pear and watching Marta bite into an apple. At first, Frovin feasted on the fat worms wriggling out of the soil. But then eyeing off some apricots, plums and berries, he stretched up to break off a particularly plump bunch of grapes. Soon his cheeks were full of sweet pulp, spurting and dripping as he chewed in newfound delight.

Marta started gathering a pile of the various nuts: walnuts, hazelnuts, chestnuts, pine-nuts and almonds. Attricus helped her. He was amused at how Frovin used his sharp teeth to crack open the hardest shells, while nudging aside his favourite—walnuts—and leaving the hazelnuts and almonds for the other two.

Now with her belly full, Marta silently thanked the elementals and sat down. But she turned her body away from Attricus, and resting an elbow on drawn knees, concealed the Lightenstone with a casually draped hand.

Meanwhile Attricus was studying her closely, recollecting all he knew about the Pentark. He doubted that her light was coming from a simple amulet. But could Marta really be carrying the Lightenstone? It seemed impossible.

He knew that the Firebird brought the Lightenstone from the sun, then collected the twelve cut outer gems from the gnomes and placed all of them in the Pentark structure. And it was generally believed that when Lord Mortimer invaded the World of the Soul, Ikoseer removed the Lightenstone and four of the outer gems, and taken them either to the Lux Mountains, or to the Queen of the Sun.

But now he was questioning that belief.

When he queried the words 'light carrier' in several books in Elodom library, he learned that the Firebird, the Queen of the Sun and Ikoseer were all light carriers. But what if that did not refer to them? What if Ikoseer was not the one that removed the Lightenstone? What if it was someone else? He needed to check out his growing suspicions about Marta's identity.

'You remind me of someone I once waited on at Elodom Monastery.'

Marta's heart beat faster. Could the soothsayer have met her mother some time in the past?

'Ikoseer was a regular visitor at the monastery,' he continued, 'especially after it became a refuge for those who fled when Lord Mortimer invaded. It was a chaotic time. I was still a novice in those days. I remember a young woman and her mother stayed overnight at the monastery before Ikoseer spirited them away on her beautiful golden palfrey, Helios. I assumed she must have taken them into the World of Man. But she seemed to treat them differently from other refugees. As if she was protecting them somehow. There was definitely a sense of secrecy and haste around them.

'You look very much like the younger woman. Perhaps it's your eyes.'

He noted Frovin's sharp glance in her direction. 'I found out later that the names of the two women I waited on were Maria and Roselin.'

Marta mumbled something. Frovin gave a snort of surprise.

Frovin knew that Maria and Roselin were Marta's grandmother and mother, because their names were spoken at the front door of Aramark Temple. And he had been partly right about her mother taking the amulet into the World of Man. Ikoseer must have taken both of them from the monastery and into hiding.

And now he felt that he must distract the soothsayer again. 'But what do those women have to do with anything?'

'I get the feeling that somehow, there's a connection between them and the Pentark. The name Roselin reminds me that roses are mystical symbols of the Pentark.'

Frovin felt panic rising. Marta had described to him the image of the ring of red roses she saw in the Well of Forgetfulness. *Here I am trying to keep everything a secret and meanwhile Attricus is working it all out.*

'Or roses could be symbols of the Ascension Mountains.' He quickly tried to steer the conversation in another direction. 'I once saw a cabbage rose on the breast of a female statue there.'

Attricus straightened. 'You *are* well travelled. So, is that where you met Ikoseer?'

'Certainly not. Ikoseer used to visit my clan's sett in Greenwood For- …'

He stopped abruptly, remembering that on the previous night he had denied knowing the Sage at all.

*Aha!* Attricus was amused by the revelation. 'Is your sett beneath a stand of golden oaks?'

'As it happens, yes. It had to be dug somewhere in the forest.' Frovin tried to sound offhand. He threw Marta a worried glance.

Attricus chuckled, his jowls wobbling. 'So, you do belong to the famous badgers of Greenwood Forest. Who's in your family tree then, old Oak Brock?'

'My great grandfather,' admitted Frovin irritably, wondering how the soothsayer could know such a thing.

Now Attricus relented. 'Your family tree is recorded in the library at Elodom Monastery.'

Frovin gave him a startled look. He had just confirmed that he came from the family of protectors of the Lightenstone. Frovin had the upper hand when he first met Attricus at The Veils, but now he realised Attricus had turned that around. Marta should have sent him on his way to Arctus.

A sudden look of understanding came over Attricus' face.

He murmured as if to himself. 'I've never made the connection before. That's not the only family tree recorded in the library at Elodom. Princess Maria and Lady Roselin are members of the maternal line of the royal family of the Kingdom of Gorthonomir. Before Lord Mortimer invaded, they must have lived in Mirraway Castle. That's why they were with Ikoseer that day. She was helping them escape into the World of Man.'

Astonished, Marta gasped. Her eyes widened.

Frovin was taken aback. *Is Marta a descendant of the royal family of Gorthonomir?* He watched as Attricus picked up a small handful of rounded pebbles, rolled them between his palms. He threw them and stared at the result.

Despite appearing calm, Frovin wanted to scatter the pebbles. He had been assigned to protect the Lightenstone and Marta in her quest and he had betrayed his mission.

After a long silence Attricus looked up at Marta and murmured gently, 'Do you still have the gnome's key?'

She nodded, reached into her pocket and gave the key to Frovin.

Attricus took it and turned it over. 'You're partly right about the connection to the statues. This key also reminds me of the crossed swords between the two statues. And the cross held in the male statue's hand.'

'Well, we are in the land of magic and everything is connected to everything else. We all know that.' Frovin replied with a sarcastic tone. He was anxious to get going.

Holding Marta's gaze, Attricus leant forward, handing her the key, 'May I see your … light?'

'I can't,' she whispered, pulling back a little and shielding it with her hand. 'It's too bright.'

Marta felt as if she had somehow failed the Queen of the Sun, but she also understood the futility of trying to keep the Lightenstone a secret from Attricus any longer. What worried her most was that if Attricus could figure out that she was carrying it, then so could the enemy.

Initially, Attricus was confused by her fear, but quickly understood. This affected them all. He peered at her over the top of his glasses. 'Your secret is safe with me, Marta.'

She nodded, suddenly remembering Snowball's approval of Attricus at The Veils. *If Snowball trusts him, then so must I.*

'No time for any of that now,' scowled Frovin, butting in. 'We have to find Snowball.'

Giving Attricus a withering look, he snatched the key. But Frovin did not notice a grape tendril running across the floor and wrapping itself around his back foot. And as he spun, twisting violently, he was pulled towards the wall and bound tight. Attricus and Marta scrambled to help as a gnome's arm suddenly punched through the vines. An open palm now hovered under Frovin's chin.

'I think they want their key back,' he said between clenched teeth. He dropped it into the gnarled hand. As the arm withdrew, a hoarse voice said, 'Rubicon'.

At once the vine loosened and Frovin shook himself free. They all looked at each other. Marta and Frovin both knew that the Rubicon River was one of the four rivers that could have an outer gem in it. And like Boris and Ferdy, neither of them had seen it marked on any maps.

Attricus' eyes brightened. 'It's the spiritual river of light that is said to flow from the Pentark.'

'And what are we supposed to do if we come across that?' said Frovin, standing up on his back legs, theatrically throwing his paws in the air. 'Although, I suppose you could always toss a few more pebbles …'

Attricus just smiled, which annoyed Frovin even more. Then he prompted Marta to take the lead again. 'We need to take whatever food we can carry.'

He gathered up his cowl as they walked, filling it with fruit from the still laden branches. Marta filled her pockets with nuts and apples, and with Frovin pushing between them again, they journeyed on. As before, Marta partly uncovered the Lightenstone, letting its brilliance flood the tunnel.

Day and night are the same underground, and they slept when they were tired, but otherwise kept a steady pace along the tunnel. Initially, Marta was refreshed by the food, but soon monotony set in.

Attricus tried to cheer her up. 'It'll take us a few days to get to Mirraway but I'm sure we're in the right tunnel. Imagine what it's like for the gnomes. They live here all the time.' He looked around at the uninviting walls.

Frovin rolled his eyes. 'Don't imagine it bothers them.'

Amused, Attricus pushed up his glasses, saying, 'In the monastery, I was taught that the gnomes showed humans where to find the marble to build Mirraway Castle. Apparently, they're sometimes freed from their enchantment when rock is mined.'

Frovin could hold his anger no longer. 'Freed? You claim to have never seen a gnome! But they must be everywhere, what with the building of all the castles in the Isle of Spheres—Mirraway, Jimpiragh, Mawdark.'

' … but then they supposedly return to the ground,'
Attricus continued unmoved.

'Sounds like a fanciful story. Done a lot of studying then?'

'Most of my life, as it happens.' For a moment he lamented the precious books he'd had to leave behind in Jimpiragh's library.

'Didn't think gnomes were such a mixed lot,' said Frovin. He was struck by the possibility that as the dwarves of Banters Den were miners, they might have liberated the gnomes so that they could help them.

The next day Frovin was the first to notice the slight vibration in the tunnel floor.

'Can you feel that?' He was worried that a rock giant was moving beneath them.

Marta stopped. 'What is it?'

Attricus eased to his knees and put his ear to the ground. 'It's an underground river.'

Soon the rumble under their feet increased to a roar. Then the tunnel suddenly ended, opening into a large cave, with wide sandstone steps that zigzagged down from the tunnel. Higher up and to their right, a waterfall gushed over a sharp drop into the river that then curved and disappeared. As they wondered what to do next Attricus pointed out a metal structure, partly veiled by the mist of the waterfall.

'That must be the bridge.' Frovin rushed past Marta and down the steps.

A finely structured bridge in the shape of an X arched elegantly over the river. The four spans of the bridge had open decks that connected to an open centre where the spans crossed and there were guard rails on the outer and inner edges of the spans.

Frovin waited for the others and then looked expectantly at Marta. But he could tell she was hesitant.

'What an unusual bridge,' she said, thinking aloud.

'It's just like the gnome's key.' Frovin was thinking that the gnomes must have built the bridge too.

She turned to Attricus. 'This has to be the Rubicon River. The legendary point of no return.'

He shrugged. 'Don't see how. This is a real river.'

'But you people in the World of the Soul believe that the spirit world is reflected in the real world. Isn't that how your readings work? You said yourself: "everything is a matter of interpretation".'

Attricus slowly nodded but he gave her a quizzical look.

'Why do you say "you people in the World of the Soul."?' As more of the puzzle slipped into place, he went on. 'You've come here from the World of Man. Lady Roselin must have been your mother.'

Now, he was certain. But he wondered: if Marta can carry the Lightenstone does that mean that Lady Roselin or her grandmother Maria could also carry it? Is that what 'light carrier' really means? He was shocked. Is it really a maternal line?

Marta interrupted his musing by pointing back to the top of the stairs and saying, 'When I first saw the bridge, it triggered an old memory.'

Reminded of Ikoseer and Yoska, Marta crouched down, smoothed a patch of river sand and drew an X with her finger, saying, 'This represents the bridge.'

Then she drew another line through the middle of the X. 'And imagine this line represents the river running under the bridge.'

Frovin frowned as she carefully drew a fourth line perpendicular to the last, creating an eight-pointed star.

'I can't see that,' he said searching her face. Then he realised that she had drawn something to do with the Lightenstone.

Marta truly felt she was at a crossroads. She took a deep breath. 'I'll show you.'

Keeping her back to Attricus, she stood between the two rising spans of the bridge. Now, fully exposing the Lightenstone, Marta let it shine across the river. The drifting mist from the waterfall created a rainbow, reminiscent of when she and Frovin met Solara, the Queen of the Sun, in the Ascension Mountains.

From the safety of the riverbank Attricus and Frovin saw what Marta had already seen: a separate bridge of shimmering light, arching over and between the two metal spans. It was the most beautiful thing that Attricus had ever seen.

'We're not expected to cross that, are we? It's not a real bridge. What if we fall through it and end up in the river?' Frovin was waiting on the riverbank, watching the water rushing past.

'If the gnomes built the bridge we'll just have to trust them,' she said.

As Marta moved closer, Attricus was forced to shield his eyes against the increasing glare. Then letting the Lightenstone hang free, she grabbed the ends of the railings, one in each hand.

'We'll have to cross this together. Hold onto my clothes. Try to stay close.' Once she felt their weight, she tentatively took her first step.

Nothing could have prepared Attricus for this moment. Clutching the decorative hem of Marta's shawl he tried to keep his eyes open but was blinded by the light. He shuffled behind her, hearing the rush of water beneath and feeling the cool mist of the waterfall on his face.

Marta stopped when she reached the edge of the midway point, where all the spans converged into an open space. She slowly swept her eyes around the cavern walls, looking for signs to guide her: a rock formation in the image of someone she knew; a symbol formed by crevices; a geometric pattern. Anything. Then she glanced at the top of the waterfall and started.

At first she thought it was an illusion. Swirling mist veiled the top of the falls so Marta turned towards the rock face and held up the Lightenstone. It was no illusion.

Snowball was neighing in joyous greeting, and with her head high and her ears up, she was pawing playfully at the water rushing over the drop.

'Snowball?' Letting go of Marta's trouser leg, Frovin looked up between the rungs on the railing. His eyes widened in disbelief at the figure standing beside her.

But there was no mistaking the band of mirror-imaged symbols embroidered down the front of the Sage's vibrant blue robe and the strange blue crown hugging her skull.

'Ikoseer!'

Attricus leant closer, both relieved and excited. 'Is Ikoseer here?' he whispered.

'Yes,' said Frovin. 'With Snowball. At the top of the waterfall.'

'Then we must hurry.'

But Marta stood her ground. 'No. I get the feeling we should wait.'

Marta and Frovin watched as the pair disappeared from view, re-emerging close to the bottom of the falls before coming to stand at the base of the light bridge on the far side. Now more silver than white, Snowball's coat sparkled in the rays of the Lightenstone, her head arched elegantly over Ikoseer's shoulder. In their few days apart she had grown even taller and finer.

Marta let the Lightenstone go and grabbed the railings, facing Ikoseer. When the Sage held the base of her staff, Gif, on the centre of the deck, the head burst into an electric blue flame, and Ikoseer's voice boomed around the cavern: 'By the power of the eight: stand within the circle.'

Frovin tugged excitedly on Marta's trouser leg. 'You were right! The bridge and river—it really is an eight-pointed star.'

As Marta instinctively bowed her head, Ikoseer began to chant an incantation, just as she did when she found the keyhole to the door in the Lux Mountains. Suddenly the circular seal of the Isle of Spheres appeared on the open deck, where the spans converged in front of them.

Although unsure, Marta let go of the railings, and with Attricus and Frovin crossed to the heart of the seal. Then Ikoseer raised Gif and lowered the flaming head onto the deck of the light bridge, sending an electric blue pathway racing to them.

With her heart pounding, Marta felt for the top of Frovin's head, reminding him to hold on again. As he glanced behind, he saw that the first half of the span was now gone. As soon as Marta stepped over the outer circle of the seal and onto the blue path, the light railings dropped and fizzled in the moving river. Now there was nothing to stop them falling in.

'Stay right behind me,' she warned.

Attricus forced his eyes open to a slit, startled by what he saw. 'What's happening?'

'Almost there.' Marta was walking carefully, focusing on Ikoseer. As they reached the end of the blue path, Ikoseer nodded to Marta, pulled Gif away and stepped back.

Marta hid the Lightenstone, so that now the only light came from the blue flame of Ikoseer's staff. Feeling relieved, she stretched up and flung her arms around Snowball's neck as the mare nickered quietly in greeting. Still amazed by the mare's continuing transformation, Marta offered her the last apple from her pocket.

Ikoseer greeted Attricus like an old friend and listened with great interest as he told her all about his escape from Onysius with Volgor and about the aquamarine they found. All this was of course news to Marta and Frovin, although Attricus got the distinct impression that Ikoseer somehow already knew the whole story.

Then Ikoseer bent down to Frovin, her brave animal helper and hugged him affectionately. Although excited and relieved to see her, Frovin wriggled free in embarrassment.

Attricus could see that Marta also knew Ikoseer well. With his newfound understanding of her, he saw that there was a kind of reverence between them, an unspoken comprehension, something powerful and deep and ancient.

Ikoseer suggested that they rest. Instructing them to put together a small pile of the larger river rocks, she used Gif's flame to ignite them and they gathered around, grateful for the warmth.

They were brimming over with their own adventures but Marta and Frovin knew that Snowball would have already told Ikoseer about their travels, so they listened fascinated as Attricus expanded on his story. He told them about his escape from Jimpiragh and the Tangled Woods and encountering the ferryman and crossing the Abyss River on his rock ponies. He described his escape from the wrake near Riverbend Village, and how he found Mortimer's army. Finally, he told them about Rhyll and his anomir.

But the location of the other outer gems was worrying Attricus. Ikoseer seemed to sense the soothsayer's inner turmoil and repeated what Artorus had told Ferdy: 'Two outer gems were cast into a river.'

'They're both in the belly of a fish then?' Attricus was twiddling the tassels on his belt.

Chuckling, the Sage shook her head. 'I wouldn't have wanted them all to end up in the Mother Sea.'

'But Volgor found the aquamarine in a salmon from the Abyss River …' Then he stopped. A new realisation suddenly dawned. 'Volgor was meant to find it.'

Ikoseer studied the blue flames. 'It takes a kurr to catch a fish. Most of our enemies wouldn't be bothered with Volgor.'

*Except Onysius, thought Attricus.*

'To save the Isle of Spheres, the Queen of the Sun has decreed that all the stones must be returned to the Pentark.'

A cold shiver ran through the soothsayer. *That makes sense. So, that's why you're here to greet Marta and Frovin. You're overseeing the restoration of the Pentark and the safe return of the Lightenstone. No wonder Lord Mortimer's army is camped on Mirraway's doorstep.*

'Is Volgor safe? Does he still have the aquamarine? Does he know it has to be returned to the Pentark?'

Ikoseer nodded. 'Your companion is safe—for now. He still has it. And he knows.'

Relief flooded through the soothsayer. Volgor must have survived the wrake attack and be somewhere near Mirraway.

'So, have the remaining outer gems been found too?' he asked eagerly.

'They are on their way.'

Now it was Frovin's turn to be flabbergasted. *How did Boris and Ferdy manage that?*

He glanced at the river. 'So … do you mean …?

'There's no need to worry, Frovin. Everything is as it should be.'

'Are we close to Mirraway?' asked Marta.

'We are. I know a short cut.' Ikoseer, grabbed her staff and stood up.

She and Attricus exchanged a knowing glance. 'Come. Helios is waiting.'

# CHAPTER 34

Ferdy was balancing on a wobbly three-legged stool, ladling out umpteen bowls of watery soup when a burly guard ordered him to stop, and instead, deliver a basket of cold meat, cheese, bread and red wine to the throne room above.

Ferdy treated the order with a mixture of suspicion and trepidation. The last time he was in the throne room was more than three weeks ago, when the Commander almost found the agate and charged Ferdy with stealing the Lightenstone for him.

He hoped that the Commander had forgotten all about it. Having more or less given up being rescued by Boris anytime soon, Ferdy had made several attempts at escape but was always thwarted by the hawk-eyed cook. Tittle-tattle was rife among the scullions, but Ferdy was sure there was a smattering of truth to it this time. Lord Mortimer and Earl Onysius were definitely here in Mirraway Castle—he assumed that he was about to deliver their lunch.

The assortment of specialty cheeses in the basket made Ferdy's mouth water. He eyed off the accompanying bread, lavishly spread with thick golden butter. He knew exactly what that tasted like. After being made to churn the precious cream nonstop for over an hour, he'd managed to sneak a finger-full while kneading in the salt.

As the guard knocked on the tall gilt doors a lump formed in Ferdy's throat. Although he had conjured up unsavoury images of both the Lord and the Earl, he really had no idea what to expect. Two more burly guards opened the doors from within and Ferdy was ushered in hurriedly. He was not sure where to put everything, so he kept his head down and shuffled to the middle of the star pattern in the floor of the large and familiar room. The demijohn of elven wine was heavy and hung awkwardly from one hand, but he did not dare to put it down.

The air was thick, the only sound an irritated tapping on the end of an armrest. Suddenly, realising he had forgotten to bow, he did so and then trotted forward.

'Put it there,' commanded the man sitting on the throne to his right. Stealing a glance at him, Ferdy put the wine and basket down between the two thrones and stepped back.

He guessed this man was Earl Onysius. Ikoseer and Artorus had spoken of him. The years of fruitless searching for the Lightenstone seemed to be etched on his aged face: the eyes distrustful, the mouth set into a thin, hard line. There was an angry red scar above his right eye. A tall big-boned man, he easily filled the huge throne.

The man on the other throne wore a crown. Ferdy assumed he was Lord Mortimer, although he was surprised to see that he seemed much older than Onysius. He was much smaller, with hunched shoulders and his head bent forward, seemingly weighed down by a hefty chain and medallion hanging from his neck.

Ferdy's presence seemed to bother him somewhat. He suddenly reached up and turning his neck a little, attempted to ease his discomfort by lifting the chain cutting into the flesh at the back of his neck.

'The Lightenstone is near,' he rasped. A long black fingernail tapped the medallion. 'Toil is telling me so.'

Ferdy instinctively reached for his waterskin and not knowing what else to do said, 'I'm terribly sorry about that … but I'm needed back in the scullery.'

He gave a curt bow and turned to go but Onysius gripped his armrests and slid forward.

'You cannot leave, Ferdy. My Commander tells me you are an accomplished thief and have agreed to … find … and steal the Lightenstone.' He gave a half-hearted flourish in the air.

'Your C … C … Commander is m … mistaken. I … I have no idea where it is. I … I'm not the thief he thinks I am,' spluttered Ferdy. He took a furtive glance around to make sure the Commander was not in the room. 'A … And I can't steal something if I don't know what it looks like.

Unable to stop himself, he added: 'Besides, if you haven't been able to find it after all these years … don't see how I can.'

A terrible sound erupted from the depths of the Earl's throat, and Ferdy stepped back, squeezing the waterskin.

Onysius swooped up an empty wine goblet nearby and roared, 'How dare you!'

Ferdy instinctively ducked as it sailed over his head and hit the floor hard, rolling until coming to rest at the foot of the startled guards. By now the Earl was on his feet, clenching and unclenching his fists. He began to pace menacingly around Ferdy, glaring at his bowed head. His hobnailed boots thudded on the marble floor. Ferdy swallowed hard. His knees felt weak and the skin on the back of his neck prickled.

'Did you know you're not the only dwarf in the castle?' said Onysius between clenched teeth. 'The other one evaded our soldiers and wrakes. And he carries a peculiar dwarf blade.'

Ferdy felt a wave of relief. It must be Boris!

'He escaped from the elf cart at the Lake Bridge,' Onysius continued, watching for Ferdy's reaction. Ferdy could only manage a vague shrug of his shoulders.

Onysius sucked on his crooked teeth. Suddenly one of the guards came forward and whispered fiercely in the Earl's ear. He gave a sly glance at Ferdy before returning to his post.

'My Commander tells me you were on your way to the Rolling Hills when you supposedly got lost. Some months back, my soldiers raided a dwarf village. Near the World of Man and south of the Rolling Hills. Banters Den. Is that where you're from?'

Ferdy felt his cheeks flush.

'N … never been to Banters Den. Or met the dwarves there. 'Sides, the Rolling Hills are over two hundred miles away.'

'Hhmm … Is that so? And what do you know about dwarf swords?'

Ferdy shrugged and spread his hands. 'They're just the same as any other …'

'Not this one. No. Seems the seal of Thrim is stamped into the blade.'

Ferdy immediately recognised this as Boris' sword, Thrust. The stamp near its hilt; the letter "T" scribed by a circle. But he said nothing.

Onysius continued, more confidently now. 'Hhmm … Thrim didn't make ordinary blades. They all serve the Isle of Spheres. This particular one was thought to be lost after the Battle of Stones.'

'Umm … Was it? Perhaps the dwarf found it somewhere …?' He knows, thought Ferdy.

'Bah! The presence of the blade confirms that the Lightenstone is also near. Or perhaps this other dwarf has one of the outer gems.'

Lord Mortimer moaned as Toil began to react. Onysius stopped. He was now towering over Ferdy, his huge hand squeezing the decorated pommel of his equally huge sword, his knuckles turning white.

'So. Now we're getting somewhere.'

The Earl could have easily killed Ferdy there and then. Ferdy was sure that he was considering it. But just then Lord Mortimer gestured for Ferdy to come closer to his throne.

'Spare him for now, Onysius. We can use him to lure the other dwarf.'

Ferdy had to step around the scowling Earl to approach the Lord, who was now looking quite ill. His skin was wan, his cheeks sunken and his eyes cloudy. But as he shuffled closer, Ferdy could not take his eyes off Toil. The medallion was now swinging ever more violently from side to side.

'Spare me some pain. Find the Lightenstone,' rasped the Lord.

It was obvious that Toil was now unbearably heavy. The wound on Lord Mortimer's neck was deep and suppurating. Despite all he knew about his cruelty, Ferdy suddenly felt sorry for him. He was clearly under the control of something darker, and Ferdy couldn't help but cry out: 'You could always take it off.'

At this a scream escaped from the Lord. And Ferdy staggered back as the neckchain yanked Mortimer off the throne and onto the marble floor.

Ferdy was close to panic. *I've only made things worse, instead of better.*

With the Lord moaning pitifully, Ferdy watched the medallion slide out from under his body towards him, and a tingling shot up his spine.

*Toil knows I have the agate!*

Even in Ferdy's dire situation he was puzzled that Onysius seemed reluctant to help the Lord. And then suddenly he turned on the dwarf. Everything seemed to proceed in slow motion: the drawing of his massive sword, the delayed reaction of the guards.

Ferdy did not know how to escape. The doors were far too heavy for him to open, and the guards were too strong to push past them anyway. He was too chubby to fit between the thrones. The life-sized marble statues on both sides of the thrones stopped him from running around them. So all he could think to do was rush past the still prostrate Lord and grab the lunch basket.

As Onysius brought his sword down, Ferdy threw the basket as hard as he could. Next, he picked up the demijohn and swung it wildly, hitting one of the guards on the head, knocking him out. As the guard collapsed, the vessel smashed and the precious red liquid spilled across the floor. The remaining goblet was his last possible defence weapon. He grabbed it by the stem and used it to block Onysius' next vicious strike.

By now the other guards were almost upon them. Onysius roared,
'Get him!'

But Ferdy jumped onto the seat of the throne closest to him and
scrambled over the decorated top. Seeing just enough room between it
and the wall, he breathed in hard and dropped. The thrones sat on a wide
marble plinth with a single step up in front. The plinth was hollow, with
strange metal framework so Ferdy squeezed into the cavity as deeply as he
could. To get him out they would have to move everything.

Onysius, enraged, tried to stab him by standing on the seats and
driving his battle sword downwards behind the plinth as Ferdy puffed
and trembled below.

Meanwhile, the thrones and plinth were so solid that he thought, with
some small comfort, that it would take an army of men to move them
and the marble statues. He could hear Onysius cursing and raging
for some time.

The door guards were replaced immediately and the Lord managed to
drag himself up off the floor and return to his throne. But, in a strange
way, Ferdy still had some control. Now, Onysius and Lord Mortimer
could not use the throne room to talk confidentially. They would
need to go elsewhere. Ferdy knew they wouldn't trust him to steal the
Lightenstone now, but on the positive side, if Boris really was in the castle,
then he might hear about Ferdy's attempted escape and work out how
to rescue him.

Before they left, Onysius leant over the throne and whispered fiercely.
'You can't escape me, Ferdy. Tomorrow, I will bring wrakes to tear all this
down—you will be their tasty reward.'

Ferdy shuddered and felt for the agate. Images from months ago rose in
his mind; when he was trussed and prepared for roasting in Greenwood
Forest. Boris and Frovin had rescued him from the wrakes then. But now,
he felt very alone and wished he was back home in Banters Den, picking
hops to make frothy beer. After the doors closed, with nothing else he
could do and exhausted from weeks of work, Ferdy dozed.

It was almost dark when something woke him. His body felt stiff and uncomfortable in the tight space, so he tried to stretch out. Then he heard soft scurrying. There was just enough light coming through the metal framework for him to see—a harvest mouse!

Ferdy liked mice. He and Boris used to catch them in the hop vines and much to his mother's disapproval, he had briefly kept one as a pet. This mouse raised its head, watching him with beady black eyes. Its ears were perked and its nose twitched. Ferdy copied it, screwing up his own nose and wiggling it from side to side.

When the mouse moved a little closer, Ferdy slid his open hand slowly towards it and smiled. The mouse jumped onto his palm and Ferdy raised his hand to look more closely at it. The moment took him back to his carefree youth and his eyes suddenly misted. Then he lowered his hand and dared to gently stroke the tiny creature with his fat stubby fingers.

'How did you get in here? If you're lucky, you might find some cheese crumbs up there.'

He spoke softly and nodded his head towards the front of the thrones, but hit his head on something hard. When he reached up to rub the spot, the mouse ran up his other arm, across his hat and jumped onto whatever the thing was. Ferdy reached for his new friend again, but the mouse curled its tail around a long metal rod to keep balance and crouched low.

Ferdy was confused, but when the mouse squeaked, he realised that it was trying to tell him something. He smiled ruefully and scratched it between the ears. 'I only speak Dwarf, not mouse.'

Undeterred, the mouse refused to move but instead, stood on its back legs, revealing a small plain knob on the metal rod. Ferdy looked closer. He twisted around further so he could reach and touched it, wondering what it was. Excitement began to rise in him, but the knob was tarnished and thick with grime and he thought it would be difficult to move. He decided to wait, hoping that the guards inside the room would eventually fall asleep, safe in the knowledge that Onysius had stationed more of them outside the main doors. It was some hours before he heard their steady snoring.

By this time, he had little light. He braced himself and with all his strength and as quietly as he could, he lifted, pushed and pulled on the knob in every conceivable direction. He groaned inwardly. He could barely budge it.

Suddenly, the mouse untwined its tail, raced around the knob in one direction and then the other. Finally, sensing that Ferdy was still puzzled, he began to scurry back and forth along the rod, which Ferdy could now see ran the full length of the thrones. By now he was certain that the mouse was trying to help him, but all this did was frustrate him.

And then he had an idea.

He twisted the knob first one way and then the other—and heard a faint click. Excitement rose, but nothing followed. *Think ... think ...* he said to himself.

The mouse ran faster, along the rod to the far left end, and waited. *Ah*, Ferdy thought.

Bracing his body, he gripped the knob and slid it slowly towards the mouse. Another faint click, but still nothing happened. The mouse ran to the far right end of the rod and stopped, this time stretching its neck out and twitching its whiskers, as if telling him to hurry.

Ferdy slid the knob back to the far right. He heard two clicks this time, one close to his ear, the other behind him. As he rolled over to face the wall behind the plinth, the mouse jumped onto his shoulder, ran down his arm and then between him and the wall.

Apart from the two statues, the magnificent thrones were framed from behind by an elaborate gilt architrave. Ferdy assumed it was just a decorative feature, but now, as he felt a draught of cool air, he realised that it was the frame of a doorway—through which the mouse had disappeared.

With excitement rising, he manoeuvered round, and leaning on his elbow, felt for the breeze. Then, putting a hand along the edge of what must be a marble door, where the breeze was strongest, he tried giving it a push.

The marble door was heavy and opened just wide enough for the mouse to go through, so Ferdy crawled out of the plinth into the small space between it and the door. With the plinth digging into his back, and barely enough room to bend his knees and plant his boots on the door, he slowly straightened his legs. As he pushed, it began to move, until, after a particularly strong push, it groaned just enough to make the guards snort in their sleep.

Ferdy forced himself to be patient and wait for their snoring to resume. Then with another shove, he was just able to follow the mouse into a secret room.

*Wait till I tell Boris about this.*

He stood up and checked the waterskin—it was secure. Feeling rather proud of himself, he gently eased the door shut, wincing each time it creaked and listening for the sleeping guards to react. A final hard push locked the door back into the framework, thus re-setting the knob under the plinth. And he only just made it. As he leant against the door, sighing with relief, the first guard woke up.

Ferdy had no idea about the room he was in, how big it was or where it went. He couldn't see anything—it was pitch dark—but he could smell oak, so he assumed it was lined with timber. He reached down to feel the floor. Cold and smooth. Marble, he thought.

He did not want to waste any more time and was desperate to get to the Pentark. He quietly called for the mouse. He waited a few moments. No response.

Standing up he whispered 'Thank you', then stretching his arms in front of him, took hesitant steps forward. *What I need is light*, he thought and as if in answer, he saw a small red glow ahead. And then a familiar aroma hit his nostrils: dwarf 'baccy'.

Ferdy was thrilled but confused. *It can't be Boris, can it? Where would he have found 'baccy'?*

'Who's there?' He crept towards the glow as it continually dimmed and brightened. But there was no answer. All he could do was follow the pungent smoke moving ahead of him.

Ferdy knew that Boris would have been more cautious. But although he did not know where he was being led—or by whom—he was desperate to get out of the castle. It seemed worth the risk.

By now the secret room had narrowed into a tunnel and the smooth even floor had given way to a rocky track. It reminded Ferdy of when Ikoseer led them through the tunnel in the Lux Mountains, to where he and the others met Potsy. That seemed such a long time ago. He began remembering some of the delicious food Potsy had prepared for them: hot vegetable soup, crusty bread dripping with melted butter, apple tart, wafers, cheese, honey oat biscuits (his favourite) and mead. His tummy started to rumble and his mouth began to water again.

Ferdy quickened his step, trying to close the distance between him and the glow, but to no avail. Eventually, the baccy smoker disappeared. Ferdy rushed forward to see who it was but there was nothing except a hovering pipe being puffed on by someone—or some thing—invisible.

Besides seeing the apparition of the Queen of the Sun, he knew nothing about ghosts except those described in bedtime stories. At first he thought this was a trick.

'Who are you?' he asked, trying to sound brave.

The ghost remained mute. Then Ferdy heard a long drawback on the pipe and a large puff of smoke revealed a face. Although it was unfamiliar, he knew immediately who it was.

'Hello, Ferdy. Twin brother of Boris, son of Ester and Leopold of Banters Den.'

'Hello … Thrim.' Ferdy could hardly speak.

'I haven't seen you since you sprinkled white daisies in front of my headstone at the Ascension Mountains.'

'The daisies were very pretty.' This was all Ferdy could manage to say.

'Boris carries my blade, Thrust. And you, the agate.' Thrim got straight to the point.

Ferdy started. 'Yes, but now Onysius somehow seems to know about Thrust too.' There was worry in Ferdy's voice.

'That's inevitable. Thrust serves the Pentark. It can't remain lost forever.'

'And because of … Toil,' Ferdy screwed up his face, 'Onysius thinks Boris has one of the outer gems.'

'Better than him knowing you have it.' Thrim blew more smoke to keep the vision clear.

'All I want to do is put the agate back and go home. I don't know why Elvendor gave it to me.'

'He gave it to you because you're a twin and the agate is the stone of Gemini, the twins in the zodiac.'

Ferdy gave him a blank look. 'We're miners, not magicians,' he protested, echoing Boris' sentiments. 'I've got nothing to protect myself with. And now there'll be a price on my head.' Ferdy's bottom lip trembled.

Thrim continued puffing. 'Boris is in the castle looking for you. He's come across one other who also carries an outer gem.'

'Another dwarf?'

'No, a creature called a kurr. Kurrs live and fish along the banks of the Bleak River between this world and the World of the Dark Night. His name's Volgor, and I'm sure he would like to go home too, if he could.'

Ferdy looked down at his boots. 'I'm not as brave as them.'

'Bravery comes in many forms, Ferdy. You're quite right about needing protection. Especially from here on. Therefore, you must steal a weapon the first chance you get. And take off your hat. The guards and wrakes will be on the lookout for it.'

Ferdy looked up as more smoke blew in his face. 'Is Boris close?'

'Yes, but you must continue on alone. Take comfort. Thrust will guide him and Volgor to the Pentark. And one body is much easier to hide than three.'

'But I miss him.'

'You will meet again soon.'

'I'm worried he's going to be killed, what with all the soldiers and wrakes.'

'Thrust will serve him well.'

*Thrust didn't save you in the Battle of the Stones.*

'It was my destiny to die that day,' said Thrim.

Ferdy was shocked. *He can read my mind?*

'Is it difficult being dead?' he asked.

The question seemed to amuse Thrim. 'Never be afraid of death, Ferdy. It's just another realm, but don't force it. When it's time, it's time. You've a lot of living to do yet and talking of that—you need to keep going. There's a door nearby. At the end of this tunnel.'

'Hope it's easier to open than that last one.' Ferdy jabbed his thumb behind. 'Where does it lead to?'

'Another room. And from there, steps lead down to a door in the outer wall of the castle, the bailey.'

'Can I get to the Pentark from there, then?'

'You can. But the Pentark is heavily fortified now.'

'What will I do?'

'You've made it this far. You'll think of something.' And then
Thrim was gone.

Left in the dark again, Ferdy remembered all the things he should
have asked Thrim.

*I forgot to ask about Ikoseer. Surely she and the Knights of Power aren't
far away. And if Frovin was here, he could protect me, like he did by
attacking that shrieking goblin in the Norfolk Woods. And where are Marta
and the ponies?*

He gave a deep sigh.

Keeping one hand on the wall, Ferdy felt his way to the door. Then he
noticed something sticking out of the lock, something shining with a
blue light. Thrim had left a key for him, a strange transparent ghost key,
marked by Thrim's monogram: the letter 'T' within a circle.

Ferdy expected his hand to go straight through the key, but it didn't. He
turned it. The lock clicked. He tried the handle and cracked open the
door. Through the crack he could see the dull yellow light of a torch.
Torches like that usually meant soldiers. He poked his head through the
door for a quick look. It was an armoury.

*This must be where they store some of their weapons. Little wonder it leads out
to the bailey, he thought. Enemy soldiers must be coming here day and night!*

He panicked a little and quickly closed the door. Now it occurred to him
that because the armoury was connected to the throne room, the weapons
might belong to protectors of the royal family. He had another look.
Not only were there weapons, but also full body armour and livery. And
everything was covered in dust.

'It sort of looks abandoned,' he whispered to himself, pushing the
door a little wider. The torch flame flickered, making creepy shadows
on the walls.

After listening for a while he decided it was reasonably safe, slipped the ghost key into his pocket and went in, carefully shutting the door behind him. It would be the perfect place to find a weapon for himself. He tiptoed along one side of the room looking for something suitable. But everything towered over him: swords, battleaxes, lances, flails, pikes and crossbows. All of them enormous.

'I need something shorter,' he muttered. He rubbed his bearded chin and swept his eyes back along the wall.

'Perhaps this will suffice?' asked a familiar voice behind him.

Startled, Ferdy spun round. His jaw dropped. Standing among the livery and hanging armour and camouflaged by a long hooded cloak, was Artorus. With a huge grin, the Knight of Power held out a sheathed short blade.

Tears of joy streamed down Ferdy's face as he flung his arms tight around the knight's legs. Artorus hugged him with equal affection. Ferdy then began to blurt out everything that had happened since he and Boris separated from the group at the Norfolk Woods.

It was quite a story and took some time to tell, but Artorus listened with great interest, taking particular notice of the tittle-tattle Ferdy could recall from the scullery and his visit to the throne room.

But Ferdy felt that somehow Artorus already knew about the agate, and he wondered if the knight had been waiting for him in the armoury. As Artorus was finding a belt for the short sword, Ferdy decided to keep his meeting with the ghost of Thrim to himself. *It's dwarf business anyway.*

The knight was by now kneeling in front of him, threading the blade's sheath onto a belt that he shortened by one notch before buckling it round the dwarf's fat tummy.

'Ever used a sword, Ferdy?'

Ferdy would have liked to be able to say 'yes', but he finally shook his head.

'Then just pretend. Your intention puts it into spirit and it becomes so.'

Ferdy gave him a doubtful look. 'Can you help me get to the Pentark?'

'I can only go with you to the bottom of the stairs. They will take you to a door in the outer wall, the bailey.'

Ferdy's face fell. 'Does the enemy know about this room?'

'Not yet. The entrance from the outer wall is cleverly hidden within a carved stone plinth. Similar to the way the architrave hides the door from the throne room. So do try to keep it a secret.'

'I will.' Ferdy took that as a gentle warning and felt a little intimidated.

Artorus took a dusty but rather smartly designed hat from a rack and handed it to Ferdy. He stuffed his dwarf hat into a pocket, dusted off the new one and put it on. The knight wrapped a matching cape round Ferdy's shoulders and tied it under his chin. It almost touched the ground.

'I'm sure I look ridiculous,' he protested.

'Well, the main thing is … at a glance, you look less like a dwarf.'

Ferdy returned an indignant look. 'Are all the Knights of Power here?'

Artorus nodded. 'Yes, but a bit like you, we're all in disguise.'

'Are Marta and Frovin still with you?' He had no reason to think otherwise. They had been with them at the Norfolk Woods.

Artorus saw the love and concern in his eyes. 'Not with me, no, but they are on their way.'

Ferdy's eyes brightened a little. Then his worried look returned. They were in mortal danger too. 'What about Ikoseer?'

Artorus hesitated. 'Why is it that some dwarves ask far too many questions? Come, Ferdy. Night has fallen. The moon is waning and the gathered clouds seem to sense that we are in need of their help.'

That's the same question Ikoseer asked me in Wayfarer's Cave, Ferdy thought, as he followed Artorus down the stairs. *Does that mean the Sage is here somewhere too?*

The mechanism that opened the door reminded Ferdy of the underside of the thrones. Artorus slowly slid a metal knob a couple of inches sideways until it stopped. He listened intently for a few moments. Deciding it was reasonably safe, he opened the stone door just enough for Ferdy to slip through.

'Do I have to lock the door after me?'

'It can be done from the outside, but the door's very heavy. It's easier if I do it from here. All I ask is that you wait briefly in front of the carved sword just outside the door, until you hear me re-lock it.'

Squeezing the hilt of his weapon for courage, Ferdy pushed through the gap and, although he desperately wanted to run, he did as Artorus said. He faced the stone sword as if he might be studying it and waited until he heard the slight sound of metal sliding on stone and watched as the knob was returned to the centre of the crossguard of the sword.

Now he could see how cleverly the door was hidden within the richly carved plinth. Once he heard the mechanism lock, he dared to lean back, and find out what was above it, but it was too hard to tell in the dark. After a furtive look around, he moved away until he could view the outer wall properly. He drew in his breath. It was a huge statue of the revered Firebird, bigger than he had ever seen. He shivered. The night shadows made it look even more fearsome: with beak wide open and huge wings swept upwards into the outer wall, the talons, opened in a menacing gesture, seemed to dare the enemy to approach.

But Ferdy had to get going. He felt for the agate and crept away, in what he hoped was the direction of the Pentark, perched on the rocky fell above the castle.

The young lad who had helped Boris into the castle and then demanded Thrust for payment, was on an errand for Onysius outside the castle walls when he caught sight of something moving. He stopped and turned to look more closely, but there was nothing there. Could have been a child, he thought at first, but then the body was too big.

He was unaware of what had happened in the throne room, but it did cross his mind that it might be Boris. Since being brought before Onysius and proudly ratting about Boris, he had been rewarded with food and more comfortable lodgings. But it had come at a cost. Now, he was constantly expected to update Onysius with meaningful information—and the Earl's demeanour frightened him. He decided to keep this observation to himself until he knew more. He could return within the hour and start his search then. He was keen for revenge, but he also had a healthy respect for the armed dwarf. The constant pain from the stab wound in his hand was a reminder of that.

# CHAPTER 35

Lighting the way with Gif, Ikoseer led Marta, Frovin, Attricus and Snowball through the mountain to join Helios. As the two horses greeted each other with a familiar blowing of nostrils and nuzzle of noses, Attricus gazed at Helios in amazement. He had last seen him twenty years ago at Elodom Monastery and had forgotten how beautiful the stallion was. And here he was again, looking just as magnificent.

Marta felt greatly strengthened by Ikoseer's presence. The images in the Well of Forgetfulness showed her helping her grandmother to remove the Lightenstone. And now, Attricus more or less confirmed that Ikoseer had taken her mother and grandmother from Elodom Monastery into the World of Man.

As if reading her mind, Ikoseer slowed until she caught up to her, saying, 'The Queen of the Sun needed to hide them somewhere safe.'

And hide the amulet too, she thought, now with greater understanding, but she said nothing, unsure if Attricus knew that the Lightenstone could be separated into two parts.

'Am I really related to the royal family of the Kingdom of Gorthonomir?'

Ikoseer nodded. 'Mirraway Castle is your rightful home.'

Marta still could not believe it. 'So, is Yoska my …?'

'Prince Mir is your second cousin. His mother, Helena and your grandmother—they were sisters.'

'Does he know who I am then?'

Ikoseer smiled and Marta suddenly felt foolish. Of course he knows, she thought.

'Tell me about the old sword that he used to protect us at the Norfolk Woods.'

'Hmmm. Honorex.'

'You said that Thrim forged Honorex—is that why the anomir was so afraid of it?'

Ikoseer stopped and faced Attricus, aware that he was listening closely. 'Do you know why?'

Attricus shrugged. 'I have a theory … but it's just conjecture.'

'Perhaps, you don't trust yourself enough,' suggested the Sage. She waited for him to continue.

Encouraged, Attricus explained, 'Each of the twelve Knights of Power carries a sword forged by Thrim. Honorex is held in trust by the reigning monarch of Gorthonomir, but it's really the thirteenth sword, the master sword of the other twelve. It's a sword of discrimination; dividing the false from the true or some might say, right thought from wrong thought. It's a sword of light, despite its physical appearance.

'Each of the knights' swords represents one of the outer Pentark gemstones and Honorex represents the Lightenstone. So I'm guessing even a common anomir somehow knew to avoid it.'

'Well, we are in the land of magic. Everything is connected to everything else,' asserted Frovin.

'Your intuition is strong, Attricus,' said Ikoseer. She gave Frovin a wry smile before she turned to take up the lead again.

Marta dropped back beside Frovin. 'Did you know that Honorex represented the Lightenstone?'

'Of course … ' The badger was busily keeping ahead of the huge hooves behind him, inches from his tail.

'You never mentioned it?'

'You had enough to deal with.'

They continued on for some time until Ikoseer slowed as they approached a wide opening to their right. The Sage halted, pointing the head of Gif into the void. Attricus jumped in fright as a tall cloaked figure suddenly stepped into view. But Marta and Frovin were excited to see the familiar face and the horses nickered in greeting as the proud black head of Famrod appeared above Artorus' shoulder.

As Artorus greeted them, Marta expected Patrayus and his mount to be with them. The knight saw her disappointment. 'Patrayus isn't with me today.'

Marta felt her cheeks flush. She looked away. Meanwhile, Ikoseer was introducing Attricus to the knight, who nodded and gave Marta a knowing smile. He ruffled Frovin's head.

'What news do you have?' asked Ikoseer.

Artorus told them about Ferdy's escape, adding, 'I've armed Ferdy with a short sword. I'm hoping he has enough strength of mind to use it when he should.'

'But, surely, they have Thrust to protect them?' Frovin had assumed that the dwarves were still together, but then he read Artorus's face. 'Isn't Boris still with him?'

'Circumstances have separated them,' said Artorus. 'But Boris is in Mirraway. Patrayus saw him recently. With another creature. A scrawny kurr.'

'Ah! That must be Volgor,' said Attricus, very relieved. He briefly told Artorus about the kurr, and their escape from Jimpiragh together.

'Volgor carries the aquamarine from the Abyss River—the Pisces gem,' explained Ikoseer.

Artorus raised his eyebrows.

But hearing that Boris and Ferdy were not together alarmed Frovin. At the Rubicon River, the Sage had said that they were not to worry about the remaining gemstones because everything was 'as it should be'. Knowing that Volgor carried the aquamarine, Frovin assumed that Boris and Ferdy had found the other three gems and were returning them to the Pentark.

'So … does Boris have the other gemstones?' he asked.

Artorus glanced at Ikoseer.

She chose her words carefully. 'Ferdy carries one of them—the Gemini stone.' She let Frovin assume that Boris had the remaining two. But this seemed like a total disaster to Frovin.

'But Boris is the more sensible twin! Hhummph! I'd never have thought he'd entrust even one of the gemstones to his brother. Hope they know what they're doing.'

'Don't worry. All will be well,' said Ikoseer. 'And besides, it was the elves who entrusted the gemstone to Ferdy, not Boris.'

Frovin immediately gave Marta an 'I told you so' look. 'Elves? What on earth have they been up to?'

'The most important thing is that the gemstones are here now,' said the Sage.

With Gif lighting the tunnel ahead, she strode on, talking to Artorus in hushed tones, and leading them ever closer to the Pentark. Ikoseer obviously knew the tunnels well and Marta wondered if there was a tunnel under the mighty Intrepid River between Mirraway Castle and the Gorthwain Mountains on the far side. Perhaps Ikoseer had used it to escape Lord Mortimer's army all those years ago.

Marta's thoughts turned to the Pentark, prompting her to place her hand over the Lightenstone. For the first time she felt a strange tugging sensation. She imagined an invisible thread, somehow guiding the Stone home and thought they must be quite close. The images from the Well of Forgetfulness were still vivid and she wanted to know more about the connection between the gemstones, the zodiac and the knights' swords. She suddenly turned to Frovin.

'Do you know which sign Artorus' sword represents?'

'The Lightenstone is my only concern.'

'It's the fire sign. Aries,' answered Attricus over his shoulder. 'The crossguard of his sword is curved like the horns of a ram.'

Marta thought for a moment. 'Then … Patrayus has the Sagittarius sword. His crossguard is curved too, but more elegant. Like the bow of an archer.'

'You're probably right,' said Attricus. 'It makes sense to have fire swords protecting the Stone.' As an afterthought he whispered, 'And animal helpers with a fire attitude.'

Marta stifled a giggle. Frovin fumed.

Hours later, Ikoseer led them into a cave. Marta looked around the walls, thinking it looked like another Wayfarers' Cave, similar to the one in Greenwood Forest. They fed and watered the horses. Artorus attended to the stallions, while she groomed Snowball, talking to her softly, still amazed by her new size and beautiful silver coat.

Attricus took wood from a stack and the Sage lit a fire. It was now clear to Marta that Ikoseer had been expecting to meet them at the Rubicon River, for the circular table was already set, with a water-filled goblet to the right of each plate. But it was not until they sat down to eat that she noticed the zodiac signs engraved around the rims of the plates, and in each base, a two-dimensional pattern of the Pentark. Her gaze met Ikoseer's as she leant across the table and placed a slice of herbed bread, topped with hard cheese and dried apple onto her plate. The Sage then gestured for them all to join hands.

Annoyed at being left on the floor, Frovin managed to scramble up and push between Marta and Attricus. Ignoring Ikoseer's frown, the badger held out both paws and closed his eyes. After a pause, the Sage began a prayer of thanks. The food was simple but delicious.

'Did this bread come from the kitchens of Mirraway?' asked Attricus, taking his last fresh mouthful. Artorus explained that resistance fighters in the castle provided all the food.

'I didn't know there were any fighters here,' said Marta.

'They've been active in the World of the Soul since the Lightenstone was removed. Potsy's been in charge of them.'

She smiled, fondly remembering the podgy old dwarf, sitting in his gilt-framed chair, toasting his toes in front of a roaring fire and reading a large book.

'And then there are the nomads from Magirus, like the ones we met on the Trading Road. And the refugees, allied countrymen and women—all commanded by the old archer that Yoska knighted in the grotto,' added Artorus.

Marta frowned. 'Sir Henry.'

'Yes. His small army is now gathering in and around Mirraway.'

'Jigs, the Gnome King, promised to help too,' said Marta.

Attricus sat back in his chair. *So, that's who gave you the key to open the door above the fen at Glen Bain.*

'And the rock giants,' added Frovin.

'They have limited capacity.' Ikoseer pushed her plate aside and folded her hands. 'After all, we don't want the mountains all crumbling around us. But others are coming.'

The Sage went on to tell them what she had learned from Sheen the owl about Volgor's meeting with Tibbs, the Captain of the tall ship *Sirius*, and of the elven army, the Arrowsmiths.

'Captain Tibbs commands a small fleet of three tall ships, the *Sirius*, the *Arcadia* and the *Sancta Maria*. He has returned from the outer islands, recruiting sailors, defectors and other willing citizens.'

'Are they close? Have they sailed up the Intrepid River?' Attricus was trying to take it all in.

Ikoseer shook her head. 'Some sections of the Intrepid are too narrow.'

'Then how will they …?'

Ikoseer held up a hand. 'Stop. The time has come. Tomorrow we leave this tunnel and head to the Pentark.'

A sudden shiver ran through Marta. She clutched the Lightenstone.

She quickly looked around the group. 'I want to know more about the Pentark. I know it uses the sun to power the light spheres. I've seen images of it being built and drawings of it. But …'

Ikoseer's voice was almost reverential. 'The Pentark is a living entity.'

Marta was puzzled.

The Sage continued. 'You already know that there are two rings that make up the bulk of the Pentark. A smaller inner ring—a five-pointed star— where the Lightenstone goes. And an outer zodiac ring—a twelve-pointed star—where the gemstones go. What you may not know is that the rings are independent of each other and revolve. In opposite directions. The outer ring revolves anticlockwise, taking a year to move around the zodiac. The inner ring rotates clockwise twelve times a year.'

She paused. She could see that Marta was thinking hard.

'So, have the rings revolved since the invasion?' she asked.

'Just the outer ring. But it moves much slower now with only eight of the gemstones in situ. The inner ring stopped the moment your grandmother took the Lightenstone.'

Shocked, Attricus drew in a breath. *So. I guessed the truth about Marta and her grandmother Maria.*

'Why hasn't the enemy removed the remaining eight gemstones?'

'Because they are protected by a magic incantation.'

Marta was taken aback. 'Does that mean we need an incantation
to return them?'

'No. Not at all.' The Sage gave her a warm smile. 'The Pentark awaits.'

Marta sat back in her seat trying to absorb all this information. When
nothing further was forthcoming, Ikoseer again said, 'Tomorrow we leave
this tunnel and head to the Pentark.'

Artorus pulled a map from under his cloak and made room on the
table to spread it out. He pointed as he spoke. 'We'll come out of the
tunnel here. And here's the Pentark. As you know it's built on top of a
rocky fell. It's steep. The only easy access is via the roadway between the
Pentark and Mirraway.'

'But is the escarpment really too steep for us to climb?' Marta recalled the
image of Ikoseer in the Well of Forgetfulness, propelling Helios off the top
of the fell and away from Mirraway.

Artorus fell silent, deferring to Ikoseer. 'No, but it would be a tough climb.
Boorlings wouldn't hesitate to pursue you. And you'll be easy pickings for
goblins on anomirs.'

Marta looked up suddenly. 'But you're with us now …' she began,
searching her face. Somehow the intricate headpiece hugging her
skull seemed brighter.

'The Knights of Power and I are to draw Lord Mortimer and Onysius
away from you,' said Ikoseer. 'They believe I have the Lightenstone. And
you've heard of the necklace called Toil?'

Marta nodded. 'Attricus told us about it. It binds Lord Mortimer to the
Prince of Darkness.'

'There is more to it. Toil is also the opponent of the Pentark stones, in
particular, the Lightenstone. Once we are out of the tunnel, Toil will sense
that the Stone is very close.'

Marta felt a terrible foreboding; the weight of her task grew heavier. Suddenly, a tingling spread throughout her body. It was clearly coming from the Lightenstone. It seemed to strengthen her.

'Guess I'll have to blend in with the enemy somehow.'

'Women have been seen carrying rations to the makeshift kitchens near the Pentark. The cooks there prepare soup and unleavened bread for the many guards.' The Sage gave her a knowing smile. 'I already have a hooded cloak for you, and a small basket of turnips.'

'But if they see Frovin, they won't hesitate to kill and eat him. And Onysius will recognise Attricus.'

Ikoseer glanced at the soothsayer. 'Attricus won't be with you. I have a special task for him. I want this cave and tunnel to be a command centre for the resistance. Also for somewhere to bring the wounded and to be a safe haven for women and children.'

'Suits me.' Attricus didn't want to be anywhere near Onysius or the coming battle.

'And Frovin?' Marta stroked the badger's striped head.

'You must separate … albeit temporarily.'

'Marta needs me now more than ever!' exploded Frovin. He placed his front paws on the table and glared at the Sage.

The Sage was unmoved. 'And you shall protect it … by being absent. Marta is right. She has to get as close to the Pentark as possible, before any alarm is raised. I have a different task for you—helping Boris, Ferdy and Volgor to get there too.'

Frovin grunted. 'They've made it this far without me. And as you have reminded me many times, the gemstones aren't my concern.'

'True, but the complete restoration of the Pentark is your concern. It's the reason we're all here.' Ikoseer swept her eyes around the group.

Marta gave Frovin a loving squeeze. 'It's alright,' she whispered, kissing the top of his head. 'I know you'll be close by if I need you.'

But Frovin was busy looking at the map thinking: *I'll be closer than you realise!*

Ikoseer looked at Frovin. She pursed her lips. 'Are my instructions clear?'

'Gemstone clear,' replied Frovin, jumping down from the table.

# CHAPTER 36

Marta left the mountains alone. With her cloak pulled tight around her shoulders and holding the small basket close, she picked her way along the gully below the Pentark. Ahead, the giant marble spires of Mirraway Castle disappeared into the fog. From Rhyll's anomir the castle had looked magnificent, but now, in first light, it just looked eerie. Her eyes scanned the steep side of the fell towards the still shrouded Pentark.

She headed towards the roadway connecting the Pentark fell to the castle. Drifting voices broke the stillness and soon a small group of guards standing around a fire came into view. One of them moved towards her.

'Who goes there?' he barked.

Marta kept walking. 'Just some turnips for the cooks.' She nodded in the direction of the fell.

'Wait!'

Marta slowed, wrapping her cloak closer to protect the Lightenstone. She turned to face the group, hoping to lure the one who had spoken away from the others. As he approached, she stole a glance at him from under her hood. This was no ordinary guard. He wore a royal surcoat, and his scabbard was richly decorated.

She held the basket out and he took a turnip, rolling it in his hands and watching her closely.

'Where did you get them?'

'The castle,' she said quickly.

He scoffed. 'Did you get lost?'

'It was dark when I left. I have no torch to guide me.'

He shoved the turnip back into the basket and ran his tongue around the inside of his mouth, considering her answer.

'Are we having turnip soup for breakfast?'

'I don't know. I'm just following orders.'

'I'm Commander of the castle's soldiers and I'm looking for two escaped dwarves. Did you see any this morning?'

'No,' she replied, too quickly.

He gripped her chin roughly and tilted it up hard to look into her face. She stepped back, pushing his arm away, glaring. His hand flew to his sword and the muscles along his jaw tightened.

'One of those dwarves worked in the scullery. A sneaky thief named Ferdy.'

'I've seen a dwarf in the scullery, but not today.' Marta was thankful that she knew about Ferdy's capture and subsequent escape.

'The other dwarf, I'm told, was last seen near the dungeon.' The Commander studied her. 'He had an unusual blade.'

*He must be talking about Boris and Thrust,* she thought.

'What's your name?'

She answered quickly. 'Rosemary.'

'I haven't seen you at Mirraway before … yet somehow …
you look familiar.'

'I'm a nomad. I travel around here with my family.'

'You speak very fine for a nomad.'

Marta said nothing. He narrowed his eyes. 'Which family?'

Marta started. 'We … we … come from … Magirus.'

'Some months back Onysius sent a nomad spy into the World of Man. Did he come from your family?'

Marta's heart was beating fast. 'Onysius uses spies from many families.'

She realised that he was referring to the gambler from Jester Alley: the one Artorus had killed. A shudder ran through her as she realised that the Commander might have been part of the raid on Brechin Village. *Is that why I look familiar?*

He frowned and let go of her chin. Water droplets covered her cloak, and the slowly brightening rays, weak though they were, clearly showed her beginning to shiver.

'Go then!' He watched her briefly before returning to the fire. But as he warmed his hands and talked with the guards, the faded pattern of the fleur-de-lis on her scarf triggered a memory.

*That pattern is part of the seal of the Knights of Power. Yes, I remember now! She's the girl I saw being held in front of a knight charging on his black warhorse into Greenwood Forest!*

Within minutes he'd mounted his horse.

But Marta had already scrambled a short way up the fell. Huddled behind a boulder she heard him venting his anger, and then the sound of his horse's hooves as he turned and galloped back the way he'd come. *Yes, he must have remembered where he'd seen me.* She glanced around the boulder and saw the vague shapes of his foot guards, coming towards her through the fog.

Clutching the Lightenstone helped her decide what to do: she would scale the fell and join the road closer to the Pentark. She discarded the turnip basket and began to climb carefully so as not to alert the guards. The rocks were wet and slippery and soon her fingers were numb. She kept stepping on the hem of the cloak but although it was cumbersome, she wanted to keep it for camouflage. Bunching the bottom of the now sodden cloak, she tied it roughly round her waist.

Visibility was so poor that she lost her sense of direction, especially when forced to skirt boulders. Although she used the increasing pull of the Stone as her guide, she wanted to climb as direct a path as possible and reach the Pentark before the fog lifted. But it wasn't to be. A jutting overhang blocked her path. She moved along it, trying to find her way around it but it seemed to have no end. She would have to wait until the sun rose higher and for the fog to clear a little so she could see where she was going.

Marta drew up her knees, wrapped the cloak tight around them, pulling the hood forward. She was damp and cold and the rocks dug into her back, but she closed her eyes and somehow managed to doze. When she finally stirred, she could hear snoring. For a moment she thought she was waking up in the comfort of Potsy's cave. But then her eyes flew open. The fog had cleared.

Marta crept out from under the overhang, sweeping her gaze below her, then to left and right and finally up as far as she could. Now she understood what Ikoseer meant about the Pentark fell being difficult to climb. It was much higher and steeper than it seemed from the air. But time was running out and she couldn't stay where she was. The snoring was still bothering her, so she inched closer to take a look.

Clothed in matching hat and cape, the snorer was tucked under the overhang, oblivious to the adolescent boy trying to peer under the hat without waking him. Marta was sure the lad was trouble, and thought the least she could do was warn the snorer. She picked up a sharp rock and threw it. The lad snapped upright and the snorer woke with a start.

She ducked out of sight, listening to the ensuing scuffle and the rocks clattering down the slope. Deciding to leave them to it, she headed back the way she'd come. She didn't know who they were and didn't want to be near the lad if he was working for the enemy.

She froze, recognising one of the voices. It was Ferdy, cursing in Dwarf. She hadn't seen him since the attack of the anomirs at the Norfolk Woods over a month ago, but now she remembered that Artorus had told her that Ferdy was on his way to the Pentark with the Gemini stone. She stood up just in time to see him wildly swinging a blade and advancing on the lad, who backed away and disappeared over the rocks.

Marta kept watching as Ferdy decided what to do. Muttering but apparently unhurt, he sheathed his blade, checked his waterskin, and pushed his hat back onto his head. Then he slumped down, looking despondent.

Her heart went out to him. 'Hello Ferdy,' she whispered.

He slowly turned his head to her and his eyes widened.

'Are you real?' Ferdy blinked as he slowly stood up to face her.

But when she smiled and moved towards him, he ran and wrapped his chubby arms around her legs, squeezing tight.

'Oh, oh … you're alright.' He was almost sobbing.

'And you too.' Marta bent down to hug him, amused by his outfit.

'Where's Frovin?' he asked, peering round her legs.

'With Ikoseer and Artorus. And Attricus.'

Ferdy leant back. 'Who's Attricus?'

'A soothsayer. The companion of a kurr called Volgor. Frovin's been given a new task by Ikoseer—to help you, Boris and Volgor make it to the Pentark safely.

'Humph. Frovin won't like that. I suppose Artorus told you about Boris travelling with that kurr?'

Marta nodded, and Ferdy suddenly realised that if Marta was here, she must be the one carrying the Lightenstone. He stepped away, searching her face, and Marta put a warning finger to her lips. Then his eyes suddenly brimmed with tears.

'What's wrong?'

'The castle's Commander expected me to steal the Lightenstone for him …' he said softly.

Marta paused, her heart skipping a beat. 'But you didn't want to.'

'Course not, one gemstone's brought me enough trouble.'

He wiped his nose on his sleeve and patted the waterskin. His immediate thought was that Marta could help him get to the Pentark, but then he realised this would increase the danger, rather than lessen it.

'Not far to go now then.'

He quickly changed the subject and pointed in the general direction of the Pentark. 'After I left the castle I found the roadway, but then I tumbled down the fell in the dark. Got lost in the fog. Have you come from Mirraway too?'

Marta shook her head and pointed across the gully towards The Veils.

Ferdy stroked his long bushy beard. 'I know all about mountain tunnels.'

'The enemy are looking for you and Boris. You must have created quite a stir in the castle.'

'It's all because I was caught spying on the Lake Bridge and then put to work in the scullery,' he replied indignantly.

'At least they have food in a scullery,' she teased.

'Don't remind me.' He rubbed his tummy.

'Tell me about Toil.' Marta was suddenly serious, remembering her conversation with Attricus.

Ferdy was startled, but then described Lord Mortimer's strange necklace in detail, adding, 'Toil knew I had the agate.'

'Then it will also know …' Her voice trailed off.

He nodded in understanding. 'It'll bring the Lord to the Pentark, that's for sure,' he said, keeping his voice low. Putting his hands on his hips, he suddenly asked, 'You don't want to carry the agate as well, do you?'

Amused, she raised her eyebrows. 'I thought Elvendor gave it to you to carry.'

He murmured. 'Suppose Ikoseer told you about the Elf King?
And other things?'

Marta said nothing. Ferdy sighed and twiddled the tassel round the neck
of the waterskin.

*Nobody wants to carry the agate. But I can't blame them. It looks like I'll have
to carry it all the way. Perhaps Boris was right after all. We should've kept
going on our way to our cousins' place in the Rolling Hills.*

'Should I wait here for Frovin then?'

Marta's skin prickled and she half turned, expecting to see him in her
peripheral vision. 'You can come with me to the roadway, but we'll have
to traverse this first.' She was scanning the overhang. 'If we can find a gap
somewhere we can climb to the ledge above and it'll lead us there.'

'Perhaps we could go back that way, as long as we don't get too close to
Mirraway.' He was pleased with the invitation and jabbed his thumb in
the direction of the castle.

Ferdy watched Marta re-hitch her cloak, knotting it in front and wondered
if he should do the same with his cape. Then he had a sudden idea.

'We could ask the rock giants to help us. Mother always insisted on
blessing their mining tunnels at our yearly festival, although Ikoseer did
say that the giants were aware, rather than awake.'

Marta thought for a moment. 'So, you know how to ask them?'

Ferdy was taken aback. Although he'd said, '*we* could ask the rock giants to
help us', he really meant, '*you* could ask.'

'No, no, no, not at all … well, I doubt it,' he replied. Then he remembered
Artorus chiding Boris when he doubted that the elves of the Norfolk
Woods would help them. Boris' doubts had been unfounded. King
Elvendor had given Ferdy the precious agate. Marta had put him on the
spot, and now all he could think to do was to echo the tunnel blessing and
hope he'd got it right.

But when he tried and nothing happened, he spread his hands in defeat.

'See?'

'Try again but close your eyes this time. Pretend you're back in Banters Den with your family and it's festival time. Visualise standing in front of the mining tunnels, and taking your mother's hand. Then ask again.'

Ferdy did as he was told and, although his eyes bulged when a few shards broke from the back of the overhang, he was still unconvinced.

'It's a waste of time,' he said, crestfallen.

'Do it again, but this time stay in the moment for longer.'

As soon as he'd closed his eyes, she stepped behind him and putting both hands over the Lightenstone, silently asked the rock giants to help them. By the time Ferdy had finished and re-opened his eyes, Marta was standing beside him again. And as she moved towards the back of the overhang, Ferdy was ready to dismiss the whole exercise again, until she pointed out a roughly hewn step at the base of the wall.

He cautiously put one foot on the step and then the other.

'See? It isn't working,' he said, in a loud whisper.

'Give them time, Ferdy.'

He looked again at his battered boots: there was a new step.

'Wait till I tell Boris about this,' he said, now pleased with himself. And Marta followed him, moving up as each new step formed, making a steep, narrow path up the vertical wall beneath the overhang.

'As you get close to the ledge, Ferdy, see if there's a gap we could both get through.'

As they neared the top, Ferdy glanced up. 'There is!'

Excited now, he began to push aside the covering vegetation. They crawled through the gap and looked back: the stairs had disappeared. And now with the sun higher and the fog lifting, Marta was able to get her bearings. From their position, crouched below the road, they could look down at Mirraway, protectively nestled within a sleeping rock giant. And the stark white marble of castle, now tinged with the golden rays of the rising sun, was absolutely breathtaking!

Marta was awestruck: *This is my true home.*

Ferdy was busy pointing out the entrance and the statue of the Firebird, and explaining about the secret door beneath. Then Marta looked behind her. Up to her right was the Pentark, just visible through the fog. They crouched, listening to the muffled sounds above: creaking carts, rattling wheels, snorting horses and a babble of different voices.

Marta leant closer. 'If we can hear them, then they can hear us.'

When he glanced in the direction of the Pentark Ferdy felt ill as images of goblins, anomirs, wrakes and boorlings filled his mind. And his bravery started to crumble.

'I don't think I can do this,' he whispered suddenly, putting his head in his hands. 'I'm sure my little agate isn't that important anyway.'

Marta put her arm around him and drew him close. 'I'm frightened too.' They sat for a few moments, holding each other tight.

'What will happen when the battle begins?'

They knew it was only a matter of time. Marta's heart thumped.

'I don't know, but you've escaped Onysius and Lord Mortimer and fought off that young lad. And if you can awaken rock giants into making steps through solid rock, then I know you can put the gemstone back. And just think: of all the dwarves on the Isle of Spheres, you and Boris were chosen to help restore the Pentark.'

'I suppose so. Hadn't thought of it like that. But Boris isn't with me, and he's the one with Thrust. And Thrust was also made to serve the Pentark.'

' … but Thrust is serving the Pentark. Boris is helping Volgor now.'

'I know … *Thrim told me.*'

Marta paused. 'You miss your brother …'

'Yes … terribly.' His chin was wobbling.

Marta felt his pain. 'I miss my father too.'

Ferdy sighed heavily. Then wiping away a tear, he broke away.

'This won't do, then,' he said, attempting to brighten their mood. 'Best get on with it I suppose, otherwise it won't happen. And you said Frovin was coming to help.'

Marta's skin prickled again and she looked around, wondering where he was.

'I'm sure he's here somewhere,' she said. 'The fog's still rising so we need to stay with it as long as we can. We'll keep going along the overhang towards the Pentark, and then climb up to the roadway.'

'But what happens once we're up there? It'll be heavily guarded. I'm sure the soldiers are on the lookout for us dwarves. I don't see how I can get through them without raising the alarm, 'specially not dressed like this. And I don't know where to put my agate anyway. And I don't like heights so I hope it doesn't have to go on top of a lith. Anyway, where's Gemini in the zodiac?'

Marta held up her hand.

'Each zodiac sign has a symbol and Gemini looks like this.' She gathered a handful of small rounded pebbles and used them to draw the symbol.

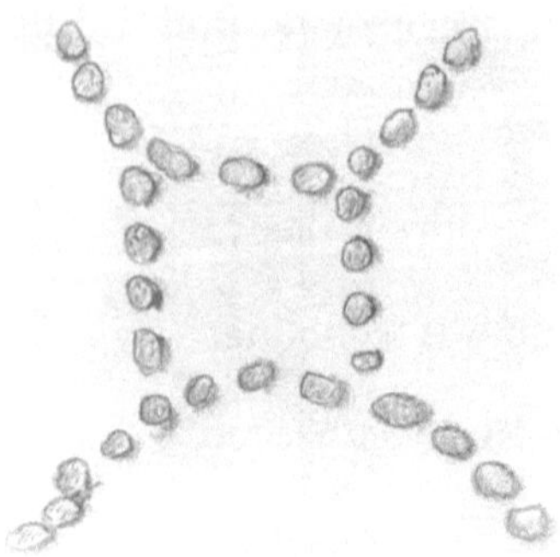

'That should be easy enough to find, then,' said Ferdy.

'But the symbol's marked in two places: on one of the Pentark's twelve outer liths and again on the Pentark itself. The outer stones are set on a circumscribed twelve-pointed star, one gemstone on each point. Your agate must be returned into the Gemini point, between Taurus and Cancer.'

Ferdy gave her a blank look.

'Between Taurus the bull and Cancer the crab,' she explained further.

'Oh, like Ranger the bullock … but I've never seen a crab.'

Marta drew both signs.

Ferdy smiled. 'Ranger's got horns just like that.' He gave a cursory glance at the crab.

'There's one other thing,' said Marta. 'Ikoseer explained that the twelve-pointed star moves, taking a year to make one full rotation of the zodiac. So your point might not be anywhere near the Gemini lith. You'll still have to look for it once you're inside the liths.'

Ferdy adjusted his hat, checked his blade and waterskin, and waited for Marta to take the lead. *At least I know where to put my gemstone now.*

They walked along the overhang until it petered out, and then clambered carefully to just below the edge of the roadway. Marta stole a quick glance ahead. Her heart sank a little. She had further to go than she had expected and there were also fewer people: this would make it harder to blend in.

Suddenly they heard the rattle of dislodged pebbles. Ferdy wanted to look but Marta grabbed his arm and shook her head. A boorling had stopped directly above them.

'I smell … young dwarf,' came the low growl of the master wrake, sniffing.

Ferdy sneaked a look through his fingers and shuddered when he saw the long black claws of the boorling curled over the edge of the roadway.

*Disguised or not, if I try to get to the Pentark now, I'll be captured and eaten in no time.* Ikoseer's warning about boorlings was ringing in his ears … *"so try not to get tangled up with one if you can help it."*

He looked at Marta and then, in a sudden moment of sheer madness—or bravery—he scrambled up the last few feet and ran under the belly of the startled enemy.

As Ferdy stumbled and zigzagged wildly among the soldiers with the mounted boorling after him, pandemonium broke out. The remaining fog was a blessing but his outfit wasn't. His hat soon fell off and he managed to undo the cord under his neck, letting his cape drop. He was frantically looking for a place to hide when he was scruffed by his jacket, pulled off his feet and spun around. His nose bumped against an armoured kneecap, making his eyes water and then a long cloak was wrapped around him. He had no idea what was going on, but thought it wise to stay still. Then he was bundled up and shoved through some leather curtains into the back of a cart. Rubbing his smarting nose, he sat up, inwardly cringing at the displeased look on his rescuer's face.

'Hello Ferdy.'

'Hello Patrayus.'

'It seems you have managed to alert the enemy before Ikoseer intended.'

Patrayus' fierce whisper made him swallow hard. He felt his face flush. 'I had to protect Marta,' he said defensively.

Now, he had the knight's full attention. 'How so?'

Ferdy leant closer. 'I was with her just now, below the edge of the roadway.'

A change came over the knight's face, a mixture of determination and … something else. It reminded Ferdy of the day Boris had come back from visiting Aster and Poppins in the stables at Alfura, when Ferdy thought the elves had put a spell on his brother. Sometimes, he'd seen the same look between his parents.

'Stay here,' Patrayus commanded. 'Hide among the onions in the back of the cart … and don't move until I come back to get you!'

Ferdy opened his mouth to protest, but thinking better of it, instead gave a dutiful nod. Patrayus gave him a warning glance and left. Ferdy had no wish to disobey him.

But he didn't want to stink of onions, even if it might help ward off the wrakes, and when he stole a forbidden peek between the leather curtains and saw the Pentark, he really wanted to get his task over with. His mind swirled with all manner of possibilities. Patrayus had clearly gone to find Marta. What would happen to him if Patrayus was killed, or didn't come back?

Patrayus was standing on the edge of the roadway, searching along the steep slope, but Marta was nowhere to be seen.

'Is this where that dwarf came from?' asked a curious soldier, joining him.

Patrayus gave a vague shrug.

'Leave him to the wrakes and boorlings,' said the soldier offhandedly. 'Onysius has sent word. Now, we're to look for a young woman.'

'Oh?' said Patrayus, feigning disinterest.

'The Commander saw her earlier this morning. Down there in the gully.' The soldier pointed, then added, 'She had a delivery for the kitchen, but then she disappeared. He thinks she's hiding on the fell.'

'Many women come to the kitchen. Why is the Earl so interested in her?'

'She told the Commander that she was a nomad, but he recognised her from Brechin Village in the World of Man.'

Patrayus started. 'The Arkfeld is weaker now,' Patrayus said quickly, implying that travel between the two worlds wasn't impossible.

'It's not that. The Commander remembers seeing her with a Knight of Power and she wears a scarf decorated with the fleur-de-lis. He wants her captured and questioned.'

Patrayus knew he needed to find Marta quickly, but he held his nerve.

'I'll start looking then.' He stepped casually off the roadway onto the slope.

'No need,' said the soldier. 'Onysius has already deployed goblins on anomirs.'

But suddenly the soldier's attention was drawn to the gully below. He squinted but it took him some moments to understand what he was seeing. Then his eyes widened in disbelief. He spun round, yelling and pointing at the moving figures below, bringing more soldiers to stare.

The soldiers had heard of Ikoseer, the Sage and her golden horse, but for most of them, the pair had seemed unreal. Now they seemed only too real, and on their flank was what looked like an armoured rider, on an equally armoured and powerful black steed.

Panic swept through the group. 'Find the Commander! Alert Earl Onysius and Lord Mortimer!'

As mayhem ensued, Patrayus moved steadily towards the Pentark. He started, looking up when a mounted anomir glided effortlessly over him and swept down the fell at great speed. He watched it wheeling and banking in the morning glow. Then another followed, and another, and another, and another.

He glanced back at Mirraway. *They don't need me down there,* he thought. *The first glimpse of Ikoseer will strike fear into all the soldiers, and soon the rest of the knights and allies will join the battle.*

His hand tingled as he squeezed the pommel of his charged sword. Determined to find Marta, he turned away, steeling himself for what was to come.

# CHAPTER 37

Mirraway Castle was a breathtaking sight. The golden rays of the morning sun painted the marble in a light yellow hue, and the warmth had dissipated the remaining fog, exposing the tips of all the spires.

Earlier, Marta had seen Ikoseer and Artorus riding along the gully towards the castle, to alert the enemy and draw them away from the Pentark. At the same time, she heard the muffled shouts from the roadway above and now, as she looked back at Mirraway, all she saw was chaos. Her heart gladdened that Snowball was not with them, and she hoped the mare was safe in the cave with Attricus. It was still early morning, so most of the enemy were asleep when the alarm was raised. Then Marta remembered the battalion of battle-weary foot soldiers they had seen when crossing the Sarsen Plain, with their heads drooped and shoulders sagging. Twenty years is a long time to maintain a war, and she hoped that the soldiers were too exhausted or disenchanted to fight.

She worried about her friends. Was Frovin helping Boris and Volgor? Did Ferdy avoid capture? His rash behaviour with the boorling and wrake had saved her life and she hoped that he had survived.

The piercing scream of approaching anomirs chilled her. She pulled her hood forward and huddled under her cloak, motionless as they passed overhead. They flew so close to the ground that she could see the anomir's talons tucked against their scaly underbellies and the war lust on their goblin riders' faces. As they swept along the natural contour of the fell, she searched in vain for Rhyll and his mount, and then thought suddenly of Yoska and his sword, Honorex. *I need you now!*

Her proximity to the Pentark made her feel as if her body was on fire, electric fire. The pull between the Pentark and Stone grew stronger with each step, and not knowing what else to do, she kept one hand pressed against her chest. *It knows I'm very close.*

She crept up to the roadway and amid the chaos stole a glance at the Pentark. Encircled by the twelve outer liths, the only section visible was through the gap between Leo and Virgo, the signs identified by large gold symbols carved into the pink granite. She felt the sudden urge to get it over with, to run between the liths and complete her mission for the Queen of the Sun. But she hesitated.

More soldiers were milling around the Pentark, making it easier to blend in but the ring of the twelve-pointed star, where the outer gemstones were set, was so high off the ground that she would need to jump up to grab it and then swing herself up. The only other way would be to somehow climb unseen, up through the centre of the structure. Ferdy and Volgor would have to do that to return their gemstones, but Frovin and Boris would be there to help them. And, once I've returned the Lightenstone, I could help too, she thought.

Marta felt the heavy weight of expectation, and looked at her trembling hands. She clenched them and closed her eyes tight; she felt vulnerable and alone, feeling there was nothing she could do to ease her burden. Despite Ikoseer's efforts, she knew that Toil would soon guide Lord Mortimer and Onysius to the Pentark. The Prince of Darkness will see to that, she thought. All I can do is return the Lightenstone before they arrive.

Absorbed in her thoughts, she didn't notice Patrayus approaching along the steep slope. He called her name softly. She startled, then turned and stared, relief washing over her.

He crouched beside her. 'I've come to help. It seems that Onysius' Commander remembered seeing you in Brechin Village. He recognised the fleur-de-lis pattern on the scarf I gave you, connected you to the Knights of Power. So Onysius has sent word to capture you.'

Marta nodded. 'Yes. I met the Commander in the gully.'

She undid the scarf, ready to hand it back to him. He briefly put his hands over hers. 'My scarf was a gift. But keep it hidden.'

She gave him a quizzical look but pushed the scarf down the front of her doublet, next to the Stone.

'Do you know why I'm here?' she asked.

'I do now,' he whispered, searching her face. 'But after we'd met you with the Sage in the Ascension Mountains, how could I have been so arrogant and proud as to challenge her about her choice of companions? If only I'd known then, what I know now.'

'At the time, I didn't know either.' She wanted to ease his pain. 'Do all the Knights of Power know about me?'

He shook his head. 'Apart from me, as Knight Commander, only Artorus—and now Scithios—know. I still believed that Ikoseer removed the central Stone from the Pentark and brought it to the Queen of the Sun. But before Ikoseer left us in the Valley of the Queen to go to White Timber Mountain, she asked Artorus to explain to me who you are as soon as he got the chance, and so he did.'

Marta thought quickly of the many others who now knew she was carrying it: Frovin, Snowball, King Jigs and the gnomes, Toros, Sheen, Mafasat, Attricus … and now Ferdy.

'Have you seen Ferdy?'

'Yes.' Patrayus briefly told her what happened after Ferdy had managed to flee the boorling and wrake.

It brought a fleeting smile to her lips. 'I doubt he'll do as he's told and stay in the cart. Have you seen Boris and Volgor?'

'Not yet.'

'Or Frovin?'

He shook his head.

'It's important that they get here safely too,' she said. 'They have the missing outer gemstones. Without them, the Pentark or light spheres won't have full power.'

'True, but they only carry two of them. Ferdy has the Gemini stone and Volgor has the Pisces.'

Marta was shocked. 'But Frovin and I thought Boris … ' she started, trying to make sense of it all. 'Why didn't Ikoseer tell us that? So, where are the other two outer gemstones, Taurus and Leo?' Her eyes were blazing.

'Who do you *think* has them?'

'I don't know,' she said, still angry.

Then she stopped, seeing a vision of herself on Toros' back, with Frovin and Snowball crossing the Abyss River, when the bull transformed from black to white and afterwards, when he took them to the Sarsen stones to meet the golden lion.

'Toros and Mafasat.'

Patrayus nodded.

'So, that means two were hidden in the Abyss River. I can understand the Pisces gemstone being in a fish in the Abyss River, but not the Earth one. Wouldn't the gnomes have had that?'

'As well as being the Bull of the Abyss, Toros is an Earth symbol, and he has the emerald.'

'And Mafasat?'

'The gnomes have been keeping his gemstone in trust—an imperial topaz.'

'So, that's why the gnomes followed us through the mountain and King Jigs was so wary of us. But then, that means that Toros and Mafasat must be coming here too. How will they get here without alerting the enemy?' It was a lot for Marta to take in.

'I don't know. But we can't wait for everyone else to arrive before you return … what you have. You have to seize the moment. Once the Lightenstone is returned, it might help the others.'

Just then they heard the high-pitched scream of approaching anomirs. Patrayus immediately wrapped his cloak around Marta and pulled her close. She leant her head against his chest, comforted by the steady beating of his heart.

'If they're still alive, you can trust one of the anomirs and its goblin rider, Rhyll,' she said softly. 'When Attricus, Frovin and I were crossing Glen Bain, they protected us from attacking wrakes and boorlings.'

Patrayus had heard about this from Ikoseer. 'How will I recognise them?'

'Rhyll has a brand seared high up on his cheekbone, a half circle beneath a horizontal line. There's also a jagged scar on his left leg. And his anomir is a female. She has lighter coloured feathers.'

'Yes, the females are also larger. Those two should be easy to spot among the other anomirs.'

Patrayus then released his embrace and lay flat beside her. He peered out just above the ridge. The soldiers around the Pentark had readied their weapons—mostly swords and crossbows—and were nervously keeping watch on the roadway leading up from Mirraway Castle. Several surly wrakes, mounted on boorlings, were patrolling the perimeter of the Pentark.

He relayed all this to Marta. 'If we can make it between the liths then I can lift you up to grab the outer ring.'

'But the wrakes and boorlings will kill us before we get there. And if that happens, then I've failed.'

He gently tilted her chin towards him. 'No task is ever given to someone who's not able to handle it.'

But Marta still had her doubts. She broke his intense gaze, wondering how to know the right time to move. But when they saw a breakfast of turnip and onion soup being delivered by horse and cart to the soldiers, Marta and Patrayus seized the opportunity. As the dray passed them, they crested the rise to mingle with the scullions before the dray halted nearby.

The scullions didn't want to be caught up in any fighting, so they were in a hurry, and, despite a few wary glances, the newcomers were immediately given tasks. Even the horses were fidgeting; they seemed to sense trouble in the air.

It was a meagre meal, a mouthful of stale bread and a small portion of watery soup. Told to break the bread and hand it out, Marta glanced at each soldier from under her hood. She sensed the uncertainty beneath their outward bravado.

But the wrakes and boorlings were definitely more dangerous. By contrast, they looked well-nourished, and one wrake and his mount were pacing back and forth behind the gathered soldiers.

Then, as Marta reached forward with the next morsel of bread, a lock of red hair fell from under her hood. She quickly pushed it back behind her ear but the wrake must have seen it, for he halted his boorling and stared directly at her. The Lightenstone juddered with a warning, the same sensation Marta felt when crossing Glen Bain, when the voice hissed in her head: *Then I will stop you and the Lightenstone will be mine!*

Patrayus had also seen the wrake dismount and with a menacing snarl, began to shove his way through the soldiers towards her. The knight gripped the pommel of his sword and swore quietly under his breath; there wasn't enough room to draw it out of its scabbard.

Meanwhile Marta was quickly handing the bread to the woman beside her, shielding her face then stepping back.

'I have to go,' she muttered to Patrayus. But the wrake had already gestured for his kin to join him, and was jostling the soldiers between him and his quarry.

Suddenly one of the jostled soldiers, hungry and irritable, pushed back, and the infuriated wrake backhanded him, the force sending the man careening into those behind him. With a scream of pain he clutched his jaw and slumped to the ground. The nearby soldiers stepped back, not daring to challenge the wrake.

As Marta ducked behind the scullions and crawled under the dray, the furious wrake was scattering the bowls and upending the large soup pot onto the rocky ground. In the resulting melee she scrambled on all fours towards the horses. With the brake on and constrained by their harness, their huge hooves were stomping on the ground. It was too risky to move between them, or even to climb up and make her way along the dray's shaft.

As she peered from under the axle, she saw the legs of the alerted wrakes, running to join the commotion. *Now is the time to go*, she thought. But she wavered, crouching down and looking longingly towards her goal. She remembered how a white feather, floating down from the trees in the Ageless Forest had told her that the Queen of the Sun was still with her. But nothing came now. Marta felt utterly alone.

She took a moment to gather herself, and then shot out from under the dray, and jumped down off the roadway and back onto the slope. She wiped the welling tears away with a fury and, moving faster now, scrambled along the steep slope, past the Pentark and headed further around the fell. The piercing scream of anomirs drifted up from the gully and she could see them coming towards her again. Directly ahead, but further down the slope, were clusters of boulders. If she hurried she could hide among those.

She refused to look behind, but her heart was racing: *Where are you Patrayus?*

∽

Marta was right about Ferdy. Despite Patrayus' stern order—' … don't move until I come back to get you!'—he'd had no intention of staying put in the cart. He wanted to be rid of his gemstone.

After the knight had gone, he searched the cart for anything useful, but there was nothing save a small pile of onions. He had seen how the onions were braided neatly into bunches in the scullery at Mirraway Castle. He scratched his head wondering how he could use them. He tied two bunches together by the stalks, thinking he could sling them round his neck or shoulders and pass off as an onion seller. I should be able to, he muttered to himself, attempting to strengthen his courage, but knowing full well that he'd be carrying the onions away from the kitchen instead of towards it.

And then another thought came to him. He cut off some of the dried stalks with his sword then pulled his beloved pointed hat from his pocket and roughly tied the stalks tightly around the point. He put his hat on, pushing the point down to the crown of his head, so that the pale stalks spilled over his face and body, almost reaching his midriff. He knew he'd look ridiculous, but no more so than when dressed in the outfit Artorus had chosen for him from the armoury room, before he escaped Mirraway Castle.

When he was finished, Ferdy sheathed his sword and peered between the leather curtains of the cart. He knew something was amiss when he heard frenzied shouting and saw that more soldiers had arrived. But he decided that this might be to his advantage. With some difficulty he managed to get the onions around his neck, but groaned when he stood up. They were heavier than expected and almost touched the ground.

Ferdy had been preparing to back out through the curtains, but changed his mind. Boris would push the onions out first, he thought. So he slipped them off his neck and manoeuvred them until they were balanced, side by side, at the end of the tray. Intending to slide them down the steps, he kept both hands on the knotted stalks, and then, to control their descent, sat down with one boot on each bunch, and gently pushed them to their tipping point.

But Ferdy didn't know that Patrayus had removed the steps as a deterrent to nosy passers-by, and so his final push sent the onions plunging to the ground. It also launched him out through the curtains. His natural reaction was to clench his hands tighter around the knotted stalks, so that when the bunches landed, the momentum flipped him over somehow and left him lying flat on his back, winded and in shock—and in full view of anyone looking on.

Horrified, he let the onions go, rolled over and scampered under the cart. Holding his sore ribs, he hid behind the back wheel and peered between the spokes towards the Pentark. As he tried to make sense of all the commotion, he absentmindedly felt for the waterskin. It was gone!

He began to panic. He crawled out from under the cart, reached for the knotted stalks, and started dragging the bunches towards him. Now he could see the top of the waterskin, protruding from under the onions. He cursed. The buckle must have broken. But he kept pulling, hoping the waterskin would come too, but the onions just slid over the top of it. Heedless of the rising danger, he wriggled out and after a quick glance around, snatched the waterskin, and retreated. But in that moment, something caught his eye.

Ferdy had seen many strange things on this adventure and now here was another. Heading in the direction of the Pentark, an odd looking creature was walking behind the cluster of tethered horses, carts, drays and hastily built shelters. By the way it moved, he initially thought it must be drunk. It was as tall as an average man but seemed disjointed somehow. The top half was thin, and the bottom half, thick. And it seemed that this odd creature was also trying to avoid the enemy.

Having no better plan, Ferdy decided to follow it. He removed the broken strap and jammed the waterskin down the front of his jacket. Giving the onions a dismissive glance and then taking his chances, he ran from relative safety, and ducked behind a crude wooden shed used for storing armour. He stopped abruptly when he ran into the legs of a soldier who was relieving himself. After an awkward moment, he scurried past. But now that the enemy had seen him he needed to run for his life.

He dived under the next cart to catch his breath. Ahead of him were the tethered war horses, already skittish because of the commotion. To avoid being kicked or trampled, he ran under their noses, hoping that their legs would hide him somewhat. They reminded him of Aster and Poppins and he felt a rare twinge of fondness towards the ponies, wondering where they were now.

He wasn't sure if the creature he had seen was trustworthy, but he wanted to get a closer look, and so he skirted around a dray and then spotted it, still bumbling along ahead. The ground was uneven and the creature was moving in an exaggerated manner, first lurching one way and then the other. Ferdy heard it puffing and blowing from exertion and suddenly felt his skin prickle. He ran closer and looked down at the creature's boots.

'Boris?' he whispered loudly.

The creature suddenly spun to face him. The upper half appeared to break off and topple to the ground, taking with it the long tunic that was obviously part of the disguise.

And suddenly the twins were hugging each other, greatly relieved.

'Thank goodness you're here,' said Boris, squeezing tight. 'We went to the scullery looking for you, but you'd already gone.'

Each thought the other looked comical: Boris was wearing the liripipe hood from Mirraway Castle, and Ferdy's hat was still decorated with dried onion stalks. Boris ran to help Volgor up, and made quick introductions. Ferdy had never seen a kurr before and screwed his nose up at the lingering smell of fish. But knowing he was also a gem carrier, he gave him a respectful nod.

The twins were bursting to tell each other of their separate adventures, but there was no time.

'We can't stay here.' Boris immediately took responsibility for the group and led them under the closest cart.

'Have you seen Frovin? Or Marta? Patrayus?' asked Ferdy.

Boris gave him a quizzical look. 'No. Should we?'

'They're here somewhere. I've seen Marta and Patrayus. Frovin's meant to help us get to … ' Ferdy jabbed his thumb towards the Pentark.

Boris raised his eyebrows. *Did that mean Marta had the Lightenstone?* But he was unsure how much Volgor knew, and so merely said, 'I doubt Frovin will help us.'

'That's what I told Marta,' said Ferdy, 'but it seems that Ikoseer has ordered him to. And don't forget that he helped you rescue me from the scouts and wrakes in Greenwood Forest.'

'A lot has changed since then. And we've made it this far without him.' Boris was defensive. Then he glanced at Ferdy's midriff and started.

'Where's the waterskin?'

Ferdy patted his chest. 'The buckle broke. And I also know where to put it when we reach the Pentark.' Turning to Volgor he said pointedly, 'But I don't know where your gemstone goes.'

Volgor fixed his bulging grey eyes on Ferdy. 'Attricus has already told me.'

Boris pursed his lips. Volgor still hadn't revealed where he was hiding it. To conceal his annoyance, Boris poked his head out from the cart and then back again.

Apart from the cylindrical leather case containing the elven map, Ferdy noticed a strange thin rope slung across his brother's chest. *Wonder where you got that?* His thoughts were interrupted by Boris. 'Soldiers are coming.'

He was already unsheathing Thrust as he searched the faces of the other two. 'You ready?'

Volgor drew the kitchen knife from his belt. Ferdy hesitated and then slowly drew his own short sword. Boris' jaw dropped a little, but he soon recovered and, with a grin, touched the others' blades with Thrust. Flames shot upwards from the tips and a cold shiver ran through their bodies.

Then Boris briefly touched his chest, where he'd secreted the lock of Yahdra's hair in an inside pocket. 'Now we're ready. 'Let's go.'

∾

Transformed into an eagle, Sheen was hovering above the reach of the anomirs, watching the trio as they ran between the Pentark's liths towards the Pentark itself. The remaining guards were ignoring Volgor—perhaps because they had seen kurrs before—but they were soon chasing after the dwarves.

Each time Boris wielded Thrust against them, Sheen saw a flash of light, and she wondered how long it would be before Boris realised that once Thrust was inside the Pentark's liths, the blade would have a mind of its own.

# CHAPTER 38

After sending Volgor on his way to Mirraway Castle with the Pisces gemstone, Captain Tibbs prepared to engage the enemy outside Mirraway Castle. He had sailed the Mother Sea with the *Arcadia*, the *Sirius* and the *Sancta Maria*, using the only navigable route for such a fleet. And then, with his small crews supplemented by a volunteer force of sailors, defectors and other willing citizens, he made his way to a bay on the western coast of the Isle of Spheres.

The glacial lake from which the headwaters of the mighty Intrepid River flowed east for a long way, then south to Werthyn Harbour, over several rapids and shallows, was also the source of a river that flowed west for barely ten miles and emptied into this bay. From here the fleet would go up-river, across the lake and then down the Intrepid River as far as Mirraway Castle.

But this also happened to be the route used by Lord Mortimer's pirates when delivering their booty to the castle, and so, as they sailed into the bay with the Jolly Roger flying, they encountered an enemy galleon at anchor. Captain Tibbs easily seized the vessel and was pleased to discover that it was loaded with food and weapons.

After the disgruntled pirates were dispatched ashore, he simply replaced the galleon's crew and put it at the head of his fleet, so that, as they came in sight of the castle, either all the ships would seem to belong to Lord Mortimer, or Captain Tibbs' ships would seem to be under maritime arrest.

But on approaching the wharf used to service Mirraway Castle, they were surprised to see that resistance fighters had already sabotaged the enemy fleet, with the crews either captured or killed, and so they had to negotiate around the enemy vessels that floated adrift like ghost ships, their anchor ropes hanging lifeless.

The Captain climbed aloft, clawing his way up the rigging of the main mast and into the crow's nest of the tall ship, *Sirius*. He pulled his spyglass from the leather case slung across his chest and held it to one eye.

Ninety feet up, with the Jolly Roger flapping above him, he adjusted his spyglass and scanned the wharf. He saw there was no time to waste. The longboats had to be lowered and the fighters rowed ashore. His ginger tail swishing rapidly, he extended a claw and roared at the crew below.

'All hands hoy!'

'Heave, ho.'

'Secure the boat plugs.'

'Prepare to slack away.'

'Aye, aye Cap'n,' shouted the quartermaster. He then barked the same orders along the chain of command to the other ships.

Satisfied, Captain Tibbs adjusted his cocked hat and swept his spyglass to the battle around the castle. He saw Helios first, charging, kicking, trampling, and apparently grabbing wrakes by the throat. Then Ikoseer and the Knights of Power came into view as they clashed with the enemy. Ikoseer wielded Gif powerfully and sparks of blue flashed each time a knight's sword struck an enemy's. The Captain wondered if Yoska (Prince Mir) was with them somewhere, brandishing Honorex.

Soldiers kept falling. And from the left flank, the nimble Arrowsmiths of the elven army were fanning out, furiously launching arrows from their longbows. But as soldiers fell, more arrived to swell the enemy's ranks.

As he swept the spyglass away from the centre of the battle, Tibbs spotted a small group of mounted boorlings gathered near the bottom of the roadway leading up to the Pentark. Their riders appeared to be having an animated discussion. Two were richly dressed and Tibbs let out a throaty growl: Lord Mortimer and Earl Onysius. But as he sharpened the image, he saw that Mortimer was hunched over in his saddle and Onysius seemed to be in charge of the group.

He lowered the spyglass and looked down at the wharf. Packed with eager fighters, the first relay of longboats was almost there.

'All hands on deck,' roared the Captain. More soldiers swarmed up through the hatches, arming themselves and awaiting their turn for a longboat as young Nipper darted to and fro, attempting to keep them in some sort of order.

As the rising breeze gently rocked the *Sirius*, Captain Tibbs slowly combed his claws through his whiskers, and turned his attention to following the flight of mounted anomirs up and over the top of the fell. That scrawny little kurr, Volgor, is up there somewhere with the gemstone, he thought. Sheen had kept him abreast of all the news, so the Captain also knew about the other stones. He assumed she was gliding overhead now, ready to alert Ikoseer about Lord Mortimer's movements. Toil is the nemesis of the Lightenstone and Ikoseer will be pushed to her limit if she has to protect Marta from that, he thought grimly.

Earlier, as the ships weighed anchor, Sheen arrived with a message from the Sage.

'Ikoseer asks you to stay with your ships, Mr Tibbs. Keep a skeleton crew on each and use them as makeshift hospitals as well as a safe haven for the elderly, women and children from the castle.'

The Captain secured the spyglass in its leather case. Swinging from the crow's nest and then onto the rigging, he clawed his way backwards down the ropes, leapt onto the deck and then up onto the gunwale. There he paced the length of the *Sirius*, observing the dip of oars and relay of longboats from his fleet. Satisfied at last, he sharpened his claws with a quick scratch on the gunwale, dropped back onto the deck, and then sprang onto the raised wooden box in the middle of the deck. The tip of his tail flicked and, with a still watchful gaze, he began to purr.

∽

Marta kept working her way around the top ridge of the fell, moving between boulders and rocky outcrops and was now safely on the western face. A natural amphitheatre of five rocky columns rose up behind the outer liths of Sagittarius and Capricorn, so she climbed between the tallest two, pulled her hood forward and cautiously looked down towards the Pentark. Although it was partly obscured by the granite liths its beauty made Marta catch her breath.

The Pentark seemed to be made of pure gold and although she had already glimpsed it from the ground, it was much wider than she realised. She checked the outer ring and noted the large zodiac symbols. Each was represented on a point of the twelve-pointed star, but closer to the inner ring, where each point lengthened and widened towards the centre. There should be no confusion as to where the gemstones go, she thought.

As she studied the inner ring, the circumscribed five-pointed star that gave the Pentark its name, her heart quickened and she clutched the Lightenstone. Her emotions bubbled to the surface as she thought of her father, of the wolfhound Wallace, and of Bloss the gentle draught mare. *If I survive all this, I can finally go home.*

A voice whispered in her head, 'But you are already home.'

Marta spun round to look down at the empty rocks. She felt a sudden chill and shivered. Turning back, she pulled her cloak tighter.

She knew to place the Lightenstone in the centre of the inner ring, but now, instead of the vacant space she was expecting, there was a gold sphere. She started by summoning the images she had seen in the Well of Forgetfulness.

*My grandmother didn't remove the Stone from a sphere. It must be somehow connected to the three light spheres on the headlands of the Isle. But do I now have to place the Lightenstone in a sphere? If so, why didn't Ikoseer tell me that?*

Around the Pentark, tension was building. The soldiers and wrakes appeared to be searching for someone, and Marta noticed darting figures on the ground, between the under structure of the rings and the outer liths.

*I hope that's Ferdy searching for the Gemini point. Perhaps Patrayus is with him. Maybe Frovin's helping the others after all.*

Furrowing her brow, she re-focused on the sphere. There seemed to be a small opening at the top. Visualising the Well of Forgetfulness again, she recalled the image that showed the petals of a central rose gently opening to reveal the face of her mother. And then she thought she understood.

*The sphere's like a flower. That's where the Lightenstone should go, in the middle of that. It must've been open and then, after my grandmother removed the Stone, it closed. And now it's slowly re-opening again; it's preparing for the Lightenstone. So, the closer I get …*

Marta shivered, sure that the enemy would notice the changes too. She instinctively looked south towards the World of the Dark Night. Menacing storm clouds were gathering in the distance and, as she hurriedly made her way back down the column, a clap of thunder rolled across the morning sky.

High above, an alert goblin rider saw something move and banking his anomir hard, he dropped away from the others for a closer look. His eyes glinted with war lust, not caring whether or not it was the woman they had been searching for, with strict orders to report her location immediately to Onysius. But instead of doing that, he circled again and again, losing height with each turn.

Marta kept moving, darting around the sparsely vegetated rocks, to find a way between the columns and get to the Pentark more quickly. As soon as she saw the sphere, she knew that she was at a greater risk of being exposed to the enemy. But as she felt the pulling forces between the Lightenstone and Pentark strengthen, the compulsion to complete her task seemed to engulf her.

The screaming of the descending anomir now made her drop and scramble onto a worn animal track that led between rambling briar bushes. Thorns snagged her cloak as she pushed her way through, until the track stopped abruptly against solid rock.

She immediately thought of the rock giants and of how the fell she had just climbed could be the bent leg of a reclining giant, while another giant could have rested their forearm against the shinbone, thereby creating the roadway up to the Pentark. Perhaps the columns I've just climbed could be the fingers and thumb of a rock giant's hand, palm up and resting on the kneecap of the other giant. Could the Pentark be built in the palm of a rock giant's hand?

With a thumping heart she pulled the Lightenstone from her doublet and squinting against the increasing radiance of light, she placed her free hand on the solid wall, saying a silent prayer:

*On behalf of Ikoseer the Sage of White Timber Mountain, and Solara the Queen of the Sun, I command the rock giants to help me.*

At once, pebbles began rattling down the columns. The giant seemed to separate its fingers enough for Marta to crawl between two of them, and then created room for her to stand. The fingers closed after her. After several moments of her eyes adjusting to the darkness, the Gnome King Jigs suddenly lumbered out of the wall just in front of her, rattling his walking sticks. She recoiled and glanced around, expecting to see black and white gnome eyes protruding from the rocks, but it seemed that the King was alone.

Meanwhile he was eyeing her warily, well pleased that there was not enough room for Snowball, the small white pony that had sprayed snot all over his royal head. But he was wondering why the badger was not with her.

'So … you actually managed to get here then?'

Marta had by now recovered from his sudden appearance, and retorted, 'And I see that you knew when to come.'

' … thanks to my *headache*.' Glaring at her, Jigs raised one stick and with a gnarled finger, pointed to the glowing-hot jewels on his simple crown.

'You asked for my help. Now that I'm here, what are you expecting me to do?'

Marta was taken aback.

'My only task is to return the Lightenstone,' she reminded him curtly. 'The Gemini and Pisces gemstones are already here, but I'm not sure where the other two gems are.'

'But you do know who has them.' His tone was matter of fact. He narrowed his bulging eyes a fraction.

Marta hesitated. 'Yes. Mafasat and Toros have one each.'

'Quite. But then who else would carry the gemstones of the Lion and Bull?'

'Are they close to the fell?' She was quite sure Jigs knew more than he was telling.

'They'll arrive when they're supposed to.'

Time's slipping away, thought Marta. But she made a point of saying, 'I'm very grateful to the gnomes. I know you've been helping us since Frovin, Snowball and I saw you last. We wouldn't have made it this far without you. Before we left The Veils to cross Glen Bain, Frovin found the gnome key in Snowball's saddlebag, and this opened the door into the mountains around Mirraway Castle. Attricus, the soothsayer told us about the gnome door.'

He gave her a sharp look.

'And then you fed us too,' she added, recalling the plants that the gnomes pushed through the tunnel walls.

The King grunted. 'Humph! I suppose you have to go. I'll see to it that I …' Stopping mid-sentence, he scratched his bulbous head and shuffled aside for her to pass.

Marta squeezed past him, not sure whether he was unwilling to tell her what he was intending to do, or if he had simply forgotten what he was going to say. But she'd noticed that he didn't seem bothered by the Lightenstone's brightness.

She stopped and faced him. 'Do you know anything about the gold sphere in the centre of the Pentark? I think it's starting to open …'

'We gnomes are very clever. We know many things. Each section of that sphere is a solidified flame. They are the remnants of the fire that consumed the Firebird … after it placed all the stones in the Pentark.'

Marta was silent for a moment. *So they're flames.*

'The enemy will notice it opening too,' she said quietly.

'Can't be helped.'

'And I'm sure … Toil will know.'

Jigs' gaze intensified and there was a moment of silence between them.

'You're a light carrier, Marta. Your mind is a star, a spark of light. Confront your fear. Use your willpower.'

He tapped the wall with a walking stick. Immediately the cavity came alive with what seemed like thousands of black and white gnome eyes peering curiously, packed so tight that they appeared to smother the rock—a very strange sight. As soon as Marta slipped the Lightenstone back into her doublet, the whites of the gnomes' eyes became soft lights, and the jewels on the King's crown seemed to brighten.

'Hurry,' he said, 'I'll get no *peace* until the Lightenstone is returned.'

'There's something else I forgot to ask.' She hung back.

'Quickly, then. What is it?'

'Do the stones have to be returned in any particular order?'

The question seemed to fluster the King momentarily. 'Well … the Firebird put the Lightenstone in first … and then the gemstones. But it won't matter this time.'

Marta hoped he was right. The rock wall facing her was now within arm's reach. She tried to keep calm, but it seemed impossible as the mass of eyes glowed and stared at her expectantly.

Her whole body seemed on edge as she attempted to shore up her courage. *I have to trust my heart.* Hardening her resolve, she stepped straight into the rock, scattering the eyeballs as the giant's fingers parted in response to her move.

Squinting against the daylight, Marta could see that the lith of Capricorn was still some distance away. She pulled her hood forward and with head bowed, made towards it. Most of the soldiers gave her only a cursory glance as she moved through them, but several followed her. Eventually one yelled, 'Hey! You there … halt!'

The command prompted others to turn and stare as she hurried the last few steps and disappeared between the liths of Capricorn and Aquarius.

'Get her!'

Marta ran under the Pentark, looking for a way to climb up. The Pentark had a simple uncluttered supporting structure that she had observed when handing out bread to the soldiers, and again just now, from the top of the rocky columns. Now that she was underneath it, she estimated that the zodiac ring was nine feet above the ground; and the diameter of the rings, double that. The central shaft appeared to be in two sections; the lower one twice the length of the top shaft, and each with five supports.

Now she received another shock.

Cracks suddenly appeared beneath her feet, followed by gnarled tree roots pushing up through the cracks and spreading out. This reminded her of the menacing trees in Greenwood Forest, snatching at her when she fled Brechin Village with Artorus. She ran to the centre of the structure, where the lowest supporting beams curved out and up from the base of the main shaft.

She stood on the closest beam and jumped up, trying to grab one of the smaller supports above and climb up to the five-pointed star, where the Lightenstone was to be placed. But now a tree trunk began to extend up the main shaft, groaning as it grew. Branches sprouted from it, twisting and winding around the supports. In desperation, Marta jumped again and managing to hang on this time, glanced down for a moment and saw a very familiar striped head.

'Frovin!' She let go and dropped. 'Look out!'

But Frovin seemed nonplussed about the tree so she held out her hand. 'Hurry!'

And then Ferdy appeared, red cheeked and puffing, running towards her for all he was worth, with Boris and someone she assumed was the terrified kurr, Volgor, just behind him. Boris was clearly planning to use Yahdra's elven rope.

Suddenly Frovin called out, 'Quickly! Grab the highest branch you can reach. The tree's growing, its branches will take you to the top.'

In that moment Marta realised that the tree was not an enemy, but was actually helping them escape—and there was no time to waste. For the wrakes had arrived, and were already swinging their battleaxes and hacking at the growing boughs, which were lashing out in retaliation: And where cut limbs fell, new shoots sprouted.

So that's what King Jigs and the gnomes had come to do, she thought, remembering what he'd said when they first met: … *the roots of plants tell us that they feel the advancing march of many feet.*

As they started to climb, Marta was thinking that the gnomes must be able to communicate with trees through their roots. And trees too had suffered at the hands of Lord Mortimer and the Prince of Darkness.

Meanwhile, since the wrake's battleaxes had no effect on the tree, the more nimble soldiers were now attempting to climb after Marta and her companions. In answer to this new assault, lateral limbs began to sprout, slowly filling the void beneath the Pentark as the outer branches thickened and lengthened, not only fashioning a barrier between the five supports, but also growing out from the tree's crown, along the underside of the rings, and once past the circumference, hanging down to create a canopy.

The wrakes and boorlings raged below them, and the soldiers' outstretched arms and stabbing swords came ever closer, but Marta and the others kept climbing up and around. Boris and Volgor soon left their liripipe hoods behind. They came to a halt when they reached the underside of the outer ring, not knowing what zodiac signs were above them.

Ferdy wanted to be rid of the agate. He poked his head out to see where it should go. As he pulled his head back in, Volgor asked if he'd seen a fish symbol.

But Ferdy shook his head and turned to Marta. 'It's like a … a set of scales. For weighing things. Like in the scullery at Mirraway.'

'No. That's Libra,' she said. 'Gemini's further around to the right.'

Volgor groaned. 'So where's the fish sign?' His grey eyes peered at Marta through his thin blond fringe. He assumed she was the young woman Boris had told him about.

'Pisces is almost directly opposite us, but look for a sign with two fish, not just one.'

Volgor felt for the aquamarine still secured in his jacket. *Where's Attricus when you need him?*

'And don't forget about the Taurus and Leo gems.' Frovin gave Boris a stern look. Ikoseer had led him to believe that Boris had them. 'Taurus is just *after* Gemini and Leo is *before* it,' he added pointedly.

'Humph!' Boris scowled. 'I don't have them. And I don't know where they are.'

Frovin's jaw dropped. His gaze flew to Marta. 'Did you know about this?'

Marta held his gaze, and gently shook her head.

Initially, she didn't know who had the remaining gems, but now she realised why Ikoseer had not revealed it: the Sage wanted Frovin to leave her and help the others, knowing he would be more likely to do that if all four gems needed his protection. But she also felt that there was more behind Ikoseer's carefully veiled deception … something deeper and wiser.

Boris was now looking smug. He knew something that the precocious badger didn't. Pointing Thrust in the general direction of the ring, he said,

'We'll just work our way further around under here until we get to the sign of the twins.'

'That's silly. It'll take forever,' scoffed Ferdy, looking through the tangle of branches. They were sure that he couldn't possibly squeeze through, and were all shocked when, by first pushing and then pulling his chubby body up through the gap, he then disappeared from sight.

Boris started. *Whatever does he think he's doing? Carrying that agate must've done something to his head!*

Now he had no choice but to follow his emboldened brother. Volgor gave Frovin an uncertain look and then he too slipped his scrawny frame through the gap after the twins.

'Be careful!' Marta shouted above the sound of the rising wind as it whistled through the branches. But they had already gone.

'Thank you for helping them to get here safely.' Marta wrapped her arms around Frovin, affectionately stroking his coarse fur as the commotion intensified.

'Hummph! They arrived all by themselves.' He loosened from her embrace. 'I've been minding my own business.'

'You've been following me instead.'

'It's my destiny to protect you and the Stone.'

'You disobeyed Ikoseer.'

'But I obeyed the Queen …'

Marta admired his courage, and despite a rising an uneasy feeling, asked, 'Did you see Toros or Mafasat on the fell? They have the other two gemstones.'

He snorted at the revelation. 'No, I did not see them. And what else has Ikoseer kept from me. Who told you about them?'

'Patrayus,' she said softly.

'So, he knew and I didn't. I should have known,' he growled. He had seen the young knight with her earlier.

'But you knew that this tree wasn't our enemy,' she said, attempting to lift his mood.

'It's a golden oak, like the one above my family's sett in Greenwood Forest.' Frovin was still irritated. 'It's evergreen and you can tell what type of oak it is by the colour and shape of its leaves.'

Marta had never seen a golden oak before. Different oaks grew in the World of Man.

'We have to go,' he said hurriedly. 'Onysius, Lord Mortimer and Toil will be here soon enough. They're already on the fell.'

Fear gripped her. 'Did you see them?'

'No, but Sheen did. She paid me a quiet visit to let me know.'

*So, Ikoseer and Artorus won't be far behind.* Marta felt somewhat relieved but she couldn't shake off the feeling of dread that kept rising from the pit of her stomach.

It was now clear that enemy reinforcements had arrived. The cursing and shouting below grew louder. The boughs shuddered with each vicious lash and low, haunting moans escaped from deep inside the tree. The oak will soon be overwhelmed, she thought, praying that she would be able to return the Lightenstone in time.

Then their eyes locked. Neither knew their future, but Frovin, steadfast and determined to fulfil his destiny, scrambled through the gap between Libra and Virgo. And Marta followed … between the balancing scales and the enveloping mother … between justice and light.

∽

As he topped the rise near the Pentark, Lord Mortimer halted his mount, groaning as Toil suddenly dug deeper into his weeping flesh. He gasped. 'The … Lightenstone … is here.'

Onysius's eyes slid to the top of the Pentark. He saw movement and licked his lips. *I have been biding my time long enough.*

He gave the Lord a sideways glance and squeezed the hilt of his favourite dagger. Soon, Toil will defeat the Lightenstone. Mortimer will be dead. Then I will be the ruler of the Isle of Spheres.

# CHAPTER 39

By now word about the coming battle and the expected return of the Pentark stones had spread throughout the World of the Soul. The soothsayer, Attricus, was busy organising a command centre for the resistance in the cave and tunnel, as Ikoseer had asked him to do.

In this he was helped by a motley crew of allied fighters: the old dwarf, Potsy, sent many from the Lux Mountains; others came from the coldest reaches of Arctus in the far north. Some came from the knight, Sir Henry, in the east. They brought not only weapons, but also woollen blankets, torches, salves, tinctures and somehow, fresh herbs for poultices and remedies.

The adults were helping to prepare for the injured by ripping cloth for bandages and slings, and simmering mandrake, hemlock, henbane and willow bark in a small cauldron over a fire. The women were also encouraging their ragged, frightened children to join in the work: running messages, fetching water from a nearby stream, stirring the warming herbs, stoking the fire and rolling bandages. Meanwhile, outside the cave under Snowball's watchful eye, the older siblings were gathering firewood.

They had never seen a horse like Snowball before. Some reached out to touch her silvery white coat, and gaped at the strange spiralled horn now parting her forelock. Frovin's guess was correct. After Frovin left the cave to find and help Boris, Ferdy and Volgor, Ikoseer had one final task before she and Artorus also left.

She placed Gif on Snowball's forehead and intoned an incantation. The horse's white coat shimmered and seemed to glow as a long spiralled horn emerged from her forelock. She was transformed—Snowball was a unicorn.

Attricus had seen images of unicorns in the books at Elodom Monastery, but believed them to be mythical creatures, and at first he was taken aback by the marked change in the mare. All he could grasp was that she looked regal, even magical. He lifted everyone's spirits by explaining that she usually lived with the Sage in White Timber Mountain.

Now, as the battle was raging, Snowball lifted her proud head as if hearing a clarion call. She pricked up her ears, whinnied, and left the cave, breaking into a gallop as she headed along the gully towards Mirraway Castle. Toros and Mafasat had arrived.

As Attricus watched her disappear, bloodied carriers arrived from the battlefield with the first of the wounded.

The enemy goblin who had earlier seen Marta moving among the rocky columns, was now circling above the Pentark on his anomir. Below there was chaos: the ground had erupted and a tree had suddenly grown from under the Pentark, seemingly to protect it from ground attack. And, after flying in ever decreasing circles, making several attempts to touch down, the goblin finally landed his anomir on top of one of the zodiac liths that encircled the Pentark.

As the creature folded its wings, its goblin rider scanned the Pentark and saw—as they climbed up from underneath the rings and made their way across the top of the Pentark—one dwarf, another dwarf, and then a kurr. The goblin's eyes narrowed as two more figures joined them: a badger and another covered in a cloak. None of them seemed to have noticed him. The goblin sneered, baring his sharp teeth.

He had seen two dwarves and a badger together once before, during an attack on a travelling group at the Norfolk Woods. That badger had killed his brother goblin, and the two dwarves had escaped when the ponies they were riding had bolted into the woods. He was sure this was the same group. As he watched them, his hatred grew and he began to tremble in anticipation of a kill.

Far above him, Rhyll was watching on his new anomir, sure that the cloaked figure at the centre of the Pentark below was Marta, with Frovin beside her. He had no knowledge of the dwarves, but he wondered about the scrawny kurr. Could this be the same one that my master Onysius, sent me to capture on that rogue anomir that bit me and then was killed by that stranger?

As he glanced east, down the sloping roadway towards the battle, Onysius and Lord Mortimer were just cresting the last rise in the road, bringing them up to the top of the fell and close to the Pentark. A short distance behind them raced two mounted horses: an unknown golden warhorse, and a black steed that somehow seemed familiar. In fact he was sure he'd seen it in the rocky gorge with Marta and Frovin when his first anomir was killed. But this time, the rider on the black horse was clad in armour, and although the rider of the gold horse looked rather old, she appeared formidable, extending before her a long staff, the head of it glowing and sparking with a bright blue light.

Now, as the anomir perched on the lith below began to open its wings in readiness to attack, Rhyll, high above, urged his ride to reach her maximum speed, stroking her scaly neck and, strangely for a goblin, speaking encouraging words.

Then, as the anomir below rose from the lith and homed in on his prey, Rhyll's command rang out: 'Strike!'

Once he was on the top of the Pentark, Volgor, despite his misgivings, easily found the fish symbol. He hurried across the centre and then along the middle of the Pisces ray until it narrowed and merged at the point. He then slid off the ray, and under the canopy of the tree, screwed his jacket around until he could use his teeth to break the stitching that secured his gemstone on the inside pocket.

Until this moment, he'd forgotten just how beautiful the aquamarine was, and the sight of it took him back to the day he'd found it in the belly of the fish in the Abyss River and held it up to the light. Now he grasped it in his long bony fingers and, peering out of the tree just far enough to guide his hand, he dropped it into what he hoped was the correct place. As soon as he felt the Pisces ray quiver, he snatched his arm back, thinking only about returning to his Bleak River home near the Raven Mountains. Keeping his knife at the ready, he decided to make his way back down through the branches. As long as I can avoid Onysius, I should be safe, he thought.

∽

Meanwhile, unlike kurrs that are used to skipping from rock to rock, dwarves much prefer walking on solid ground, and so Boris and Ferdy were wobbling precariously around the inner circle of the zodiac star, stepping on the centre of each ray in turn as they made their way towards the Gemini symbol, and being careful not to fall back down into the tree canopy. As they passed the sign of Cancer, Ferdy recognised it: 'Gemini's next.'

'Hope you know what you're talking about,' whispered Boris, now staring suspiciously at the new symbol. 'They look more like the columns at the entrance to Alfura court—not twins.'

'Perhaps, but it's still the Gemini sign. And I know because Marta drew the shape for me with pebbles,' said Ferdy. Then facing the outer circumference of the Pentark, he moved towards the tip of the ray. *'Keep watch while I try and remove my agate.'*

Boris was still behind him. Sitting down close to the point, Ferdy hurriedly pulled the waterskin out from the inside front of his jacket. But as Boris turned around, he was startled to see an anomir perched directly opposite him, on one of the outer liths. Fortunately the goblin rider seemed to be concentrating on Marta and Frovin at the centre of the Pentark.

Boris yelled, 'Anomir!' and holding Thrust out in front of himself, made towards them.

But the blade suddenly ripped from his grip as it had done in the garderobe in Mirraway Castle, when he'd first met Volgor and the two blades had become one. And now, as if deciding what to do next, Thrust was hovering in the air in front of him. In a panic, Boris spread his fingers and held his hand out, willing it to return to him, but when it didn't move, he baulked at making a grab for it, recalling the words of the Queen of the Sun, *"Keep it safe and use it well … for all its secrets are not yet revealed."*

And then he heard the same musical note he'd heard only twice before: the first time in Alfura, the elven enclave, before King Elvendor gave Ferdy the agate. The second time was in the garderobe in Mirraway Castle when Volgor had his gemstone. And now it was alerting him again to the presence of an outer gemstone. *Does this mean that the two missing gemstones of Taurus and Leo are here too?*

But without Thrust, Boris's only weapon was Yahdra's elven rope, still slung across his chest. When he saw the anomir open its wings, he swallowed hard and pulled the rope up and over his head.

Lord Mortimer moaned, desperate for the pain to end. Fresh blood now trickled from his festering neck, staining the collar of his garment a darker red.

'Take it off,' he gasped.

Onysius leant closer to the Lord.

'You spoke, my Lord?'

'Take it off!'

As Toil dug even deeper, the Lord slumped forward in his saddle.

Onysius wrapped one arm across the Lord's back to support him and grabbed the only bit of Toil's chain that he could still see and pulled it over the Lord's head. He wrenched it back through the festering flesh, and, as the Lord screamed and collapsed, Onysius hurled Toil into the air. Drawing his dagger from its sheath, and keeping it concealed from the accompanying wrakes, he drove it deep under Mortimer's rib cage and up towards his heart.

As the Lord's body slid to the ground, and Toil sped through the air towards the Lightenstone, Ikoseer and Artorus came up the rise behind them, closely followed by another armoured rider: it was Yoska, holding aloft the mighty sword, Honorex.

Crouched in the centre of the Pentark, Marta's hands were shaking as she reached inside her hood and slipped the chain over her head. She was about to pull the Lightenstone out from her doublet when she was alerted by Boris' shout. She glanced up, relieved that the anomir she saw was larger than other anomirs, with pale coloured feathers.

'It's only Rhyll,' she said quickly to Frovin beside her. 'Boris doesn't know about him or his anomir.'

She needed to hurry. The solid flames of the central sphere were now fully opened and she could see where to place the Stone.

Badgers have such poor eyesight that Frovin couldn't see either anomir, but his excellent sense of smell was alerted by their scent, blending with those of their rider goblins, boorlings, wrakes, and now … something very different. He lifted his nose into the air and sniffed furiously. But Marta now pulled out the Lightenstone, and shielding her eyes, pushed it down hard into the receptacle.

Instantly, vibrations spread from the centre of the Pentark in several directions; along each ray to the outer circumference of the zodiac ring and down the central shaft, then radiating along each of the ley lines and out to the three spheres on the headlands of the Isle, rumbling and shaking the ground.

And then, Frovin realised what he could smell.

Meanwhile, startled by Boris' warning about the anomir, Ferdy hastily pulled the stopper out of the waterskin, and then holding his hand under the opening, he tipped the skin upside down and shook it, expecting the purple agate to drop into his palm. But the agate seemed to be stuck somehow on the inside. In a panic Ferdy squeezed the skin, feeling for the gemstone. Weeks earlier, when interrogated by the Commander in Mirraway Castle, Elvendor's incantation had somehow kept the agate safe, but now Ferdy silently cursed the elven King.

'I'll have to try and split the seam to get it out,' he muttered, but then, thinking to use his newly charged blade, he placed the tip of it between the two edges of the seam at the bottom of the waterskin and pushed.

He didn't know how Boris and Thrust had managed to sharpen his short sword, but now it split the seam like a hot knife through butter. Ferdy wriggled his chubby hand down inside the skin, pulled out the agate and shoved it into the Gemini point.

At the same time, Rhyll's anomir struck the attacking anomir and goblin rider, slamming them to the ground. And as Rhyll's anomir squeezed its talons tight around the scaly throat of the other madly flapping anomir, the shocked and injured goblin rider crawled away.

As Onysius slid his bloodied dagger back into its sheath and turned from the murdered Lord to glare, he immediately recognised Rhyll. But by this time Ikoseer and Artorus were upon them. As the other wrakes swung their boorlings to face the Sage and knight, Onysius spurred his own boorling away from the group, raging and slicing his sword in a wild arc over Rhyll's ducking head as they passed.

Although unsure of what he was going to do with the elven rope, Boris hurriedly created a noose on one end and re-coiled the rest of the rope against it. Struggling to keep his balance, he headed towards Marta and Frovin.

He'd totally lost control of Thrust. The dagger continued to hover in the air near him until the moment Marta returned the Lightenstone, and the Pentark shuddered into life. Then Thrust suddenly flew out and, as if on a trajectory, began to speed around and around between the Pentark and the liths, creating a sound so strange to Boris' ears, that he felt weak and dizzy and sank to his knees.

Having returned the agate, Ferdy flinched when Thrust sped past him, seemingly inches from his nose, and then, hearing a very strange noise from Boris, he turned towards his brother just as he collapsed. Horrified at the thought that Boris had been struck by an arrow, he grasped the hilt of his short sword and began to scramble to help him.

As thunder rolled across the darkening sky and lightning crackled, the atmosphere seemed charged with an enormous energy.

Meanwhile, finally ready to leave the Pentark, Volgor began to weave his scrawny frame back down through the oak branches when he stopped and peered below. The enemy's concentration around the Pentark had increased greatly, and in a way this made it easier for him to leave without being noticed. But once Marta replaced the Lightenstone in the Pentark, the tree began to shake, the ground rumbled and the howl of the wind rose even higher. Now Volgor saw bewilderment turn to terror on the soldier's faces as they turned tail and fled, leaving the wrakes and boorlings to fight alone.

And then his already bulging eyes widened.

From between two of the outer liths emerged three animals: a huge golden cat that seemed to have flames around its neck and down its chest, a white bull, and a fine silvery white horse with a strange pointed horn protruding from its forehead.

Volgor was transfixed. He'd seen bulls and horses before and was pretty sure that the cat was really Mr Tibbs, now somehow grown to an enormous size and changed colour from ginger to gold. But the bull, flanked by the cat and horse, now tossed his head with its massive horns and trotted straight towards him. When it stopped in front of the oak, pawing at the ground and bellowing low and loud, Volgor shrank back into the branches.

Could these animals have something to do with the missing gemstones? Although Attricus had never mentioned them, Boris had. And so had the badger. No matter, Volgor wanted nothing more to do with the Pentark, or with Mr Tibbs and his sailing ships. He just wanted to go home. But when the bull pushed his muzzle through the branches and opened his mouth, Volgor could see a gemstone resting on his tongue. It was the same shape as the Pisces gem but green in colour.

He now understood very well what the bull was expecting him to do, but could only stammer. 'I … I'm just a simple kurr. I … I've done what Mr Tibbs asked me to do. So now I'm going home to Bleak River.'

Suddenly, the huge gold cat leapt up onto the back of the bull. It held Volgor's gaze with eyes like liquid amber.

'Take the emerald!'

'Mr Tibbs?' squeaked Volgor hopefully.

'I am Mafasat the lion. Take the emerald!'

Volgor then remembered seeing a stylised image depicted on the crest of the Knights of Power in Jimpiragh Castle, and now realised that the image was that of a lion. Had the Knights of Power sent these animals? His pulse racing, Volgor reached forward to put his open hand into the hot, wet mouth of the bull. Wrinkling his hooked nose in disgust, he plucked the emerald off the rough tongue with his long bony fingers.

As he stared at the gem now resting in his palm, he saw that, just like his aquamarine, it was very beautiful.

'Hurry! Onto my back!' demanded Mafasat.

'B … but I'll be burnt!' Volgor protested. He watched as the flames around the lion's neck licked the air, and expected them to set the tree alight.

Seeing Volgor's hesitation, Mafasat opened his mouth, and thrusting his head forward, let out a strange deep sound. Volgor stared at the four huge fangs.

'Now!' Mafasat roared, lowering his flaming head as Volgor closed his hand around the emerald.

It must have been a strange sight: the lion standing on the back of a pure white bull, and the kurr emerging from the oak tree's branches to step awkwardly between the horns of the bull and then leap over the neck flames of the lion onto its back.

'Sit down. Grab my mane. Hold tight.'

Volgor tentatively grabbed a flame in each hand, thankful that they were not actually hot. Mafasat then leapt onto the top of the Pentark and made for the Taurus point, leaving Snowball and Toros below to help fight off the wrakes and boorlings.

As they leapt past Pisces, Volgor recognised his gemstone, now glowing bright and strong. *I'm almost back where I started*, he thought despondently as they passed Aries and stopped at Taurus.

'The sign of the bull,' said Mafasat.

Not waiting to be told, Volgor hurriedly slid off and pushed the emerald into the point. It began to pulse.

'And now onto Leo,' said the lion.

Volgor was unaware that there was also a lion symbol in the zodiac. Reluctantly, he pulled himself back up onto Mafasat, and held tight as they bounded past Gemini, Cancer, and then stopped at Leo. In a blur, Volgor could see Ferdy attending to Boris; there also seemed to be a mighty clash at the perimeter of the Pentark.

Mafasat dropped his head, opened his mouth over the Leo point, and coughed. As the lion lifted his head, Volgor saw yet another gemstone, a very strange one, intense golden yellow to reddish orange. He thought it was the most beautiful gem he'd ever seen, but he also noticed that it was slightly askew. He dismounted, aligned the gem and pushed it into place.

'So you see,' said Mafasat, 'even a simple kurr is worthy enough to help restore the mighty Pentark.'

Their attention was suddenly arrested by a heartbroken wailing.

∽

Thrust was fighting Toil at the perimeter of the Pentark, trying to wrap the chain of the bloodied necklace around itself in an attempt to take it far away, even back to the World of the Dark Night where it belonged. But now that it was free of Lord Mortimer, Toil seemed to have increased in power.

Frovin heard the clash and turned instantly, protectively keeping his back to Marta. The Lightenstone has been returned, but the Prince of Darkness will not give up so easily, he thought. Although the Lightenstone was home, the chain was still loosely attached. Squinting against the brightness, Marta was hastily undoing the chain and re-clasping it around her neck.

Thrust now split once again into two blades, both fighting valiantly against the adversary, but Frovin saw Toil suddenly break away and come towards him. In that moment, he understood that the power emanating from Toil was a hate-fuelled power, a vengeful power. The motley band of travellers had done what Toil and the Prince of Darkness couldn't: they had found and returned the Pentark's stones.

Frovin flung his paws wide to protect Marta as she worked to free the chain from the Lightenstone and took the full brunt of Toil against his chest. The force of it pushed Marta onto the Stone and she turned to Frovin, seeing him struggling and writhing in agony. In desperation she held one hand over the Lightenstone. Feeling the light surge through her, she grabbed for Toil.

But she was too late. Frovin, mortally wounded, submitted to his destiny. Marta's cry of utter love filled the air. Her heart was full of pain and anger and hot, salty tears of unimaginable grief streamed unhindered.

'No! No!' she sobbed, gathering Frovin's lifeless body to her own, pulling him to her heart, cradling him, rocking him, pressing her face into his dense coarse fur.

She shouted to the dark angry sky. 'No! No!'

'This cannot be,' she wept, her shoulders heaving with each anguished breath, for she loved him so, her brave and faithful companion. Not even the Lightenstone could save him.

Bereft and numb with sorrow, she didn't notice Boris and Ferdy beside her. As they rushed to help, Thrust returned to a single blade, and the twins now wrapped their arms tight around Marta, sharing in her unfathomable grief. Volgor joined them too but stood apart, unsure of what to do, while Mafasat stood guard.

Below them, on the ground surrounding the Pentark, Ikoseer and all the others were still fighting the remaining enemy. The ground still rumbled a little, the howling winds abated and the sky began to clear, but the Pentark was complete once more. Terrified of Yoska's blade Honorex, all but one of the anomirs and their rider goblins fled, following Toil as it hurtled back to the World of the Dark Night.

From the edge of the roadway, the group watched as Onysius, mounted on an injured boorling, careened away from the carnage and down towards the gully, away from the taunts of Rhyll and his anomir.

Ikoseer had no interest in pursuing the ageing Earl. She knew that even if he lived long enough to return to Jimpiragh Castle, he could only brood and rage over the defeat. The Sage glanced at the murdered Lord Mortimer: perhaps Onysius would go to live in Mortimer's castle, Mawdark, in the World of the Dark Night. There, if he also is tempted by the sly Prince of Darkness into wearing Toil, that will be the end of him too.

She already knew of Marta's heartbreak, having foreseen Frovin's death. She had even attempted to thwart it by ordering his brave animal friend to help return the outer stones instead. When Sheen warned her that Lord

Mortimer was nearing the Pentark, she and Artorus left the battle at once to protect Marta from Toil.

Patrayus brought his warhorse to the perimeter of the Pentark and grabbed the outer span of a ray to pull himself up. As he approached them, Mafasat, Boris and Ferdy all stepped away from Marta, and watched as Patrayus gently picked her up, with her arms still cradling Frovin's body, and carried them both across the Pentark to Ikoseer, as she waited to take them both on Helios.

Ikoseer was well aware of the young knight's affections and as soon as Patrayus was mounted on his warhorse, the Sage sidled Helios up beside them. She gently placed Marta and Frovin on the knight's horse.

Ferdy's chin wobbled and he wiped brimming tears from his eyes as he watched the group heading down the roadway to Mirraway Castle. Scithios and the remaining Knights of Power were by now at the Pentark, where they began the grim task of supervising the removal of the dead bodies and tending to the wounded.

Having completed its task, the golden oak quickly withdrew into the earth, leaving Boris, Ferdy and Volgor still high on the Pentark—with Mafasat.

'Onto my back, all of you,' ordered Mafasat.

Unsettled by Frovin's death and understandably wary of the huge cat, they shifted uncomfortably while the flaming lion stalked back and forth before them.

'We don't need your help … we can use my rope to climb down.' Boris held up the elven rope.

He didn't have an arrow to secure it to the Pentark, as Yahdra did under the Lake Bridge. But he knew that Thrust's blade could do the job, and he was sure that once he and Ferdy were safely on the ground, Thrust would return to him on command, bringing the rope with it.

Mafasat stopped, allowing Volgor to grasp a flame in each hand and climb up. He gave them a hard stare.

'Toros and Snowball are waiting.'

'Snowball?' said the twins in unison. They hadn't seen her since the attack of the anomirs at the Norfolk Woods.

Mafasat snarled, again revealing his fangs.

Ferdy was alarmed. 'Come on. Imagine what stories we can tell when we get home. It's not every day that you get to sit on a gold cat with flames around its neck.'

'My name is Mafasat and I am a lion,' corrected the cat, as Boris reluctantly sheathed Thrust and slipped the coiled rope back over his head.

Once all were aboard, Mafasat leapt off the Pentark, first onto Toros' back, and then to the ground. Then the lion headed back down the fell and through the former battlefield to Mirraway Castle. Once inside the barbican, Mafasat took them to the stables where the scruffy moor ponies were waiting, much to Boris' surprise, for he thought they were safe in Alfura.

Snowball stood beside the ponies and the twins found it hard to believe the changes in her. Ferdy even wondered if anything strange had also happened to Aster and Poppins, but it seemed not.

The twins thankfully slid off Mafasat, warily extending a hand in greeting. Snowball dropped her silvery head and nuzzled their palms. They dared to touch her protruding horn but snatched their hands away, zapped by an electric charge. Stepping back with a respectful nod they flung their arms around the ponies' necks. As they nickered in tender greeting, Boris had the strange sensation that he was being watched. He slowly turned round and saw Yahdra, the princess elf, leaning casually against a stable door, cheekily grinning at him. And then it was Ferdy's turn to show his disbelief, as Boris ran to her, first hugging her and then standing on tiptoes and kissing her full on the lips.

Ferdy's jaw dropped even further as the gathering crowd parted for Elvendor, the King of the elves. Thinking quickly, he stepped away from Poppins and stood bowing before the King.

'I … I returned the gemstone you gave me, b-b- … but I'm afraid that I left your waterskin at the Pentark. It's split open now, you see?' Ferdy spluttered, unable to think of anything else to say.

'You have done well … for a dwarf. But I have come for my elven map and my daughter … and it seems, even my rope.' He glared at Boris, who now faced Elvendor, feeling his face turn bright red.

Boris swallowed hard. *So, the rope that Yahdra gave me at the Lake Bridge really belongs to her father, the King?*

'Soon my army, the Arrowsmiths, shall be returning to Alfura. Perhaps the pair of you, along with your ponies would like to go with them as far as the Norfolk Woods. Then you can follow the Eastward Road from there to Banters Den … where you belong,' he said with heavy emphasis.

'Certainly,' said Ferdy, trying to reassure him. 'Our parents will be pleased to have us back home.'

'In the meantime, Ikoseer has requested your presence, along with that of the kurr, Volgor.' Elvendor also acknowledged Mafasat with a slight nod.

Coming forward but avoiding eye contact with the displeased King, Boris removed the leather case with the elven map and pulled the rope from over his head. He handed them back to him.

With Yahdra now beside him, Elvendor turned on his heel and strode ahead, forcing the twins to trot in order to keep up. But, as they stopped before the huge throne room doors, Yahdra turned, puckering her nose at Boris. Then she gave him a brazen wink.

# CHAPTER 40

Soon after the Lightenstone was returned and the victorious group gathered in the throne room at Mirraway, Ikoseer spoke to the Knights of Power.

'The battle is over but there is still much to do. We must ensure safe passage for any survivors returning to the World of the Dark Night, and at the same time show mercy to any of the enemy's forces that we find wounded or displaced. They can all return via the portal that the Prince of Darkness created in the Arkfeld. The Queen of the Sun will ensure that it remains passable until the last of them are through. We will also allow them to bury their dead, or otherwise take them home for burial. The rock giants will open graves for any remaining bodies and then close the ground for you. The Arrowsmiths will help until the work is done.'

Patrayus stepped forward. 'And what about any enemies that wish to stay here?'

'They must first go to live in the World of Man until their soul is cleansed of their inner darkness. The Arrowsmiths will escort them to their new home in the World of Man when they leave in a few weeks. But until then, keep them under guard.'

News spread fast throughout the World of the Soul and there was much rejoicing. Within a few weeks of the Lightenstone's return, the bare ground was lush with new grass, the animals emerged from hiding, and the forests were once again safe for travellers.

But for those who had known Frovin, there was a lingering sadness over his death. Ikoseer allowed Marta time to grieve and rest, but eventually went looking for her.

As she entered the high-walled garden at Mirraway Castle, the hinges on the heavy oak door groaned. Then the Sage made her way to the central inner garden, slipping between the clumps of white lilies that seemed to guard the narrow entrance. The walls of this garden were also built of dry stone, and the climbing rose that had been struggling now had new leaves, and was already smothered with heavily scented double blooms. Colourful rows of rosemary, iris, marigold and violets decorated the curved inner border. The autumn chill brought on by Lord Mortimer's attack and the removal of the Lightenstone was now transformed into brisk spring weather.

'Your grandmother and mother used to come here,' said Ikoseer, sitting down on the wooden seat beside Marta and stretching out her long legs.

As Marta acknowledged Ikoseer, she sensed how the Sage suddenly seemed content. Her eyes were brighter, her skin more lustrous, and the strange crown hugging her skull now seemed to have an undertone of gold beneath the blue.

'You knew that Frovin was going to die.' There was anger in her accusation.

She looked into Marta's eyes and replied tenderly. 'If you search your heart Marta, so did you.'

'It wasn't supposed to end like this. Life can be so cruel.'

'Life teaches us many things, but your love for Frovin is eternal and written in the stars. Like your mother, he's now a star in the night sky.'

Tears welled and there was a slight tremor in her voice. 'He'll have to be buried but I don't understand … why hasn't his body started to … decay?'

'Your attempt to save him by holding your hand over the Lightenstone has preserved his body.'

'Oh.' Marta was taken aback. 'His family will want him returned to Greenwood Forest. Or perhaps he should be buried near Thrim, among the kings, queens, knights and elven lords in the cemetery near the Ascension Mountains. He deserves that.'

'Indeed, he does,' conceded Ikoseer, 'but his family will decide.'

'So, you already knew him before our quest started.' Marta was trying to piece everything together.

'Yes, he was the incarnated protector of the Lightenstone. Whenever I was travelling between this world and yours, I used to visit his family in Greenwood Forest. Once the Queen of the Sun decreed that the Pentark be restored, then it became urgent that I find him. It proved to be quite difficult, even for me. He was never at home and always up to something.'

Marta smiled as she remembered how she had met him. 'Just before our quest, Boris found him somehow. I once asked Frovin how that had happened but he was vague about it all.'

Ikoseer chuckled. 'That's because he disobeyed my order. Even then. He was supposed to be waiting for me in Wayfarers' Cave, but he'd instead gone on a soiree to sample the apple cider his cousin was fermenting.'

Marta raised her eyebrows. 'He was drunk when Boris found him?'

'Tipsy, more like. Apparently the cider was quite good and he was sleeping it off, unseen under a mound of leaves beside the Greening Road. Ferdy had just been captured by the Commander and his wrakes, and Boris was wondering what he was going to do about it when he heard Frovin's snoring. So he went to investigate. It seems that Boris accidentally stepped on him.'

'Yes, Frovin told me that much.'

'According to Boris, he was jolted so violently into the air that he lost his footing and fell flat on his back into a damp pile of rotting leaves. Then he opened his eyes to see the badger's front paws planted firmly on his chest. Frovin was giving him a very angry stare.'

Marta smiled again. 'So, that's why there always seemed to be a bit of tension between them.'

After a pause, she began again on a more serious tone, 'I know that my home is here in Mirraway now. But I do want to return to the World of Man, not only to gather some things, but also to explain everything to my father. It's been several months since Brechin Village was attacked, and he must be beside himself with worry. I was thinking I might travel with Boris and Ferdy when they return to Banters Den with the Arrowsmiths.'

'You could take Frovin's body back to his family in Greenwood Forest.' She paused for a moment. 'And don't worry about your father. I've already sent word to him. He knows where you are and also that you're quite safe.'

'Oh … thank you.'

'But talking of the twins …' Ikoseer continued in a lighter tone, 'it seems that Boris and Princess Yahdra, the elven King's daughter, have somehow fallen in love. Of course, Ferdy's bewildered by the whole thing and King Elvendor is, at best, displeased.

'And … ' There was a twinkle in her eyes and she gave Marta a knowing look. 'When you return to the World of Man, you should also take one of the knights with you. Patrayus perhaps?'

Marta blushed. She was watching a pair of wrens flitting among the roses and added, 'And what about Attricus and Volgor?'

'Attricus intends to continue his studies in Elodom Monastery, and Rhyll has offered to fly Volgor back to his family at Bleak River near the Raven Mountains. It's quite a long way.'

Marta gave an involuntary shudder. 'And it's close to the World of the Dark Night. Won't Rhyll and his anomir still be in danger of being attacked by the other goblins on anomirs?'

'Like Toil, the remaining anomirs, wrakes and boorlings have already fled back to their maker, the Prince of Darkness. And I expect that the rider goblins have either returned to Mawdark Castle, or to Hammerlock, their enclave in the west. Even the wolves of Skag have returned to the Raven Mountains.'

At the mention of Toil, Marta felt her anger rise. She fiddled with the empty chain around her neck.

'Pay them no heed, Marta. Any energy we direct at them just strengthens them.'

'Why didn't the Firebird help us during the battle?' she said in a low, almost bitter, tone. 'The power of the Pentark when it was first built may have consumed it, but I know it still exists somehow. I saw an image of it in the Well of Forgetfulness. It took the outer part of the Lightenstone from the Queen of the Sun and was flying it to Aramark Temple.'

'You have been shown a great mystery,' confirmed Ikoseer. 'The Firebird does still exist, but only Solara can summon it.'

'So, why didn't she summon it again, this time? Frovin could have been saved.'

Ikoseer gently touched her forearm. 'Even the highest of beings cannot interfere with anyone's destiny.'

Marta fell silent, watching bees gather nectar as she took in all that Ikoseer said. Neither of them spoke for several moments. Wanting to change the subject, she asked another question: 'Are the three spheres on the headlands glowing again now?'

Ikoseer nodded.

'Even the sphere in the World of the Dark Night?'

The Sage paused. 'Yes. The sun shines on both good and evil.'

'So, the inhabitants there do have hope,' Marta said earnestly.

'They do.'

'And is the portal in their Arkfeld closed now too?'

'Soon,' she said. 'Once the last of the enemy are through it.'

'So, what will stop the Prince of Darkness from using sorcery to breach the Arkfeld again?' She remembered what Frovin had told her, what had started all the strife.

'The Queen of the Sun has already strengthened it.' Ikoseer spoke reassuringly, but her mind was elsewhere, recalling a message she'd received that morning:

*Greetings from Potsy. The old dwarf requests that you visit him on your return to White Timber Mountain, for he has something for you.*

Marta was looking down at her hands. 'I've heard that the royal family has now arrived from the Ascension Mountains, and that tomorrow you're crowning Yoska's father, Prince Galway, the new King of Gorthonomir.'

Noticing that she still referred to Prince Mir by his nomadic name, Ikoseer nodded. 'His mother, Helena, will then be Queen, and you'll also meet his sister, Princess Moira. The coronation will take place in the Great Hall at noon.'

'I should help with the preparations, then.' Marta stood and drew a deep breath of the heady scent of the roses. 'And I must also find Ferdy.'

The pair made their way back through the beautiful garden. The hustle and bustle at Mirraway Castle reminded Marta of Brechin Village's market day and she found Ferdy in the scullery, not slaving over a sink as before, but perched on a stool and sampling, with an opinion, every morsel being prepared for the coming coronation feast.

He looked up as Marta approached, and with a broad grin, offered her a buttery biscuit topped with a slice of hard cheese and a generous blob of quince paste. He was still wearing his battered dwarfish hat, but his beard seemed trimmed and that, at least, appeared to have been combed.

They hugged. 'I have something for you,' she said, 'but you have to give me your vest.'

Giving her a curious look, Ferdy complied. As he handed over the vest, he leant forward and whispered fiercely, 'Boris is under the influence of elven magic. He's fallen in love with an elf called Yahdra and she happens to be King Elvendor's *daughter.*'

'I see.' Marta suppressed a smile, with the clear impression that Ferdy wanted her to *do* something about it.

But she said nothing more. She pulled a needle and thread from her pocket and then she took out the button with blue threads.

'Where did you get that from?' Ferdy thought that the button looked suspiciously elvish in design.

'I found it in a deserted farmhouse on the way to the Ageless Forest.'

'Oh, I've never heard of that forest.'

He watched her closely as she knotted the new thread and then pushed the needle through the fabric, testing it by pulling the thread taut. The needlework was reminding him of his mother and making him feel homesick, when Patrayus suddenly appeared beside Marta, putting his arm around her shoulder.

She looked up and smiled at him. Ferdy was reminded again of the same faraway look that Boris had in Alfura after coming back from the stables.

Just as Ferdy was thinking that he'd better go home as soon as possible, lest he get the same silly look, Patrayus handed him a small white cloth, now somewhat the worse for wear. It took a moment for Ferdy to realise that this was the handkerchief that his mother had embroidered with his name. She had tearfully pressed it into his hand just before he and Boris left for the Rolling Hills. He'd lost it somehow early on in their quest.

'You've found it!' he said delighted.

Patrayus gave Ferdy a mischievous look. 'Actually,' he teased, 'it was the enemy that found your handkerchief. It was in the saddlebag of Onysius' abandoned warhorse. The Knights of Power only discovered it after their fight with Onysius and the wrakes and boorlings in the Valley of the Queen.'

'I don't know how it got to the Valley of the Queen,' blurted Ferdy innocently. 'I'd already lost it before we reached the Lux Mountains …'

Then he reddened as he realised that at the time he'd probably alerted the enemy to their group's whereabouts. He'd kept his loss a secret from everyone, except Boris.

Patrayus grinned. 'No doubt the enemy would've seen our tracks on the plateau anyway.'

'Yes, of course. That's quite right. They would've done.' Ferdy agreed, a little too quickly and with a sheepish expression.

But then, as he shoved the handkerchief into his trouser pocket and out of sight, he happened to touch Thrim's ghost key: the one that had miraculously opened the armoury room in Mirraway Castle. Until now, he'd completely forgotten about finding it and using it to get inside that room.

Marta handed him the repaired garment. He glanced at his new button then wriggled back into his vest and buttoned it up.

*I'll be able to tell quite a story to the youngest dwarves of Banters Den about my strange buttons. I've got several mismatched ones on my shirt and now two on my vest—but I won't be sharing any stories about this key.*

The coronation of the new King of Gorthonomir was a grand and joyful affair with Elvendor keeping Boris within his sight, especially after the banquet had finished and the musicians started playing. And even Ferdy, having been approached by several starry-eyed scullery maids since he was now famous, warily joined in the merry dancing.

It was another fortnight before Captain Tibbs left Mirraway, sailing his small fleet back along the Intrepid River to the Mother Sea, down the western coastline and around the southern cliffs, through the Berthing Gates and finally back into Werthyn Harbour.

Trade with the outer islands of the archipelago had already resumed. Together, Toros and Mafasat travelled south-east: Toros to guard the Abyss River and Mafasat to guard the Sarsen stones. The oppression in the World of the Soul had lifted and the Pentark was at full power once again. Any remaining enemy had by now returned to the World of the Dark Night and the portal in the Arkfeld was closed.

Around the same time, the Arrowsmiths were preparing to leave for Alfura. Attricus was helping with the packing, and Boris, Ferdy and Yahdra were grooming Aster and Poppins for the journey, when Ikoseer arrived at the stables with a surprise for Marta.

Marta threw her arms around Snowball's neck exclaiming, 'Oh, she's back to normal again!'

'I don't think the World of Man is quite ready for a unicorn.' Ikoseer was beaming as she handed her the reins.

'So, does that mean she'll remain a pony from now on?'

'Who can say what will happen,' she teased.

Their big adventure now over, the twins were now happily heading home again too. Meanwhile their parents, Ester and Leopold, were concerned by the flurry of rumours now reaching Banters Den, about twin dwarves and elves being somehow involved in the return of the gemstones to the Pentark.

'It can't be our precious boys,' insisted Ester, waving a sticky jam spoon in her husband's direction. 'They're tucked up safely in the Rolling Hills. Besides, dwarves and elves never mix.'

'So true, my dear … so true,' he agreed.

But his heart was bursting with pride. He was sure that the rumours were indeed true. After all, he had secretly given them Thrust—just in case they did find themselves in danger.

# CHAPTER 41

Ikoseer used Gif to open the door into the Lux Mountains and led Helios through the tunnels to visit Potsy once again. The old dwarf seemed to have known she was coming, for he was already waiting at the cave entrance and greeted the Sage with his usual gusto.

'Welcome, my dear friend,' he said, shaking Ikoseer's hands vigorously, 'I see that you've received my message. We have much news, but first there's a meal to be shared.' He swept his arm towards the table already set for two. 'So please make Helios comfortable in my stalls over there and then we shall eat.'

After attending to Helios, Ikoseer sat down and watched (with some amusement) as Potsy busied himself on feeding his honoured guest.

First, he sliced the hot Maslin bread straight from the oven and, as always, spread it with so much butter that it melted and pooled on their plates. Then from two warming pots near the roaring fire, he spooned turnip mash and rabbit stew onto the hot bread on each plate, and placed the loaded plates on the table. Humming with satisfaction, he then set down two goblets, filling them to the brim with spiced mead from a jug that was ready and waiting near the fire. Then Potsy took his seat opposite Ikoseer and raised his goblet.

'To the Pentark.'

Ikoseer also raised her goblet and the goblets touched. 'To the Pentark,' she echoed.

As they ate and drank, Potsy chatted on about the logistics of gathering resistance fighters, and also quizzed Ikoseer about everything that had happened since their last meeting. He was particularly interested in the twins and Thrust and laughed uproariously when told that Boris and Yahdra had fallen in love.

'King Elvendor won't be too happy about that,' he chuckled.

Then, as Potsy was mopping up the last of the gravy with his remaining crust, Ikoseer finished her mead and sat her empty goblet down.

'You wanted to show me something.'

'Yes, I do,' said Potsy as he chewed. 'But I didn't want to spoil our meal. However, now that we've finished, I suppose …' His voice trailed off and he suddenly seemed distracted.

He swallowed his last mouthful. 'Come, let's sit by the fire.'

Ikoseer moved to one of the two high-backed, gilt-framed chairs set back from the fire, while Potsy fussed over the fire before joining her. Between the chairs was a low round table, with several books of note on it: The Dwarf's Guide to Practical Mining; Herbs and Other Useful Plants; The History of the Isle of Spheres; Military Warfare and on top, The Complete Guide to White Magic.

But beside the books there was also something wrapped in white silk. Ikoseer gazed at it, knowing immediately what it was: the Adamas, the talisman that the Prince of Darkness fashioned so many years ago to create a portal in the Arkfeld. Without it, Lord Mortimer could never have invaded the Kingdom of Gorthonomir.

'How did you come by this?'

Potsy nervously cleared his throat. 'It was brought to me by a rabbit hunter who found it in the Valley of the Queen, after Onysius and his wrakes and boorlings had an altercation with the Knights of Power. I can only assume that Onysius was carrying it that day and it must have fallen somehow when he escaped. Thankfully, the hunter had enough sense to keep it wrapped up and I've since added another covering of silk for my own protection.'

Ikoseer nodded her approval, wondering if Lord Mortimer had given the talisman to Onysius. If so, had he ever been told that the Earl had lost it?

Potsy interrupted her thoughts, raising his bushy eyebrows. He was obviously anxious to get it out of his home: 'Perhaps you should take it to the Queen of the Sun …?'

'Hhmm … Perhaps,' said Ikoseer thoughtfully. 'But I think I'll return it to the rock giants instead. There's a diamond on the tip of it, formed under intense pressure and heat from the carbon in the pure hearts of some of our …'

'Yes, yes, my dearest friend,' interrupted Potsy. 'But just talking about it is starting to give me indigestion. So, now that we've settled the question of where the Adamas should go, what say we have some dessert? I'm most interested to hear more about Mr Tibbs and his sailing ships. I've never seen ships—or the ocean—or a cat, you see.'

In the kitchen Potsy piled a plate with honey oat biscuits, and on returning to the fire, was shocked to see that Ikoseer had removed the strange blue crown hugging her skull and placed it over the talisman. It was the first time Potsy had seen the Sage without it.

Then, putting the plate on top of the books and feeling much better about things, Potsy grabbed a handful of biscuits and settled back in his chair. With the biscuits balanced on his belly he listened, fascinated, as Ikoseer told him about Mr Tibbs and his small fleet of ships; about Werthyn Harbour and the Berthing Gates; about salty water; and, the most amazing of all, about a giant sea creature with eight arms.

THE END

www.ingramcontent.com/pod-product-compliance
Lightning Source LLC
Chambersburg PA
CBHW050102120726
47904CB00004B/1179